BOUNDARY
WATERS

Also by William Kent Krueger

Iron Lake

Available from POCKET BOOKS

BOUNDARY WATERS

WILLIAM KENT KRUEGER

POCKET BOOKS
New York London Toronto Sydney Tokyo Singapore

POCKET BOOKS, a division of Simon & Schuster Inc.
1230 Avenue of the Americas, New York, NY 10020

Copyright © 1999 by William Kent Krueger

ISBN: 0-671-01698-9

First Pocket Books hardcover printing May 1999

10 9 8 7 6 5 4 3 2

POCKET and colophon are registered trademarks of Simon & Schuster Inc.

Printed in the U.S.A.

RRDH/✶

For Diane, a promise kept;

and

for my parents, Marilynne and Krueg,

who taught me not to be afraid to adventure or to love.

ACKNOWLEDGMENTS

My thanks first and foremost to the Anishinaabeg. In this book, I have relied heavily on their rich storytelling tradition, if not the stories themselves. The Iron Lake Band of Ojibwe is not real. However, I hope that the spirit with which I rendered these people captures respectfully the courage and integrity of the real Anishinaabeg.

As always, I owe a huge debt of gratitude to the members of the mystery writing group that calls itself Crème de la Crime: Carl Brookins, Julie Fasciana, Betty James, Michael Kac, Joan Loshek, Jean Miriam Paul, Betsey Rhame, Susan Runholt, and Anne B. Webb. Without their suggestions and their blessing, this book would not be.

In the course of writing this manuscript, I had the very good fortune of stumbling on Steve Masten, an attorney for the state of Minnesota, whose client is the Department of Natural Resources. I've never known anyone more knowledgeable in the ways of the wilderness. From knife blades to ballistics, from wolves to the watershed of the Boundary Waters, he has been generous with his expertise. His editorial comments hit the bull's-eye every time. "Up to Green River," Steve. And thanks.

For their guidance in the ways of a county sheriff's office and of search-and-rescue operations in the Boundary Waters Canoe Area Wilderness, I am grateful to Chief Deputy Mark Falk and Judy Sivertson of the Cook County Sheriff's Department.

Acknowledgments

Because anonymity was requested, I will refrain from identifying the helpful source of much of the information concerning the reality of the policies and procedures of the FBI.

In that clean, well-lighted place called the St. Clair Broiler, in the early hours before dawn, this book was written. If you're ever in St. Paul, drop by for a cup of coffee and an earful from the regulars and to say hello to Jimmy Theros and Elena and the staff. They'll treat you well, I promise, even if you don't tell them Kent sent you.

BOUNDARY WATERS

1

HE WAS A TOUGH OLD BIRD, the redskin. Milwaukee allowed himself the dangerous luxury of admiring the old man fully. He was smart, too. But way too trusting. And that, Milwaukee knew, was his undoing.

Milwaukee turned away from the Indian and addressed the two men sitting by the campfire. "I can go on, but the Indian's not going to talk. I can almost guarantee it."

"I thought you guaranteed results," the nervous one said.

"I'll get what you want, only it won't be coming from him."

"Go on," the nervous man said. He squeezed his hands together and jerked his head toward the Indian. "Do it."

"Your ball game." Milwaukee stepped to the campfire and pulled a long beechwood stick from the coals. The end of the stick glowed red, and two licks of flame leaped out on either side like the horns of a devil held in Milwaukee's hand.

The old Indian hung spread-eagled between two small birch trees, secured to the slender trunks by nylon cords bound about his wrists and ankles. He was naked, although the night was cool and damp enough to make his blood steam as it flowed down his skin over the washboard of his ribs. Behind him, darkness closed like a black curtain over the rest of the deep woods. The campfire lit the old man as if he were a single actor in a command performance.

Or, Milwaukee thought as he approached with the burning stick, *a puppet who'd broken his strings.*

Milwaukee grasped the long gray hair and lifted the old man's head. The eyes flickered open. Dark almond eyes. Resigned but not broken.

"See." Milwaukee brought the angry glow inches from his face. "Your eyes will bubble. Just like stew. First one, then the other."

The almond eyes looked steadily at Milwaukee, as if there were not at all a flame between them.

"Just tell us how to get to the woman and I won't hurt you anymore," Milwaukee offered. Although he meant it, he'd have been disappointed in the Indian if he broke; for he felt a rare companionship with the old man that had nothing to do with the business between them but was something in their spirits, something indomitable, something the nervous man by the fire would never understand. Milwaukee knew about the old man, knew how he was strong deep down, knew the information they were after would never come from him. In the end, the living would still be ignorant and the important answers, as always, would reside with the dead.

The second man at the campfire spoke. "Gone soft?" He was a huge man with a shaved head. He lit a fat Cuban cigar with a stick much like Milwaukee held, and he smiled. He smiled because next to himself, Milwaukee was the hardest man he knew. And like Milwaukee, he tolerated the nervous man only because of the money.

"Go on," the nervous man commanded. "Do it, for Christ's sake. I've got to know where she is."

Milwaukee looked deeply into the eyes of the old man, into his soul, and wordlessly, he spoke. Then he tipped the stick. The reflection of the fire filled the old man's right eye.

The old man did not blink.

2

WENDELL WAS THREE DAYS LATE. The woman's anger had passed and worry had set in, a heavy stone on all her thinking. Wendell Two Knives had never been late before.

In the early afternoon, she stepped from the cabin and walked along the little creek down to the lake. Like many of the lakes in the Boundary Waters, it was small. Long and narrow—a hundred yards wide and little more than half a mile long—it lay in a deep trough between two ridges of gray stone capped with aspen. A week ago, the aspen leaves had been yellow-gold, every tree like a match head struck to flame. Now the branches were mostly bare. The scattered leaves that still hung there shivered in the wind over the ridges, and one by one, they fell away. The water of the lake was very still. Even on days when the wind whipped the aspen trees high above, the narrow slit of water remained calm. Wendell told her the Anishinaabe called the lake Nikidin, which meant vulva. She often looked at that narrow stretch of calm whose surface reflected mostly heaven and smiled at the sensibility of Wendell's people.

But now she stared down the gray, rocky corridor with concern. Where the hell was Wendell?

He'd come ten days before, bringing her, as always, food and the batteries for her precious tape recorder. He'd told her his next visit should be his last; it was time for her to go. He said if she stayed much longer, she risked a winter storm, and then it would be hell getting out. She'd looked at the aspen, whose leaves had only just turned, and at the clear blue sky, and at the calm water of the lake that was warm enough still for a brief swim in the afternoons, and she'd laughed.

Snow? She'd questioned. *But it's absolutely beautiful, Wendell.*

These woods, he'd cautioned darkly, *this country. No man can ever say for sure. Better to be safe.*

She was almost finished anyway with the work that had brought her to that secret place and so she agreed. On his arrival the following week, she would be ready. She gave him a letter to mail, as she always did, and watched his canoe glide away, silver ripples fanning out behind him like the tail feathers of a great bird.

Now there were thin, white clouds high up in the blue, and along the ridges a constant wind that she couldn't feel but could plainly see in the waving of the aspens. She pulled her jean jacket close around her and shivered, wondering if the smell in the air, something sharp and clean, was the approach of the winter storm Wendell feared.

For the first time since she'd come to that lost lake and its old cabin, she was tight with a sense of urgency. She turned and followed the thread of the creek back through a stand of red pine that hid the cabin. From its place on the rough-hewn wood table near the potbellied stove, she took her tape recorder and turned it on. There was a red light in the lower right-hand corner that blinked whenever the batteries were getting low. The red light was blinking. She lifted the recorder near her mouth and held it in both hands.

"Saturday, the fifteenth of October. Wendell still hasn't come."

She sat in the empty cabin a moment, aware of the silence of the afternoon, terribly aware of her aloneness in the great wilderness.

"He said he would be here and he's the only man who's

ever kept his promises to me," she said into the recorder. "Something's wrong, I know it. Something's happened to him."

The red light blinked off. But she left the recorder on, not knowing if it captured at all her final confession: "Jesus Christ, I'm scared."

3

CORK WAS BREATHING HARD and feeling great. He'd been running for an hour and he was nearing home. Each stride landed on a mat of fallen leaves and each breath filled him with the dusty smell of a long, dry autumn. He kept to a gravel road that paralleled the Burlington Northern tracks. The tracks ran through the town of Aurora, Minnesota, and in doing so, shadowed Iron Lake. In the late afternoon of that mid-October day, the lake was dead calm, a perfect mirror of a perfect sky, blue and piercing. The trees along the shoreline were ablaze, bursts of orange and russet that exploded again on the still surface of the water. In boats here and there, solitary fishermen cast their lines, shattering the mirror in brief silver splashes.

Cork cleared a small stand of gold-leafed birch and aspen that surrounded the ruins of an old foundry, and Sam's Place came into view. It was a Quonset hut, second world war vintage, that had been turned into a burger stand by an old friend of Cork's named Sam Winter Moon. The front of the hut was decorated with pictures of burgers—Sam's Super Deluxe, especially—and fries and ice cream cones. Cork lived in the back part of the long hut. He'd inherited the place a couple of years earlier after his old friend was killed by a scared little man with a big rifle.

As he crossed the tracks, he heard a scream come from Sam's Place. He kicked into a sprint and ran.

Behind the sliding screen of the serving window, his

twelve-year-old daughter, Annie, jumped up and down wildly.

"What is it?" Cork called.

Annie ripped the headphones of her Walkman from her ears. "Notre Dame just scored! Yes!"

She was tall, athletic, and very freckled. She had red hair kept austerely short. At the moment she wore blue-jean cutoffs and a T-shirt with colorful block letters that spelled out LOVE KNOWS NO COLOR. Her enthusiasm for Notre Dame was long-standing and legendary. Annie was more Catholic than the pope. There were times when Cork envied her profound and simplistic faith because it was not a thing he shared anymore. On that afternoon, however, the perfection of the day had given him a sense of spiritual peace as profound as anything that came of Christian prayer.

> Straight is my path.
> Straight is my mind.
> Straight is my heart.
> Straight is my speech.
> Kind will I be to my brothers and sisters.
> Kind will I be to beast and bird.

He remembered the words of the drum song old Henry Meloux sang. That seemed to just about cover it all as far as Cork was concerned.

"Where's Jenny?" Cork asked. He'd left his two daughters in charge while he went for his daily run. Annie had stayed at her post. Jenny was nowhere to be seen.

"She said it was too slow and she went for a walk."

Cork could tell his daughter disapproved. To Annie, authority was important, rules existed for good reason, and any breach in protocol was always to be viewed with a disapproving eye. She was a wonderful Catholic.

"Has it been slow?"

"Dead," Annie admitted.

"Good for you, though," Cork observed. "You've been able to listen to the game without being bothered."

Annie grinned and put her headphones back on.

"I'm going to shower," Cork said. The salt in his sweat was crystallizing and he felt gritty.

Before he could move, a delivery truck bounced over the railroad tracks, kicked up dust along the unpaved road to Sam's Place, and pulled to a stop a half-dozen yards from where Cork stood. The truck was painted gold and bore a big green shamrock and green lettering that read CLOVER LEAF POTA- TO CHIPS. Charlie Aalto, a large, potbellied Finn, stepped out, wearing a gold shirt and gold cap, both of which bore the same green shamrock logo as the truck.

"What d'ya say dere, O'Connor? Training for another marathon, looks like."

"One a year is enough, Charlie," Cork said. He'd run in the Twin Cities marathon only a week before. His first. He hadn't broken four hours, but he'd finished and that had been just fine. "What're you doing out here? Monday's your usual drop-by."

"On my way in from Tower. Figured I might as well save myself a trip. How's business?"

"Been good. Slow at the moment, but the best fall I've ever seen."

Charlie opened the back of his truck, where boxes of potato chips were stacked. "Gonna pay for it," Charlie said. "Snow by Halloween, betcha. Bunch of it. And one tough bas- tard of a winter after that." He pulled down two boxes, one regular, one barbecue.

"What makes you think so, Charlie?"

"I was just shootin' the breeze with old Adolphe Penske. Over to Two Corners, you know. Runs a trapline up on Rust Creek. Says he ain't seen coats on the muskrats in years like what they're gettin' now."

"Means good ice fishing," Cork considered.

"Yah," the Finn said, nodding. With a look of envy, he eyed the nearest fisherman on the lake. "Been a busy year. Ain't had near enough time in my boat. Like to be on the lake right now, fishin' like dat son of a gun out dere." He watched a few moments more. "Well," he decided, "maybe not like him."

Cork glanced at the fisherman on Iron Lake. "Why not?"

"Hell, look at 'im. Don't know squat about fishin'. Usin' a surface lure, looks like. You know, a topwater plug. Supposed to hop the dang thing across the surface, fool them Northerns into believin' it's a frog or somethin'. Dat guy's lettin' it sink like it was live bait. Ain't no fish dumb enough to hit on that." He shook his head in misery. "God save us from city folk."

"Come to think of it," Cork said, "he's been out there the whole day and I'll be damned if I've seen him pull anything in."

Charlie handed Cork a pen and a receipt to sign for the chips. "Now you tell me why any fisherman, even a goddamn dumb one, would stay in the same place the whole day if the fish ain't bitin'."

Another scream burst from Sam's Place.

"Dat Annie?" Charlie asked.

"She's listening to the Notre Dame game. They must've scored again."

"Still plannin' on bein' a nun?"

"Either that," Cork said, signing for the boxes of chips before Charlie took off, "or the first female quarterback for the Fighting Irish."

Sam's Place stood on the outskirts of Aurora, hard on the shore of Iron Lake. Sam Winter Moon had built a simple, sturdy dock where the pleasure boats that supplied most of his business tied up. Directly north was the Bearpaw Brewery, separated from Cork's property by a tall chain-link fence. Cork didn't much like the brewery, but, in fact, it had been there longer than Sam's Place, and in the hard economic times before the Iron Lake Ojibwe built the Chippewa Grand Casino, it had sustained lots of households in Aurora. So what could he say?

Cork eyed the nearly empty lake as he passed the chip boxes through the window to Annie. "What do you say we call it a day," he suggested.

"What about Jenny?"

"She knows the way home."

"We're supposed to stay open another hour," she reminded him. "What if someone comes expecting to eat and we're not here?"

"What's the use of being the boss if you can't break the rules once in a while?" Cork told her. "Let's shut 'er down."

Annie didn't move. She nodded toward a car pulling into the place vacated by Charlie Aalto's chip truck. "See? A customer."

The car was a rental, a black Lexus. The man who got out pulled off his sunglasses and walked their way.

"Corcoran O'Connor?"

He was a big man, late fifties, with thin hair going gray and a thin, graying mustache. He had a long, jowled face, not especially handsome, that reminded Cork a little of a bloodhound.

"I'm O'Connor."

The man was dressed in an expensive leather jacket, light brown suede like doe hide, with a rust-colored turtleneck underneath. His clothes were the color and weight for a normal fall day. Too warm for that day, but the long, hot autumn had them all surprised. Despite the quality of his clothing, he seemed—maybe because of his easy, lumbering gait—like a man who'd be at home staring at the rump of a mule all day while he wrestled a plow through red clay.

"My name's William Raye." He offered Cork his hand.

"I know," Cork said. "Arkansas Willie."

"You remember me." The man sounded pleased.

"Even without the biballs and the banjo, I'd recognize you anywhere. Annie." Cork turned. "Let me introduce William Raye, better known as Arkansas Willie. Mr. Raye, my daughter Annie."

"Well, hey there, little darlin'. How y'all doin'?"

His voice was slow, like his gait, and all his words seemed to be gifted with an extra syllable. It was a voice Cork remembered well. Twenty years ago, every Saturday night, Cork had managed to clear his schedule to be in front of the television for *Skunk Holler Hoedown*. The program was syndicated, a country music review full of guitars and fiddles and banjos and enough corn to feed a hungry herd of cattle, broadcast from the Grand Ol' Opry in Nashville and hosted by Arkansas Willie Raye and his wife, a woman named Marais Grand.

"Sugar, I wonder if you'd pour me a little water there," Raye asked Annie. "My throat's dry as a Skunk Holler hooch jug come Sunday mornin'."

"Still entertaining, Mr. Raye?" Cork asked.

"Might as well call me Willie. Most folks do. Nope, don't even do charities anymore. I put away my biballs and banjo after Marais died." The hurt was old, but the man's voice carried a fresh sadness. He put his hands in his pockets and explored the inside of his cheek with his tongue. "I have a recording company now," he said, brightening. "Ozark Records. Biggest country label in the business. The Blacklock Brothers, Felicity Green, Rhett Taylor. They're all on Ozark."

"Here you are, Mr. Raye." Annie passed a big Sweetheart cup full of water and ice through the window.

"I thank you kindly, honeybunch."

"Up here for the color?" Annie asked.

"No, actually I'm up here to see your daddy." He turned to Cork. "Is there a place we can talk for a few minutes? In private."

"Mr. Raye and I are going to walk a bit, Annie. Hold down the fort?"

"Sure, Dad."

They strolled to the end of the dock, where sunnies swam in the shallows. The water was rust colored from the heavy concentration of iron ore in the earth. Raye looked out over the lake, smiling appreciatively.

"I only made it up here once. When Grandview was being built. It's every bit as beautiful as I remember it. Easy to see why Marais loved it like she did." He set his water cup down on the bleached planking of the old dock and pulled a compact disc from the pocket of his leather jacket. He handed the disc to Cork. "Know who that is?"

"Shiloh," Cork said, remarking on the woman whose picture filled the cover. She was a slight woman, young, very pretty, with smooth black hair like a waterfall down her back all the way to her butt. "One of Annie's favorites."

"My daughter," Raye said. "And Marais's."

"I know."

Raye regarded him earnestly out of that long, hounddog face. "Do you know where she is?"

Cork was caught off guard. "I beg your pardon."

"If you do," Raye rushed on, "I only need to know she's all right. That's all."

"Willie, I'm afraid I don't have the slightest idea what you're talking about."

Raye's big shoulders dropped. His face glistened with sweat. He shrugged out of his jacket and hung it on one of the posts that anchored the dock. He wiped his forehead with the back of his hand. "I've got to sit down."

Cork hooked his foot around the leg of a small stool he sometimes used when fishing from the dock and nudged it toward Raye, who sat down heavily. The man picked up a golden leaf that had blown onto the dock and idly tore it into little bits as he spoke.

"Marais sometimes talked about the people back here, the people she grew up with. When she talked about you she called you Nishiime."

"Means 'little brother,'" Cork said.

"I guess she thought a lot of you."

"I'm flattered, but I don't understand what that has to do with Shiloh."

"The deal is this: My daughter's been missing for a while. Several weeks ago, she canceled all her engagements and dropped from sight. The tabloids are having a field day."

"I know. I've seen them."

"She's been writing me. A letter every week. All the letters have been postmarked from Aurora. Two weeks ago, the letters stopped."

"Maybe she just got tired of writing."

"If I thought that, I wouldn't be here."

"She didn't say in her letters where she is?"

"Nothing specific. She didn't want anyone to know. She

was here for something she called . . . I don't remember exactly. It sounded like *misery*."

"Misery." Cork pondered that a moment. *"Miziweyaa,* maybe? It means 'all of something. The whole shebang.' Does that make sense to you?"

"Not to me." Raye shrugged. "Anyway, she talked about a cabin way out in the Boundary Waters. And she said she'd been guided there by an old friend of her mother, someone with Indian blood. That's why I thought it might be you."

"I don't know anything about your daughter, Willie. What's your worry exactly?"

"See, Shiloh's been under the care of a psychiatrist for a while. Drug abuse, depression. She's tried suicide before. When the letters stopped . . . " He looked up at Cork like a man staring out of a deep well hoping to be thrown a rope. "All I want is to know for sure my daughter's alive and okay. Will you help me?"

"How?"

"You could start by helping me find the man who guided her in. That's all."

Out on the lake, a motor kicked in. A couple of hundred yards from shore, a boat began to troll, gently wrinkling the perfect surface, leaving a wake that rolled away from it like a blue silk flag on a listless breeze.

Cork shook his head. "A man with Indian blood? That could be a pretty tall order. Half this county has some Anishinaabe blood in them. I'm not the sheriff around here anymore. I just run a hamburger stand. I think you should go to the proper authorities on this one."

"I can't take a chance on publicity," Raye said, looking stricken. "If word got out that Shiloh was somewhere up in the woods here, those tabloid reporters would be on this place like dogs on a ham bone. No telling who'd be out there looking for her. Shiloh gets more than her share of letters from psychotic fans. My God, it would be like open season." He threw away the remains of the leaf he'd torn apart. The broken pieces drifted away, shuddering as the sunnies nibbled at them, fooled by their size and color and sudden appearance, which mimicked insects lighting on the water. "Look, I know you don't really know me. But I'm not just asking this for me. If Marais were still alive, she'd be the one doing the asking."

Cork rubbed his arms to generate some heat. He could feel in his legs and shoulders the stiffness from his run. "I have a business, Will. And I don't do police work anymore."

Raye stood up and desperately took hold of Cork's shoulder. "Help me find her and I'll pay you enough to retire tomorrow."

"I don't know if I could help you find her."

"Will you try? Please?"

Behind the serving window, Annie screamed. Cork looked her way. The scream had been one of excitement, not terror, but it made him think. What if Annie were the one out there? Or Jenny? One of his own. He'd be desperate, too. Circumstance alone had saddled Willie Raye with this burden. It wasn't Cork's business or responsibility, but he said, "You say you got a letter every week. And all were postmarked Aurora?"

"Yes. There wasn't much in them that I could see would be any help. But maybe there's something y'all would pick up on. You're welcome to look at them. They're back at my cabin."

"Where are you staying?"

"Grandview."

"Grandview? Been a long time."

"I know. Told myself lots of times to get shut of the place. It's the past. But Marais, she loved it so. I just couldn't bring myself to let it go."

Cork said, "I'll stop by this evening. I want to shower and eat first. Say, seven o'clock?"

"Thanks." Raye grabbed his hand and pumped it hard. "Thank you kindly."

After Arkansas Willie had driven away, Cork returned to the serving window. "How's the game going?"

"Over. Notre Dame won." Annie gave a big victory grin.

"What do you say? Think we can shut 'er down?"

Annie started about the business of closing. "What did Mr. Raye want?"

"A little help finding something. I'll take care of it."

"He talks like a hillbilly. Is he?"

"Don't let him fool you, Annie. I'm sure he's made a fortune sounding like a hayseed."

Cork cleaned up outside, pulling the big trash bag from the barrel by the picnic table and hauling it to the Dumpster near the road. As he headed back toward Sam's Place, he noticed that the fisherman also appeared to be packing up his gear and calling it a day. Cork considered him a moment. Charlie Aalto's question had been a good one. Why would a fisherman, even a goddamn dumb one, spend the whole day in a place where the fish weren't biting?

4

ALTHOUGH IT WAS THE BEST FALL anyone could remember in years, the town of Aurora was prepared for the worst. In that far north country, winter was always on the mind. Cords of split wood were stacked against garages and porch walls. In the evening, the air was heavily scented with the smell of wood smoke. A sign in the window of Mayfair's Clothing on Center Street warned, DON'T BE FOOLED! IT'S COMING. WINTER COATS 20% OFF! Rows of snowblowers flanked the bin of Halloween pumpkins outside Nelson's Hardware Hank. Heading down Oak Street as he took Annie home, Cork spotted Ned Overby up on his extension ladder affixing Christmas lights to his gutters.

Cork pulled onto Gooseberry Lane and into the driveway of the two-story house where he'd been raised. Stepping from his Bronco, he considered the porch swing, empty now in the shadows. For Cork, the approach of winter wasn't palpable until he'd taken down the swing and stored it in the garage for the season. He stood on the lawn, considered the brilliant red of the maple tree against the clear blue afternoon sky, and took in with long, deep breaths the warm autumn air. He decided that despite Charlie Aalto's warning of heavy snow by Halloween, it would still be a long time before he put that swing away.

Annie sprinted through the side door into the kitchen. Cork followed and found himself in a house that, except for Annie and him, seemed empty.

He hadn't lived in the house on Gooseberry Lane for nearly a year and a half. He'd grown used to living alone at Sam's Place, but it wasn't the way he'd choose to live if the choice were his alone.

Annie had the television on, tuned to highlights of the Notre Dame game. Cork passed through the living room and called up the stairs, "Anybody home?"

"In here." Jo's voice came from her office just down the hall.

Nancy Jo O'Connor sat at her desk, papers spread out before her, a pen in her hand. She was dressed in faded jeans and a denim blouse with the sleeves rolled up to her elbows. Her blond hair was short and a little disheveled as if she'd run her hand through it in frustration. She wore her glasses, which made her ice-blue eyes big and startled looking. She smiled at her husband as he stepped in.

Jo wasn't alone. Near her at the desk sat a tall man with the black hair, almond eyes, and light bronze skin of the Ojibwe Anishinaabe. He sat back a little from Jo as soon as Cork stepped in.

Jo took off her glasses. Her eyes grew smaller but no less blue. "I didn't expect anyone for a while."

"No customers," Cork explained. "We shut down early." He nodded toward the tall Shinnob. "Afternoon, Dan."

"Hello, Cork." Daniel Wadena offered him a cordial smile. Wadena was the manager of the Chippewa Grand Casino, an enterprise operated by the Iron Lake Band of Ojibwe. He wore a red T-shirt that read CASH IN AT THE GRAND across the front in black letters.

"Business on Saturday?" Cork shook his head.

"We're trying to get the contracts together so we can actually break ground for the casino hotel before winter sets in," Jo said. She'd been counsel for Iron Lake Anishinaabe for years.

"Better hurry," Cork cautioned. "Word is, snow by Halloween."

Wadena glanced outside. "Did you get that from the weather service?"

"Muskrats," Cork said.

Jo stretched. "I think that's it for me today, Dan."

"A good day's work," Wadena concluded and stood up. He carefully placed a number of documents in his briefcase, clicked the latch, and stepped away from the desk. "Monday?" he asked Jo.

"I'm in court most of the morning. After lunch?" she suggested.

"Fine. I'll see myself out. Take 'er easy, Cork," he said as he exited.

Cork walked to the chair Wadena had vacated and plopped himself down. He watched Jo as she arranged the papers on her desk.

"He's taken with you, you know."

"I know." She opened her desk drawer and put away her pens. "I don't encourage him."

"He's what I believe they call a catch."

"Like a mackerel?" She looked at him directly. "The last thing I need in my life right now is another man." She put her glasses back on and made a notation on her calendar.

Cork heard the front door open, and a moment later, his sister-in-law Rose slumped against the doorway of Jo's office, a small sack of groceries in her arms. Rose was a large, plain woman with hair the color of road dust and a heart as big as Gibraltar. She was unlike her sister Jo in almost all respects except for the way she loved the children. She'd helped raise them from the beginning, and although they hadn't come from her body, a great deal of who they were had been born from the goodness of her spirit. Cork had never felt anything but love and an overwhelming gratitude toward the lumbering woman who stood puffing in the doorway.

"Stevie ran practically the whole way," Rose said, breathless. Beads of sweat popped out on her forehead and temples and followed the plump contours of her cheeks. "This weather has him crazy."

"Where is he?" Cork asked.

"I'm right here!" Six-year-old Stevie squeezed through the doorway past his aunt. Of Cork's children, Stevie most clearly carried the signs of his Anishinaabe heritage. His hair was straight and dark, his cheeks high, his eyes thick lidded. He smiled eagerly at his father. "Annie said she'd play some football with me if you will. Will you?"

"Sure," Cork agreed. "For a little while. Meet you guys in the front yard."

Stevie cried, "Yippee!" and vanished back through the doorway.

"I'm going to start dinner," Rose said. "Cork, will you join us? Just burgers on the grill."

"Thanks, but I haven't had a chance to shower after my run this afternoon. I'll just toss the ball a bit with Stevie then head back to Sam's Place and get myself cleaned up."

"We've rented a video," she tried again. "*The Lion King*. Stevie's favorite, you know."

He glanced at Jo, who gave him a nod. "Maybe I'll make it for that. But don't wait for me."

Rose turned and carried the groceries away.

"Didn't Jenny come home with you?" Jo asked.

Cork shook his head. "Went for a walk; never came back."

"She went to see Sean, I'll bet," Jo said.

"Speak of the devil."

Jo's eyes shifted to the window where Cork's attention had been drawn. Jenny and a teenaged boy had stepped into the backyard from the alley. They stood together near the end of the lilac hedge and they kissed. Cork moved closer to the screen.

"Don't spy," Jo said.

"I'm not spying. I'm assessing the quality of their relationship."

Every year, Jenny grew to resemble her mother more: slender, blond, bright, independent. At fourteen, she'd been keen on piercing her nose, had dyed her hair purple, and had chosen most of her wardrobe from the Salvation Army. Now almost sixteen, she spoke no more of nose studs, had washed the dye from her hair, and bought her clothing at mall shops. She'd stumbled onto *The Diary of Anaïs Nin* and was saving all her money to move to Paris just as soon as she graduated from high school. Jo said she'd change her mind about that, but Cork wasn't so sure. Like Jo, once Jenny had decided a thing, it was as good as done. The boy with her, Sean Murray, was a tall, lanky kid with long black hair and a lot of dark fuzz along his cheekbones. Whenever Cork saw him, Sean was dressed entirely in black.

"What does she see in him?" Cork asked. "He looks like a burned matchstick."

"He writes her poetry. And he's a nice kid."

Cork leaned to the screen. "Jenny," he called. "Could I talk to you a moment?"

Jo gasped. "Cork, get away from there."

"That nice kid's hand was on her butt," Cork said.

When he returned to Sam's Place, the first thing he did was to head for the basement.

Cork shared Sam's Place with a monster he called Godzilla, an ancient oil-burning furnace that occupied a good deal of the space beneath the old Quonset hut. Godzilla had a temperamental disposition that generally required giving the burner a kick now and then. Whenever the old furnace rumbled on in the winter, a shudder ran through the pipes above that often gave Cork's visitors a start. He'd hoped to have enough money from the season's profit to replace Godzilla with something new and quiet that burned clean natural gas instead of smelly heating oil; but employing Annie and Jenny all summer had eaten whatever savings he might have put away. Considering how much he'd enjoyed the company of his daughters in those months, he felt it was a trade that was more than fair.

Cork pulled the cord on the overhead light and stepped around Godzilla. He went to a black trunk shoved against a wall beneath a couple of shelves of jars. The jars were gifts from Rose. They contained tomato preserves, chokecherry jelly, sweet corn relish, pickled watermelon rind. Despite the fact that Cork was separated from her sister Jo, Rose continued in her own ways to take care of Cork with a vengeance.

He opened the trunk. On top lay a rolled bearskin. He lifted the skin, felt the weight of it that was in large part due to the Smith & Wesson .38 Model 10 military and police special wrapped in oilcloth inside. Both the bearskin and the gun were ties to the two most important men in his past. The gun had been his father's when he was sheriff of Tamarack County, and Cork had worn it during his own tenure in that office. The bearskin had been left to him by Sam Winter Moon and was a constant reminder of how the man had saved his life—in so many ways—after Cork's father was killed. They were violent symbols, to be sure. Yet upon the memories they represented rested much of the foundation for Cork's understanding of what it was to be a man.

Underneath the rolled bearskin was folded a yellowed wedding dress, his mother's. The trunk, before it had come into his possession, had held mostly his mother's treasures. When, at his wife's insistence, he'd left the house on Gooseberry Lane, the house he'd grown up in, the trunk was one of the few nonessentials he took with him. He'd failed in so many duties that keeping safe the things his mother had valued was one he would not forsake. Cork lifted the wedding dress and laid it gently on the bearskin. A great deal of the space remaining in the trunk was taken up by boxes of old photographs. When she was alive, his mother was always planning to sort through the photos, organize them, place them in the pages of albums. It never happened. What she left behind was a jumble of lives seen in scattered moments. Cork began to sift through a box. He couldn't remember the last time he'd looked at the collection, and if he hadn't been so focused in his mission, he'd have lingered over photographs, puzzle pieces that formed his history. It took him almost an hour and three boxes to find the photo he was looking for. It was black-and-white and taken with an old Kodak box camera that Cork remembered well. The photograph showed the O'Connor house on Gooseberry Lane circa 1961. In the front yard, squinting into the sun, wearing calf-length print dresses, were his mother, his mother's cousin Ellie Grand, and Ellie's twelve-year-old daughter Marais. They'd come that year from the Twin Cities to live in Aurora after Ellie had finally given up trying to live as an urban Indian. No one seemed to know about Marais's father, or if they did, they never spoke of him. For reasons Cork never really knew, Ellie Grand hadn't been welcome on the Iron Lake Reservation, so Cork's mother had offered her sanctuary in the house on Gooseberry Lane. For almost a year, Ellie Grand slept in the guest room and Marais, in the sewing room.

Marais Grand had not been like any girl Cork had known. She reminded him of an East Indian princess—long black hair; gold-dust eyes; soft, fine features; and skin a darker hue than that of any Ojibwe he'd ever seen. He loved her immediately. Marais, nearly three years older than he, had found him amusing. At first, she called him Odjib, which meant "shadow" or "ghost," for he followed her everywhere. Later, she'd dubbed him Nishiime, "little brother."

He dug some more in that same box and came up with a shot of Ellie's Pie Shop, the old house on the edge of town that Cork's mother loaned the money for and that Ellie Grand turned into an enterprise much favored by the summer tourists. He found a photograph he recalled taking himself at the Windom Bluegrass Festival the year Marais took first place. She was sixteen, beautiful, happy. All the tragedy was still far ahead.

Cork was tired by the time he came across several articles clipped together. They'd come from the *St. Paul Pioneer Press* and were a series that reported on the murder of Marais Grand at her home in Palm Springs. He skimmed the articles, refreshing his memory. The primary suspect had been a man named Vincent Benedetti, owner of a Vegas casino called The Purple Parrot and reputed to have had connections with organized crime. In the rumor mill, he'd been linked romantically with Marais. The articles followed the investigation until it was ultimately dropped, officially leaving unanswered the question of who'd killed Marais Grand.

Cork carefully placed everything back in the trunk except the early photo of Marais on the front lawn, and the bearskin. The photo he slipped into his pocket. The bearskin he held a while, considering the weight of what it concealed. Sam Winter Moon had once told him that all things created by Kitchimanidoo, the Great Spirit, had many purposes. A birch tree supplied shelter for animals, bark for canoes, sticks for cooking fires. A lake was a home for fish, water for drinking, a cool place on a hot day.

But a gun. What purpose did a gun serve except to kill?

Cork put the bearskin back, closed the trunk, and turned away from one more unanswered question.

5

He WAS STEPPING OUT OF THE SHOWER fifteen minutes later when the phone rang.

"Cork? Wally Schanno."

Cork rubbed a towel across his chest. The towel smelled musty and he made a note to do some wash.

"Yeah, Wally. What's up?"

"Can you drop by my office? Soon?"

"How soon? I haven't had any dinner yet, and I'm starved."

"Grab a burger. You can eat it here."

"I eat burgers all day long. What's it about?"

"I'll tell you when I see you. Just get over here."

"How about a please?"

Sheriff Wally Schanno was quiet on his end of the line. "Please," he finally grunted.

Twenty minutes later, Cork pulled his Bronco into the parking lot of the Tamarack County Sheriff's Department. Inside, the night desk officer, Deputy Marsha Dross, buzzed him through the security door.

"They're in the sheriff's office," she said, nodding toward a closed door.

"They?"

"I make 'em to be FBI, maybe BCA. Poles up their asses for sure."

"Any idea what they want?"

She shrugged. "Search me. But every time the sheriff pokes his head out, he looks like somebody gave his colon another crank."

Cork knocked on the door and opened it when he heard Wally Schanno grumble from the other side.

Schanno sat at the desk Cork had occupied for almost eight years himself. Too much time had passed for Cork to feel any antipathy toward the man who'd taken his place. Schanno was about one gray hair shy of retirement anyway. He was a Lutheran, staunch Republican, and not a bad sheriff. A big man, he wore special-order shoes, had huge hands with long crooked fingers. At the moment he was dressed in a white shirt, gray pants, black suspenders. He looked tired, but he often looked that way. His wife Arletta suffered from Alzheimer's, and between his duty to the voters and his duty to his wife, Schanno had those huge hands of his more than full.

He waved Cork in like an impatient cop directing traffic. "Close the door behind you."

"Good evening to you, too, Wally," Cork said.

Three men were in the office with Schanno. Two were black, one white. They wore suits, although a couple of them had their coats off, ties loosened, sleeves rolled back. The windows were closed. The air in the office was warm, a little rank from the sweat of worried men. They'd been huddled in front of a map taped to Schanno's wall. When Cork came in, they turned. He felt their eyes go over every inch of him, but their faces registered about as much emotion as if he were nothing but a draft of air.

The tallest of the men was the first to move toward Cork and offer his hand.

"Mr. O'Connor, Special Agent in Charge Booker T. Harris. FBI. I appreciate your coming."

Like the deep measured tone of his voice, his handshake was firm and purposeful. A man used to command. His hair was short and for the most part black, although gray had begun to flair along his temples. His skin was light, like maple wood.

"Agent Harris," Cork said, and nodded.

Harris turned to the nearest of the others, a man whose skin was dark brown with just a hint of red, like cinnamon tea. "This is Special Agent Sloane."

Sloane reminded Cork of a linebacker he knew in college, a man low to the ground and solid. But if Sloane had indeed played football, his best games were thirty years behind him. Much of his muscle had gone to fat, although there was still a lot of power visible in his big chest and shoulders. Cork and Agent Sloane exchanged a decent handshake. The man's eyes were a liquid brown and tired. His sleeves were rolled back and his huge forearms were covered with white scar tissue like long scratches on mahogany.

"And Special Agent Grimes."

Grimes was lean and grinning. He had red-brown hair in a military crew cut, a jawbone sharp as a machete, blue-white eyes like hot steel, a calloused hand. His face carried the tan and sharp creases of a man who spent a lot of time in the sun.

"Have a seat," Schanno said.

Cork sat down and looked carefully at the map taped to the wall. A topographic map of the Boundary Waters.

"I'll get right to the point, O'Connor," Harris said. He leaned back easily against Schanno's desk, in a pose that made the office seem familiar to him, as if the space had very quickly become his personal territory. "The sheriff has assured me you're a man who can be trusted. We've got a problem on our hands, and we're going to need your cooperation."

"Go on," Cork said.

Harris reached into a briefcase on the floor, pulled out a folded tabloid newspaper, and handed it to Cork. The major headline read $10,000 REWARD! It appeared above a huge color photo of the woman called Shiloh. The photograph was the kind anyone—man or woman—would have begged to have burned. Shiloh's skin was bright and oily, her eyes angry, her face twisted in a snarling remark in the instant the glare of the flash had caught her. She looked positively demented, nothing like the soft CD cover Arkansas Willie Raye had shown him that afternoon. Beneath the photo the caption read HELP US FIND SHILOH AND YOU POCKET TEN GRAND!

"It's a gimmick," Harris said. "This rag's been updating the world on Shiloh sightings ever since she dropped out a couple of months ago. New York City, Paris, Sante Fe, Graceland. We have reason to believe this woman is, in fact, somewhere up here, O'Connor."

"What reason?" Cork asked. He returned the paper to Harris.

"Good reason," Harris said, and let it drop.

"All right," Cork said. "Assuming she is up here, what do you want with me?"

"We know she was guided into the Boundary Waters Canoe Area Wilderness some time ago by an Indian. We need to identify this man so that we can locate her. Sheriff Schanno believes you can help us with that."

The room was too warm. Cork wanted to tell Wally Schanno to open a window, let in some cool evening air and let out the smell of the worry.

"You say she dropped from sight," Cork said. "Voluntarily?"

"Yes. We've spoken with her publicist and her manager. They both say the move was her choice but that they don't know anything more. She was apparently very secretive about the whole thing and very sudden."

"Then why look for her? Seems to me if she wants privacy, she's entitled to it."

"We have our reasons," Harris replied.

"Good reasons," Cork finished for him. He stood as if to leave. "Gentlemen, it's been interesting, but you're on your own."

"This is a federal investigation, O'Connor," Harris warned him.

"So take me to court."

"Look, if you want his help, tell him what's going on," Schanno broke in. "Just be straight with him."

Harris gave Schanno a sharp look, considering the advice as if it were about as enticing to him as a spoonful of sulfur. His eyes flicked toward the other two agents, and they appeared to have a wordless conference. Harris gave a grudging nod.

"Okay, the Bureau's interest in this case, and its jurisdiction, comes from the RICO statute. You know what that is?"

"Sure. Racketeer Influenced and Corrupt Organizations Act. How does that tie in with the woman in the Boundary Waters."

"Fifteen years ago, this woman, Shiloh, was the only witness to her mother's murder."

"We all know that," Cork said, and he sat back down. "Her mother was a local."

"Then you probably also know that she's always claimed she couldn't remember what happened that night. Post-traumatic amnesia. Not unheard of. A few months ago, she was ordered by the court to undergo treatment for substance abuse. She's been seeing a psychiatrist named Patricia Sutpen. You may have heard of her. Lots of famous clients. Been on *Oprah*. Her psychological bag of tricks includes regression therapy. We believe that in the course of her treatment, Shiloh may have finally recalled the events of the night her mother died."

Harris picked up the tabloid from where it lay on top of Schanno's desk and slapped it down, hard.

"This piece of trash appeared a couple of weeks ago. Almost immediately, the reporter—if you can call anyone who stoops to this kind of journalism a reporter—in charge of this story gets a call from a woman named Elizabeth Dobson. She's a studio musician for Shiloh. Plays the violin."

"In country music, they call it a fiddle," Grimes put in quietly and with a grin.

"Whatever." Harris waved it off and went on. "Elizabeth Dobson claims to have letters from Shiloh. Claims that not only do they tell where she is, but they contain some pretty juicy revelations as well. The reporter arranges to meet her at a restaurant in Santa Monica. She doesn't show. He gets her address from the phone book, goes to her apartment, but gets no answer to his knock. He greases the building manager's palm, they open her door, and find her lying dead on the living-room rug. Strangled. It appears to be a burglary, lots of stuff missing. Including the letters she claims to have had. LAPD, while investigating, stumbles onto a diary Elizabeth

Dobson kept right up to the day she died. Entries indicated that Shiloh was somewhere in the Boundary Waters. She was being supplied by a man she referred to only as—uh—"

"Ma'iingan," Agent Sloane said.

Cork was surprised at the agent's correct pronunciation.

"Means 'wolf,' in the Ojibwe language," Sloane said.

Grimes had taken a pack of Juicy Fruit from his shirt pocket. He folded several sticks into his mouth. "You're a regular encyclopedia," he told Sloane, speaking thickly around the wad of gum.

Harris gave them both a sharp look, then addressed Cork again. "We're concerned that whoever killed this woman may be after Shiloh."

"Got any idea who that 'whoever' might be?" Cork asked.

"That's where RICO comes in. The primary suspect in the murder of Marais Grand was a man named Vincent Benedetti. Owns a casino in Las Vegas."

"The Purple Parrot," Cork said.

"Yes." Sloane looked surprised. "How'd you know?"

"Lucky guess. Go on."

Harris glanced at Schanno, who only looked back blankly, then the special agent in charge proceeded like a man on a ride he couldn't stop. "Before her death, Marais Grand and Benedetti were romantically linked. At the time of the woman's death, Vincent Benedetti was under investigation for racketeering. We've always believed the two events were related. Now Benedetti's nowhere to be found. If Shiloh has remembered what happened that night, we're here to make certain she has the opportunity to testify."

"Why is it you think I can help?" Cork asked.

"The diary makes it quite clear that Shiloh's somewhere in the Boundary Waters and that the man who guided her in is an Indian. When we explained the situation fully to Sheriff Schanno, he suggested you might be our best hope for identifying this man."

"Because I'm part Ojibwe?"

"And," Harris added pointedly, "because he insists you're smart and can be trusted."

"Smart?" Cork smiled at Schanno. "You actually said that, Wally?"

"Well?" said Harris, interrupting. "Can we count on you?"

"Could I see the diary?"

"Give him the photocopies," Harris said to Sloane.

Sloane lifted an expensive-looking leather attaché case from where it sat on a chair, snapped it open, and took out a folder. He closed the case and carefully put it back down. He crossed to Cork and held out the folder, which was labeled in small, precise, block letters DOBSON DIARY.

The diary entries went back several months. Someone had gone through them already and neatly highlighted in yellow those passages that pertained to Shiloh. Elizabeth Dobson wrote like a romantic. Her script was florid, with big loops above the line and elaborate flourishes that ended each sentence. Her writing leaned heavily to the right. Optimistic. The passages that hadn't been highlighted talked about mundane things: loneliness, whether she should get a cat, worries—a lot of them—about her mother's health and the cost of caring for her. He found the reference to Ma'iingan, but, in his cursory look, found little else that was very helpful.

"Before I agree," Cork said. "I'd like a few minutes alone with Sheriff Schanno."

Harris shook his head. "This is my case. Whatever you've got to say about it, I'd like to hear."

"Your case, my office," Schanno pointed out. "If Cork wants to speak with me alone in here, he'll speak with me alone. You gentlemen can wait outside."

Harris chewed on the decision a moment, then jerked his head for the others to follow him. When they stepped outside, Cork closed the door.

"Hate these guys," Schanno said. "Waltz in here like they own the place."

"You ID them?" he asked

"Yeah, Harris anyway. Why?"

"Doesn't it seem odd, them showing up here this way, no introduction from the local field office?"

"I thought the same thing. So I made a call to Arnie Gooden, the field rep in Duluth."

"I know him. A good man."

"He worked in the L.A. office for a while. Said he didn't know anything about this investigation, but he did know Harris. They spoke on the phone a few minutes. Gooden promised to help if Harris needs anything. Look, Cork, you put it all together, it adds up pretty well. If this girl is in the kind of trouble they say, I'd hate to leave her hanging."

Cork stood at the window. Across the street, the bell tower of the Zion Lutheran Church was lit with floodlights, blazing white against the dark evening sky. There was something wonderfully simple in the solid colors and the straight lines, and Cork stared a long time. He wondered if he should tell Schanno about Arkansas Willie Raye.

"Anything else?" Schanno asked.

"I guess not," Cork answered.

He opened the door. Only Harris and Sloane came back in.

"Well?" Harris said.

"I'll do what I can," Cork told him. "But if I'm going to help, I'll do things my way."

"Elaborate," Harris said.

"The people I'll be talking to are Ojibwe. They won't trust you. I'll talk to them alone."

"I'd prefer one of us accompany you," Harris insisted.

"You're strangers," Cork reminded him. "More than that, you're federal law. It would be like throwing a skunk at these people—no offense. If I do this, I have to do it alone."

"He's right," Schanno said.

Harris crossed his arms, his hands fisted and sheathed in the bends at his elbow. He looked like a man who'd invited himself to dinner only to discover that the special of the day was a plateful of shit.

"All right," he finally agreed unhappily. "Just remember, whoever murdered the Dobson woman may be here now. They could be after Shiloh at this moment. We don't have much time."

"In that case," Cork said, "I'd best get started. How do I contact you?"

"We've got a cabin at a place called the Quetico. Here's the phone number." He wrote it on the back of an FBI business card. "One more thing, O'Connor. We've tried to keep a lid on this. But the tabloid that posted the reward for Shiloh has a front-page story on the Dobson death ready to go. By mid-week, your little town here is going to be middle ring in a three-ring circus."

"I'll keep that in mind," Cork said. He held up the photocopied diary of Elizabeth Dobson. "Mind if I hang onto this?"

Harris waved him an okay. "We've got other copies."

At the desk outside Schanno's office, Deputy Marsha Dross handed Cork a brown paper bag. "Fried chicken," she said, and smiled. "Sheriff's orders."

Outside the county building, Cork found Grimes waiting for him. The man leaned against Cork's Bronco and watched him approach.

"A word of advice, O'Connor," Grimes said, stepping out to intercept him.

Cork held up and waited.

Grimes chewed while he talked, moving the wad of Juicy Fruit around in his mouth like it was chaw. "I've seen local lawmen screw up more times than I care to remember. Working with them is always like trying to dance a ballet in diver's boots. You understand what I'm saying? So what do you say you do us all a favor: Just give us what we ask for and try to stay out of the way the rest of the time. Comprende?" Grimes took the wad of Juicy Fruit from his mouth and dropped it.

Cork stared into his blue-white eyes. "Comprende," he said. "Comprende real good." He nodded down at the gum on the parking-lot cement. "Careful there. You might end up stepping in your own mess. Comprende?"

He shoved past Grimes, who stood grinning in his wake.

6

GRANDVIEW WAS A GREAT DEAL MORE than just a summer cabin. It was an estate built of yellow pine logs, a huge two-story structure that dominated a southern inlet of Iron Lake called Snowshoe Cove. Marais Grand had had it constructed at the height of her fame; but she'd had little opportunity to use it. Now, it was generally rented in season by wealthy families out of the Twin Cities or Chicago. As far as Cork knew, no one connected with Marais Grand had stayed there since her murder. The place was hidden from the highway by an acre of hardwoods, mostly maple. As Cork approached Grandview, the wind ran through the trees, shaking down crimson leaves that fell into his headlights like drops of blood.

He knocked at the front door, waited, then knocked again. He checked his watch. A couple of minutes past seven.

"Willie," he called at the curtained front window. "It's Cork O'Connor."

He heard an outboard purring on the lake behind Grandview, the sound growing distant. He followed the flagstone walk around to the deck in back. From there, he could see the long stretch of darkness that was Iron Lake at night. Far across the water, the lights of the Quetico marked the newest resort complex on the lake. Condominiums, tennis courts, a par-three golf course, a pool in a Plexiglas dome, a large marina with a flotilla of rental boats, the best wood roast restaurant north of the Twin Cities. There were cabins, as well, isolated in woodland settings, each with its own Jacuzzi and sauna and one hundred twenty-five channels on a big screen television.

Much of the shoreline of Iron Lake was being devoured in this way. The success of places like the Quetico was a direct result of the success of the Chippewa Grand Casino. The casino attracted money, lots of it, for the whites as well as the Anishinaabe. Although Cork was happy to see that many good things had come from the new wealth—upgraded services and an increase in the levels of health and education on the reservation, and an economic boom to the rest of Tamarack County—it made him uneasy. Money changed things. Usually for the worst. He'd loved Aurora in part because of its isolation. He felt a deep sadness as he realized a world of strangers was slowly pushing in.

The gas lamps on the deck were turned low, creating lighting that would have been perfect for a romantic dinner at the big picnic table. The table was empty. Cork mounted the steps and approached the sliding glass doors. The doors were closed, but the curtain was drawn back slightly.

"Willie?" Cork called again, and tapped on the glass.

He peered through the slender gap where the curtain hadn't closed completely. He saw a big brown leather sofa, a coffee table, a beige carpet, a brass lamp, a fireplace without a fire. Grandview looked empty.

Then he felt a slight shaking of the deck. And he heard something.

He grasped the sliding door. It opened easily.

From the other end of the cabin came a sudden, jarring thump followed by a muffled cry. Cork followed the sound down the hallway. Just past the bathroom was a heavy cedar door with a temperature control mounted on the wall next to it. A sauna. The sauna door had been wedged shut, a length of two-by-four jammed between it and the opposite wall of the hallway. As Cork looked the situation over, the door shook from a blow delivered from the other side. Inside the sauna, Willie Raye swore loud and long. Cork slipped under the board and pried it loose with his shoulder. As soon as the door was freed, Raye burst out, naked. His silver hair lay plastered to his forehead. His body, surprisingly lean and powerful for a man of his age, glistened with a thick sheen of sweat. His right shoulder was reddened where he'd slammed uselessly against the door. He gulped in the cool air of the hallway.

"Goddamn, I'm going to sue somebody," he swore breathlessly, as he rubbed his shoulder. "That sauna's a menace. Christ, somebody could get killed in there, door sticks like that."

"It wasn't stuck, Willie." Cork held up the two-by-four. "Somebody used this to make sure you couldn't get out."

Raye stared at the board. "Shee-it." His face suddenly lit with the fire of a fearful thought. "My things." He shoved past Cork and made for the stairs.

Cork followed and caught up with him standing dead still in the doorway of an upstairs bedroom.

"Jesus," Raye gasped.

The room was torn apart. The drawers had been thrown open and a lot of Willie Raye's clothing had been tossed on the floor.

"Sons of bitches cleaned me out," he said with disbelief. He checked the top dresser drawer. "Except . . . they didn't take my wallet or Rolex." He turned suddenly to the open closet. The racks of clothing looked untouched, but Willie Raye slammed an angry fist against the wall so hard his naked flesh quivered. "Them goddamn sons of bitches. They took my briefcase. It was in the closet. The ball-less bastards took my briefcase." From the pile of clothes that had been thrown on the floor, he grabbed a pair of boxer shorts, some socks, a pair of jeans, and a white pullover sweater. He began hurriedly to tug the clothing on.

"What are you doing?" Cork asked.

"Hell, I'm going after 'em."

"That won't do any good, Willie."

"You don't understand," Raye said. "Shiloh's letters were in that briefcase."

"Whoever it was, they're gone," Cork told him.

Willie Raye slumped onto the bed. "What do we do now?"

"In her letters, did Shiloh ever mention anybody out here by name?"

"Nope. She seemed pretty careful about not doing that."

"What about the name Ma'iingan?"

"That's a name?"

"It might be."

"Never heard it before."

Cork walked slowly around the room, noting where fingerprints might have been left, where, if he'd still been in charge of investigations, he would have made sure they dusted. "What did Shiloh talk about in her letters?"

"The past mostly. Our past."

"Her mother?"

"Not really. She doesn't remember much about her mother."

"Willie, do you know a woman named Elizabeth Dobson?"

"No. Should I? Why all these questions, Cork?"

Cork stood in the closet doorway. A big walk-in closet. A closet bigger than his entire kitchen at Sam's Place. The walls were lined with cedar. He turned back to Arkansas Willie Raye.

"I just had a talk with some federal agents. They're here looking for your daughter, too."

"Federal agents? What on earth for?"

"This woman, Elizabeth Dobson, was apparently a friend of Shiloh and had been receiving letters from her, too. She's been murdered, Willie. The FBI thinks it was because of those letters."

"I don't get it."

Cork continued moving around the room. Near the window, he bent and studied carefully a yellow birch leaf that lay on the rug.

"The therapy that Shiloh was involved in might have brought back the memory of the night Marais was killed. Or at least that's what the federal agents are speculating." He picked up the leaf. "They think someone might be trying to make sure she doesn't leave the Boundary Waters."

"Christ, Marais died fifteen years ago. Shiloh was only six. What could she possibly remember that would be of any use now?"

"Maybe it's not important what she remembers. Maybe what's important is what someone is afraid she remembers."

Willie Raye's eyes settled on the board Cork still held in one hand. His mouth opened and he took in a quick breath. "Jesus, Mary, and Joseph. I guess I was lucky."

"Luckier than Elizabeth Dobson," Cork agreed. "I'm going to have a look around."

Cork checked the rest of the inside of Grandview, then went outside and followed the flagstone walk as it curved toward the lake. He passed through a small stand of birch where a pile of boards lay, a lot of them two-by-fours, that looked like debris from a building project. Finally, he came to the dock. The water stretched away in unbroken darkness. The nearest signs of life were the lights of the Quetico on the far shore. Cork considered the outboard he'd heard when he arrived. A small boat could easily have pulled up unseen and left the same way. He thought it interesting that Harris and the other agents were staying just across the water, and that the interview with the FBI in Schanno's office had delayed him just long enough for someone to steal the letters from Grandview.

Raye was fully dressed and watching through the sliding doors when Cork came back.

"I'm going to leave you now and go talk to someone who may be able to help us."

"Who?"

"Just a man I know. You'll be okay here?"

"I'll be fine. But Cork, if someone is after Shiloh, we don't have much time." Arkansas Willie's long face seemed longer, drawn down by the weight of his worry.

Cork reached out and put a hand reassuringly on his shoulder. "We'll find her, Willie." He started through the sliding door, but turned back. "One more thing."

"Yes?"

"Do you smoke cigars?"

"No. Vile habit. Why?"

"Just wondered. Lock up," he said, and tapped the latch on the glass door.

Almost a year before, Cork had been a heavy smoker, more than a pack a day. But he'd made a promise to someone he'd loved very much that he would reform. Now he ran every day, and he hadn't had a cigarette in nine months. He'd become supersensitive to the smell of tobacco smoke. It had been faint in Raye's bedroom, but definite. Whoever it was who'd been there, they had a fondness for cigars.

7

Cork DROVE NORTH OUT OF AURORA, passed the Chippewa Best Western, Johannsen's Salvage Yard, and finally the last streetlamp of town. Three miles farther, he turned right onto a county road that followed the shore of Iron Lake. In another ten minutes, he came to a graveled access that led to an old resort hidden among the trees. A long time had passed since he'd been out that way, and he slowed as he approached the access, then stopped, killed the engine, and stepped out.

The moon above the dark pines was waning, lopsided, like a balloon leaking air. The night was still and without a sound. Cork couldn't see the buildings of the old resort, but he knew how they lay. The big cabin set back from the shoreline. Six small cabins flanking the lane down to the lake. And there, where the black water met the sand, the sauna. All of it had been built by the old Finn Able Nurmi, Molly's father, and left to Molly when he died. When Molly died, there'd been no one to pass it on to, and now the old resort just sat, disintegrating with each season, the wood going soft with rot so that it would all collapse someday and go back to the earth and there would be no sign that Molly Nurmi had ever been. In the time before the cold science of the whites came to Iron Lake, the Anishinaabe believed the water was bottomless. There was a tradition among the Iron Lake Ojibwe. Before they were married, a couple would take strands of their hair and braid a cord. On the day they were wed, they tied the cord around a stone, canoed to the middle of the lake, and dropped the stone into the water. The stone descended forever, they believed, its spirit bound by the braid of their hair, and forever there would be a thing that bore the memory of them together. In a way, that's how Cork thought of Molly and him. Forever bound in spirit. As long as he had memory, Molly would always be.

He drove on, putting the old resort behind him. Two miles farther, he came to a double-trunk birch off to the right of the road. He pulled onto the shoulder and stopped. From the glove compartment, he took a flashlight, locked up the Bronco, and headed toward the birch, which marked the trail into the woods to the cabin of Henry Meloux.

Meloux was a *midewiwin,* an Ojibwe medicine man. He was also said to be a *tschissikan,* or magician, although that was a claim Meloux himself never made nor admitted to. He was the oldest man Cork had ever seen, and he had seemed that old for as long as Cork could remember. As far as Cork knew, except for his dog Walleye, Meloux had always lived alone in his cabin on a small rocky peninsula on Iron Lake called Crow Point.

Although Cork brought the flashlight, he didn't turn it on. The trail was easy to follow, lit by the moon and beaten nearly bare by the feet of others who, like Cork, had sought out the old man for his succor and advice. Cork walked for half an hour in the stillness of the woods, crossing at some point from national forest land onto the reservation of the Iron Lake Band of Ojibwe. As he approached the cabin, he could see light through the windows and he smelled wood smoke. He paused, waiting for Walleye to bark and announce his presence.

When no sound came from the cabin, Cork moved nearer.

"Henry!" he called. "Henry Meloux! It's Corcoran O'Connor!"

A small animal whine came from the woods to his left. In a little clearing visible in the moonlight stood a small dark structure. Cork headed that way.

Walleye, Meloux's old hound, lay beside the door. He

lifted his head casually as Cork approached and his tail lazily thumped the ground. From the tiny building behind the dog came a long, grumbling fart.

"Henry?"

"You're early," the old man accused from inside.

Cork didn't argue. He'd long ago learned that Meloux had a way of knowing when someone would come to him.

"Getting so a man can't take a quiet crap anymore."

"Sorry," Cork said.

After a momentary rustling behind the door, the old man emerged from the outhouse buttoning the last strap on a pair of gray overalls. "That's all right," he said, waving off Cork's apology. "Wasn't going so good anyway."

Meloux led the way back to his cabin, Walleye at his side. Inside, the cabin was a simple affair. One room, a bunk, an old cast-iron stove, a rough-hewn table and three chairs, a sink with a pump. The walls contained an assortment of items—snowshoes, a reed basket, a *midewiwin*'s drum, a big bear trap, and a Skelly calendar from 1948 with a drawing of a buxom woman in tight shorts inadvertently entertaining a gas-station attendant as she bent to the sideview mirror to apply lipstick. The cabin was lit by two kerosene lamps, and the smell of the burning oil was mixed with the scent of burned cedar.

"Been purifying, Henry?" Cork asked.

The old man didn't answer, only nodded toward one of the chairs for Cork to sit. He went to the sink and brought back two blue speckled enamel cups, then to the stove where a coffeepot sat heating. He poured hot coffee into the cups. When he returned and sat at the table, Cork handed him a pack of Camel unfiltered cigarettes. Meloux accepted them with a smile and a nod. He broke open the pack and held it out to Cork, then took one for himself. Kitchen matches stood in a small clay holder on the table. Meloux struck one and lit his cigarette.

Cork held his own cigarette gingerly. He hadn't smoked since Molly died. It was the last promise he'd ever made to her and he wanted to keep it. But it would be an insult not to join

Meloux in the smoking of tobacco, a thing that for the old man had nothing to do with an addictive habit.

Meloux watched Cork with silent interest. Cork finally reached for a match and lit the cigarette. Only nine months, but as soon as the smoke hit his lungs, it seemed like nine years. Cork realized how much he'd missed the old habit. He closed his eyes and the smoking felt like a visit with a deliciously sinful old friend.

They smoked in silence for a while. Walleye lay sprawled on the old wood floor, snoring loudly.

"Walleye didn't bark when I came," Cork noted. "He's old, Henry. Is he going deaf?"

"You think he didn't hear?" The old man grinned and shook his head. "He heard. He just didn't care. He's old like me. He's finally learned that what comes, comes. Why bark?"

The old *midewiwin* exhaled a flourish of smoke and watched it rise to the ceiling. "They tell me you are a running fool."

"Running fool? Well, I do run, Henry."

"The wolf runs after the deer. The deer runs from the wolf. In this running, there is reason."

"Believe it or not, there's reason in my running, too. A lot of things are clearer to me when I run."

Meloux considered this for a moment. "A walk in the woods makes clear a lot, too."

"It's hard to explain, Henry. In a way, it's part of a promise I made to Molly to make my life healthier."

"Ah, Molly Nurmi." He nodded as if that explained it just fine.

The cedar-and-kerosene-scented silence descended comfortably once again. Cork finally decided it was time to approach Meloux with the reason for his visit. But before he could speak, Meloux said, "I have been purifying the air to clear my mind. The wind speaks these days, a warning I do not understand. I hear the trees groan, but their complaint is lost on me." He looked at Cork, and within the dark eyes, sunk deep in lined and wrinkled flesh, was a look of concern. "*Majimanidoo,*" he finished.

"Evil spirit." Cork translated the Ojibwe word.

Meloux nodded. "Powerful. Very powerful," he cautioned. "It is this that has brought you to me?"

"Maybe so, Henry."

"What do you need?"

"Information. There's a woman missing. Noopiming," Cork said, using the name the Anishinaabe gave to the Boundary Waters area. *Inland, in the woods, up in the north.* He waved a hand in that direction. "A Shinnob guided her in. This man comes and goes there often. I think the woman may be in some danger and I need to find her guide."

The old man put his cigarette down, sipped his coffee, and passed a little gas. In the corner, Walleye growled in his sleep.

"I have heard that Wendell Two Knives visits there often."

"Wendell Two Knives." A good name to hear. A good man. And it made sense. Wendell Two Knives was of the Wolf Clan. Ma'iingan.

"This *majimanidoo* is puzzling," the old man said. "Even cedar smoke does not make him clear to me. Be careful, Corcoran O'Connor. Be especially careful of the water. Pay attention to the wind that blows across the water. It can tell you much."

"What comes, comes." Cork finished his cigarette in a final, pleasing lungful of smoke. "Isn't that what you said?"

"Okay advice for an old man like me. But if I was you," the *midewiwin* cautioned, "I would keep a barking dog."

8

SHE WATCHED THE WANING MOON RISE above the rock wall at the end of the long, narrow corridor that held the lake. *That's east,* she thought. It was a pathetic little piece of information, but with everything so uncertain, that one solid fact was reassuring. Far enough east, she knew, and she would hit Lake Superior and civilization. How far and how long it would take if she were to attempt it were mysteries to which she had no clue.

Wendell had left her a map, a complicated thing, black and white with confusing lines and rings all over it. Nothing like a road map. *You might as well give me a book in Chinese,* she'd said, laughing. He'd tried to explain to her the lakes, the portages, just in case. She'd pretended to listen.

Stupid, stupid, she thought of herself now. *You never listen to the right people.*

Somewhere on the cliffs along the shoreline far down the lake, an owl called. She tried to pierce the darkness to see where. The light of the moon gave the gray rock of the corridor a bleak, haunted look. The color reminded her of gravestones. Death was something she'd thought about a great deal alone in those woods. She'd examined carefully the time she tried to take her own life. Wrapped deep in the scent of pine and the sweet smell of the lake water, with the wind and the birds giving her music, her suicide attempt seemed bewildering, like the action of a stranger. Wendell told her the woods

44

could heal if she let them. In that, as in everything, he'd been truthful.

You should have listened more, she thought bitterly, remembering the map. She'd been so careful to make sure no one knew where she was going. She'd been so clever, so complete in her escape. In a way, she realized, she'd dug her own grave.

Then she remembered something Wendell said to her near the end. She'd walked with him down to the lake to see him off. He'd talked of her mother that visit, of the things he remembered about her. They were good things, and she'd been grateful to hear them. Before he'd shoved off in his canoe, he'd said, "We don't die. In the things we pass on to our children, we go on living. There's a lot of your mother alive in you."

Thinking of that, she pulled herself together and pushed away her useless recriminations. She couldn't sit and wait for Wendell forever. Her food was low. Soon the snow Wendell feared would come. She would have to think of a way out on her own.

From its hidden place in the rocks, the owl called again: *Who.*

The woman drew herself up in the darkness. *Me,* she thought. *Shiloh.*

9

CORK TOOK THE LONG WAY HOME through the Iron Lake Reservation, where he stopped at the mobile home of Wendell Two Knives. Wendell didn't answer his knock. Cork checked the door. Unlocked, as he suspected it would be. The Anishinaabe did not believe in locking doors. He called inside. No response. He checked the trailer briefly but found nothing that caused him concern. On the back of a car-wash receipt, he wrote his phone number. *Call me,* he added. *Urgent. Cork O'Connor.* Then he put the note on the door with a bit of silver duct tape from the toolbox in his Bronco.

He left the reservation and drove around the southern end of Iron Lake toward Grandview. Will Raye opened the door as Cork approached along the flagstone walk.

"What'd you find out?" Raye asked.

"I think I know who guided Shiloh in. A man named Wendell Two Knives. A good man."

"A good man," Raye nodded gratefully. "That's something."

"I stopped by his place tonight. Nobody home. I left a note for him to call."

"If he doesn't?"

"I'll head over first thing in the morning."

"We'll head over," Raye said.

"Not a good idea," Cork told him. "On the rez, people tend to be suspicious and tight-lipped around strangers."

46

"She's the only family I have, Cork. I can't just sit here and wait."

Once again, Cork found himself imagining what it would be like if he were in Raye's shoes and it were Annie or Jenny out there.

He relented. "All right. If Wendell calls, I'll let you know. Otherwise I'll be here at eight-thirty to pick you up."

"Thank you." Raye looked out at the night beyond Cork. "What if he's not there in the morning?"

"Then I think we try his nephew Stormy. If anybody would know where Wendell is, it's Stormy Two Knives."

Raye slumped against the doorjamb, as if the waiting had already exhausted him.

"Get some sleep if you can," Cork advised.

It was late by the time Cork returned to Sam's Place. He got himself ready for bed, turned out the lights, and lay down. He lived in one big room in the back of the Quonset hut. Simple amenities. A kitchen area with a gas stove, old refrigerator, sink. A small table and two chairs Sam Winter Moon had made of birch wood. A single bed. A writing desk and three shelves of books. A small bathroom with a toilet and shower stall. Everything smelled of french fries and grilled hamburgers. A couple more weeks and he'd probably close up for the winter, something he wasn't looking forward to. He liked the business. He liked it a lot. It was easier pleasing customers than it had ever been pleasing voters when he was sheriff. A bad hamburger was a simple thing to get rid of. A bad law was something else. He loved having the girls help him. And he liked the fact that he was self-employed. He could close up shop any time he wanted and just go fishing. Or searching for a lost woman.

He thought about the woman in the Boundary Waters. Whether he liked it or not, she was his concern now.

It was going to be hard to sleep. In the days when he smoked, this would have been the time to light a cigarette. Instead, he got up, put on a pot of coffee, and sat down at the birchwood table with Elizabeth Dobson's diary in front of him. He went over everything carefully. What he noted most significantly was that there was a great deal missing. Whole days. Whether Elizabeth Dobson had decided not to confide in her diary in those times or whether the pages had simply been excluded from the copy Cork was given, he couldn't say. He didn't like the feel of things at all, didn't trust Agent Harris or the others, had such an overwhelming sense of having been diverted from the heart of something important. But what? He hadn't reported the break-in at Grandview—something that went against all his professional training—not only because he suspected nothing substantial would be found but also because he was reluctant to trust the authority of the FBI until he had a better sense of what he was really dealing with.

As usual, Meloux had given him plenty to think about. *Majimanidoo.* Evil spirit. What the hell did that mean?

The coffee finished perking. He went to the counter to pour himself a cup and took a moment to stare out the window toward the lake. What was it Meloux had warned? Pay attention to the wind that blows across the water?

The moon had risen high and grown smaller. The light that came from it was weaker now and less revealing. On a calm night, Cork could usually see stars reflected on the surface of the lake like sugar crystals sprinkled over dark chocolate. But there was a breeze ruffling the water, just enough so that nothing reflected from the sky, and the lake spread away from the shore in a darkness that was like the vast empty space between planets.

Then a star appeared on the water. One red-orange star. As Cork watched, it bloomed brighter, like a nova, then dimmed.

Someone on the lake, maybe fifty yards out, was smoking.

Cork jammed on his socks, grabbed a flashlight, and hurried outside. At the edge of the water, he flicked on the beam and shot it where the ember glowed. He couldn't make out much; the boat was too far away. But whoever it was who was watching didn't seem particularly disturbed that Cork was watching back. An outboard motor kicked over and, leisurely, the boat began to glide into the dark well beyond the range of the flashlight beam. Cork flipped off the light. Shivering in the cold, he listened until the sound of the motor was too far away to be heard anymore.

He wasn't certain, but he could almost have sworn that the breeze across the lake carried on it the faint odor of cigar smoke.

10

SHILOH DIDN'T SLEEP WELL. A nightmare had jarred her awake, a visitation from an old enemy. The Dark Angel.

Most of her life, her dreams—the worst of them, anyway—had been dominated by a frightening, faceless figure in black. In the dreams, she inevitably found herself trapped, backed against a dead end—a city alley, a blind desert canyon, a dimly lit hallway, a cave. The Dark Angel approached her. Like the Grim Reaper or the Ghost of Christmas Future, the Dark Angel never spoke, never touched her. Shiloh had always believed with a deep, paralyzing terror that if the Dark Angel ever laid its hand on her, she would die. She usually woke screaming, soaked with sweat. Until she discovered drugs, she had never been able to go back to sleep after a visit from the Dark Angel.

Therapy had helped. Dr. Sutpen had guided her well to an understanding of this terrible figure that haunted her. The nightmares had subsided. Her whole time in the woods, Shiloh had not once been tormented by the Dark Angel.

Until now. In the dream, the Dark Angel had trapped her against a wall of trees she could not break through, trees red with what she thought were autumn leaves, but when the leaves fell, they formed a pool of blood at her feet.

She woke in a sweat and couldn't go back to sleep. At first light, she didn't feel rested at all. She rose and fixed herself a breakfast of coffee, oatmeal with raisins, and some toast, all cooked on the cabin's old cast-iron stove. Every morning, the cabin seemed colder and the little stove less able to heat the one room.

On the rough table, she spread the map Wendell had given her, wrapped her hands for warmth around the tin cup of coffee, and tried to figure where she was and where she would have to go. Wendell had marked the cabin on the map with an X and had put arrows across the map showing her the way home. Where the arrows hit the land, he put a series of small x's to denote a portage. There were seven portages in all. The mix of the contour lines, the arrows, and the x's confused her. She felt hopelessness sweeping over her like a heavy air mass, and for a moment, she could hardly breathe.

"You can't stay here," she said, speaking aloud so that it was as if the advice had come from outside herself. "Wendell's not coming. He can't, or he'd be here by now. That's why he gave you the map. Just in case."

She stared down at the jumble of lines and found where he'd written "Wendell's Place" beside a big circled X in the bottom right-hand corner of the map. It looked like a long way and as labyrinthine a route as a maze in a puzzle book. She closed her eyes and imagined herself already there, Wendell smiling as she came. She imagined hugging him, and she could almost smell the leather of the old vest he always wore.

"You can do it," she heard a strong voice say.

Opening her eyes, she found she was still alone.

She packed her thermal underwear. Before he would take her into the Boundary Waters, Wendell insisted she buy the underwear, although it was hot summer. Now, with the chill in the air, she was thankful for his foresight. In her backpack, she placed a small cooking pan, some utensils, a waterproof container of kitchen matches, a Swiss army pocketknife (a gift from Wendell), a flashlight, and the last of her packaged food—two packs of dehydrated vegetable soup, a bag of apple chips, three granola bars, and a tin of tuna fish. She also packed a change of clothing. She put the map in a side pocket and tied on her rolled-up sleeping bag.

She knew she had to leave her guitar. It had been a good friend in her isolation, but would be a burden on her journey out. The cardboard box full of the tapes she'd recorded she put on the table beside the four big notebooks full of her writing. She thought about the portages, about carrying her pack and the canoe, and she knew she couldn't cart the other things, too. She decided that when she reached Wendell's place, she could arrange to retrieve her guitar and the work she'd done. The larder of the cabin, a box sunk into the floor in one of the corners, was empty now. She put the cardboard box and the notebooks there and placed an old mat woven from cedar bark over the larder lid so that it was hidden.

She took a final look around. This had been a good place for her, the hidden cabin, just as Wendell had promised when he first invited her to the woods. Although it was small and rugged, with but a single room and no running water, she felt a greater fondness toward it than she did either of the big homes she maintained outside those woods. Like a rough old friend, like Wendell himself, it was a place stripped to the essentials and it had helped her get clear.

She hefted the pack, stepped outside, and closed the door. There was no lock, yet she'd never been afraid.

"Good-bye," she said, not feeling silly at all in addressing the place. All things had spirit, Wendell had taught her, and this spirit was good. "Thank you."

She turned and followed the stream to the lake.

The morning sun hadn't climbed above the gray rock ridge, and the lake lay in cold shade. For most of its length, the water was edged with sheer cliffs. To reach the far end, Shiloh followed a steep trail upward through the pines and boulders to the top of the ridge. The air was crisp and clear. Her hands were already chilled, so she slipped her gloves on and began to climb. The woods were quiet. The sound of her own heavy breathing and the clomp of her booted feet seemed an intrusion. For some reason, the scent of the evergreen was sharper to her than ever, and she wondered if in preparing to leave it all behind, she'd become suddenly aware of how pervasive and wonderful it was. She followed the trail half a mile to the other end of the narrow lake. There, a small gap in the ridge had long ago allowed the stream to flow through freely. Now a jumble of rock debris filled the gap, creating a dam across the stream that had flooded what was once a small canyon. Water seeped through the debris, flowing over rocks that were covered with slippery green algae. On the forest floor far below, the stream gathered itself again and ran another quarter mile until it spilled into a lake so large and so convoluted with islands and wooded points of land that the true far shore was impossible to see. Wherever that shore was, miles lay between it and Shiloh. She remembered canoeing in with Wendell, how for most of a day they'd been on that lake weaving among the islands until she had no sense of where they were going or where they'd been.

The sun hit the great lake with a painful brilliance that made her look away. She turned her gaze back to the little lake Wendell called Nikidin. It was so familiar she wanted to go back, to convince herself to wait a bit longer, to believe that Wendell would come after all. But she'd spent so much time there searching for the truth that she couldn't lie to herself. Wendell wasn't coming. God alone knew why, but she was on her own.

Carefully, she began to descend the slick rocks. By the time she reached the bottom of the ridge, she was sweating hard. She dropped her pack and slipped off her gloves and jean jacket. She tied the jacket around her waist by the arms, hefted her pack once again, and followed the stream.

Where the stream spilled into the big lake, the shore was lined with smooth stones. Shiloh put down her pack, went to a thicket of vines not far away, and pulled at the covering to a narrow blind. Inside, a green canoe lay upside down, its gunwales cradled across two logs. Wendell had showed her the canoe so that she could, if she wanted, explore the lake. She'd been so awkward with the paddle and so afraid of getting lost that she'd never gone far. She lifted the bow and raised the canoe as she walked under it. The midthwart was fitted with a padded yoke for ease in portaging. She settled the yoke pads onto her shoulders as she tipped the canoe and balanced the weight to carry it. After she'd put the canoe in the water, she returned for the paddle. She tossed her pack in, shoved off from the shore, and settled herself into the stern.

At water level, all the islands before her created the illusion of a wall across the lake. The sun behind them cast their trees and slopes in shadow so that the wall looked dark and impenetrable. She pulled out the map and studied the line of arrows Wendell had drawn among all the confusing contour lines.

"Too bad you couldn't have put them right on the water, Wendell. Like in a cartoon." She surprised herself with a laugh.

Returning the map to the pack, she dug her paddle into the still water.

And so it began.

11

CORK WAS UP AT FIRST LIGHT, into his sweats, and running. The air was brisk. Frost crisped the grass and the bushes. The sun was red-orange, like a lava flow spilling through the trees along the eastern shore of Iron Lake, and where the flow met the still lake water, the confluence blazed.

He ran north along Center Street, heading toward the outskirts of town. In the early morning, the street was quiet and almost empty. He loved the town in this hour when, like the living thing it was, it slowly woke and showed a face unadorned and innocent, beautiful as a waking child. He passed Lew Knutson delivering Sunday papers from the tailgate of a station wagon driven by his father Karl, and he waved to Cy Borkmann, who was making the rounds in a sheriff's department cruiser. He passed the garage where Harold Svendsen had worked for years repairing the cars and trucks of Aurora before a massive coronary hit him while he was shoveling snow and put an end to his expert tinkering. The garage sat abandoned for years until a young couple from Des Moines bought it, renovated the building, and turned the place into a shop serving fresh-baked goods, sandwiches, and gourmet coffee. They called it Mark and Edie's Gas Pump Grill. When Cork was a kid, the air around Harold Svendsen's garage had been heavy with the smell of drained engine oil, thick and black. Now when he ran past, he was treated to the aroma of fresh-brewed coffee and croissants.

Just at the edge of the old town limits, Cork came to the new Best Western and stopped. The motel complex had been built to accommodate the influx of outsiders coming to Aurora to gamble at the Chippewa Grand Casino. Much of the ground the big motel sat on had once belonged to Ellie Grand. The old house that had stood there had been both her home and her business. When the bulldozers razed the house to make way for the motel, Cork had felt a deep sadness, but who was he to argue with a destiny for the town that profited so many. New tracts for housing had been cleared, moving the edges of Aurora further into the forest. Stores were doing record business. Even Sam's Place had had an outstanding season. Unfamiliar faces populated the streets every day. Cork was often at a loss to distinguish the tourists and gamblers from the permanent transplants, the growing number of urban escapees with enterprise in their eyes. Aurora had no less than three gourmet coffeehouses now. Even Johnny Pap was serving cappuccino at the Pinewood Broiler.

The old house had been abandoned for years when Ellie Grand bought it. The paint was blistered, flaking away. The boards in most places had weathered to a sun-bleached white. The porch sagged like the back of an old horse with a broken spirit. A lot of the windows were empty of glass. The yard around it had gone over to timothy and thistle.

The work of renovating had been done mostly by Cork's father and Wendell Two Knives. Cork's father labored at the urging of his wife, Ellie Grand's cousin. Wendell, who was the husband of Ellie Grand's aunt, Lenore, did it for family. In the way of men in those days and in that country, both Cork's father and Wendell knew about carpentry. They did a bang-up job of helping to create Ellie's Pie Shop.

Behind the shop, Ellie Grand had planted a huge garden full of raspberry vines, strawberries, pumpkins, rhubarb. Whatever was in season filled her pie crusts. The tourists who returned to Iron Lake every year made Ellie's Pie Shop part of their annual pilgrimage. Cork had spent a lot of his paper-route money on slices of Ellie Grand's pie. But he hadn't gone just for the pie. Like a lot of the other young men in Aurora, he'd gone because Marais worked there behind the counter, helping her mother.

When the young men came around, and sometimes older men, too, Ellie Grand was harsh. How a woman so bitter about men—about anything—could make pies so sweet, Cork couldn't figure. As far as he knew, there were only two men Ellie Grand didn't consider cohorts of the devil—his father and Wendell Two Knives. She even distrusted the priest at St. Agnes, Father Kelsey, who, she fiercely maintained, looked at Marais in a way that would make holy water boil.

He remembered a time—he must have been twelve or thirteen because his father was still alive—when he sat at one of the tables while Marais worked the counter. It was late summer. He was eating a piece of strawberry-rhubarb. Marais hummed to herself, hummed beautifully. Cork, as always, tracked her every move. She was fifteen or sixteen then. Straight black hair that hung to her butt. Dark, East Indian princess skin. She wore cutoff jeans and a tight red jersey top. Three young men came into the shop. Tourists, or sons of tourists. Eighteen, nineteen years old. They asked what kind of pie Marais recommended. She offered several good options. They took the blueberry, Cork recalled.

"What do you do when you're finished here for the day?" the one who gave her the money asked.

"That depends on what my choices are." She didn't smile, but Cork was certain there was an invitation in her gold-dust eyes.

"We've got a speed boat," another one said. "Come for a ride."

"Or a swim," the third suggested. "Bet you look great in a swimsuit."

"Oh, I do," Marais said. She looked him over briefly and added, "Too bad I can't say the same for you."

The other two laughed.

The first one pressed her. "So, what do you say?"

She gave them the pie and change. "Got a cigarette?"

"Sure," the second one said. He reached into his shirt pocket and brought out a pack of Marlboros.

He was holding the pack out to Marais when Ellie Grand burst from the kitchen, a pie server gripped murderously in her hand.

"Out," she cried. "Get out of my shop. All of you."

"Hey, wait a minute—" the first one began.

Ellie Grand pushed Marais aside and leaned over the counter, the pie server only inches from the heart of the kid who held the cigarettes. "I said get out. And don't ever let me see you in my shop again."

They backed away, glanced at Marais, who offered them only slight sympathy with a shrug of her shoulders; and left the shop.

"They only asked if I'd like to go for a boat ride," Marais explained casually.

"Men always start out asking small, but in the end they want everything." Ellie Grand aimed the pie server at her daughter. "Don't you be fooled, Marais. Don't ever let them use you. You do the using. Understand?"

"Yes, Mama," Marais said.

When Ellie Grand returned to the kitchen, Marais looked to Cork, laughed silently, rolled her eyes, and said, *"Giiwanaadizi, nishiime." She's crazy, little brother.*

When Marais Grand had been a star on television, the town council had voted to put up a sign at the town limits declaring it the HOME OF MARAIS GRAND. Ten years after her death, when annexed land extended the town limits, the old sign, full of rusted holes from a .22 target pistol, had been removed.

Cork continued his run, veering from Center Street where it became once again the state highway, and following a county road that paralleled the lake. He was a mile or so outside of town when a black Lincoln Town Car drew alongside him and the charcoal-tinted rear window slid silently down.

"O'Connor?"

The man whose face filled the frame of the car window looked to be in his late twenties, maybe early thirties. He had thick black hair, a rich man's tan. His left ear had been pierced, and he wore what appeared to be a diamond stud. Cork had never before set eyes on him.

"Yeah?" Cork put his hands on his hips and stood at the side of the road, breathing hard.

"Mind getting in?" the tanned man said with a smile. He had very white teeth. Although they were unnaturally even, the smile they formed seemed easy and genuine. However, Cork's mother had taught him early the danger of getting into a stranger's car. It was a rule that had stood him in good stead for over forty years. He didn't see a particularly compelling reason to disregard it now.

"I'm in the middle of something here," he pointed out.

"I'd like to talk to you about Shiloh," the man said.

That was one pretty compelling reason. Then through the window of the Lincoln, the man aimed a very large handgun right at Cork's nose. That made two pretty compelling reasons. The door swung open and Cork got in.

The other man in the car, the one behind the wheel, appeared to be in his midthirties, blond, a neck full of more muscle than most people had in their whole bodies. Cork thought he could outrun the big man if he had to, but if the guy ever caught him, he'd take Cork apart like his bones were nothing but soda straws.

The handsome man smiled and put the gun on the seat between them.

"Sorry. This is really a friendly visit," he said. "I just had to get your full attention. This won't take long; then you can finish your run."

"You said you wanted to talk about Shiloh." Cork glanced at the gun. He could have reached for it easily enough, but he decided he wanted to hear what the man had to say.

"There are some things you need to know. For your own good." The handsome man tapped the driver's shoulder. "Take off, Joey. We don't want to attract attention."

Good luck, Cork thought. In Aurora, a Lincoln Town Car would be as inconspicuous as a nun in a G-string.

Joey drove north along the lake.

The man in back was clean-shaven and smelled of a good,

subtle aftershave. He wore calfskin boots, tight jeans, a red chamois shirt under a dark green sweater.

"My name is Angelo Benedetti. You probably already know my family's name. You spoke with the FBI about us? Last night, I believe."

"And if I did?"

"Then they told you a lot of lies, mostly about my father."

"Vincent Benedetti?" Cork said. "What kind of lies do you believe they told me?"

"That my father killed Shiloh's mother. Look, they've been after my father, my family, a long time. Isn't that right, Joey?"

"Long time," Joey said into the rearview mirror.

"They never get anything, but that doesn't stop them," Benedetti said. "They're like flies. They hang around and make a nuisance of themselves."

"If they're only a nuisance, why are you here?"

"To help you. And to help Shiloh."

"Yeah," Joey said, turning his thick neck and speaking over his shoulder, "you're in deep shit."

"Shut up, Joey." He lightly slapped the back of Joey's head.

"Sure thing, Angelo."

"The feds told you about Libbie Dobson, I'll bet." Benedetti waited for Cork to confirm but went on when Cork only stared at him. "I'll bet they didn't tell you about Dr. Sutpen. Shiloh's psychiatrist."

"What about her?"

In the front seat, Joey made a noise, a boy noise, the kind Cork often heard from Stevie in his play when he pretended something was exploding. Joey laughed to himself.

"She's dead." Benedetti allowed a dramatic moment before he went on. "Killed in a gas explosion at her Palm Springs office that burned the place down and destroyed all client records. Authorities are listing it officially as accidental."

Joey swung the car into a turnaround and headed back in the direction from which they'd come.

"You don't think it was an accident," Cork said.

"Highly coincidental, don't you think? I don't know about you, Cork, but I don't believe in coincidence."

"Only my friends call me Cork."

"That's what I'm here to tell you. In this, you won't know who your friends are."

"You claim the FBI lied to me. Why would they?"

"My father believes they're protecting someone. Someone big."

"Who?"

"He doesn't know. He believes whoever it is, they were responsible for the murder of Shiloh's mother. Back then, Marais Grand had a powerful friend, someone who pulled a lot of strings for her. My father never knew who it was, but he thinks Marais was killed to keep that friendship from being exposed. Now they're trying to kill Shiloh."

"Why?"

"Come on, Cork. The feds filled you in on that part. Shiloh's shrink helped her remember things about the night her mother was killed." Benedetti held up his hands in easy guilt. "It's not hard to find these things out. Cops are civil servants and terribly underpaid."

"Why isn't your father here taking care of this business himself?"

"He's not a well man. The flight here was hard on him. He's resting. But my words are his."

Cork looked straight into Benedetti's eyes. They were green with flecks of gold. Women no doubt found them compelling. "Elizabeth Dobson was probably killed because someone wanted the letters she'd received from Shiloh. Some more letters from Shiloh were stolen last night."

Benedetti didn't flinch at all. "I'm not going to lie to you, Cork. Yeah, I know people who know how to steal. I know people who can set fires that look like accidents. I know people who kill as easily as you or I brush our teeth. But then, so does the FBI."

Cork looked away from Benedetti, watched the placid morning surface of Iron Lake glide past. "Why should I believe you?"

Benedetti folded his hands to his lips as if he were praying. In the moment of silence inside the big Lincoln, Cork heard the snap of bubble gum from Joey up front.

"I hear you're that rare bird, Cork—an honest man. They say you have integrity. If the FBI goes into those woods after Shiloh, she won't come out alive. You're her only hope as far as I can see. Even if you don't believe me, what harm can it do to help her?"

"Help her how?"

"Go in and bring her out before the FBI can get to her. That's all. No other strings attached. If you do this, my father will pay you fifty thousand dollars."

"Fifty thousand dollars." Cork let his surprise show. "What's his interest?"

"If Shiloh does remember who killed her mother," Benedetti said, "my father wants to know the name."

"There's one problem. I don't know where she is," Cork said.

Benedetti lifted his hand as if to silence Cork's objection. "If everything I've heard about you is true, you will." He reached under his sweater and drew out a card from the pocket of his shirt. "Joey, a pen."

Joey handed a gold ballpoint over the seat. Benedetti wrote on the back of the card, then handed the card to Cork. On one side was a lithographed purple parrot in a gold cage and under it Angelo Benedetti's name. On the other side, Benedetti had written a telephone number.

"My cell phone," he said. "Call me when you know something."

They'd returned to the place where Cork had entered the Lincoln. Joey stopped the car.

"Like I told you," Benedetti said. "You make sure Shiloh comes out safely and my father will be very grateful. Joey, is my old man grateful or what?"

"His gratitude is boundless," Joey confirmed. "You should take the money," he advised, grinning over the seat at Cork. "Keep Angelo's old man happy. Cuz when he ain't, he's one mean son of a bitch."

Cork noticed that this time Benedetti didn't tell Joey to shut up.

"Tell your father to keep his money. Whatever I do, I do for my own reasons." Cork opened the car door and stepped out.

Benedetti leaned out after. "I've been as straight with you as I've ever been with any man. Help Shiloh. Please."

The door closed. The big Lincoln pulled away.

Cork started running again, back toward Sam's Place. He'd told Meloux things became clearer to him when he ran. But the way the situation stood now, he could run all the way to the fucking moon and everything would still be a mess.

12

AT GRANDVIEW, Willie Raye opened the door to Cork's Bronco and stepped in.

"Morning," he said cheerfully.

"Tell me about Vincent Benedetti," Cork said.

Raye looked startled. "Benedetti? Why do you want to know about *him?*" The last word was full of poison.

Cork explained his morning meeting.

"Don't ever trust a Benedetti," Raye said. He stared at the trees that isolated his cabin and worked his jaw as if he were chewing on something old and bitter. "I never knew for sure if it was him who killed Marais. But if he wanted her dead, he knew how to get it done."

"What do you know about him?"

"I haven't seen him in years. Not since—well, not since Marais's funeral. The bastard had the gall to be there, looking innocent as a lamb," Raye said. "Man like that," he added in an acid Ozark twang, "got hisself a cast-iron soul and a shithole for a heart."

Wendell Two Knives' mobile home sat on a patch of green lawn that rolled gently down to the reflection of blue sky that was Iron Lake. Under the windows were flower boxes that held red geraniums still in full bloom. The whole place was surrounded by birch trees, trunks white as icicles, leaves gold as freshly minted doubloons.

The note Cork had left the night before was still taped to Wendell's door. Cork knocked, but Wendell didn't answer. He crossed the lawn to the big corrugated shed that Wendell used as a garage and peered in at a window. He beckoned Willie Raye over.

"Wendell drives a Dodge Ram pickup," Cork said. "Pickup's gone. But take a gander at what's sitting in its place."

The floor of the shed was covered with fragments of birch bark, and the shed itself was full of tools that Wendell used in the building of birch-bark canoes, an art he'd practiced his entire life. Mallets, wood chisels, buckets, sawhorses, brushes— all hung on racks or sat on benches. In the center was a cleared area large enough for a truck to park. Instead of Wendell's truck, a small red sports car sat there, highlighted in a long shaft of sunlight that came through the window on the far side of the shed. A coating of dust dulled the sheen of the car's finish.

"Shiloh loves sports cars," Raye said.

Cork walked around to the back of the shed where there stood a canoe rack with spaces for four canoes. Only one space was filled.

"What do you think?" Raye asked.

"I think he's gone for a while."

"To Shiloh?"

"Let's hope so. Come on."

"Where to?" Raye asked as he followed Cork to the Bronco.

"To Stormy Two Knives. He's the only other person I can think of who might know where that is."

Two miles up the road, just beyond the far outskirts of Allouette, Cork pulled into the drive of a small log home set among white pines growing in planted rows. A sign posted beside the drive advertised firewood for sale. Next to the house, a woman stood at a clothesline, her arms lifted, holding a wet sheet. A slight northwesterly breeze had picked up and the ends of the hung linen ruffled leisurely. The woman finished pinning the corner of the sheet to the line with a clothespin, then shielded her eyes against the sun as she watched the two men approach.

"*Anin,* Sarah," Cork greeted her.

"*Anin,* Cork." Her reply was polite, but not warm. She was a small woman in her early thirties with high cheeks and dark red hair that she wore long. She had on Nikes, neatly creased jeans, and a blue denim shirt. Her attention glanced off Raye, then quickly settled again on Cork.

"I'm looking for Wendell," Cork explained. "We stopped by his place, but he's not home."

Something cloudy passed briefly across her face. "You'd better talk to Stormy."

"That's what I figured, too. Where can I find him?"

"Him and Louis are cutting firewood. On the old logging road at the bridge over Widow's Creek."

"Thanks, Sarah."

"I'm not saying he'll talk to you, Cork," she cautioned.

"I understand."

As they pulled back onto the road, Raye asked, "Why wouldn't he talk to you?"

Cork turned east out of Allouette and began to follow a dirt road that cut through thick forest. "Stormy's got a temper," he explained. "A few years ago he got into a fight, killed a man. Afterward, he panicked and ran. Holed up in a shack up north on Iron Lake, threatened to shoot anyone who tried to come near him. The sheriff talked his way in and convinced Stormy to give himself up. Assured him he'd get a fair trial. As it turned out, he didn't. Stormy spent five years in the prison at Stillwater."

"That still doesn't explain why he wouldn't talk to you."

Cork pulled across an old wooden bridge over a small creek and stopped behind a dusty blue Ford Ranger parked at the side of the road. "I was the sheriff."

The biting whine of a chainsaw chewed through the stillness of the woods near the creek. Cork followed the sound until he came to an area where a number of big dying firs stood brown among the other evergreens. Several trees had already been felled, their dry branches splintered against the ground. Stormy Two Knives was moving swiftly down one of the horizontal trunks, a big yellow McCulloch in his gloved hands, carving away the limbs and slicing the trunk into sections. The air smelled of oil and gas and sawdust. A boy of ten followed on the ground gathering the debris into piles. The boy noticed them first.

Cork waited in a big patch of sunlight until Stormy Two Knives cut the motor of the chainsaw and lifted his safety goggles. Two Knives saw the boy looking, and he looked, too. He stepped off the fallen tree.

"*Anin*, Stormy," Cork said. "*Anin*, Louis," he said to the boy.

Two Knives set down the chainsaw. He took off the ball cap he was wearing and shook his head vigorously. Sweat flew off him like a dog shaking dry after a bath. "You don't have to pretend the Indian shit with me, O'Connor."

"*Anin*," Louis Two Knives said.

His father shot him a stern look.

Stormy Two Knives was slightly smaller than Cork but outweighed him by fifty pounds. He stood hunched a little forward from overdeveloped back muscles, a characteristic of men who'd cut timber most of their lives. In the years he'd been in prison, Two Knives had used his time to develop the rest of his body as well. His chest was massive. The sleeves of his plaid flannel shirt were rolled back, revealing sinewy arms. But prison had also developed something else in Two Knives, and it showed in the coldness of his dark eyes.

"Sarah told us you'd be here. I need to talk to you, Stormy."

"I'm busy."

"It's important. It's about your uncle."

Two Knives reached down to where a thermos sat on a stump. He poured cold water into the thermos cup and took a drink. He offered the cup to his son.

"Wendell? What about him?"

"Have you seen him lately?"

"Why?"

"It's important I talk to him."

"Haven't seen him."

Louis Two Knives handed the thermos cup back to this father. "He's in the Boundary Waters."

"Louis," Stormy Two Knives snapped.

"He's been gone a long time," the boy continued, ignoring the hard look from his father.

"Stormy," Cork said. "He may be in trouble."

"The only trouble an Indian is ever in is with the law. Has my uncle done something?"

"He guided a woman into the Boundary Waters. We think somebody may want to hurt her, and they might try to use Wendell to get to her."

"We?" Two Knives coldly scrutinized Arkansas Willie Raye, looking directly into his eyes, an unusual thing for an Ojibwe. But prison had changed Stormy Two Knives in a lot of ways. "I know you."

"Call me Arkansas Willie," Raye said. He thrust a hand out, but Two Knives only looked at it.

"Used to watch you on TV," Stormy Two Knives said. "Didn't know you were still alive." He turned his attention back to Cork. "I don't know anything about my uncle."

"Stormy, this woman's life may be at stake. Your uncle's, too."

"My uncle can take care of himself."

"I've been told he goes in and out of the Boundary Waters frequently. I think he must take supplies to this woman. Louis says he's been gone a long time. That makes me worried."

"Look, what do you care, O'Connor? You're not the sheriff anymore. You don't make the laws around here."

"I never did, Stormy."

"Like I said," Two Knives went on, lifting his chainsaw, "I'm busy. Hand me that bar tool, Louis. I want to tighten this chain."

"I'll pay you," Willie Raye said.

Two Knives paused. "How much?"

"A thousand dollars."

"We get an allotment from the casino profits now." He

hefted the saw and plucked at the chain to gauge the tension. "You can take your thousand dollars and shove it up your ass."

Willie Raye moved forward a step. "I didn't mean to insult you. I'm just plumb scared, Stormy. I got me a little girl out there, lost as a blind kitten in a kennel full of hounds. I'd give my left nut just to know she's okay. A man loses his family, doesn't matter what else he's got. He's got nuthin'. There's no reason you should help me. No reason on earth. Except you're the only one who can."

Stormy Two Knives stared at him. "You her father?"

"I'm her father."

Two Knives' face was impassive as he stood considering. Louis reached out and touched his father's arm. Two Knives bent down and the boy whispered.

In the quiet, Cork heard the crack and pop of twigs as someone approached from the direction of the old logging road. In a moment, Booker T. Harris and Dwight Sloane appeared. They walked to where Cork and Raye stood and Harris addressed Stormy Two Knives.

"Is your name Hector Two Knives?"

The skin around Two Knives' eyes went tight as old leather. "Everyone calls me Stormy. Except cops."

"Is that your Ranger parked out there?"

"That's my Ranger."

"Mr. Two Knives," Harris said, taking a pair of handcuffs from his coat pocket, "you're under arrest."

13

"UNDER ARREST?" Two Knives' eyes flashed toward Cork. "What for?"

"Sloane," Harris said.

Agent Sloane held out his hands. He wore black gloves. Cradled in the palms of his gloves was a big handgun. Cork guessed, from its size and square trigger guard, that it was probably a Ruger Super Blackhawk, .44 magnum. Not an uncommon handgun.

"I found this in the toolbox in the back of your truck," Sloane said.

"You have a search warrant to look in the toolbox?" Cork asked.

"The lid was up," Sloane said.

"That's not mine." Stormy stood rigid, the saw poised in his hands.

"You can argue that from your prison cell. This is a parole violation, Hector. You're going back to hard time," Harris said. "Put that saw down."

Stormy didn't move. "You didn't find that in my toolbox."

"I will testify under oath that I did," Sloane said. He put the gun in a plastic evidence bag.

"What's this all about, Harris?" Cork demanded.

Stormy shot Cork an angry glance. "You know them?"

"FBI," Cork said. "That's Special Agent in Charge Booker

T. Harris. And that's Agent Dwight Sloane. They're looking for the woman, too."

"Too?" Harris said. "I thought we were working together on this, O'Connor."

"So did I," Cork said. "I thought we agreed to do it my way."

Stormy Two Knives regarded Cork as if he had murder on his mind.

"Read him his rights," Harris said to Agent Sloane. He stepped toward Stormy with the cuffs in his outstretched hands. "Unless he wants to tell us where the woman is."

"I don't know where the woman is," Stormy said.

"Then how do you explain this?" Harris took from Sloane another plastic evidence bag. Inside was a brown envelope, approximately nine by twelve inches. Harris slipped black leather gloves on his hands, carefully took the envelope from the bag, and held it delicately by one corner as he removed the contents—a stack of hundred-dollar bills and a piece of plain typing paper. "Care to read what the note says? Out loud, if you please." He held the paper out for Cork to read.

"'As agreed. For making sure our little wood nymph doesn't leave the forest. Split it with Stormy anyway you want.'"

"There's fifteen thousand dollars here," Harris said, waving the stack of bills in the air.

"Where'd you get that?" Cork demanded.

"The trailer you just left. The door was open. Envelope was on the kitchen counter."

"How convenient," Cork responded.

Stormy Two Knives glared at the money. "I don't know anything about it. And my uncle would never have anything to do with something like that."

"You have a search warrant for Wendell's trailer?" Cork asked.

"It was in plain sight," Harris said. "And we had reason to be suspicious. Even if it doesn't hold up in court, it'll still be a long time before Two Knives breathes free air again. Unless he decides to help us find the woman."

"You're on reservation land," Cork pointed out. "Jurisdiction here is local. You have no right to arrest this man."

"Bullshit, O'Connor. Reservations are under federal authority," Harris countered.

"Not this one," Cork said. "Jurisdiction here is in the state of Minnesota. Approved by Congress. Public Law 280, passed in 1953."

"I'm here on an investigation under the RICO statute. Hauling him in on a parole violation involving a firearm is well within the scope of my authority. Two Knives wants to argue jurisdiction, he'll have to do it from a jail cell."

"The hell he will." Cork stepped between the men and Stormy Two Knives.

Sloane drew a weapon from a shoulder holster under his coat. "We will arrest you, all of you, if we have to," he said carefully and earnestly. "It would be easier if you just cooperate."

"I don't know where the woman is," Stormy told them. Again.

"Too bad. Sloane." Harris nodded toward Stormy.

"You have the right to remain silent," Sloane began.

"I know where she is."

Everyone stopped and looked at the boy.

"Hush, Louis," Stormy said.

"No," Harris said. "Go on, son."

"Louis," Stormy warned.

"I don't want you to go back to jail," the boy said.

"They won't—" Stormy began.

"Like hell we won't," Harris cut him off. "I'll slap your daddy's ass in jail faster than you can say Geronimo, boy."

Louis looked at the federal agent fiercely. "He was a Chiricahua Apache. We're Ojibwe Anishinaabe."

Harris seemed almost on the edge of laughing. "So you are. So you are." He knelt down to the boy's level. "Unless we get some cooperation, Louis, I'm going to have to put your father back in jail. I don't have a choice. You know where the woman is?"

Louis Two Knives nodded.

"Where?"

"Nikidin."

"What's that?"

"It means 'vulva,'" Cork said.

"Vulva?" Harris laughed. "You mean like in vagina?"

"I don't understand," Sloane said.

"It's a place, I imagine. Somewhere in the Boundary Waters," Cork said.

"A place?" Harris still looked pretty amused. "They named a place vagina. Jesus."

"Can you show us this place, son?" Sloane asked. "Can you show us on a map?"

The boy looked uncertain, then shrugged.

"Get us a map," Harris told Sloane.

Agent Sloane holstered his weapon, turned, and hurried back toward the logging road.

Cork said to Harris, "You followed us. How?"

"Technology, O'Connor."

"A transmitter of some kind? Planted on my Bronco?" Cork looked to Stormy. "I didn't know. I swear it."

Sloane came back with a map. He unfolded it and laid it out on a stump.

"Come over and take a look, Louis," Harris said. He beckoned the boy to him. Stormy Two Knives made a move toward his son, but Sloane stepped in to block his way. Harris put his arm around the boy's shoulders. "How old are you, Louis?"

"Ten."

"Know what this is?"

"Sure. It's a map."

"A map. That's right. A map of the whole Boundary Waters Canoe Area Wilderness. Can you read this map?"

Louis took a long look at the map. Finally he shook his head.

"Take your time. I'll help. We're right here." Harris put his finger on a spot near the center on the bottom.

"We never used a map," the boy said.

"We?"

"Uncle Wendell and me."

"You've been there?"

"Yes," the boy said.

Cork said, "Louis, do you remember the names of the rivers and lakes you crossed to get to where the woman is?"

Louis nodded. "Aaitawaabik. Zhiigwanaabik. Bakwzhi-ganaaboo."

"Hold it." Harris lifted his hands. "Those don't look like any places I see on this map."

"Ojibwe words," Cork said. "Louis, did Uncle Wendell tell you stories about the rivers, about the lakes?"

"Yes."

Cork explained. "Wendell Two Knives is, among other things, an *aadizookewinini*. A storyteller. I'm guessing he made up stories about the rivers and lakes, gave them names that fit the stories he told Louis. Maybe they're real names to the Anishinaabe. Maybe they're just Wendell's inventions. It would be hard to know."

"So you're saying Louis can't tell us how to get there?" Harris turned his attention once again to the boy. "How far is it?"

"A long day by canoe."

"Can you take us there?"

Stormy exploded. "No! My boy's taking you nowhere. There's no law can force him to go."

"No?" Harris looked toward Sloane. "Give me the gun."

Agent Sloane handed him the bag with the .44 he'd claimed to have found in the toolbox. Harris knelt again, putting himself at the boy's level.

"Louis, see this gun? We found it in your father's truck. It's against the law for him to have this gun and he should go back to jail. But I'll make a deal with you. If you take me to where the woman is, I give you my word your father will be all right. I won't tell anyone about the gun."

"You son of a bitch," Stormy spat. He yanked the cord on the McCulloch. The saw roared to life and Stormy thrust it toward Harris. "Get away from my boy, or I swear I'll cut you in half."

Sloane's gun was out of his holster in the blink of an

eye. "Drop it, Hector," he hollered over the roar of the chain-saw.

For a long moment, no one moved. Stormy Two Knives held so still, so tense that the veins on his huge arms stood out like rivers on a map. Sloane was like a tragic geometric equation, body vertical, arms horizontal, the barrel of his gun trued on a line directly to Stormy's forehead. Then Harris made a surprising move. He stood up slowly, looked at Stormy with something very near to sympathy, and asked, just loud enough to be heard over the crying of the saw, "Do you really want your son to see this?"

Stormy glanced at Louis, who stood slightly behind Harris looking terrified. He killed the engine of the McCulloch and put the saw down.

In the relief of the stillness that followed, Cork said, "If the boy goes, his father goes with him."

Stormy glanced at Cork and nodded almost imperceptibly.

Harris thought it over briefly. "Fair enough."

"And him." Stormy gestured his gloved hand toward Cork. "O'Connor?"

Cork understood. Stormy was already confronted with a system weighted to Harris's advantage. Once out in the woods, Harris could do anything he wanted, and who was there to challenge him?

"Yes, me," Cork said. "And him." He nodded at Willie Raye.

"Christ," Harris said, noting Raye carefully for the first time. "I'll be damned if it isn't Arkansas Willie. I thought you were dead."

"Those reports were greatly exaggerated," Raye said without smiling.

"What are you doing here?" Harris asked.

"Shiloh's my daughter," Raye said.

Harris gave him a smile without a thimbleful of humor in it. "Is that so? Seems to me I heard once upon a time that when it came to husbandly doings, you were more likely to be doing husbands."

Arkansas Willie's face darkened, as if he'd entered a tunnel. He came out on the other side looking mean and hard. "She's my daughter, you son of a bitch. You're not going after her without me."

"No way." Harris shook his head adamantly.

"Arkansas Willie doesn't go," Cork said, "I don't go. I don't go, Stormy doesn't go. Stormy doesn't go, the boy won't go. Long way for you to come, to not get where you're going, Harris."

Harris regarded them all. "Ah, shit." He stepped away and turned his back to the men while he considered.

Stormy motioned Louis to his side. The boy obeyed and took shelter under his father's arm. Raye mouthed a "thanks" to Cork. Sloane had lowered his weapon and was waiting.

"All right," Harris finally agreed, swinging back around. "But this is how it's going to be. We give the orders. You do exactly as we say or we'll nail your asses. Understood?" Harris waved Agent Sloane toward the logging road. "Get on the radio. Put it together."

14

"Shit."

Jo O'Connor stood in a bright square of kitchen sunlight, glaring down at a cherry pie that flaunted its perfection from the pages of Rose's opened cookbook on the counter. Flour and dough surrounded the cookbook as if there'd been a battle in a bakery. Jo's fingers were doughy, her jeans starred with floury handprints. Her conversation earlier that morning with Rose played again and again in her mind, like a bad tune she couldn't shake.

"You don't really want to try this," Rose had said, eagerly offering her sister an out.

"I wouldn't have offered if I didn't want to," Jo replied.

"At least let me give you a few tips."

"Tips? I'm thirty-eight years old, Rose. I make a living deciphering legal gobbledy-gook. I can certainly follow the instructions in a cookbook."

"But—" Rose had tried.

"No buts. This is my pie."

Rose had started to argue, then shrugged, opened her arms toward her kitchen, and proclaimed darkly, as if inviting an army to ravage that which she best loved, "Fine, then. Be my guest."

Jo jammed her fists on her hips and eyed the mess she'd made of the kitchen. "Sweet Jesus," she whispered, and rued her own stubbornness with Rose.

The territories of their interests had been established early. Their mother, an army nurse, moved them a dozen times when they were growing up, and a dozen times they'd faced the obstacle of being new in a place. Rose had been a plump child, freckled, terribly picked on by other children, and possessed of a gentle and uncertain spirit that kept her from fighting back. Jo had done that kind of fighting for both of them. When she was thirteen, she broke the nose of the son of a full colonel at Fort Sam Houston who'd goosed Rose, grabbed her purse, pulled out a tampon, and taunted, "Plug the ugly dyke!" Jo had been afraid her mother, whom she and Rose both called the Captain, would be angry. The Captain wasn't. The colonel's son not only apologized to Rose, he asked Jo to the movies. She turned him down.

For Rose, each home was a haven, and she learned to care for each respectfully and well. From early on, she did the cooking. Jo fixed the leaky faucets. Rose did the laundry. Jo changed the oil in the car. Rose sewed. Jo mowed the lawn. In school, Rose was content to pass her courses without attracting attention. Jo battled to be at the top. They were so different—in appearance and interest—that except for the fact they loved one another fiercely, it might have been hard to believe they were sisters.

Jo was in her third year of a full scholarship to Northwestern University when the Captain suffered a stroke that left her paralyzed on the entire left side of her body. Rose, who'd just begun a major in home ec ed at Eastern Illinois, dropped out to care for her mother. For more than seven years, that was the focus of her life. A few months before Jenny was born, the Captain passed away, another stroke, massive this time. Jo was about to begin her final year of law school at the University of Chicago, and Rose offered to come and help with the baby. She'd been an integral part of the O'Connor household ever since.

Jo looked down at herself, dusted with flour, barnacled with bits of dough. She was sorry she'd insisted on tackling the pie. But there was motive in her madness. The pie, along with other desserts prepared by the women of St. Agnes, was to be served that evening at a church gathering honoring Elysia Notto, a local girl who headed a Benedictine mission in Togo and who was visiting her home parish for a brief while. Jo knew the women of the church had long ago opened their arms to Rose. Her kindness, her firm, gentle spirit, and her proficiency at skills those women admired had helped her overcome fairly quickly the hurdle of being an outsider in Aurora. It didn't hurt, Rose was always the first to put in, that she was also heavy, unattractive, and no threat whatsoever where their husbands were concerned. Whatever the reasons, Rose had found her place, as if she'd always belonged in that isolated, far north town. But Jo never felt accepted in the same way. Although the women of Aurora were always cordial, Jo sensed a half-built wall there. Rose believed this was because the women didn't understand Jo. Part of it, she argued, was that from the beginning Jo had chosen to represent the Anishinaabe in proceedings that were often at odds with the interests of the citizens of Aurora. Also, she worked in an arena generally populated by men and was extremely successful there. And, finally, she was very attractive. That, Rose told her bluntly, was a lot to overcome.

If there had indeed been a wall, events of the last year had begun to make it crumble. Cork's affair with Molly Nurmi, something known to the whole town now, had brought Jo a good deal of sympathy. Although she felt guilty—if people knew the whole story, there would be little sympathy—she was touched by the warmth of the concern suddenly showered on her, and she found herself trying, often in awkward ways, to reciprocate.

The pie, in some pathetic twist of thinking, was one of those ways.

Now she looked down at the ruins of a crust that refused to do for her even something as simple as roll flat on waxed paper. She swore quietly.

"Is Rose dead?"

Jo turned around and found Cork standing in the kitchen doorway taking in the devastation.

"At church all day. I'm cooking," Jo said gravely.

"You?"

"I've cooked before. Remember?"

"Believe me," Cork said. "I remember."

She'd been notoriously bad, had had a reputation among their Chicago friends for possessing a flair for the soggy, the lumpy, the burned. Consequently, Cork had done most of the cooking before Rose came to live with them. He was pretty good at it; she'd always been the first to admit it.

Cork took a couple of steps into the kitchen. "What are you making?"

"Cherry pie. For the St. Agnes Guild tonight."

Cork scanned the counter, the whole mess, and Jo was afraid he was going to offer her advice. He didn't. Just nodded and glanced at the potato peelings lying in the sink. "Cooking dinner, too?"

"Yes." She recalled the looks of horror on the faces of the children when they'd heard the news. "Shake 'n Bake chicken, mashed potatoes, canned corn, and gravy from a jar," she confessed. "Want to stay?"

"Can't," he said.

"Coward."

"No, really. I just stopped by to tell Jenny and Annie I won't be opening Sam's Place today."

Jo turned back to her recalcitrant crust and lay on it with the rolling pin. "Going fishing?"

"Hunting's more like it. A woman's lost in the Boundary Waters. I'm going in to help find her."

The crust rolled up with the rolling pin as if it were metal and the roller a magnet.

"Jenny's at Sean's. You can reach her there. Annie's helping Rose at church. They should be home pretty soon. I heard Arkansas Willie Raye's out at Grandview. Annie said he stopped by Sam's Place yesterday."

"He wanted to shoot the breeze about Marais and the old days," Cork said.

"I didn't even know he was still alive."

"He definitely is," Cork said. "And kicking."

He leaned against the stove, watching Jo struggle with the pie crust. She wore a powder blue sweatshirt with the sleeves rolled up. A small trickle of sweat crawled from her blond hair onto the soft down of her temple and then her cheek. He studied the curves of her hips as they rolled to her labor. He felt an old desire rising up, one that hadn't visited him in quite a while, tempting and, at the same time, frightening.

"I'd better go," he said.

Before Cork could move, Stevie burst through the back door. He ran and leaped into Cork's arms. "Daddy!"

Cork nuzzled his son, who smelled of sunshine and dry leaves.

"Can you play football?" Stevie asked eagerly.

"Sorry, buddy. Not today."

Disappointment flooded Stevie's small face.

"I have to go away for a while. A day or two. When I come back, we'll toss the old pigskin until our arms fall off. Okay?" He tousled Stevie's black hair.

Stevie pushed out of Cork's arms. "Okay," he said, but his voice betrayed him.

Jo put down her rolling pin and knelt to Stevie. "Tell you what. Right after dinner, we'll make some cookies shaped like footballs, you and me, then we'll toss them down our mouths till our arms fall off. What do you say?"

"Cookies?" Stevie's dark eyes were pools of concern. "Yours?"

"We'll make them together. They'll be ours."

"All right," he finally agreed. He turned around and drifted back outside.

"Smooth, counselor." Cork smiled.

"I'm great at negotiations. Especially when the opposing party is six years old."

She followed Cork to the front door and they stood a moment, awkwardly, as if they were on a first date.

"I'll stop by soon as I get back so I can keep my promise to Stevie."

Jo nodded. "Fine."

Cork started down the walk. He was dressed in loose

khakis and a red T-shirt. In the last year, he'd lost weight, and he looked good and strong. He'd stopped smoking, too. A promise to another woman—Jo knew and accepted.

A couple of weeks earlier, Jo had taken the girls and Stevie down to the Twin Cities so they could cheer Cork on in the marathon. Although she didn't say anything to anyone, she felt a good deal of admiration for him—a man in his mid-forties, running his first marathon. In the best of ways, he was like the old Cork, before so many circumstances had come between them, split them apart, sent them both into the arms of other lovers.

"Cork," she called suddenly, and went quickly to him as he stood by the Bronco.

He turned to her. Although his face was full in the sun, there seemed so much in it that was shadowed, so much unspoken between them.

"What is it?"

She felt foolish, not certain at all what she'd meant to say. "Just—oh, just take care of yourself." Then she surprised them both. She leaned to him and kissed him lightly on the cheek.

"Thanks." He looked slightly bewildered. "I—uh—I will."

She watched the Bronco pull away. The street was quiet. Sunlight dripped over the houses along the block like butter melting over stacks of pancakes. From across the street drifted the aroma of Birdie Frank's sauerbraten and the sound of Birdie in her kitchen whistling "That Old Black Magic." Jo felt empty and out of place.

A moment later, she heard Rose call out. Turning, she saw her sister and Annie approaching along the sidewalk from the other end of the block.

"Was that Dad?" Annie asked.

"Yes. He stopped by to say don't come out to Sam's Place. He's not opening today."

"I'll bet you didn't even invite him to dinner," Rose said.

"I did," Jo replied. "He declined."

"Wisely," Annie said. Then she ducked, as if her mother were going to swing.

"For that, you get to set the table." Jo pointed an admonishing finger toward the house.

Jo stood with Rose in the sunlight after Annie went in. She was looking where the Bronco had gone.

"Why don't you just ask him back?" Rose suggested. "He'd come in a minute."

"He'd come for the children. I don't want that."

"Look in his eyes, Jo. He'd come for you, too."

"You're an incurable romantic, Rose." Jo turned away and headed toward the shadow of the house. She felt suddenly weary, though it was not even noon.

"If you'd just listen to your heart for once, darn it—" Rose began to say.

Jo closed the front door before Rose could finish.

Rose stormed into the house behind her. "You're so damn stubborn." She followed Jo to the kitchen and stopped abruptly, staring about her in disbelief. "My God. What are you trying to do?"

"Make the cherry pie. I'm just having a little trouble with the crust."

Rose smiled. The smile turned to a giggle, the giggle to a full-blown laugh that Rose couldn't stop. She shook like a sack full of puppies. She laughed hard and crossed her legs. "I think I'm going to pee."

"What's so damn funny?"

Rose went to the refrigerator and, from somewhere near the back, pulled out a package that she held out to Jo. The package contained two round—perfectly round—and flat— perfectly flat—premade pie crusts.

"I haven't made my own crust in years, Jo. Pillsbury does it for me. And so much better than I ever did."

15

THE DIRT AND GRAVEL ROAD cut alongside a wide meadow full of marsh grass and cattails. The grass was yellow in the late afternoon sun and redwing blackbirds perched on the swaying cattails. Cork took stock of the sky. Long wisps of feathery clouds trailed across the blue. High cirrus clouds. Ice crystals.

"Much farther?" Willie Raye asked.

"Couple of miles."

"You're sure this is the way Shiloh went in?"

"Louis is." Cork swerved to miss a turtle. "You ever been in the Boundary Waters?"

"Never."

"It runs all the way to the border. Continues on the other side, but the Canadians call it the Quetico there. More than two million acres of tall trees, blue lakes, and fast rivers."

A white RV came toward them. Cork waved as they edged past one another on the narrow road.

"It's funny," he went on. "Spring, you battle ticks. Summer, it's the mosquitoes and no-see-ums. Then come the black flies. Acid rain is killing the fish and trees. But people still line up for permits like this was Disneyland. There's something about this country that's like nowhere else on earth."

"Do you go into the Boundary Waters often?"

He used to. With the kids and Jo. They'd all loved it.

"Not much anymore," he replied.

Booker T. Harris was already in the parking area at the terminus of the road, along with Agents Sloane and Grimes. The two agents were dressed in jeans and long-sleeved wool shirts. Harris had on a tasteful blue sweater and Dockers and didn't look at all ready for a trip into the wilderness. Stormy Two Knives and Louis were there with Sarah, all keeping to themselves. As Cork pulled up, Sheriff Wally Schanno got out of a Land Cruiser with the Tamarack County Sheriff's Department seal on the door. He sauntered to where Cork parked the Bronco and he leaned in at the window.

"Harris is staying behind," he told Cork. "Sloane and Grimes'll be going in with you. They've already got the canoes in the water and loaded up."

Cork turned to his passenger. "Willie, why don't you head on over. I'll be right there."

Arkansas Willie Raye took his big Duluth pack from the backseat of the Bronco and walked toward the others.

Schanno studied him, then said, "Isn't that—"

"Yeah."

"What's he doing here?"

"He's the woman's father."

"How'd he get wind of all this?"

"Long story. Bottom line is he's going in, too."

Schanno didn't look happy with Cork's cursory explanation. Cork thought he was probably wondering what else had been kept from him, but Wally didn't push it. "Heard how those agents buffaloed Two Knives. Any wonder the Ojibwe have a healthy suspicion of lawmen?" Wally Schanno glanced at the sky. "You heard the latest weather forecast? Rain tomorrow. Maybe turning to snow by nightfall."

On the far side of the graveled lot, Harris stepped toward Stormy and Louis and Sarah Two Knives. The three formed a tight group when they faced him. Cork was moved by the way they held together, had held together despite all the circumstances that might have torn them apart. How had they managed it? How did anyone, white or Ojibwe?

Schanno kicked at the gravel. "I sure don't like the feel of this whole thing. Taking a boy like Louis on something like this. You watch those agents, Cork. Look after that boy." He leaned close and asked, "You carrying?"

"My thirty-eight. Cleaned and oiled it last night."

"Good." Schanno shoved his big hands helplessly into the pockets of his khakis. "Good." He eyed the agents again. "Harris says they've got regular radio check-in times set up. He'll be monitoring it himself on this end."

"Did they set up a command post of some kind at the department?"

"No, didn't want anything to do with us local lawmen."

"O'Connor!" Harris waved Cork toward him.

Cork pulled his gear out of the back of the Bronco and joined the others.

"Special Agent Sloane's in charge out there, O'Connor. You make sure you do what he says. Am I clear?"

"Clear," Cork said.

"Good. Canoes are in the water, rest of the gear's loaded. It's time to get rolling." Harris pointed to Stormy and Louis. "Two Knives, you and the boy first. The rest of us are right behind you."

Sarah touched Stormy's arm. Only that. But she leaned down and gave her son a long, tight hug. "You do what you're father tells you, understand? *Akeeg-ow-wassa*," she said. *Be careful.*

Stormy led the way along a corduroy path of logs toward the lake that was invisible beyond the tall swamp grass and cattails. Louis followed closely.

"You two next," Harris said to Cork and Raye.

"I want to speak with Sarah a moment," Cork replied. "You go on."

Harris tried a withering look on him, but Cork turned away and walked to Sarah Two Knives. "Make it quick," Harris snapped, then jerked his head for Sloane and Grimes to accompany him. They took off after Stormy and the boy.

Sarah watched the agents as they headed into the tall grass. Her face showed nothing, but her eyes raged. "That gun wasn't Stormy's."

"I know," Cork said.

"You won't let anything happen."

"It'll be fine, I give you my word," he said.

"Those men—they're *majimanidoog*."

"I know." Cork hefted his pack, grunting as he slid into the straps. "A couple of days, Sarah, and it'll all be over."

"We are Anishinaabe," Sarah Two Knives reminded him. "It never ends."

There was not much he could say to that, so he turned and moved down the long corridor through the tall grass the others had followed before him. Willie Raye brought up the rear.

A hundred yards into the grass, they came to the small bay. The canoes were in the water, the gear secured under the midship and stern thwarts. Stormy Two Knives and Louis stood beside one canoe, Sloane and Grimes beside another. Harris looked at his watch irritably.

Cork nodded agreeably at the canoes that had been chosen. Eighteen-foot Kevlar Prospectors. He said to Raye, "Sturdy, but light for portages."

"Will we have to portage much?"

"I can't say for sure because I don't know where we're going. But you can't go far in the Boundary Waters without having to portage some. I assume this one's ours, Harris?" Cork moved to the last canoe.

"You and Raye. Two Knives and the boy in that one. Sloane and Grimes in the other. Stow your gear and get started," Harris ordered.

"Reminds me of a sergeant I had back in 'Nam," Raye said under his breath. "He didn't last long, and it weren't Charlie that got him."

Cork secured the packs under the thwarts. "You know how to handle a paddle?" he asked Raye.

"I've run a few rivers in the Ozarks in my day," Arkansas Willie said. "But if you don't mind, I'd just as soon you take the stern."

"Okay by me."

"Two Knives and the boy'll take the point," Agent Sloane said. "Grimes and I will follow. O'Connor, you and Raye bring up the rear."

Cork steadied the canoe as Willie Raye got in.

Stormy and Louis's canoe glided onto the lake, moving fast and smooth. Sloane made his way awkwardly to the bow and nearly tipped his canoe before he took up his paddle. Grimes shoved them off and they moved out.

Arkansas Willie dug his own paddle into the smooth water of the little bay and asked over his shoulder, "What was it the woman called those guys? Magic something?"

"Not magic," Cork said. *"Maji. Majimanidoog."*

"Majimanidoog. What's that mean?"

"Majimanidoog." Cork considered it as they cleared the bay and followed the other canoes onto the body of the lake. "Well, in the Christian tradition," he finally replied, "I guess you might call them devils."

16

IN THE AFTERNOON, a wind rose up, not strong but steady, and it fought her as she tried to work the canoe across the lake. She was making for a big island with a tall gray cliff along the southern edge and pines over it all, thinking she would stop there awhile and rest. It didn't seem far, but the wind made everything a struggle.

In the house in Malibu, she had a weight room. She worked out every day, paid a trainer to guide her toward a perfect body. She did it for business, so that before she went onstage, she could slide into clothing that fit her like a surgical glove. In the Boundary Waters, she didn't worry about how she looked. She hiked. She swam. She cut wood. She didn't think of it as exercise, something she had to build into her schedule. The feeling it gave her was different—better—than any workout she'd ever done.

But she was tired now. She'd been on the lake for hours. The steady wind slapped the water against the bow, and she fought to keep the canoe moving straight. Her arms ached, and she felt blisters rising on her hands. Still, the big island got no closer.

She remembered crossing the lake with Wendell many weeks before. He'd given her the stern, told her to take them across. The wind had been against them then, too.

"Yield a little," Wendell had counseled. "Don't fight a losing battle. Give in to the wind." They'd come around and moved with the wind until they reached the lee of an island and used its protection to reset their course.

She gave up battling, chose a small gathering of rocks to the north, and let the wind help her there. She dragged the canoe half out of the water and lay down on sun-warmed rocks. The wind, no longer an enemy, cooled her. She stared up into the sky and marveled at all the unnoticed elements of the air that drifted by—a long gossamer thread spun and cast by a spider, bits of milkweed fluff, the yellow dust of pollen. After a while, she took a granola bar from her pack and ate it, then drank from her water bottle. She wished she had her guitar. In the hidden cabin, she'd fallen in love again with her music.

When she was young, especially after her mother had died, she'd used music to grieve. It had flowed out of her like tears. Willie Raye had seen this and encouraged her. Those days were good between the two of them. Later, they fought, often and hard. Willie claimed she was ungrateful and wrong-headed, and maybe she was. But she didn't see it that way. He sent her away, to boarding schools where she learned to use her music to rebel. At fifteen, she had her own band. Angry punk rock lyrics from a girl who sang with a Tennessee drawl. She didn't like the music, but it was a formidable weapon. Eventually, Willie Raye offered her a grudging compromise: tone down her music, return to her country roots, and he'd produce her work.

She was in love again with the music she made and so were those who bought her first CD. It had gone platinum. For a while, she and Willie Raye felt almost like a family again. As near to a family as they'd ever been, anyway. But as always, Willie had to run the show. Eventually, they ended up back at the place where they'd started, on opposite sides of angry words, she screaming that he was not her real father and had no business controlling her life, he hauling up a wretched refrain that was always a variation on ungrateful. At eighteen, with her platinum CD propelling her, she put together her own show and left for Branson, Missouri. And, oh God, did they love her there.

After Branson, she'd gone to L.A. The heavy drinking and the up-and-down ride on a carousel of drugs had started then. She moved away from her heart, away from the place where her music flowed up like the cool, pure springs of the Boundary Waters. She could write a song in a drugged haze. Her producer would take it, graft on harmonics and instrumentation, give it grit, and she would grind it out for the business, make a video she'd slide through like a snake. Her music sold, sold big, but she hadn't loved it for a long time. It was like living with a man she loathed but couldn't leave because he paid the bills.

She studied the glittering blue of the lake, worked her cramped hands, rolled her aching shoulders. Pulling the map out of her pack, she looked at it a long time, and at the lake, and after a while she began to understand a thing or two. She found the big island with the cliff on the south, found the small protrusion of rocks where she was. She had drifted north of the arrows Wendell had drawn across the lake. The wind would make it hard to get back on line. But if she yielded, if she let the wind help her to the eastern shore, she could hug the shoulder of the land as she worked her way south, to the blue line called the Deertail River that, according to the map, would be her way off the lake.

She'd grown chilled as she sat idle and she put her jean jacket back on. There was also a chill to the wind itself. She looked up at the sky. High cloud wisps were caught on the sky like down feathers on a blue blanket. Something about the sky disturbed her, although she couldn't say what, and she drew herself up and moved back to the canoe.

On the water, she paused a moment. Every part of her body hurt, but there was no help for that now. There was work to be done, and no other to do it but her. She took a breath, shoved down the pain, and dug her paddle into the lake.

17

STORMY TWO KNIVES set a hard pace. He never seemed to tire. Partly, this was due to his build, his massive upper body with its foundation in cutting timber and its elaboration in the boredom of prison life. Partly, it was his anger. He stabbed at the water like a man in a killing mood. Louis didn't complain. When he was tired, he rested his paddle across the gunwales. The canoe never slowed.

Cork watched the two agents closely. Grimes was an easy read. If he were a dog, he'd have been a pit bull. He struck Cork as an odd type to have been successful in the Bureau. Too independent and dangerously glib with his authority. Cork wondered what his service file looked like. Rife with reprimands he cared little about, probably. But Cork could tell why Grimes had drawn this assignment. He knew wilderness. He handled a paddle like he was born to it. He was strong on the portages. Cork suspected it was Grimes who'd chosen the canoes and selected the agents' gear. In a fight, Cork would have appreciated the man on his side.

Agent Dwight Sloane was a harder read. The authority of the big black man was quiet, considered, even a little reluctant, which was as odd in its way as the heavy-handed enthusiasm of Grimes. He let Louis lead them without comment, questioning the boy occasionally on distance and direction. With Stormy, he was different—hard and watchful. He kept father and son apart on the portages and eyed Stormy intently whenever they rested. Cork knew the gun and the money the agents claimed to have found were part of a frame. Although he'd never stooped to such tactics himself when he'd been a cop, he knew plenty who did and who didn't feel such zealousness was wrong in the pursuit of justice. Cork had often seen distrust of Indians in the eyes of white men, but it surprised him in Sloane, in the man who'd taken the trouble to learn the meaning of the word *ma'iingan*.

By the time sunset was at hand, they'd portaged three times, the longest a muddy hundred rods over bad trail. They double-portaged, leaving some packs behind to be retrieved when the canoes had been successfully carried to the next body of water. It took longer and was harder than Sloane must have imagined. Although he said nothing, his big body moved slower and slower with each hour and each portage.

The sky was a pure evening blue with the high clouds pink as flamingo feathers when they completed their final portage along a shallow creek called Sandy's Gold and reached the big body of water Cork knew as Bare Ass Lake.

"We need to stop," Sloane grunted. He eased out of the Duluth pack he was carrying that held most of the food and sat down with his back against a tall jack pine. "We should eat something. And I need to do a radio check-in." But he made no move to do either. He simply closed his eyes.

Cork scanned the lake. Sandy's Gold emptied into a small inlet. Beyond that, the water opened up in a rough circle that stretched away to the horizon unbroken by a single island. Officially, it was named Embarrass Lake, and the story was that it was embarrassed because it had no islands. It was known locally as Bare Ass Lake. Same reason.

"Which way do we go from here, Louis?" Cork asked.

The boy pointed due north.

"What's that mean?" Sloane asked. His eyes were open, just barely.

"It means we should keep going," Cork said. "It'll be a hard paddle to reach the other side before dark, especially if the wind changes."

"Why would the wind change?" Sloane asked.

"I'm not saying it will. But if it does, we could be in trouble."

"Then we stay here," Sloane said.

"We'll reach the woman faster if we don't," Cork said.

Sloane let out a big sigh. "Fifteen minutes won't make much difference either way. Grimes, what have we got to eat?"

Grimes bent to the pack Sloane had shrugged off. "Jerky," he said. He glanced at Louis. "And how about a Snickers bar, kid?"

"What do they call this lake, Louis?" Arkansas Willie asked. He'd been asking every time they reached a new lake. He seemed to love the sound of the Ojibwe names and the stories Louis recounted that he'd been told by his Uncle Wendell.

"She Does Not Weep," Louis said.

Willie Raye sat down on the trunk of a fallen pine. He kneaded the muscles of his upper arm. "Pretty name."

"Yeah," Grimes said. "So what gives?" Although he didn't seem anxious to admit it, he'd listened as closely as Raye to the stories Louis told.

Between bites of his Snickers bar, Louis related the story his uncle had told him.

"Once there was a great hunter who lived here with his wife and children. Everyone said he was the greatest hunter in the world. Nanabozho heard this and was angry because he considered himself the greatest hunter in the world."

"Who's this Nanabozho?" Grimes asked.

"He's a spirit full of tricks," Louis said. "He's always causing trouble."

"You ought to relate," Raye said to Grimes.

Grimes only flashed him a grin. "Go on, kid."

"One day, when the children were playing alone, Nanabozho disguised himself as a bear and came and snatched them. He hid them in a cave far away, then he returned to the hunter's wigwam disguised as an old man. He told the hunter he'd seen a huge bear carry away the children. The hunter's wife was very upset, but her husband assured her she shouldn't worry. He would hunt the bear and he wouldn't come back until he found the children. Nanabozho thought it was all very funny. He followed the hunter, and he was surprised at how well the hunter tracked. Within a few days, the hunter had found the cave where Nanabozho had hidden the children. He had won Nanabozho's admiration. But when they went into the cave, the children weren't there. The hunter found tracks of the Dakota, a warring tribe, leading from the cave. He vowed to pursue the Dakota until he'd rescued his children. He told Nanabozho, who was still disguised as an old man, to return to his wigwam and give his wife this news. Ashamed, Nanabozho returned. The wife listened and remained very calm. Nanabozho was amazed by her reaction, but she explained that her husband was the greatest hunter in the world and he would bring the children back, even if it took years. She grew old waiting, but she never cried, because she kept on believing in her husband. In the end, Nanabozho turned her into this beautiful lake where she still waits without tears for the return of her husband and her children."

"That's a great story," Willie Raye said. "And you tell it well, Louis."

Grimes scanned the lake, a deep unbroken blue in the late afternoon light. "She Does Not Weep. No tears, right? And those would be islands?" He thought a moment. "So tell me, kid—how does a place get a name like vagina?" and he laughed.

While Sloane had been on the radio, Cork had been watching the sky. "We should go now," he said when Sloane finished his transmission.

Sloane must have heard the urgency in his voice. He looked where Cork was looking and saw what Cork had seen. Rising on the horizon like smoke from a great fire was a thick bank of clouds.

"On your feet, gentlemen," Sloane said. "Let's move out quickly."

18

Near sunset, the wind shifted suddenly and clouds appeared. They swept out of the northwest, red in the last light of day, angry looking. Halfway across the sky, they turned a sinister black. They swallowed the stars and headed hungrily for the rising moon. Dark came fast. Shiloh didn't reach the Deertail River, where she would finally leave the big lake. Instead she found a small cove, drew the canoe onto shore, and settled in behind a clumping of big rocks that provided some protection from the cold the shifting wind had brought. She gathered wood. Using her knife, she cut shavings for kindling, one of the first things Wendell had ever taught her, and she built a fire. She poured water into the small cooking pot she'd brought and dumped in one of the packs of dehydrated vegetable soup. When she finally sat down beside the flames to watch the soup warm, she was dead tired. Blisters welted her palms. Her lips were dry and cracked. Her long black hair felt like mowed, dried hay.

But she knew where she was. And she knew how she'd gotten there. And she'd begun to believe, really believe, that she could get herself out.

The soup bubbled. The smell of it made her mouth water. She used her gloves as pot holders and moved the small pot off the fire and onto a flat stone. While the soup cooled, she lay back against her own quivering shadow on one of the tall upright rocks and closed her eyes. She'd been afraid to leave the familiar little cabin that morning, but the morning seemed so long ago. Now, full of the day, full of the distance she'd traveled alone on her own, she smiled and felt like singing.

"Oh, the water is wide," she began softly with her eyes closed. "I cannot cross o'er. And neither have I wings to fly. Give us a boat that will carry two. And both shall cross, Shiloh and I." It was a song her mother used to sing to her, and it was one of the first Shiloh had ever learned to play. All her life, whenever she needed comfort, whenever she wanted to express a deep inner peace, whenever she felt—or needed to feel—connectedness, she sang the song. Although she remembered very little of her mother, the song was like an unbroken cord between them.

She let the feel of the song linger a minute, then she opened her eyes. In the trees ten yards beyond the fire, two embers glowed. Puzzled, she leaned forward and looked carefully. She made out the moist black muzzle between the glowing eyes and, a moment later, caught sight of the flash of huge white canines.

Terrified, Shiloh stared at the great timber wolf. Out of the darkness, the timber wolf stared back.

19

THE DARKNESS THAT SWALLOWED THE MOON, and the wind that rose behind the darkness changed things. Cork moved his canoe to point and used a compass to hold their direction. At first he tried to keep them on line, but eventually he turned west by northwest and quartered across the wind. They couldn't see the shoreline, nor could they see one another. Cork lashed a flashlight to the stern thwart and called out to the others to do the same so they wouldn't lose anyone.

Although Louis had not been able to give any location names recognizable on the map, Cork believed they were headed to the Little Moose River that ran north of Bare Ass Lake. It was a common route to the lakes deeper in the Boundary Waters. To reach the Little Moose, they needed to make a landing in an inlet called Diamond Bay. Once they'd made the landing, the portage to the Little Moose would be easy. But in the dark and fighting the wind, who knew where they'd hit shore?

Cork was tired. He worried about the others. Stormy could probably paddle through the night and not miss a stroke. Grimes and Sloane, who brought up the rear now, had been struggling to keep pace, mostly, Cork suspected, because Sloane was weakening. Cork had no way of knowing how far they'd all come or how much farther they had to go. But there was nothing to be done about it except put their shoulders into the effort, stroke after stroke.

For nearly an hour after the hard dark hit, they plunged through the night. Finally Cork felt a slack in the wind. He knew they'd moved into the protection of the trees on the northern shore. He unlashed the flashlight and cast the beam ahead of them. An unbroken line of rock and trees stretched into the darkness on either side of the light. The other canoes drew up alongside.

"Well?" Sloane grunted. He looked as if he didn't have another stroke left in him. His paddle lay across the gunwales and he leaned on it heavily. His face was slack with exhaustion.

"We're west of Diamond Bay," Cork told him.

"How far?"

"Can't say."

Sloane turned and stared into the dark of the east. He took a long breath, lifted his paddle and said, "Let's get to it."

They weren't so far as Cork had thought. In fifteen minutes, they entered Diamond Bay and easily located the landing. They drew the canoes up onto shore. Sloane inspected the area with his flashlight. "Good enough," he said wearily. "We camp here."

"The Little Moose is less than twenty rods down that trail," Cork said. He shot his flashlight beam down a narrow corridor through a stand of birch. The trail was covered with fallen leaves so golden they made it look like the yellow brick road. "There's an official BWCAW campsite there."

Sloane shook his head. "No more tonight. We stay here."

"You might want to think about moving on," Stormy suggested.

Sloane gave him a dismissive look. "And why's that?"

"Because," Stormy replied, "we're being followed."

Grimes took a good long look behind them at the vast black of the lake. "Bullshit," he said.

Cork looked there, too, and saw nothing but a deep, impenetrable emptiness. Sloane moved up beside him and peered a long time before he asked Stormy, "Why do you think we're being followed?"

"Ask Louis," Stormy said.

Sloane knelt down. "What is it, son?"

"There's a star on the water," Louis said.

"A star? I don't see anything."

"It comes and goes," Louis said.

"A star that follows us, that comes and goes." Grimes laughed. "Sounds like another one of your Indian tales, kid."

Cork continued scanning the dark of the lake. "I'm not so sure. Could be that someone back there's smoking and Louis saw the ember."

"What do we do?" Arkansas Willie asked.

"I think Stormy's suggestion is a good one," Cork said. "We portage to the Little Moose. That's the only trail on this part of the lake. If they're really following us, they'll have to portage down it same as us. We'll be waiting."

"I'm giving the orders here, O'Connor," Sloane reminded him sharply.

"Fine," Cork said. "What do you suggest?"

"If there is someone out there, they've probably got nothing to do with us."

"And if they have?"

Sloane considered. "Grimes, you position yourself here, somewhere out of sight so that you can monitor any activity at the landing. The rest of us'll go on to the Little Moose and set up camp."

He handed Grimes the rifle he'd carried himself on every portage. From the pack that contained the agents' gear, he pulled a box slightly smaller than a loaf of bread and took out a scope. Infrared, Cork guessed. Or maybe night vision.

"Use your head back here, okay?" Sloane handed Grimes a walkie-talkie. "Check in at fifteen-minute intervals."

"Might as well leave me the radio, too," Grimes said. "Less for you to carry. I'll bring it down when I come."

Grimes took his pack, the rifle, and the radio and settled himself at the edge of the landing behind the trunk of a fallen birch that was covered with a thicket of raspberry vines. The others grunted into their packs, maneuvered the yokes of the canoes onto their shoulders, and began the portage to the

Little Moose. Louis bent under the weight of the food pack, a heavy load for the small boy, but he didn't complain. He brought up the rear and held a powerful electric lantern in his hand that he shined ahead on the trail so that the men with the canoes could see the ground they walked over. They went slowly. The portage was flat, dry, and well worn. In less than ten minutes, the liquid sweep and gurgle of the Little Moose could be heard ahead of them.

Cork had been on that river before. It was a swift flow, tea colored because of the seepage from bogs along its watershed. There were tough sections on it, funnels where the water thundered between high cliffs, but along those sections there were trails for portage. In season, the river was a good, deep passage to the lakes farther north. This late in the year and with the weather as dry as it had been, Cork wasn't sure how smooth that passage might be.

They found the campsite beside the river at the end of the trail. They set down the canoes and the packs. The first thing Sloane did was check in with Grimes via the walkie-talkie. Grimes had nothing to report.

"Think you can build us a fire, O'Connor?" Sloane asked.

"That's not such a good idea." Cork kept his voice low so Louis wouldn't hear. "By firelight, we'd all be pretty good targets."

"For the record, O'Connor, I'm inclined to agree with Grimes. The kid's story is bullshit."

"Why'd you post Grimes back there?"

"I'd be a fool not to make absolutely certain."

"Then let's be certain before we build the fire," Cork said.

Sloane looked like he was tired of arguing. "Get the wood," he said. "We'll wait on the fire."

Cork untied the small ax from his pack and removed the sheath. "Stormy," he said. "Mind cutting us some firewood?"

"I don't want that man to have an ax," Sloane barked.

Cork waited a moment for the brief flair of his own anger to pass. "Stormy was born with one of these in his hand," he explained as calmly as he could.

"Nothing's going in that man's hand that could be used

as a weapon." Sloane reached for the ax, but Cork drew it back.

"If I wanted to kill you," Stormy said to the agent, rolling his shirtsleeves back over the great muscles of his arms, "I wouldn't need an ax."

Sandwiched between Cork and Stormy Two Knives, Sloane looked from one to the other. Finally he gave a brief, grudging nod. "All right. But the boy stays here with us."

Stormy took the ax from Cork and spoke to his son. "Louis, put up the tent." He grabbed a flashlight, slung his jacket over his shoulder, and headed into the woods.

From his own Duluth pack, Cork pulled a tightly rolled tent, a two-man Eureka Timberline. "Ever put up one of these?" Cork asked Willie Raye.

"Not far outta Skunk Holler," Arkansas Willie replied, lapsing purposely into a deep Ozark twang, "in the heart of the blessed Ozarks, God give us the best campin' country a man could ask fer. Hell yes, I can 'rect one of these."

"Good. I'm going to give the greenhorn over there a hand." Cork indicated Sloane, who was looking doubtfully at his own tent bag.

"I've got another chore first," Arkansas Willie explained. "Nature's been calling for the last hour. You'll excuse me?" He lifted a bag of toiletries from his pack, took a flashlight, and hurried into the woods.

Cork approached Sloane. "Let me give you a hand. It's not hard once you've seen it done. Why don't you hold the flashlight for me."

Sloane didn't argue.

As Cork pulled the rolled tent from the bag, he asked quietly, "Why are you so hard on Stormy?"

"He's an ex-con."

"And that's all you know about him?"

"That's all I need to know."

Cork rolled out the tent and found the pegs and flexible rods for the frame. "What do you think of Louis?"

"He knows how to get us where we're going."

"And that's all you need to know, right? Help me spread

this out. Make sure there's nothing sharp on the ground first."
As they spread the tent, Cork asked, "You a family man,
Sloane?"

"What I am right now is a law enforcement officer."

"Just another working stiff. A guy just doing his job.
What if something happens to the boy?"

"Nothing will happen."

"You have a crystal ball? You know everything that's out
there? Then who's been following us?"

"For my money, nobody."

"Here. Use this peg to secure that loop to the ground."
Sloane did as he was instructed.

"Why would the boy lie?" Cork asked.

"His father told him to."

"Why on earth would Stormy do that?"

"Ex-cons don't need a reason to lie. It's as natural to them
as pissing." Sloane pushed another peg into the soft earth.
"Besides, if I'm looking behind me to see who's there, I'm not
looking at Two Knives."

Cork said, "I know the gun you claimed to have found in
his truck was a frame."

"The fifteen grand wasn't. You explain that one to me."

"Somebody set Wendell up. And Stormy along with him.
I'm not sure why. But I can tell you this, I'd trust Stormy and
Wendell with my life."

Sloane sat back on his haunches. "Now I'll tell you something, O'Connor, something I'm surprised you never learned
as a cop. Never turn your back on an ex-con. Let me remind
you that only this morning that man threatened to cut Harris
in half with a chainsaw."

Cork shook his head. "I wonder about you, Sloane. I find
it interesting that you took the time to learn the meaning of
the word *ma'iingan.*"

"A few hours of research in a library doesn't make me a
bleeding heart when it comes to Indians, O'Connor. Especially
one who's done time for manslaughter."

"Now the tent frame." Cork reached for the flexible rods.
"Hold that flashlight steady and let me tell you about Stormy

Two Knives. I've known him all my life. He used to run his own logging operation. Had a dozen men working for him, white and Shinnob. Didn't matter to him what a man's heritage was so long as he was a hard worker. Stormy wasn't rich, but he paid his men and his bills on time."

Cork lifted the tent and began to secure it to the frame.

"A few years back, the forest service opened a tract of national forest land for logging. It was a bid system. Highest bidder cut the timber. The reservation council members approached Stormy and asked him to bid. He told them he wasn't interested in logging the area. Turned out they weren't interested in having it logged either. In fact, they wanted the land protected from logging because there's a stand of virgin white pine there hundreds of years old. They're called Nimishoomisag, Our Grandfathers. It's an area important to the Anishinaabe because it was a traditional site for *giigwishi-mowin*."

"What's that?"

"In the old days, when an Ojibwe boy was ready for manhood, he left his village and entered the woods for a period of fasting. During that time, he dreamed the visions that would guide him through his life."

"Sort of a rite of passage," Sloane said.

"Exactly. Stormy agreed to help the council and placed a successful bid. The man in charge of the bidding for the forest service was a guy named Douglas Greene. A lot of folks considered Greene more a logging-company man than a forest service agent. Anyway, when he learned that Stormy didn't intend to log but to leave the area untouched, he nullified Stormy's bid and gave the contract to the next highest bidder, a big logging firm out of Bemidji. They were going to cut every one of those fine old pines for a hundred dollars apiece.

"Now Stormy's never been real big on his Ojibwe heritage, but he's always had a strong sense of what's right and wrong, and a temper that suits his name. He was fit to be tied. There'd been bad blood between him and Greene before because of Greene's chummy association with big lumber. Stormy hightailed it down to Duluth to confront Greene, but

Greene refused to see him. Didn't matter. Stormy waited for him in the parking lot all day. When Greene finally came out, they had words. Stormy testified that Greene began the scuffle, swung at him with a lug wrench. The lot security guard testified that it was Stormy who started things. Anyway, Greene fell and hit his head against the cement base of a lamppost. According to the medical examiner's report, he died almost instantly. In the end, the question came down to who the jury believed—a white security guard who'd seen things from a distance of forty or fifty yards over a bunch of parked cars or an Indian."

"A jury of his peers," Sloane pointed out.

"Hardly," Cork said. "There were no Native Americans on the jury. In fact, there wasn't a single person of color."

"What do you expect me to do?" Sloane asked. "Cry for the man?"

"Just quit riding him."

Cork finished erecting Sloane's tent and stood back.

"Speaking of Two Knives," Sloane said, swinging the beam away and into the woods, "where is he? I haven't heard that ax for a while."

The crack of a firearm came from the direction of the landing. Cork and the others stopped what they were doing and stared into the darkness down the trail. A moment later, the sound came again.

Arkansas Willie stepped back into the campsite. "What's that all about?"

Sloane grabbed the walkie-talkie. "Grimes, do you read me? What's going on? Grimes?"

20

"WHERE'S TWO KNIVES?" Sloane shouted.

"Stormy!" Cork called toward the woods.

Sloane dug in his pack and brought out an ammo clip and a handgun. "O'Connor, watch the boy. He goes nowhere, understand?" He grabbed a flashlight and headed up the trail toward the landing.

Arkansas Willie Raye stood motionless beside his half-erected tent and whispered, "Jesus."

From his own pack, Cork pulled out his Smith & Wesson .38 police special and a box of cartridges. He filled the cylinder and was very glad he'd cleaned and oiled the weapon the night before.

"Turn out your flashlights," he instructed the others. He put his arm around Louis and said calmly and quietly, "Why don't we all move back of the canoes."

They crouched together behind the overturned Prospector that Cork and Raye had paddled all that long afternoon. Although the canoe was made of Kevlar, the same material used in bulletproof vests, Cork knew the hull was too thin to stop a bullet. It might, however, keep them all from being easy targets, if it came to that.

"My dad," Louis whispered.

"He'll be fine," Cork told him. "He can take care of himself."

Raye leaned very close to Cork. "What do you think's going on out there?"

"Those were rifle shots," Cork said. "Probably Grimes."

"Why didn't he answer on the walkie-talkie?"

"I don't know."

They hunkered down in silence. Cork strained to see into the dark where the trail opened toward them. He struggled to catch every sound. Although there was little wind on the ground, high in the trees above them the branches swayed and groaned and bullied out most other noises.

He felt a sudden stir of the air at his back and he whirled. Stormy Two Knives knelt beside his son.

"You okay, Louis?" Stormy asked.

Louis nodded.

"Heard the shots," Stormy told Cork. "What's happening?"

"We don't know. Why didn't you answer when I called?"

"If somebody was taking a notion to shoot at us, I wasn't eager for them to know where I was." He gripped the ax in his hand and held it ready.

They heard the snap of twigs breaking underfoot, someone approaching rapidly from the landing. A shape, blacker than the dark of the night, moved out from the corridor between the birch trees and immediately dropped to the ground. Cork sighted his .38 on the spot where the figure went down.

"O'Connor?"

Sloane's voice came from that spot.

"Over here," Cork called back, low.

Sloane stood up and his flashlight blazed full on them, blinding Cork.

"Two Knives!" Sloane cried. "Drop that ax, you son of a bitch!"

Stormy set the ax on the hull of the overturned canoe. The weight of the ax head carried it down until it hit the keel.

Cork put up his hand, attempting to block the light. "What's going on, Sloane?"

"Turn around, Two Knives," Sloane ordered from behind the glare. "Hands behind your back. Do it now or I'll drop you where you stand." He shoved his gun into the light.

Stormy did as he was told.

"Cuff him, O'Connor." A pair of handcuffs landed on the hull beside the ax. "Cuff him, or by God I'll shoot you both."

"Go on, Cork," Stormy said. "He means it."

Cork snapped on the handcuffs, then turned angrily toward Sloane. "What the hell's going on? Where's Grimes?"

"You want to see Grimes?" Sloane's voice had climbed to a tremulous pitch. "I'll show you Grimes. I'll show you all Grimes. Up the trail." He shoved his light toward the landing, ushering them that way.

Louis followed the beam, falling in step next to his father. Cork put his hand on the boy's shoulder. "It's a mistake. We'll get it straightened out."

Without the load they'd carried in, they went much faster. In a few minutes, they reached the lake. To their right lay the fallen birch covered with raspberry vines where Grimes had hidden. Sloane illuminated the thicket. The vines at first glance looked ready for harvest. Among the leaves, glimpses of wet red flashed, like dewy berries in the light. But harvest was long past and whatever berries had filled those vines had weeks before been the feast of birds and bear.

"Let's take a look at your handiwork, Two Knives," Sloane said, and shoved Stormy ahead of him.

"Louis, you stay here with Willie," Cork said. He followed Sloane and Stormy to the other side of the thicket.

Grimes lay fallen forward into the thorny raspberry vines.

"Look here," Sloane said hoarsely. He brought the flashlight close to Grimes's neck.

The wound was deep, nearly severing the head from the body. It looked as if it had been cleanly done with a single blow, one powerful bite of an ax swung by an expert hand. The spray of arterial blood still dripped from the raspberry vines.

"Stormy didn't do this," Cork said.

"The hell he didn't," Sloane shot back. "Whoever did it knew Grimes was waiting, and knew exactly where. And look here." He moved the light so that the smashed radio lay in the middle of the circle the beam made on the ground at Grimes's feet. "Rifle's gone, too. Probably hidden somewhere he can get at it when he decides to do the rest of us. I'd bet he fired those shots himself to distract us, give him time to hide it."

"There was somebody behind us on the lake," Cork said. "Grimes had an infrared scope. Maybe they had infrared, too, and spotted him first."

"There was nobody back there, O'Connor."

"Look, Sloane," Cork argued. "If Stormy killed the man, why doesn't he have any blood on him? A wound like that would have sprayed blood on the killer."

Sloane looked at Stormy a moment, pondering viciously. Then a cold light came back into his eyes. "Where's your jacket, Two Knives?"

"Jacket? I guess I left it where I was cutting wood."

"Right," Sloane said, disbelieving.

"Why would I want him dead?" Stormy asked.

"You had fifteen thousand reasons, remember?" He towered over Stormy Two Knives and looked himself ready to murder. "Raye!" he shouted. "Get the spade from my gear at the campsite. Bring it back here."

"What're you going to do?" Cork asked.

"We can't take the body with us and we're not turning back," Sloane said. "So we're going to do the only thing we can. Bury him here."

"Don't go, Willie." Cork kept his voice calm, although he wanted to grab Sloane and shake sense into him. "Listen to me, Sloane, it's crazy to separate us. There's somebody out there with a rifle and a nightscope."

"There's nobody out there, O'Connor. It's Two Knives and you know it. You're protecting him." Sloane looked at Cork, his brown eyes wild with accusation. "I told you, never trust an ex-con. Maybe I should've made that never trust an Indian." He swung his gun menacingly toward Raye. "Now go get that fucking shovel."

"I'll go for the shovel," Cork said.

"No, that's okay." Arkansas Willie stepped away from

Louis. "I'll go, Cork. I think you need to stay here." He nodded toward the boy, who looked scared.

"Take this, then." Cork handed him his .38. "Know how to use it?"

"Point and pull the trigger, right? I think I can just about handle that." He gave Cork a grin, saluted him with the barrel of the gun, then turned his flashlight down the path and headed back toward camp.

"Sloane," Cork tried again, "you're making a big mistake."

The agent was staring at the dead man whose raspberry blood colored the vines. "My only mistake," he replied, "was letting Two Knives out of my sight."

They buried Grimes near the landing. Stormy Two Knives dug the grave, all of it, with Sloane standing over him. It was shallow. Two feet below the surface, the spade began to spark against gray gneiss, ubiquitous fragments of the great Canadian Shield that underlay all the living things of the Boundary Waters. They covered the body with dirt and stacked a foot of stones over that to keep the animals from digging.

"Was he a religious man?" Arkansas Willie asked when they'd finished.

"I don't know," Sloane said.

"I thought maybe we should say something. A prayer or something."

"Prayers are to comfort the living." Sloane shined the flashlight down on the mound of stones and the light reflected back, giving his skin an ash gray pallor that made him appear as grim and unrelenting as a visitation of Death. "When this is over, we'll give him a decent burial among his own people. They can pray all they want then. Right now, we're going back to camp and get some sleep. We've still got a long way to go."

Raye, Louis, and Stormy moved ahead down the trail. Cork hung back and spoke quietly to Sloane. "You're wrong about Two Knives. And that means there's someone out there who knows how to kill."

"I'm not wrong," Sloane said.

"You're sure of that? One hundred percent?"

"One hundred percent." Sloane walked away.

"I've got two suggestions," Cork said.

Sloane stopped.

"I still say no fire. And I think you and I ought to take turns on watch through the night."

Sloane thought a moment. Without turning back he said, "All right."

They ate a cold meal—peanut butter on crackers, beef sticks, dried fruit, granola bars—in a cold silence. They washed it down with water. When they were done, Cork said, "I'm going after Stormy's jacket."

Sloane looked as if he were about to object, but he ultimately nodded.

"Where were you cutting, Stormy?"

"There's a little trail follows the river to a creek about fifty yards that way. Stand of aspen there. Some good dry wood. Left my jacket slung over a log."

"I'll find it."

"Pissing in the wind," Sloane grunted.

Raye had returned Cork's .38. Cork took it, and a flashlight, and headed down the trail Stormy had indicated. He found the creek and the stand of aspen. He found several downed trees and a small pile of branches Stormy must have cut. But he found no jacket.

He shined the light on the creek. It was a clear flow, a few inches deep, three feet wide. Fallen aspen leaves, dragged along by the current, crawled the bottom like banana slugs. Cork spotted the print of a boot lightly embedded on the bank. Looking closely, he realized the footprint was on a faint path that followed the little creek. He began carefully to move through the underbrush, the beam of the flashlight illuminating the path, leading him, he knew, toward Bare Ass Lake.

In a few minutes, he stood on the shore. The lake water slapped against rocks at his feet. The wind moved the trees around him, and their branches touched and scraped, making a sound that seemed like a language Cork couldn't understand. He edged along the shoreline and, after about thirty yards, reached the landing where Grimes had been killed.

Cork retraced his steps along the shore toward the faint path. Before he reached the juncture with the little creek, he saw something riding the surface of the water, nudged between a couple of boulders. He reached down and lifted Stormy's jean jacket. The lake water had done nothing to clean the material. The front was streaked with dark splashes, nearly black as they mixed with the dark blue denim.

"Find anything?" Sloane asked when Cork stepped back into camp.

"Nothing," Cork said. He moved past Sloane without looking at him.

"Should've saved yourself a lot of trouble and just listened to me, O'Connor."

"You found the stand of aspen?" Stormy asked, puzzled.

"I found it," Cork said. "Your jacket wasn't there."

"I could have sworn," Stormy said. "Are you sure, Cork?"

"I'm sure."

Sloane stood up, groaning with the effort. "We ought to turn in, get some sleep."

"My jacket should have been there," Stormy insisted.

"I give you my word, Stormy," Cork told him wearily. "Your jacket wasn't in the aspen stand."

"Go on, Two Knives. Into your tent. I'm leaving those cuffs on," Sloane said. "And leave the flap open," he instructed Louis as the boy crawled into the tent with this father. "I don't want that man out of sight. You still want to stand watches, O'Connor?"

"Yes," Cork said.

"Probably a good idea, just to keep an eye on him."

At that moment, the bark and howl of wolves carried across the Little Moose River from the woods on the far side. Sloane swung the beam of his flashlight in that direction, illuminating only an empty forest. "Great. On top of everything else, now I've got to worry about wolves."

"You don't have to worry about them," Louis said defiantly from inside the tent. "They're a good sign. We are Ma'iingan. The Wolf Clan. Those are our brothers."

"Son," Sloane replied coldly, "they ain't no brothers of mine."

21

By NINE O'CLOCK, Jo was nodding. She sat in the rocker in Stevie's room, *The Indian in the Cupboard* open on her lap, her head down, her eyes closed.

For a moment, she dreamed.

A glimpse of a long church aisle, candlelit, with someone's shadow elongated on a dark red wall. Then she realized the aisle was a corridor through a forest, and the red walls were trees drenched with blood.

She woke with a start and heard the front door open downstairs. Jenny greeted her Aunt Rose happily. Annie joined them and said something Jo couldn't quite hear. They all laughed.

Jo closed the book and left it on the rocker. She pulled the covers over Stevie, who was sleeping soundly, turned out the lamp on the nightstand, and turned on the night-light near the door. The wind had risen in the evening. Clouds had crowded out the blue of the sky and left the day with a brooding feel. Now the elm in the backyard shifted and groaned and shed its leaves in a golden weeping.

Downstairs, Rose had the television turned to AMC. A Burt Lancaster film. He was young, and when he smiled, those magnificent teeth looked ready to tear raw flesh.

"Where are the girls?" Jo asked.

"In the kitchen." Rose had a bag of microwaved popcorn in her lap. "Sean just brought her home."

"I heard. What's the movie?"

"The Killers."

The girls stood by the cookie jar on the kitchen counter. The cookie jar was a ceramic replica of Ernie from *Sesame Street*. Cork had bought it years earlier when Ernie was Jenny's favorite guy in the whole world, next to Cork. The lid was off. The girls each had a chocolate chip cookie in hand. They were laughing over something, but they stopped when Jo came in.

"Did you have a good day with Sean?" Jo asked. She slipped between them and reached into the cookie jar herself.

"Yes," Jenny answered with a dreamy smile.

Jo bit into her cookie. "What did you do?"

"Talked, mostly. Mom, he's so . . . sensitive. It's like, you know, I don't even have to say anything, but he knows exactly what I'm thinking."

"I'll bet I know exactly what *he's* thinking." Annie wiggled her eyebrows wickedly.

"It's not like that," Jenny said, and gave her sister a gentle push.

"Oh, yeah? What's it like, then?"

Jenny looked to her mother for help.

"I know what you mean," Jo assured her.

And she did. Being in love, especially for the first time, felt like being part of something wholly new to the universe. It had been like that with Cork. A long time ago.

"I'm happy for you." She hugged Jenny tightly and so suddenly that the hand that held Jenny's cookie got caught between them. Jo pulled away with crumbs down the front of her sweater and laughed.

The doorbell rang. Jo glanced at the clock on the stove— nine-fifteen, rather late for a visitor. She heard Rose at the front door, and she went to see who'd come calling.

Sarah Two Knives stepped in from the porch. The wind came in with her like a rude guest, mussing her hair and pushing at her clothes. Rose quickly shut the door.

Jo knew Sarah Two Knives, although not well. In her representation of the Iron Lake Anishinaabe, she'd spoken with Sarah on occasion at meetings called by the tribal council to discuss issues affecting the rez. What she knew of Sarah, she liked. Sarah was a strong woman who'd raised her son for several years alone while her husband was in prison at Stillwater.

Sarah looked distressed, then she looked behind her toward the closed front door. "I think someone's watching your house."

Jo followed her eyes. "You're sure?"

"I saw someone in the shadows by your lilac bushes when I parked the truck."

Jenny and Annie had joined them in the living room. Annie went to the window and peered through the slit in the curtains.

"See anything?" Jenny whispered.

"Everything's moving around in the wind. It looks like everything's alive." Annie left the window. "I'm going outside to see."

"We'll all go," Jo said and moved toward the door. "Rose, why don't you stay here. In case Stevie wakes up."

"I'll stay by the phone," Rose suggested. "Ready to call Wally Schanno's office."

"I'm sure that won't be necessary," Jo said.

The wind hit their faces when they stepped outside. They moved together—Jo, Sarah, Jenny, and Annie—toward the lilac hedge.

"There." Sarah Two Knives pointed at a dark place where the hedge cornered toward the driveway.

At the urging of the wind, the tree in the yard next door, a tall poplar, leaned over the hedge. Its long shadow moved in and out, merging and unmerging restlessly with the shadow of the hedge. Jo thought it might be mistaken for a tall man lurking there.

"If someone was there," she said, "they're gone now."

"Maybe it was one of the neighbors," Jenny said.

Annie tried to sweep the hair out of her face. "Yeah, Mr. Gunderson, probably. He sometimes forgets where he is and stands awhile talking to his dead brothers."

"Maybe." Sarah Two Knives nodded. But it was obvious she wasn't convinced.

"Anything?" Rose asked anxiously when they'd returned to the house.

"Nothing now. Probably just Mr. Gunderson a little confused." Jo turned to Sarah Two Knives. "You didn't come out this late to patrol my house, Sarah. What can I do for you?"

"Can we talk?"

"Sure. In my office. Would you like something? Coffee or tea?"

"No, thank you."

Jo led the way to her home office and switched on a lamp. The window was open, and papers on her desk, held down by a rock paperweight Stevie had painted for last Mother's Day, ruffled in the wind that rushed through. Jo closed the window.

"Have a seat, Sarah. What is it you wanted to discuss?"

Sarah sat at the desk across from Jo. She held herself very erect, a trait Jo admired in the Anishinaabe. "Some men—FBI men—came today and forced Louis and Stormy to take them into the Boundary Waters to look for a woman who's lost there."

"Forced them? How could they do that?"

Sarah told her about the gun the men claimed to have found in the toolbox of Stormy's truck and the money in the trailer home of Wendell Two Knives.

"The bastards," Jo said. Then she thought about what Cork had said that morning. Hadn't he, too, been going into the Boundary Waters to look for a woman lost there?

"Was Cork with them?"

"Yes."

"He didn't stop these men?"

"He couldn't, I guess."

Jo stood up and began to pace. "This is wrong. This is an absolute travesty."

"I only want to make sure my son and my husband are safe."

"Who else went with them?"

"Two FBI." Sarah's eyes narrowed to hard, dark slits. "*Majimanidoog*, those two. Also, there was a man who wasn't a policeman."

"The woman they're looking for. Do you know who she is?"

"She's called Shiloh."

"Shiloh?" Jo blinked at the name. Then the pieces began to fall together.

"The man who wasn't FBI. Was his name Willie Raye?"

Sarah Two Knives shrugged. "He's the woman's father. That's all I know."

"Do you know where they're going?"

"A place called Nikidin."

Jo gestured, a small flip of her hands, to indicate she didn't understand.

"It means 'vulva,'" Sarah explained. "A place Stormy's uncle knows."

"Wendell?"

"Yes."

"Is that why they forced Louis and Stormy to go? Do Louis and Stormy know the way?"

"Louis does."

"Do you?"

"If I did, I would be out there instead of my son."

Jo stood at the window and realized the wind had passed. The big elm in the backyard was peaceful. Whatever was behind the wind would be on them soon.

"I wonder if Sheriff Schanno knows about this."

"He was there when the men left this afternoon."

Jo reached for the phone. "Let's find out what he has to say."

The night desk officer, Marsha Dross, told Jo the sheriff was gone. Jo tried Wally Schanno's home phone. No answer. She left a message on the machine, then tried the sheriff's office again and questioned Deputy Dross, who maintained she knew nothing about Cork's or anyone else's going into the Boundary Waters. The deputy was convincing.

Jo came around her desk and sat on the edge, leaning

earnestly toward Sarah Two Knives. "I don't think there's anything we can do tonight. First thing in the morning, I'll kick down a few doors. I swear I'll do my best to make sure those men bring Louis and Stormy back safely."

"Thank you," Sarah said.

"Are you alone tonight?"

"Yes."

"Would you like to stay here, Sarah? We can put you up in the guest room."

"No. I'll be fine at home."

Jo walked her to the truck parked at the curb. "I'll do everything I can," she promised again.

"Migwech," Sarah Two Knives said before she pulled the truck away. *Thanks.*

Inside, Rose was still sitting in front of the television, but she was watching Jo instead of Burt Lancaster.

"What is it?" she asked.

"I'd like to look at your collection of tabloids," Jo told her.

"You hate those."

"That's true. But they might tell me a few things that I need to know right now."

Every week when she did the shopping, Rose bought at least one of the gossip rags that screamed headlines at the checkout stand. She was furtive about it and read them alone at night. Jo could hear the rocker in the attic room squeaking back and forth as Rose turned page after page of miracles, magic, and mud. Upstairs, Rose opened a cabinet Cork had built into the attic room wall. There were half a dozen stacks of tabloids. Rose gave Jo an apologetic little smile.

"I'm not sure what you're looking for," she said

"Something recent. About Shiloh."

"Oh. Here."

Rose pulled one of the papers off a stack to the right and handed it to Jo. The headline, over an awful picture of the woman named Shiloh, read $10,000 REWARD! Jo skimmed the article.

"Thanks, Rose." She handed the tabloid back.

"There's an interesting piece in there about a woman in Albuquerque who sees the image of the Virgin Mary in her swimming pool."

"I'll skip it, thanks. I've got what I need."

She heard the phone ring downstairs. A moment later, Jenny called up, "Telephone, Mom. It's Sheriff Schanno."

Jo took the call in her bedroom.

"Jo, I got your message," Schanno said. "What can I do for you?"

"You can start off by telling me why you stood by and let those federal bullies force Louis Two Knives into leading them into the Boundary Waters."

"I didn't just stand by," Schanno said. "It was a done deal by the time I heard about it."

"Damn it, Wally, how could you let it happen? A boy, for Christ's sake, exposed to God knows what dangers."

"Hold on, Jo. Cork's with him."

"That's another thing. What's Cork doing out there? He doesn't carry a badge anymore."

"It's the way things played out. The way Cork wanted it."

"You're the sheriff here, Wally. What happens in this county is up to you."

"Look, Jo, in the first place, no crime has been committed here. And I don't have any jurisdiction in a federal investigation. The FBI is in charge, and there's not a thing any of us can do about that. Now, those men are in communication by radio. If we need to, we can get a float plane out to them in less than an hour, bring 'em all in. I swear to you, Jo, I'm not going to let anything happen to that boy, or anybody else out there."

They were both quiet. Jo heard the television in the background at Schanno's end of the line. The evening news out of Duluth.

"Whenever I hear something, I'll pass it on to you. I'll let you know everything I know," Schanno offered. "How's that?"

"Deal," Jo said.

"All right, then. Good night, Jo."

"'Night, Wally."

Downstairs, Jo took a flashlight from a kitchen drawer and went back outside. She headed to the shadows where the lilac hedge cornered toward the drive and she searched the ground with the light. She didn't know what she expected to find, if anything. But so much was uncertain now, she wanted to settle it in her own mind. The ground yielded nothing, but the hedge itself was a different matter. She found a ragged area of broken branches that looked as if someone had pushed hurriedly through. Maybe to escape as the women had come from the house earlier? Not the action of a befuddled old neighbor.

Although the big wind had died, there was still a light breeze out of the northwest, cold and with a wet feel to it. Fallen leaves skittered across the cement of the drive, making a sound like the scrape of bones. Jo was concerned, and she was angry. Why hadn't Cork told her things? Why hadn't he trusted her? How could he stand by and let Louis and Stormy be taken that way?

It didn't make sense.

No more sense than someone's lurking in the shadows outside her house.

She felt herself shiver. And as quickly as she could, she headed back inside.

22

THE RAIN BEGAN AROUND MIDNIGHT, a steady drizzle so fine it fell without a sound. With the moon and stars obliterated, the darkness was profound. Cork could make out the three tents but almost nothing outside the triangle they formed. He sat with his back against the hull of an overturned Prospector, the careless gurgle of the Little Moose behind him. He'd changed his clothing, dressing himself against the rain and the damp cold that came with it. Put on thermals, wool pants and sweater, a rain slicker. On his head was settled an old wool felt hat with a broad brim. The rain gathered along the brim and funneled to a constant drip an inch beyond his nose.

He wanted a cigarette in the worst way. Instead, he'd taken to chewing on a pine twig. It wasn't the same thing.

He'd been thinking about the jacket he'd thrown back into the lake. About how that action went against everything he'd been trained to do when he was an officer of the law. About how he'd believed for a long time in the need to gather evidence at all costs. To be inordinately cautious at crime scenes. To be painstaking in his efforts to uncover truth. But it was a funny thing. Holding that bloodstained jacket in his hand, he'd known that although it was probably evidence, it had absolutely nothing to do with the truth.

He heard the zipper sizzle down the front of the tent he shared with Arkansas Willie Raye. Raye—or a black form Cork assumed to be Raye—emerged and stood up.

"Cork?" Arkansas Willie kept his voice to a whisper.

"Over here."

Willie Raye turned and peered hard in Cork's direction. "Sumbitch," he whispered. "Like the inside of Jonah's whale."

"Straight ahead," Cork told him. "Three or four steps."

Raye trusted him, and three paces toward Cork he gave a little "oh." He sat down next to Cork and he, too, lay back against the canoe hull.

"Been raining long?" he asked.

"An hour or so. Can't sleep?"

"Naw." Raye looked up toward a sky he couldn't see. "Think it'll keep up?"

"Yeah, I think."

Raye sat quietly. The drizzle gathered on the branches of the pines above them and formed drops that fell and hit the canoe like nervous fingers drumming erratically.

"You know, Cork, I'm having a hard time believing it was Stormy Two Knives killed Grimes. He just doesn't seem like a cold-blooded killer to me. I mean, just look at the way he cares for his boy."

"I don't believe it for a moment," Cork said.

"Then—" Arkansas Willie stared out at the dark around them.

"That's right," Cork said.

Willie Raye took a good long breath, let it out slow. "Leastways, whoever's out there is blind as us."

"I wish that were true, Willie. Whoever it is out there, they've got an infrared scope on that rifle they took from Grimes. We're so clear to them we might as well be wearing neon bull's-eyes."

Willie Raye drew his legs up as if to shield his chest.

"Who are they?" he asked.

"You tell me."

"Benedetti?"

"More likely, someone in his pay."

"Wouldn't be the first time he hired someone to do his dirty work," Raye said with a nasty little snarl.

"Marais?"

"The police could never prove it, but if it wasn't him, then the earth's flat and Robert E. Lee was a goddamn Yankee spy."

Cork felt Raye shiver against the hull of the canoe as if he were freezing cold.

"Why don't they do something?" Arkansas Willie asked.

Cork spit out shreds of the aromatic pine twig. "I've been thinking about that. They could have picked us all off out there at the landing. Or any time since. I don't think they want us dead. I think they just want to keep us from communicating with Aurora. I think they mean to isolate us out here, to keep anyone from knowing our exact location."

"Why?"

"Because they need us. Or they need Louis anyway. They don't know where Shiloh is either. They want us to lead them to her."

Cork focused intensely on the dark, trying so hard and deliberately to see a thing he couldn't that his eyes burned with little flashes like lightning. He relaxed.

"Like I said, they could have picked us off any time they wanted, easy as shooting bottles off a rail. But since they haven't, I'm thinking they won't do anything more until we've found Shiloh."

"You think Shiloh's safe for now?"

Cork imagined the look of hope that must have lit Arkansas Willie's face.

"I hope so, Willie," he replied. "I hope so for you and for her and for that man under those rocks out there."

A splash at their backs caused them both to bolt upright. Cork had his .38 in his hand, and he used the canoe to brace his arms as he aimed into the darkness in the direction of the Little Moose. He listened and heard the trumpet of a great blast of air.

"Christ, what is it?" Raye asked.

Cork drew in his .38. "It's what the river's named for, Willie. A moose."

Willie Raye started laughing, trying hard to keep the sound to himself. Cork laughed a little, too.

"You should be getting some sleep," Cork suggested. "You worked hard out there today. Handled yourself well. You swing a mean paddle."

"You mean for an old coot," Raye said, settling once again against the canoe. Then he added, "And a queer."

"I mean period."

"You don't care, then?"

It wasn't an apology, Cork understood. Raye was just making sure it was a settled thing.

"Your life," Cork shrugged.

Arkansas Willie spoke as if the weariness of the day was suddenly overwhelming him. "It didn't used to be."

"Mind if I ask you a question?"

"Shoot," Raye said.

"Did you love Marais?"

"Not that way." Arkansas Willie snapped a twig, and Cork could make out in dark profile that he, too, was chewing on a bit of pine. "We were friends. The best. The only. The marriage, well, that was something that helped us both out of a pickle. You see, we were negotiating this TV deal. Standard entertainment contracts back then contained a morals clause. It was the studio or network or record label's out if you embarrassed them by behaving badly. There were rumors about me, always had been. But I was careful, so that's all they were, rumors. Marais, now she really went and stepped in a pile of pig shit. Got herself pregnant just before we were going to sign. She refused to consider an abortion. There was a lot of Catholic in her even though she tried to deny it. We decided getting married was the perfect solution. We became a good television couple."

"You're not Shiloh's father." Cork stated the obvious because he'd been caught so off guard.

"Biological, no. But I raised her like she was my own. Her real father couldn't love her any more than I do."

"Do you know who her real—sorry—biological father is?"

"Marais would never say. It was the era of free love, you

know, and Marais was just about as free as they came that way. Jesus," Raye said with a sigh. "Shiloh's like her in so many ways. I mean," he went on quickly, "headstrong. Beautiful. But a streak in her mean as a wild pig when she doesn't get her way. Between running Ozark Records and raising that child, I had my hands full. Hell, I tried everything—nannies, nuns, boarding schools. Shiloh went through 'em like a cannonball through a cornfield. I finally figured getting her into the business was at least a way of channeling all that energy. She had talent, even more than her mother. Cut her first album for Ozark when she was fifteen. Went platinum. After that, she was, well, I guess she was beyond me. We've been—estranged—for a few years now."

The dark shape of Arkansas Willie Raye bent forward as the man hugged his knees. Cork understood how it felt to be separated from what you loved, from what had helped define who and what you were. It was the worst kind of loneliness.

Willie Raye spoke again. "I was surprised when I started getting Shiloh's letters from this place. Pleased me no end. She sounded so—I don't know—so peaceful with herself finally. Like she'd found something here I couldn't give her. I always wondered if maybe a real father would have done better."

"All fathers make mistakes, Willie. And I'll bet you dollars to doughnuts all good fathers lose sleep wondering if they're doing it right."

"Yeah?" Raye thought about it. "Probably."

A bit of wind rose up, only a moment's worth, but it shook the branches enough to make it feel like a heavy rain was falling. When it had passed, Raye said, "So what happens when we find her?"

"Don't worry about that, Willie," Cork assured him. "I've got a trick or two up my sleeve. Go on and get some sleep if you can. We've still got a ways to go tomorrow."

Raye left him and crawled back into the tent. Cork sat then, chewing hard on the pine twig.

A trick or two up my sleeve, he thought. *Sure, and monkeys fly out my butt.*

23

AT TWELVE FIFTY-SIX A.M., Jo O'Connor finally gave up on the idea of sleep. For hours she'd been awake worrying about Louis and Stormy and Sarah Two Knives. And about Cork. As an attorney, she was used to dealing with worry by sinking herself completely into the facts of a situation. Her strength lay in her ability to scrutinize circumstances from every angle and to anticipate the moves of an opponent. But she didn't have facts and she didn't know her opponent, and all she was left with was the worry.

She got out of bed, threw on a robe, went downstairs, and made herself a cup of chamomile tea, one of the few things she knew how to do in a kitchen without risking disaster. She turned on the television to the cable country music station and sat watching, hoping to see Shiloh, the woman all the fuss in the Boundary Waters was about. She knew the Aurora legends of the woman's mother—Marais Grand, local girl who'd hit it big, who'd run (it was rumored) with the mob, and who'd met a brutal and mysterious death that had (perhaps) been witnessed by her daughter.

Before Jo's cup of tea was half finished, a Shiloh video came on. It featured the young woman singing a lively, sassy country tune in which she warned a no-good truck-lovin', beer-drinkin', dog-smellin', lie-tellin', heart-breakin', runaround man to ". . . keep away from my bed cuz I'm warnin' you, honey, the sheet's gonna hit the fan." Jo found herself liking Shiloh, at least the Shiloh in the video. The woman was attractive in an unusual way. She seemed an amalgam of strange genetic blendings. Her hair, long and black and snapping about like a whip as she turned defiantly away from her cheatin' man, might have adorned any woman on the Iron Lake reservation. Her face was exotic rather than beautiful. A long slender nose saddled with nostrils that flared broadly, like little wings on the spine of a tiny bird. There was something electric about the eyes, such anger and insolence that Jo thought the young woman was either a superb actress or had truly felt, as most women ultimately did, the utter betrayal of love. The color of Shiloh's skin seemed to vary with the lighting. In the shadows of a room with an unmade bed, her skin was dark as an almond. But when she stepped outside, abandoning the old house and the man who'd walked all over her heart, her face danced in sunlight and glowed with a color that reminded Jo of the sky at sunset when summer fires burned the forests and everything was bathed in a smoky red-brown hue.

The song at the center of the video wasn't deep, but Jo liked its simple sensibility and it made her wonder a little if she'd missed something by ignoring country music for most of her life.

She went back to bed and slept fitfully until the clock radio clicked on at six A.M. Outside, the morning was still black, and against the windowpane, a light rain fell. She thought about Cork in the Boundary Waters, about the rainy times she'd spent there with him and the children. In the tent all day, playing games—twenty questions, spades—reading aloud or quietly to themselves, telling stories. Somehow they'd managed never to be bored.

Cork didn't have the luxury this outing of riding out the rain in a tent. All of them who'd gone, Louis included, had a driving purpose that would propel them onward. Her anger flared again as she thought of the men who'd used their power over Stormy to induce Louis to lead them. She was determined to bring an action on behalf of Sarah Two Knives when it was all over. The law wasn't perfect, but anytime those who had the power to twist it did so, it grew more grotesque. With all its flaws, the law was still something she had faith in. She'd been a part of making it work, and she believed, as strongly as she believed anything, that in the end it was one of the few powerful weapons available to common people.

Jo heard Rose lumbering down the stairs to the kitchen to begin breakfast preparations, and she threw back the covers and went to wake the kids.

Her car was the first in the lot of the Aurora Professional Building. She used her key and let herself in. She hit the lights, illuminating the hallway that was long and empty. The odor of wet wool hung in the air and she recalled that the carpeting had been cleaned over the weekend. She felt a little guilty walking to her office because her feet left wet tracks on the carpet. Jo turned on the lights, hung her coat, and set her briefcase temporarily on her secretary's desk. The cold, wet morning had made her desperate for coffee. She took the pot from the coffeemaker and went to the women's restroom down the hall to fill it with tap water. Coming back, she saw that hers were no longer the only wet footprints on the carpet. Several more sets trampled her own, and between them ran four deep, mysterious grooves. They all led to her office.

A white-haired man sat in a wheelchair facing her as she entered. The thin hands that held the arms of the chair trembled violently. Although his head wobbled a bit, he eyed Jo steadily. Two men flanked him, standing respectfully with their hands folded in front of them. They all wore dark, tasteful suits.

"Good morning, Mrs. O'Connor," the white-haired man greeted her. Coming from such a shaky body, his voice was surprisingly clear and strong. "My name is Vincent Benedetti. I believe we should talk."

Whether it was simply the surprise of finding strangers in her office so early or something about the strangers themselves, Jo wasn't sure, but she didn't like the situation or the feeling that gripped her gut.

"Do you have an appointment?" she asked.

"Appointment?" One of the standing men—a huge, broad-shouldered guy with blond hair and an idiotic smirk on his face—gave a horsey laugh.

"Hush, Joey." The white-haired man studied her eyes. "You're afraid. Someone told you to be afraid of Benedetti."

The door was open at her back. Jo calmly turned and closed it. "I'm not afraid, Mr. Benedetti. Should I be?"

"Of me, no. I've come a very long way and I'm very tired. I'm here to save your husband's ass."

Jo moved to the coffee machine so that he wouldn't see her surprise. She emptied the pot of water into the reservoir, then faced Benedetti. "I have no idea what you're talking about."

"Husbands have secrets," he said. He looked at her dead on, like an animal he had in his sights. "I know you understand that."

Suddenly, she wanted only to be rid of them. "What exactly can I do for you?"

"It's what we can do for each other, Mrs. O'Connor." The white-haired man motioned with his head and the big blond guy moved the wheelchair nearer Jo so that Benedetti spoke to her as if in strictest confidence. "I have information that will help save your husband's life. In return, you'll help save my daughter."

"Your daughter? Do I know your daughter?"

"Everyone knows my daughter. Her name is Shiloh."

Except for the fact that the man regarded her as seriously as an undertaker, she might have assumed he was joking. "Am I understanding you correctly? You claim to be the father of Shiloh—*the* Shiloh—the country singer?"

"I just said that, didn't I?" he replied with annoyance.

"I'm sorry if I seem a little slow on the uptake here, Mr. Benedetti, but that's quite a claim."

Benedetti reached inside his suit coat and brought out a shiny leather wallet, from which he extracted a photograph. He handed the photo to Jo. The picture was of a little girl, maybe eighteen months old, in a pretty white dress, posed in a photographer's studio. "Read the back."

Vince—Our little girl. She's walking up a storm. Has my hair and skin, your eyes and temper. Marais.

She studied the photograph, then looked at the white-haired man. Despite the trembling in his body, she thought she could detect in his eyes the same insolence she'd seen in the eyes of the woman in the video. She handed the photo back.

"Does she know?"

He shook his head. "Marais never told her. As far as Shiloh's concerned, Willie Raye is her father."

"Why didn't you ever say anything?"

"Promises. To Marais. To my wife, Theresa."

"She knew? Your wife knew?"

"Oh, yeah. I never understood how, but she knew. She threatened to leave me for good if I ever tried to do anything about Shiloh. After Marais was murdered, it seemed best just to let Raye take that little girl back to Nashville. He's queer as a purple dog, but there are worse kinds of fathers."

"What does all this have to do with my husband?" Jo asked.

Benedetti waved forward one of the men at his side. The man was good-looking in an obvious sort of way. Dark brown hair, curly and expertly razor cut. A strong jaw. A beauty mark on his right cheek. A diamond stud in his left ear. He wore an emerald tie that matched his eyes perfectly. Green eyes. Confident. She'd been aware of his eyes. They'd followed her every move. Men often watched her that way. Even when they respected her abilities, spoke to her as a colleague, their eyes were hiking up her skirt.

"My son, Angelo," Benedetti explained to her. "Tell her, Angelo."

"Your husband went into the Boundary Waters yesterday, Ms. O'Connor," Angelo Benedetti informed her. "He was accompanied by several men. Two of them your husband believes to be agents of the FBI. They're not."

"No?"

The coffee machine gurgled suddenly at her back and Jo jerked, startled. At the same moment, the office door opened and Fran, her secretary, came in. Fran halted abruptly, surprised at the gathering, and glanced at her watch.

"It's okay, Fran," Jo said. "An early unscheduled conference. We were just moving to my office. Would you do me a favor? When the coffee's done, bring some in for us?"

"Sure, Jo."

"Gentlemen, if you'll follow me."

Jo led the way into her office. It was a large room lined with shelves of books and dominated by a big cherrywood desk that she'd brought with her from Chicago. The desk had been in storage during Jo's first two years in Aurora as she struggled to establish a practice. In those years, she worked out of her small office in the house on Gooseberry Lane. She was the first female attorney ever to hang a shingle in Tamarack County, and it had taken a long time to become something more to the people of Aurora than Cork O'Connor's wife. She'd made a name for herself by taking impossible cases, cases no one else wanted—those of the Anishinaabe, for example. Her success in court gave her the professional recognition she sought, but she still felt as if she were waiting for some door in the town to open for her that maybe never would.

"Would you care to sit down?" With a gesture, she offered chairs to the two standing men. They declined and remained at Vincent Benedetti's side like palace guards. Jo sat at her desk and leaned forward. "You said the men who are with my husband aren't FBI."

"That's right," Angelo Benedetti said.

"Who are they, then? And why are they out there?"

"One of them, Dwight Sloane, is a big man with the California State Police. The other, Virgil Grimes, calls himself a security consultant. Both men were involved in the investigation of the Marais Grand murder fifteen years ago."

"Involved in what way?"

Angelo Benedetti tugged the cuffs of his shirt into place. "Grimes was one of the detectives in charge of the investigation for the Palm Springs Police Department. Sloane investigated on behalf of the state. There is one legitimate agent of the FBI here in Aurora. His name is Booker T. Harris. He's out of the Los Angeles field office. Fifteen years ago, Harris represented the FBI in the murder investigation."

He tilted his head slightly to one side and gave her a moment to consider. It was a gesture that struck her as calculated, disingenuous, something he might use on women after he'd propositioned them.

"If you don't believe me," he said simply, "check it out. And while you're at it, check with the FBI on the official status of this investigation. You'll find that there is no official investigation, Ms. O'Connor. Booker T. Harris, the only legitimate representative of the Federal Bureau of Investigation, is officially on personal leave."

"These men are out to cover their asses," Vincent Benedetti broke in. "I'd bet my own ass they were paid off when they investigated Marais's murder. Now they're running scared that Shiloh might have remembered something that will finger them."

"Paid off by whom?"

Benedetti began to cough, a fit that racked his withered body. Angelo drew a clean white handkerchief from his coat pocket and stuffed it into his father's hand. Vincent Benedetti shoved it over his face as if it were a mask.

"Paid off by whom?" Jo asked when the coughing was well past.

"Marais was smart. She always told me she'd cultivated friends in high places." He managed a smile.

"What's so funny?"

"Marais didn't have friends. Everyone was just a step on a ladder to her."

"Do you know who any of these people in high places were?"

"She was careful never to mention names. They were all men, of course."

"Marais Grand was an opportunist?"

Benedetti smiled again and nodded. Whether it was approval or simply an uncontrollable muscle twitch, Jo couldn't say. "A lot people would have said *tramp,* but I never thought of her that way. She was a very talented woman in a business full of very talented people. She used all of her assets to ensure her success. I never faulted her for that." He dabbed at his lips with the handkerchief and studied the crumpled linen with interest. "Men are most vulnerable when you inflate both their egos and their dicks. A hard truth, but she accepted it."

Under other circumstances, Jo would have nailed him on that one, but their business was about something else. "You're saying you believe one of these . . . friends . . . murdered her."

"Or had her murdered."

"And paid off the police who investigated."

"That's what I'm saying, yes."

"Who, exactly?"

The old man's eyes closed a moment. His son leaned to him. "You okay, Pop?"

"Just tired."

A light tap came at the door, and Fran entered carrying a tray with a coffee server and several cups. She put them on a small table near the desk.

"Thanks a lot, Fran."

"You're welcome, Jo. Anything else?"

"Not at the moment."

After Fran had gone, Jo offered coffee, but only Angelo Benedetti took her up on it. As she handed him the cup, his hand brushed hers and he smiled pleasantly. Perfect teeth. Of course.

"I have a theory about who's guilty, Mrs. O'Connor, but I don't want to go into it. All I want is to get your husband some help so he can bring my daughter out safely."

"I'd rather you go into it," Jo said, stirring cream into her own coffee. "I'd rather have all the facts. Or whatever."

"My father's tired, Ms. O'Connor," Angelo Benedetti began.

Vincent Benedetti held up his hand. "No, no it's all right. A fair request. I only ask that you keep an open mind."

Jo sat back down. "It's wide open and waiting."

"The FBI agent—Booker T. Harris—has a brother. I didn't know this when Marais was murdered. The information didn't come to me until we knew Harris was out here and I had him looked into thoroughly. His brother is Nathan Jackson. You know the name?"

Jo knew it. Attorney general for the state of California. Nationally known crusader for civil rights. Jo had heard him talk at an ABA conference in Chicago. Splendid speaker. Inspiring. A handsome man, too. And if the national press was correct, he was the top choice for the Democratic nomination in the next gubernatorial election.

"Why different last names?" she asked.

"Their mother was widowed and remarried. They have different fathers."

"Okay. Go on."

"When Marais was first negotiating with the television people, she was subpoenaed to appear before the Williams Commission. You remember it?"

"Vaguely. Investigated corruption in the entertainment industry, I believe."

"Exactly. Marais was called to testify because of her rumored connection with me. Rumored." He seemed to find that funny and gave a wheezy laugh before he went on. "She was afraid that if she appeared, the television people would back off. She got to somebody inside. Her name was dropped from the witness list. You have any idea who the chief counsel for the Williams Commission was?"

"Nathan Jackson?"

"Bright girl."

Jo sipped her coffee. The caffeine didn't seem as necessary as it had when she'd first arrived. She felt wide awake. "You're trying to tell me that Nathan Jackson had Marais Grand killed to keep her quiet about that?"

"No, I think Marais was trying to squeeze him again for something else. Just before she died, she borrowed a substantial sum of money from me to set up a recording company. Ozark Records. She swore she could get a sweet deal—tax breaks, business incentives—because she was Indian and she had this connection inside that would make sure things happened for her. Jackson was in his first term as attorney general. I think something went sour, Marais made threats, and Jackson had her killed."

"Do you have anything to back up these accusations?"

"I didn't even have these accusations until a day ago. The different last names—Harris and Jackson—threw me off. I never saw the connection before. But look at it. Same men who investigated the murder are here now. And not officially. Tell me that doesn't smell rotten to you."

Jo turned away from them in her chair and quietly studied the gray morning beyond her window. Cars drove past on the street. She could hear the swish of their tires on the wet cement.

"What do you want from me exactly?" she asked.

"Whoever the law is in these parts, talk to them," the white-haired man said. "Get somebody out there to cover your husband's ass while he finds Shiloh."

"Why don't you tell them yourself?"

"Booker T. Harris looks good. People believe him. Me," and he gestured toward his wobbling body, "I'm just a crooked old jellyfish. But people who know you here, they'd listen to you. Angelo tells me you have a reputation for integrity. That's a rare thing anywhere."

She looked at Angelo Benedetti, who gave her the slightest of nods.

"Mrs. O'Connor," Vincent Benedetti continued, "if a lot of people find out Shiloh's out here—especially those rags— it'll be open season on my girl. There'll be a stampede and your little town will be right in the middle of it. You need to act quickly. I'm leaving you a card. Angelo." He snapped his fingers, and Angelo Benedetti pulled a business card from his coat, wrote a number on the back, and handed it to her. "Call me and let me know what's going on."

She looked at the card. A purple parrot on the front with Angelo Benedetti's name embossed below in gold. On the back, a telephone number.

"Where are you staying?" she asked.

"Just call," Benedetti said. "Do we have a deal?"

"I'll check it out. If I think you're telling me the truth, I'll be in touch. If not, I'll have the authorities looking for you. Deal?"

Vincent Benedetti offered her a hand that quaked like an aspen leaf. "Deal."

24

CORK HEARD THE TENT FLAP QUIETLY LIFTED, and he was instantly awake.

"It's light," Sloane said through the mesh of the tent door. "Time to move."

From behind Sloane came the crackle of a fire. The smell of wood smoke and fresh coffee drifted through the opened flap.

"Louis built a fire at first light," Sloane explained. "I figured there wasn't any reason not to at this point. The coffee's ready. And water for oatmeal. Let's move it, gentlemen. We've got a long way to go."

The drizzle had ended, but thick clouds lay against the treetops and ragged gray wisps drifted among the trunks and along the riverbank like lost souls. Except for the crackle of the burning wood and an occasional word that passed between Stormy and Louis Two Knives as they stood by the fire, the forest was quite still.

Raye crawled out of the tent after Cork. He arched his back and stretched his arms. "You know, Louis," he said with a little grin, "I dreamed all night long I was being chased by a *majimanidoo.*"

Louis had been sipping hot chocolate. He lowered the cup from his mouth and a serious darkness entered his young eyes. "What do you know about a *majimanidoo?*"

Raye poured himself coffee in a hard plastic mug. "Not

much. Except that according to your mother, it looks exactly like Agent Sloane there." He lifted the mug to his nose and took in the good hot smell of the coffee.

"What's a *majimanidoo?*" Sloane asked. He was already at work taking down his tent. When the boy didn't answer, he stopped and looked to Stormy Two Knives. "Well?"

Stormy shrugged. "My son is the expert on his Ojibwe heritage. Me, I just have it in my blood."

"What's a *majimanidoo,* Louis?" Sloane asked.

"A dark, evil spirit," Louis reluctantly answered.

"You mean because of my color?"

Louis shook his head. "Spirit. Evil spirit."

"A devil, Sloane," Raye offered. "An Ojibwe devil."

"If there is a devil in these woods," Sloane said, casting a cold eye on Stormy Two Knives, "he's for goddamn sure met his match in me. Cut the talk now. Get food in your bellies and let's get going."

Cork was mixing instant oatmeal in a bowl. "What'll happen when you don't check in with your people in Aurora?"

"For a while, nothing," Sloane said.

"Then?"

"Then they send someone to the last coordinates I gave and they start looking."

"That was the other side of Bare Ass Lake. We'll be a long way from there," Raye said.

Louis asked, "Do they know how to read trail signs?"

"Trail signs?"

"Notches on trees, rocks set in a line, that kind of thing," Louis explained.

Sloane actually smiled. "That's a little primitive for them, son." He shrugged. "But what the hell, it's worth a try. I'm putting you in charge of trail signs, Louis."

Within an hour, they'd shoved the canoes into the sweep of the Little Moose River. The water was swift, clear caramel beneath them and silver gray ahead. Between them and Wilderness, the first and largest of the lakes north along the Little Moose, lay more than a dozen miles and two unnavigable rapids. Cork had the point, paddling his canoe.

Stormy and Louis came next. Raye and Sloane brought up the rear.

Cork had been thinking a lot about who killed Grimes. Whoever they were, they had some knowledge of the woods they were traveling. Except for the glimpse of the ember Louis had seen on the lake, they'd kept their presence hidden. Although they would have had to stay pretty far back to remain unseen, they'd followed exactly, at every turn and every trail juncture. Cork decided it was likely they knew where Louis was leading them—at least to a point. But they must not have known the whole of it, Shiloh's exact location. As he'd told Raye the night before, Cork believed that whoever they were, they wouldn't do anything further until Shiloh was found.

Cork was certain that after that, whoever it was shadowing them, *majimanidoo* or otherwise, they would strike.

25

SHILOH SAT UPRIGHT WITH A JOLT and listened. She stared straight ahead and blinked away the blur of sleeping. A thread of white smoke curled upward from a circle of ash near her feet and she realized she'd let the fire burn out. Panicked, she looked around desperately for the yellow eyes of the timber wolf who'd watched her from the darkness of the trees. A wet mist cloaked the woods and lake, and she could see nothing beyond a dozen yards. She reached for the knife she'd clutched much of the night, the Swiss army knife Wendell had given her as a gift. Although the blade wasn't long, it was sharp, and it was all she had in the way of a weapon. She probed the mist and strained to hear again the sound that had awakened her.

The night before, soon after she first saw him, the wolf had slipped away, vanishing as silently as he'd appeared. She'd risked a moment to feed the fire, and when she'd looked back, the eyes had been gone. She held tight to the knife, blade extended and gleaming in the firelight, and tried to see everything all at once—left, right, behind her. Although she seemed alone, she felt watched. All night, she felt watched. After a long time had passed, she knew she had to prepare for the cold, wet hours ahead. As Wendell had advised, she put on the thermals to wick moisture from her body. Over that a layer of wool—sweater and pants. Then her jacket, and finally a slicker as the light rain began to fall.

When she finished, she clutched the knife in her gloved hand and settled herself against the big rock at her back. Before she knew it, she'd given in to sleep.

Her sleep was restless, haunted not by fearsome images of the wolf but by an old visitation. She was in Wendell's cabin. Safe. Outside, a light rain fell. She could hear it against the windows. She'd laid a fire in the stove, which had warmed her. The sound from the burning logs, the hiss and pop of sap, was like a song. A knock at the door disturbed her. Who would come so far to visit? Who would know how to find her in that hidden place? In the prescient way of dreams, she knew that it wasn't Wendell and that she should not open the door. But the dream had a terrible momentum of its own. She watched herself cross the cabin floor and reach out to the latch. When she swung the door open, the Dark Angel swept in on black wings. Shiloh fell back. As always, the Dark Angel had no face, only a deep emptiness, black as a starless night, where a face should have been. From within that emptiness came a powerful force like the suck of a tornado trying to pull her into the void. She fought, uselessly, and felt herself being drawn into a place she knew was death.

She woke before she was swallowed, drawn out of her sleep instantly by a sound.

It came again, from the wall of gray mist that blocked the lake, the noise that had yanked her from her sleeping. A hoarse cough, somewhere out on the water. She tried to stand, but her whole body objected, every muscle cramped and knotted. Slowly, painfully, she stretched herself out. Carefully, she stood.

It was like a prison cell, the small area she could actually see. Drab gray and menacing. Beyond the rock, the lake was flat and solid as iron plating. The mist shifted slowly of its own accord in the windless morning.

A crow's sudden cawing broke from somewhere out in the gray and startled her. She listened.

Only that, she thought, relieved.

Then a watery plop, followed by, "Shit, Roy, I can't see my damn hand in front of my damn face. The fish can't see nothing neither. No wonder we're having the luck God give a three-legged racehorse."

A minute later, Shiloh heard the sizzle of fishing line played out fast from a reel and the splash of a big fish breaking water.

"Got him!" the voice exclaimed triumphantly.

"Well, hell, don't tip the damn canoe, Sandy. You'll lose him for sure."

"I ain't tippin' nuthin'. Shift the other way, goddamn it."

"Play him, Sandy boy," the second voice urged. "You really hooked that son of a bitch."

"We're tippin', Roy!" Sandy shouted.

"I got it under control. My butt's practically in the water over here. Just land the damn fish!"

The two voices barked back and forth a while until the splashing stopped.

"What d'you figure, Roy? Eight, ten pounds?"

"If it's an ounce."

"Didn't I tell you they come big up here?"

"Yeah, but you didn't tell me fishing from a canoe was going to be such a royal pain in the ass."

Shiloh called into the mist. "Hello?"

She was greeted with silence.

"I need some help," she tried again.

Out of the gray, a wary voice queried, "Who are you?"

"Help me, please."

"Hell, Sandy, can't you hear it's a woman? Put that damn fish down and grab a paddle."

Shiloh heard the water break with rapid strokes. A moment later, they emerged from the mist. Two bulky men, bearded, wearing down vests and billed caps. They came at the shore fast, then backpaddled hard before they hit the rocks. The man in front looked up at Shiloh with concern.

"You okay, miss?"

"I am now," Shiloh replied.

The two men exchanged bewildered glances as she broke into great sobs of relief.

26

WALLY SCHANNO REMINDED JO OF ABE LINCOLN. Not because he looked like the Great Emancipator, although in his height and gauntness there was a certain similarity. It was more that Schanno seemed like one of those rails Lincoln had spent so much time splitting in his early years. Thin, dry, tough. Suited to the purpose of being part of a structure that delineated something. In the case of Lincoln's rails, they were property fences. In Schanno's case, he was the law in Tamarack County.

When he opened the front door of his home to Jo, he was dressed in a white shirt, dark tie, gray pants held up by gray suspenders. He gripped a coffee cup in his hand and he smelled of Old Spice aftershave.

"I'm sorry to bother you so early, Wally."

"That's all right, Jo. Just finishing my morning mud." He held up his cup. "Come on in." He stepped aside and put a finger to his lips. "Arletta's sleeping."

"How is she?" Jo asked in the foyer.

Schanno took her coat and hung it in the closet. "About the same. I count it as a blessing that she doesn't seem to be getting much worse. Doc Gunnar says Alzheimer's is like that sometimes. Plateaus, you know."

Arletta Schanno was one of the finest, prettiest women Jo had ever seen. She'd been a schoolteacher before the disease hit her. Annie and Jenny had both passed through her classroom, and both still said third grade was the best year they ever spent at Aurora Elementary.

"May's here now, you know," Schanno said, speaking of Arletta's sister. "She's a big help."

May stepped in from the kitchen. She was a dark-haired woman in her early fifties. She came from Hibbing and Jo didn't know her well. She seemed a stern woman, not given to smiling, the way Arletta had always been. But she was obviously capable and willing to help. Goodness came in all kinds of packages.

"Would you like some tea or coffee?" May asked. It was a polite question, but not especially warm.

"Thanks, no, May. I just want to talk to Wally briefly."

"All right." She disappeared into the kitchen immediately, as if the room had sucked her back in.

They settled in the living room. Schanno took the big easy chair. Jo sat on the edge of the sofa.

"The men who went into the Boundary Waters with Cork. I think they may not be who they claim to be. You spoke with them. Did you ask them for identification?"

"Sure, I did. But—" A dour look came over his long, raggedy face.

"What is it, Wally?"

"I'm not saying anything for sure, but I have a strange feeling in my gut about this whole thing. Why are you asking?"

Jo told him about her visit from Benedetti and his entourage. Schanno listened quietly through the whole thing. Jo couldn't recall hearing the man ever swear before, but when she finished, Schanno said, "Jesus." He rubbed his clean-shaven jaw. "Like trying to decide which side of the razor blade to grab hold of."

"There must be a way to check on these men," Jo said.

Schanno sat back and thought a moment. "I'll call Arnie Gooden. He's one of the resident FBI agents in Duluth. He promised help if we needed it. Where can I reach you?"

"I'm in court all morning. You can leave a message for me at the courthouse." She stood up and went to the closet with

Schanno. As he handed over her coat, she said, "You told me last night if you had to, you could get to Cork and the others quickly."

"Less than an hour."

Jo felt a measure of relief. "Good."

Schanno put his huge hand lightly on her shoulder. "If there's anything strange going on, Jo, we'll get their butts out of there fast, I give you my word."

27

THE MIST LIFTED, but the heavy gray that overhung the Boundary Waters didn't. Shiloh followed Roy Evans and Sandy Sebring to their camp, where the Deertail River flowed southeast out of the big lake. They pulled the canoes onto shore and Roy set immediately to stoking the fire with dry wood.

"You know," Sandy said, tugging on his beard, "you sure look familiar. Do I know you?"

"I don't think so," Shiloh said.

She sat on a rock near the fire and watched the smoke begin to rise as Roy bent and blew on the embers. In a moment, a crackling flame popped up.

"That long hair," Sandy said, moving slowly behind her. Shiloh put up the hood of her rain slicker.

"You alone out here?"

"Quit yammerin', Sandy. Get me some food so I can fix her something to eat."

"All right, all right." Sandy went to a nearby tree—a pine deeply scarred from a lightning strike—undid a rope, and let down a pack that hung from a high branch. "Bears," he explained to Shiloh. "You like bacon?" He began digging in the pack.

"Bacon would be fine," she replied.

"And eggs?" Roy asked. "They're dehydrated, but you scramble 'em up and can't hardly tell the difference."

"Whatever," Shiloh said.

Without the mist, she could see a distance across the lake. The expanse of water suddenly looked huge and impossible. The islands lay on the surface like dark beasts watching. She was surprised she'd come so far so well.

"Me and Roy live down in Milaca," Sandy said. "Work at the Wright Lumber Company there. Roy talked me into coming. Said we'd have the whole woods to ourselves. Said we'd be catching walleyes big as my thigh." He handed Roy the food. "Shiloh!" he said suddenly, and his hand, full of bacon, froze in the air.

"What the hell's that supposed to mean?" Roy said.

"Son of a gun." Sandy broke into a broad smile, his thick lips nested among the wild hairs of beard. "You're Shiloh. My wife's got every album you ever put out. I knew there was something familiar about that hair. Roy, we got us a real celebrity here."

Roy dropped the bacon on the skillet and it sizzled immediately. "Shiloh? You mean the country singer? She ain't Shiloh, Sandy. Hell, Shiloh's—" He looked up from the bacon. "You ain't Shiloh, are you?"

Shiloh shook her head. "It's not the first time I've been mistaken for her."

"Yeah?" Sandy moved to her side and looked at her carefully. "Well, if you ain't Shiloh, who are you, then?"

"Nagamon." It was the name Wendell had bestowed on her. It meant 'song.'

"Nagamon? What kind of name is that?"

"Ojibwe."

"You Indian?"

"Partly."

"Yeah?" Sandy eyed her good and snickered. "What part?"

"Sandy, will you just shut up?" Roy said. "Sorry, ma'am. He's a good camping partner, but he's got all the tact of a chainsaw."

"That's all right," Shiloh said.

The smell of the bacon was wonderful. The sound, too.

148

Pop and sizzle. It was like music. She couldn't help smiling, believing that now it would be all right. She wondered if she should ask the men about going back for the things she'd left behind, the important work she'd hidden at the cabin. They could be over and back in a day. She'd pay them. Pay them well. After she'd eaten, she would ask. They might not do it for Song. But maybe they would for Shiloh.

"How 'bout some coffee while you're waiting for breakfast?" Roy said. He lifted the pot off the fire, poured some into a hard plastic mug, then looked at the lake and paused. "Got us some more company, Sandy."

Out on the lake, a yellow craft approached them. It was bright against the gray water. The man in it used a double-bladed paddle and the little craft darted toward them swift as a water bug. A few feet from shore, he brought the craft to an abrupt stop, stowed the paddle, and waded to shore, drawing the craft carefully onto the rocks.

"Morning," the stranger said.

"What the hell is that?" Sandy said. "Is that one of them duckies?"

"That's one name for them," the stranger smiled. "It's an inflatable kayak."

The stranger wore camouflage fatigues that gave him a military appearance. He had on a camouflage flotation vest and a dark green–billed cap that displayed the U.S. Marine Corps insignia. He wasn't big, but he carried himself with the confidence of a big man.

He looked toward Roy, who still held the coffeepot. "I saw the fire and smelled the coffee. Couldn't beg a cup, could I? Been on that cold lake since before dawn. Feels like I've got ice over every bone in my body."

Roy shrugged. "Guess we could spare a little. Come on over."

The stranger smiled at Shiloh. "Morning, miss."

"You on maneuvers or something?" Sandy asked.

"Not in the service anymore," the stranger replied. "But whenever I'm roughing it, I still feel more comfortable in these."

"Know what you mean," Sandy said. "Still got a bit of soldier in me."

"Yeah," Roy agreed. "At the mill, we call him the general. General nuisance." Roy laughed.

The stranger sipped his coffee. He nodded. "You make a good cup of java."

"How's that rubber duckie there work?" Sandy asked. He grinned at the term.

"For maneuverability, it can't be beat. And on a portage, it's like carrying a piece of cloud."

"Don't see any fishin' gear," Roy noted. "Just up for the scenery?"

"The scenery," the stranger said.

Sandy stuck out his hand. "Name's Sandy. Sandy Sebring. This here's my partner Roy Evans."

"How do you do?" The stranger looked at Shiloh.

"Oh, and this here's . . ." Sandy stumbled a moment, then gave up. "Oh hell, I can't remember how you say your name."

"It's Shiloh, isn't it?" the stranger said.

"See. See there, Roy? I ain't the only one thinks so."

"We already been over this," Roy explained to the stranger. "She ain't Shiloh, but folks mistake her for Shiloh. Ain't that right?"

The stranger looked at her steadily, as if he knew her lie. His eyes were earth-colored, a dark mix of brown and green. There were little specks of gold, too. "That's not true, is it? You are Shiloh."

She didn't answer but looked away instead.

"Well, I'll be," Roy said. "It is you, isn't it?"

"Son of a gun!" Sandy hollered. "Son of a gun! What did I tell you? Shiloh. You're cooking for a celebrity, Roy." This time he actually did a little dance.

Roy smiled. "Forgive him, Miss Shiloh. He don't get out much."

The stranger shook his head. "Someone like you out here in the middle of nowhere. Who would've thought? Say, would you mind if I shot a picture? Nobody'd believe it otherwise."

"Not like this," Shiloh said, waving toward her matted hair.

"Come on," the stranger said with a smile. "Up here, everybody looks a little bedraggled." He turned back toward his yellow kayak.

"Please, no." Shiloh put out her hand as if to stop him.

"Well, then," the stranger said, pausing to unzip his vest, "if I can't shoot you, how 'bout I shoot your two friends here?"

He reached to his hip and his hand came up wrapped around something dark. He turned to Sandy, who looked at him with a little smile, as if he didn't quite get the joke. The handgun gave a startling crack. A red explosion tore out the middle of Sandy's back and he crumpled in a heap next to Shiloh.

Roy's eyes grew huge. "What . . . what the . . ." he stuttered before the pistol cracked again. He grunted as if he'd been hit with a log, then he fell facedown on the ground.

The barrel swung toward Shiloh. "I've been looking for you," the stranger said.

28

THE BACON POPPED AND SPIT in the frying pan. The stranger holstered his weapon and walked to Shiloh's canoe. He lifted out her pack, dumped everything onto the rocks at the water's edge, and spent a few moments sorting through things. "Damn," he said quietly. He moved to the fire and took an appreciative look at the bacon.

"Crisp," he said. "Perfect."

Gingerly, he plucked a strip from the hot grease and began to eat.

Shiloh stared first at Roy, then at Sandy. "Oh, God," she whispered. She looked up at the stranger.

"You should eat, too," he said.

"Eat?"

The flow of blood to her head seemed to have stopped. She couldn't think, couldn't put together in a way that had any meaning the senselessness of the last few minutes. She couldn't make herself move.

"I'm guessing we have a distance to go. You look beat as it is. You'll feel better if you eat."

"I can't," she said dully.

"Suit yourself. I haven't had any breakfast." He took another strip of bacon, then picked up the coffee cup from which Roy had been drinking and held it out to her. "At least have some coffee. It'll help."

She looked at the cup—dark blue plastic—in his hand,

and she acted without thinking. Her own hand shot upward and slammed the hot coffee into his face, and then she was up and running for the woods. She hadn't gone half a dozen strides when she was jerked backward by her long black hair.

He grasped her arm and quickly twisted it behind her, immobilizing her. His other hand tugged on her hair until she was afraid he'd rip it out. She screamed.

"You think I'm hurting you because I'm angry." He spoke quietly into her ear. "I'm not angry. What you did was a natural reaction, something I would expect. Did you ever break a horse?"

He let up slightly on her hair, gave a bit of slack, then yanked brutally. "No!" she cried.

"No? Country girl like you?"

Her head burned. Her voice was choked with crying. She could barely breathe from the crush of his arm around her.

"The key to breaking a horse is to make absolutely clear to the animal that it can't throw you, escape you, or outlast you. Do you understand what I'm saying?"

She tried to answer, but only a thin, inhuman sound came out.

"Say the word." He snapped her head back with another yank of her hair.

"Yes!" she cried.

"Good. Next time you try something like that, I'll hurt you in a different way."

He let her go and she dropped to her knees. She vomited onto the golden birch leaves that covered the ground. For a while, she knelt weeping over the mess that steamed in the cold wet morning air.

"Here." He was beside her again, offering the dead man's coffee to her once more. "Like I told you, it'll help."

She looked at the cup and shook her head.

"Come back to the fire," he told her.

She didn't move.

"I just want to get away from the puke," he said. "So we can talk."

He put his hand around her arm and lifted her forcibly.

She staggered up and stumbled ahead of him to the fire. The bacon was burning now, gone black and hard as the skillet it cooked in. Blackish smoke poured upward, mixing with the gray wood smoke.

"I can't sit here," she said, looking away from the two bodies.

"Stand over by the water, then. It's all the same to me."

She walked to the shoreline where the canoes were drawn up and waiting. She stared out at the lake, at the islands that lay like dead things on the water.

He spoke at her back. "I'm here to kill you. That's the first thing you need to know. But I want something from you before I do. That's why you're alive and your companions aren't. So you have some time left. In that time, you have a choice to make. When I kill you, I can kill you very quickly and quite painlessly. I promise you. I can also drag it out and you'll beg me to kill you. I have no feeling either way. The choice is yours."

"What do you want?" she asked without facing him.

"Two things. I've told you one—your life."

"I guess it doesn't matter much what the other one is."

"On the contrary, that's what matters most. You've been at work on something while you were up here. I believe you called it—just a minute."

She glanced back, saw him take a folded letter from his shirt pocket.

"'A discovery of the past,'" he read aloud. "'I see now what I never saw before, the truth I couldn't face.'"

She recognized her own words. "Where did you get that letter?"

"I killed a woman for it."

Shiloh felt her chest go tight, as if the stranger had her in his grasp again. "Please, not Libbie."

"Her name wasn't important to me. She was just a woman who had something I wanted."

"Like me."

"Exactly."

Snow began to fall, a flake here and there. She felt the

light touch on her cheek, the cold moment of turning as the perfect shape melted into something that trickled away.

"How did you find me?"

"The letters. Then a friend of yours brought me part of the way."

"Friend?"

"Probably the best friend you've ever had, judging from how hard he tried to protect you."

She caught her breath. "Wendell?"

"I've known a lot of strong men. None stronger than Wendell Two Knives."

"Where is he?"

"That depends on your religious belief. As I understand it, his own people would say he's walking the Path of Souls."

"You killed him."

"I killed him."

Her legs felt too weak to hold her up. She dropped to the ground. She put her hands to her face, and they were filled with tears for Wendell Two Knives.

The stranger walked to his inflatable kayak, reached in, and pulled out a small radio transmitter.

"Papa Bear, this is Baby Bear. Do you read me?"

A moment of static. Then, "Papa Bear here. Go ahead."

"I've got Goldilocks. Repeat, I've got Goldilocks. That herd of deer you've been tracking, it's time to bring 'em down. Do you copy?"

"Loud and clear, Baby Bear. Papa Bear out."

The stranger stepped to her and touched her hair. She jerked away.

"Good," he said. "You're learning. It's time for us to go."

"Where?" she managed to say.

"Wherever it is you've hidden the past and whatever hopes you had for the future."

He smiled and offered her his hand.

29

A LITTLE OVER TWO HOURS along the Little Moose, Stormy and Louis came alongside Cork in their canoe.

"Louis says we've got to put in."

"What's up?" Cork asked.

"Bad stretch of river around that next bend."

"That's where Uncle Wendell always stopped." Louis pointed ahead to a break in the pines on the eastern bank.

Cork gave Sloane and Raye an exaggerated hand signal to follow and headed for the landing.

"We take a break here," Sloane called out to him.

They lifted the canoes from the water and tipped them onto the wet bed of pine needles that covered the landing. The ground was spongy and ringed with lady's slippers long past blooming. Cork sat on a fallen pine and pulled the water bottle from his pack.

"Everyone should drink," he cautioned. "In weather like this, it's easy to ignore your thirst and get dehydrated."

Sloane looked beat. He sat with his back against the trunk of a red pine and eyed the sky miserably. Drizzle wetted his face. A couple of white flakes drifted down, then vanished on his skin.

"This weather," he said, as if he were cursing.

"Where are you from?" Cork asked.

Sloane closed his eyes and didn't answer.

"Come on," Cork said. "That can't be classified."

Sloane's eyes opened slowly. "California," he finally said.

"The Golden State," Louis said.

"That's right, son."

"Are you from Hollywood?" Louis asked.

Sloane smiled briefly. "'Fraid not. Grew up in a place called Watts."

"Have you ever been to Disneyland?"

Sloane seemed to think about not answering. "Used to take my girls a lot when they were about your age. Ever been there?"

"No," Louis said.

"Someday, maybe," Sloane offered hopefully.

"How long's this portage?" Raye looked at the trail that climbed a slope steeper than anything they'd encountered so far.

"I'm not sure," Cork said. "It's been years since I've been this way. Louis?"

"Me and Uncle Wendell always made it in about half an hour," Louis said. "It's not far, but it's kind of hard because it's high and rocky. We always stopped here to rest and look at the moccasin flowers."

Raye gave him a puzzled look. "Moccasin flowers?"

"Lady's slippers," Stormy told him. He pointed at the plants around the edge of the clearing. "Some people think the blossoms look like Indian moccasins."

"It's hard to believe anyone would do this for pleasure." Sloane spoke mostly to himself and shook his head wearily.

"Where the river ends is a big lake. She's near there," Louis told him.

"We ought to get going," Cork said. "Once we're back on the river it should be only an hour or so to Wilderness. That's Louis's big lake."

The sound of a small plane came from the gray downriver. It passed near them but was hidden by the overcast. Cork knew it was a yellow De Havilland Beaver, a float plane belonging to the U.S. Forest Service.

"Think they're looking for us?" Raye asked.

"No," Cork said. "They're too high. They always stay

above four thousand feet unless they're on a search-and-rescue. Even if they were looking for us, they'd have a snowball's chance in hell of spotting us in this weather."

Sloane heaved a sigh and pushed himself up.

"You doing all right?" Cork asked.

"Fine, O'Connor," Sloane said. "Just fine. You worry about yourself." He considered the trail ahead of them. "This is how it's going to be. O'Connor, you first, then Two Knives, then Raye. You'll have the canoes. Then you, Louis. I'll bring up the rear. O'Connor, you and Two Knives carry a pack. Louis, you take one. I'll haul the last one. We'll need only a single portage that way."

"You'll be carrying a lot of weight," Cork pointed out.

"Like I told you, O'Connor, just worry about yourself."

Sloane hefted his pack onto his back, then had Louis help him sling the additional pack that carried food and cooking utensils across his chest. Cork could see the strain the weight put on him, but it was the man's choice. The others slipped into their own packs and shouldered the yokes of their canoes. They started upward along the trail in the arrangement Sloane had dictated. The going was slow not only because the slope was tough, but the ground was mostly rock and the drizzle that wetted everything made the footing slippery. The woods were quiet. Cork could hear the occasional grunt of the others behind him as they struggled to keep from slipping or stumbling. He could hear the water of the Little Moose, out of sight now, as it became an unnavigable rush compressed between rock walls and split by a scattering of sharp-edged boulders. In the cold air wetted with mist, the smell of the pines all around them seemed especially strong.

As he climbed, Cork found himself thinking about the lady's slippers. They reminded him of another trip in the Boundary Waters, long ago—the last time he'd ever spoken in an important way with Marais Grand.

At the end of every summer, when Cork was in his teens, the St. Agnes CYC made a canoe trip into the Boundary Waters. It was always eight or ten teenagers accompanied by two or three adults. Cork's first year on the outing was Marais's last. He'd just turned fifteen. Marais had just graduated from Aurora High. There were four other boys on the trip that year, all older than Cork. They'd argued among themselves who would be Marais's canoe partner. She'd settled it herself by choosing Cork. Marais asked him to take the stern, and he felt honored. His position allowed him to watch her constantly. In the heat of the afternoon, she often took off her shirt and paddled in her tank top. Her hair was black and long. Her skin was like finely polished walnut. Cork became fascinated with the curve of her shoulder blades, outlined at every stroke, as the bone captured and channeled her hair. Sometimes she sang while they canoed, leading the others in familiar songs or singing her own compositions. Every day, Cork fell more in love.

The last night of the trip that year was beautiful. They camped at a site on a point of land jutting into Lake Saganaga, less than a day's paddle from the Gunflint Trail that would take them home. The sky was cloudless, the stars brighter than Cork could ever remember. Long after dark, the moon rose, full. All the stars around it vanished as if the moon were a bucket that had scooped them up, filling itself to overflowing with their silver light. The hour became late. They doused the campfire and all turned in. Cork lay awake a long time listening to his tent partner, a boy named Duane Helgeson who was plagued by enlarged adenoids, snort in his sleep like a rutting bull moose. In a moment of rare dead quiet, Cork heard the rustle of a tent flap and the step of someone leaving camp. He peeked out and saw by the moonlight that it was Marais.

He followed along a path that cut through a stand of poplars to the other side of the point. Where the path broke from the trees, lady's slippers grew in great profusion. He crouched among the flowers watching Marais as she sat down on a big rock at the water's edge. Her head dipped foward a moment. Her face flashed in the glow of a match. She began smoking a cigarette.

Beyond Marais, the moonlight turned the water to silver and silhouetted her perfectly. She sat back, exhaled smoke. To

Cork it was like watching the shadow of her soul pass from her lips. He'd never wanted anything so much as he wanted Marais to love him. He knew he should go back, but he couldn't bring himself to move that way. Instead, to his own surprise, he stepped forward.

She didn't seem angry that he'd disturbed her solitude.

"*Anin,* Nishiime," she greeted him. She looked up at him briefly, then back at the water.

Cork sat down. Not too near.

"Smoke?" she asked.

"Sure."

She took a pack of cigarettes from her shirt pocket and handed it to him. He pulled out a cigarette, gave the pack back. He struck the match she handed him and lit up. Cork had never smoked before. He tried to take a big drag into his lungs but ended up having a coughing fit. He was afraid he'd made a fool of himself, but Marais said nothing. Her feet were bare. She dangled them in the water, making the moonlight bounce around her ankles.

A loon called from somewhere out on the lake.

"Hear that?" she asked. "No other bird sounds the same. That's what I want my music to be like. When someone hears it, I want them to understand that no one else but me could have made it."

"I love your music," he said.

"I want to tell stories with my songs. Did you know that some people believe Homer was a woman? And that the *Iliad* and the *Odyssey* were meant to be told accompanied by music?"

He shook his head in the dark, then tried another small puff from his cigarette.

"They're Players," she said.

"What?" Cork asked.

"The cigarettes. They're Players. British. I have a friend who gets them for me."

What friend? Cork wondered jealously.

She was quiet for a long time then. Cork wasn't sure if he should say something, but the truth was that he was happy enough just being alone with her.

"I'm trying to take it all in," she told him. "As much of it as I can. I don't know if I'll ever be back."

"Sure you will," he said. Then, "Where will you go?"

She turned her face to the part of the sky that hadn't been swallowed by moonlight. "Where I can't see the stars, I expect."

"I'll be leaving someday, too," Cork said.

She laughed, gently. "Don't you like it here?"

He did. He liked it a lot. But if getting out was what Marais thought was important, then it seemed like a good idea to him, too.

"I'm not leaving because I don't like this place."

He held the cigarette between his fingers, but he didn't want to smoke it anymore. "Why are you leaving, then?"

"Do you know what destiny is?"

"Sure. I guess."

"That's why I'm leaving. Destiny, Nishiime. Mine's out there. I've always known it. There's something waiting for me, something great, and I'm going to find it."

"You'll be famous, Marais. I know you will."

"Do you really think so?" She finished her cigarette and flicked it out into the water. "I think so, too."

She leaned to him and kissed him lightly on the cheek.

"Go back now," she said.

"Why?" He was confused by the kiss and by being pushed away so suddenly after.

"I want to be alone. Go on."

He crushed out the ember of his cigarette on the rock. He didn't want to leave it there, or to dirty the lake with it, so he put it in his pocket.

He was pulled back suddenly from the remembrance by the smell of smoke. Not like the smoke of the cigarette Marais had given him, nor campfire smoke, as he would have expected in that place. Another smell, faint and so different from a campfire that it was like an alarm. Cigar smoke. He reacted quickly, tilting the weight of the canoe onto his left hand, freeing his right hand to reach back to his pack, groping for the .38. At the same moment, he heard Sloane grunt behind him and Louis let out a squawk.

Cork heaved the canoe off his shoulders to the side of the trail. He spun and saw that Stormy had done the same. Behind them, beyond Arkansas Willie Raye, who still carried his canoe, they saw Sloane down, flailing his arms and legs like a beetle on its back. A few feet beyond him, Louis hung like a puppy in the grip of a giant dressed in military camouflage. The man stood at least six and a half feet tall, weighing a good two hundred and seventy pounds, all of it lean. His head had been shaved like Mr. Clean, and like most men with shaved heads, his ears seemed too large. His free hand held a pistol— a .45 Colt military issue, Cork figured. Mr. Clean was grinning around the last two inches of a lit cigar.

"Put all the canoes down," he ordered. "Let me see your faces."

Willie Raye complied, carefully unburdened himself of the canoe, and turned to the man.

"That's good," Mr. Clean said. He set Louis down, but he kept the muzzle of his gun against the back of the boy's head.

"Help me up." Sloane held out a hand to Willie Raye. When he was back on his feet, he glared at Mr. Clean. "Who the hell are you? And what do you want?"

"It doesn't fucking matter who I am. And as for what I want, well, I've got that."

The woman, Cork thought. *Shit.* His .38 was in his pack, on top, just under the flap. He'd put it there—a mistake, he now knew—because he hadn't brought his holster and had no easy way to carry it and had convinced himself that this kind of ambush wouldn't happen until they'd located Shiloh. Now there was no way he could get to it before Mr. Clean put a bullet through Louis, and probably the rest of them as well.

"Louis?" Sloane asked, confused.

Mr. Clean rolled his eyes. "Shiloh, you dumb fuck."

"Who sent you?"

"Jesus. You guys. I swear, after I kill you, you'll be grilling Satan about whether he's got a license for his fucking pitchfork."

"You hurt my son, I'll rip you apart," Stormy said.

"You make a move in this direction, Chief, and I'll blow his head off. Then yours."

Between Cork and Mr. Clean stood Stormy, Raye, Sloane, and Louis. Cork thought desperately that if he could get behind them for just a moment, out of sight, he might be able to reach into his pack for the .38. He began to ease himself behind Stormy.

"Hey, burger man. Where the fuck do you think you're going?"

"Just going to drop my pack, that's all. Getting heavy."

"Won't be heavy much longer." Mr. Clean grinned.

"What do you want with the woman?" Sloane asked.

"Business. This is all just business." Mr. Clean shrugged off a rifle that had been slung over his shoulder and set it against a stump at the edge of the trail.

"That rifle," Sloane said. "You got that rifle from Grimes. It was you."

"No shit, Sherlock. First time I ever killed a man with an ax. I kind of liked it."

"How'd you track us?" Cork asked. He was interested, but mostly he wanted to keep the man talking while he tried to figure something that might stop what he knew was about to happen.

"Training, burger man. It's all in what you learn."

"Where's Shiloh?" Raye asked.

"Right where we want her." Mr. Clean grew suddenly sober. "I think we've talked enough."

Cork knew that was it. No matter what they did, they couldn't sidestep it. He felt responsible. He felt sorry for young Louis.

Then the boy's eyes shifted toward the woods. At the edge of his own vision, Cork saw what had drawn Louis's attention. A blur of gray.

Mr. Clean saw it, too. Startled, he swung his weapon in that direction for an instant. Sloane leaped on the opportunity, grabbed the boy, and shoved him back into the arms of Willie Raye. He put himself squarely between Mr. Clean and the others.

The barrel leveled on him; the next shot sent him staggering back. He fell in a heap, rolled over, and lay still, wedged between the big packs strapped front and back on him. Sloane's sacrifice gave Stormy just enough time to catapult himself at the giant in camouflage fatigues. Stormy wrapped his powerful lumberjack's hands around the wrist of the huge arm that held the gun and forced it skyward. Another round exploded from the Colt and tunneled into the low clouds above them. Stormy was more than a head shorter and a good seventy pounds lighter than the other man, but the force of his body and the added weight of the pack propelled them both backward. For a moment, it looked as if Stormy had him. Then Mr. Clean delivered a deft knife-hand strike to Stormy's neck, a powerfully calculated blow that buckled Two Knives.

Cork was there to take his place. A running head butt threw the big man back a couple of steps so that he stumbled over the top of a big gray rock slab jutting from the ground. Cork leaped on him. He drew back for a right cross to the big man's jaw, but the pack on his back slowed him. Mr. Clean hit first. The blow caught Cork just behind the ear, boomed into him hard as a cannonball. Cork tumbled off. He tried to stand, but the toe of a boot caught him brutally in the diaphragm and knocked the breath right out of him.

Gasping for air, he saw Stormy fly at Mr. Clean again. Stormy grasped the big man from behind in a powerful bear hug and lifted him off the ground. He was about to do a body slam when Mr. Clean's arm shot back, hard as the piston on a steam engine, and his elbow rammed Stormy's nose. Stunned and bleeding, Stormy struggled to hold on, but Mr. Clean broke loose. He delivered a kick to Stormy's solar plexus that lifted Stormy off his feet.

Cork staggered up, too slowly. Mr. Clean had Stormy's head pulled back, throat exposed. In his right hand he brandished a large hunting knife.

"Time to fucking end this," he growled. His hand flicked toward Stormy's throat.

The blade never touched Stormy. Three shots popped in quick succession. The camouflage jacket Mr. Clean wore exploded in a spray of fabric and blood. The man folded like an empty flour sack.

In the profound quiet of the moment after, in the moment when there was nothing he could do but catch his breath, Cork heard the splash and tumble of the Little Moose just out of sight, the small whimper of Louis still caught up in Willie Raye's arms, the gasp of the man on the ground as he curled around his pain, and the disbelieving whisper of Sloane, who'd managed to shuck his packs and stood frozen with the gun in his hand. "Jesus. Sweet Jesus."

Stormy drew himself up. Louis ran to him and threw his arms around his father. Stormy wrapped his boy in a hug. Blood ran in a thick stream from his nose and reddened his upper teeth. He looked at Sloane, and said, "Thanks."

Sloane wobbled, then sat down hard and sudden.

Cork moved to him as quickly as his own hurting body would let him. "Are you hit?"

"I don't know." Sloane stared down at his chest, then put a hand under his coat and felt around. "No blood." He looked at Cork, his face an ashen color. "How could that be?"

Arkansas Willie Raye knelt at the packs Sloane had carried. "Are you a religious man?"

"Why?"

"Cuz lookee here." Raye reached into a pack that had a bullet hole through it dead center. He hauled out the shattered pieces of a heavy cast-iron skillet and a sack that leaked flour from what looked like a big worm hole bored in one side. Raye stuck a couple of fingers into the hole, fished around, and brought out a flattened slug.

"Something—" Sloane looked toward the woods. "Something drew his fire."

Louis turned in his father's arms. *"Ma'iingan."*

"Wolf?" Sloane asked.

"I saw it, too," Cork said.

A sound leaked from the man on the ground. Not words, but an attempt maybe. He rolled to his back and held his side. His hands were bloody as butchered meat.

"Stormy, take Louis down the trail," Cork said. "Why

don't you clean up your face and see what's broken and wait for us there."

The father and the boy picked up their gear. Stormy shouldered a canoe, and they moved on.

Sloane knelt next to the man on the ground. He examined the wounds, then shook his head at Cork. "From the way he's bleeding, I'd guess I hit an artery."

"There's nothing we can do." Cork glanced at Willie Raye, who stood nearby, staring down at the dying man. "Why don't you head along with Stormy and Louis."

"No. If he knows something about Shiloh, I want to know what it is."

"I don't think he'll be saying much." Sloane sat down on the wet ground. The man beside him stared up at the sky.

"Can he hear us?" Raye asked.

"I don't know what he can hear."

"Ask him about Shiloh."

Sloane leaned to the man and said, "Do you know where Shiloh is?"

The eyes—blue-white, like snow at first light, Cork thought—rolled slowly in Sloane's direction. Sloane bent very near and listened.

"What did he say?" Raye asked.

"He told you to fuck yourself."

The dying man's face contorted and his body tensed, then relaxed.

"Is he dead?" Raye asked.

Sloane felt the carotid artery. "Not yet."

Cork knelt beside the man and checked his pockets. "No identification. Nothing." He sat down heavily and tenderly felt himself where he'd been kicked. Nothing seemed broken. "This could take a while," he said to Sloane.

In his hand, Sloane still held the gun. He looked at it, appraising it from several angles as if it were an instrument he didn't understand at all. "A cop for thirty years and I never shot anyone till now."

"He was going to kill us," Cork said.

Sloane put down the gun. "Christ, I could use a cigarette."

"Me, too," Cork said.

Sloane grew quiet, studied the close, gray clouds. Cork looked down the trail in the direction from which they'd just come. He thought about the ambush.

"Why didn't he just shoot us?" he asked.

"What?" Sloane seemed pulled back from a far place.

"He was going to kill us, that was obvious. Why didn't he just shoot us while we had our hands full of the canoes? He could have done it in a few seconds."

Sloane thought about it. "Maybe he likes people to be afraid before they die. I've profiled killers like that."

"They've got Shiloh," Willie Raye broke in, pleading. "This man's gonna die anyway. You said there ain't a thing we can do 'bout that. We should move on. We should move on now."

"He's right," Cork said.

"I don't feel right about it," Sloane said. "I wouldn't leave a wounded animal to die like this."

"You could shoot him again," Arkansas Willie suggested.

Cork and Sloane both looked at him.

"It's what you do with a wounded animal," Raye said. "It's that or leave him. Hell, my girl's still out there. And if what he said is true, if they got her, then we need to find her fast. We can't wait around for this man to take his time in dying."

Cork said quietly to Sloane, "We've got a chance of saving Shiloh. We should do everything we can for the living."

"I'm not going to shoot him again." Sloane took a sweater from his pack, rolled it, and put it under the dying man's head as a pillow. "I don't suppose it'll make much difference." He put his gun away and lifted the scoped rifle that had been taken from Grimes.

Shouldering their loads, they burdened themselves again and moved out along the portage, leaving one more man to mark with death their passage through that wilderness.

30

THE TAMARACK COUNTY COURTHOUSE was built in 1896 with timber money. Constructed of honey-colored blocks quarried in the Minnesota town of Sandstone a hundred miles south, the courthouse stood three stories high and was crowned by a beautiful clock tower. If the passage of time were truly marked by the tower clock, the town of Aurora would have been standing still for thirty years. For three decades, time had been frozen at twelve twenty-seven. The story was that the hands had stopped at the exact moment Corcoran O'Connor's father died. It might have been true. Both the clock and William O'Connor were hit during a wild exchange of gunfire between officers of the sheriff's department and two escapees from the state prison in St. Cloud. The men had paused in Aurora on their flight to the Canadian border in order to rob the Citizen's National Bank. Sheriff William O'Connor and two deputies responded to the silent alarm. Cork's father put himself between a round from a stolen deer rifle and Louise Gregory, a short-tempered old woman deaf as a brick, who'd walked unknowingly into the melee. Every few years, the town council debated fixing the clock—debated renovating a lot of the old courthouse—but they always balked. Partly this was because the clock was seen as a kind of monument to something noble and heroic, and partly it was due to the fact that the repair would have cost a small fortune. So, like much in Aurora, things stayed pretty much the way they were.

However, there were new names on the roster of the town council and new revenues coming in from business generated by the casino, and people seemed more willing—eager, even—to put a new face on the town. There was talk of a whole new county court complex that would house the sheriff's department and county jail as well.

All this was possible, Jo O'Connor granted, but as she sat in court that gray October morning listening to the ancient heating pipes cough and grumble, passing gas and water like old men, she knew nothing changed very quickly in Aurora. And, she was surprised to realize, she liked it that way.

The pipes, Judge Frank Dziedzic had warned after he convened the proceedings, were going to be distracting. He apologized and promised that the heating system was being worked on and urged all parties to be patient and make the best of it. By the time Wally Schanno appeared in the back of the courtroom shortly before noon and signaled to her, Jo was more than ready to request a recess. She didn't have to. Opposing counsel Earl Nordstrom, while attempting to introduce into evidence a waiver of easement rights signed by the Iron Lake Reservation tribal council, was finally drowned out in a clatter of rattling metal that made him crush the document in his hands. Judge Dziedzic was favorably disposed to granting his request for a continuance until the heating was fixed.

Jo gathered her papers and turned as Schanno approached the plaintiff's table.

"Got some interesting news," he told her. "The Bureau people I know did some checking for me. At least some of what you were told is true. Special Agent in Charge Booker T. Harris of the Los Angeles field office is officially on personal leave. There's not, at this time, any official Bureau involvement in the investigation of the deaths of Elizabeth Dobson or Dr. Patricia Sutpen. And there are currently no Bureau personnel with the names of Virgil Grimes or Dwight Sloane."

Jo snapped her briefcase shut. "Special Agent in Charge Harris didn't go into the Boundary Waters, did he?"

"No, he's out at the Quetico."

"I think we should pay him a visit, don't you, Wally?"

Schanno drove them out in a sheriff's department cruiser. The wind that had come the night before, bringing the clouds and the cold, had stripped the color from the trees. Wet leaves plastered the roadways. The limbs of the birch and aspen that lined the shore of Iron Lake were absolutely bare. Jo stared at the trees as they passed, and the bared branches made the world look fractured.

Like all the cabins at the big new resort called the Quetico, Harris's cabin stood on the very shore of Iron Lake, surrounded by hardwoods and evergreen in a way that made it feel completely isolated. It was a beautiful pine log structure, two stories, with a screened porch in front and wide glass windows all around. Smoke poured from the stone chimney. All the curtains were drawn.

Jo opened the porch door and stepped in. Schanno followed. The porch was furnished with cane chairs and table, a bentwood rocker, and a standing brass lamp. The wood burning in the fireplace inside the cabin scented the air. Jo knocked on the door, waited a five count, then knocked again. As she raised her fist a third time, the door opened. Booker T. Harris filled the doorway.

"Agent Harris," Schanno said. "We need to talk."

Harris didn't reply. His eyes shifted toward Jo.

"This is Jo O'Connor. Corcoran O'Connor is her husband," Schanno told him.

"Ms. O'Connor." He nodded politely, but his courtesy had a grim edge.

"We'd like to ask you a few questions," Jo said.

"I'm afraid that will have to wait. I'm busy at the moment." His gaze shifted again to Schanno. "Couldn't we arrange to speak in your office later, Sheriff? Say in an hour?"

"The answers we need can't wait," Schanno replied.

"It's impossible for me to talk to you now."

"Impossible?" Jo said. "I'll tell you what's impossible. To believe anything that you tell us is the truth, that's what's impossible. So far, you've misrepresented facts, framed an innocent man, and may very well have put in jeopardy the lives of several people, including a child."

Schanno said, "We talk now, here, or I'll place you under arrest and we'll all go down to my office and talk there."

"Arrest me for what?" Harris asked.

"Something along the lines of criminal misconduct, pending an investigation by the Bureau's OPR. I called the resident agents in Duluth. They contacted the L.A. field office. There is no official investigation here."

"Ah." Harris looked behind him and to his left. "Just a moment." He waited, his eyes tracking something neither Jo nor Schanno could see. "Maybe you'd better come in," he finally said.

Harris pushed the door open wide and moved away. Inside, the cabin was plush. Wormwood paneling on the walls, thick beige carpeting, brown leather sofa and love seat facing a big fireplace made of brown stone. The far wall was mostly glass looking onto a scene in which the gray water of Iron Lake and the gray drip of the sky merged in a dismal, seamless curtain. The room was lit with lamplight and the flicker from logs burning in the fireplace.

Harris wasn't alone in the cabin. The other man was slender, early fifties, his hair long and silver and pulled back in a ponytail. He wore a hooded gray sweatshirt, the hood thrown back, with STANFORD printed in red across the chest. His jeans were neatly creased and he wore expensive Reeboks. He stood near the fireplace, beside a map—a topographical map of a section of the Boundary Waters—taped to the wormwood paneling. On a table near the long glass windows sat a large radio transmitter, a laptop computer, and several other pieces of electronic equipment.

Although the room was full of the smell of the burning pine logs, there was another odor in the room, less appealing to Jo. Cigar smoke.

"Jerome Metcalf," Harris said, introducing the man with the silver hair.

"Another agent?" Schanno said skeptically.

"A consultant," Harris clarified. "Communications, electronics, that kind of thing. Jerry, this is Sheriff Wally Schanno and Jo O'Connor. Corcoran O'Connor's wife."

"How do you do?" Metcalf made a slight, gracious bow with his head.

"Not too well, thanks," Schanno said. "I feel like a trout being jerked around on a line. I need some straight answers."

"We'll see what we can do, Sheriff," Harris said.

His brown skin wore a sheen of perspiration that glistened in the firelight. His blue work shirt was wet at the collar. The room was warm, Jo thought, but not that warm. The man was scared.

"Why don't we start with a simple question," Jo suggested. "There is no official FBI involvement in the investigations of the deaths of Elizabeth Dobson or Patricia Sutpen. So why are you here?"

Harris opened his hands as if to show the sand-colored palms concealed nothing. "I assure you, we're here at the request of the California authorities."

"Which authorities?" Jo asked.

"I beg your pardon?"

"Isn't it true that your involvement is at the request of one authority? Your half brother, Nathan Jackson?"

"Where did you hear this?"

"Is it true?"

"I'm not prepared to answer—" Harris began to say.

"And isn't it true that your involvement in the investigation of the murder of Marais Grand fifteen years ago was also because of your brother? Were you trying to cover up your brother's relationship with Marais Grand, Agent Harris? To save his political career? Maybe even to help him get away with murder? And is that why you're here now?"

She was out on a limb, and she knew it. One of the first tenets she'd ever learned in cross-examining was never ask a question to which you don't already know the answer.

"These are serious accusations," Harris cautioned.

"I don't hear you denying them," Schanno said.

Harris walked to the window. Against the gray outside, he looked like a shadow as he stood considering. But Jo's attention was momentarily captured by a slice of light that appeared at the top of the stairs, as if someone down a hallway there had opened and closed a door very quickly.

"You have a reputation as a strong advocate of civil rights, Ms. O'Connor." Harris didn't turn, speaking instead as if Jo were beyond the glass he faced. "You've got an impressive history of helping the Chippewa people here."

"They prefer to be called Anishinaabe," she told him. "Or Ojibwe. *Chippewa* is a white term."

"Whatever." He slowly turned around. "My point is that you understand the importance of the issue of civil rights."

"Actually, I'm having trouble understanding your point."

"Sheriff, do you mind if Ms. O'Connor and I have a word alone?"

"I mind," Schanno replied.

"Ms. O'Connor, I'd rather speak to you in private. It's important. And I promise, your questions will be answered."

Jo figured what the hell. "Wally?"

"I don't like it."

"Please," Harris said. And he seemed sincere.

"You want me to leave?" Schanno asked.

"No. We'll just step upstairs. Jerry, get the sheriff some coffee or whatever he'd like. Ms. O'Connor, if you'll follow me."

Harris led the way up the stairs, turned down the hallway, and knocked at the second door. Inside, someone called out evenly, "Come in."

He was over six feet tall, the man who waited in the bedroom. Early fifties, trim and fit. He wore indigo jeans, a yellow lamb's wool sweater, and a gold chain. He stood with his hands clasped behind his back, appraising her as if he were an officer gauging a new recruit. His eyes were quick and intelligent in a face so lightly colored and softly featured that he could have passed for a beachcomber instead of an African American. Except for the gray that salted his hair, he looked no different from the first time Jo had seen him many years before in Chicago.

"Ms. O'Connor," Nathan Jackson said, "I suspected it was only a matter of time before we met."

Harris offered her a chair, but Jo preferred to stand.

"Then it's true," she said. "You were involved with Marais Grand."

Nathan Jackson held a cigar in his left hand and gestured with it as he talked so that he seemed to write in the air with smoke. "Marais and I were lovers for a time, yes. But I certainly didn't have anything to do with her murder. Nor would I ask my brother to compromise himself by participating in a cover-up of any kind. I'd be very interested in knowing how you came to make these accusations."

"I had a visit this morning from Vincent Benedetti."

Jackson froze and cast his brother a cold look. "Here? He's here?"

"That explains a lot," Harris said grimly.

"Explains what?" Jo asked.

"What did Benedetti say?" Harris pressed her.

Jo eyed them both. For brothers, they were not much alike. Harris was small, dark, broad in the features of his face. Jackson was tall, light as a chamois cloth, and as smooth. But then, they'd had different fathers. However, they were both the same in how they regarded her, with eagerness and concern.

"I'll make you a deal," Jo told them. "You tell me why you're here, and I'll tell you what I know."

Harris gave his brother a quick shake of his head. But Nathan Jackson said, "I don't think we have much choice, Booker. Ms. O'Connor, I'll put a condition on this. What I tell you doesn't leave this room. I'll be perfectly candid, but I want your promise—your word—that you'll keep this information confidential."

"I don't think I can agree to that."

"The lives of people we both care about are at stake here," Jackson said. "For you, your husband."

"And for you?" she asked.

Jackson collected himself before he spoke, as if he'd been holding this in for a long time. "My daughter. Shiloh."

"*Your* daughter?" Jo knew surprise lit her face like a flare, but the statement caught her so off guard.

The sky had darkened more. Against the bedroom windows, the drizzle began to mix with flakes of snow. Harris turned on a lamp on the stand beside the bed.

Nathan Jackson settled his cigar in an ashtray on the stand by the bed and offered Jo a photograph from his wallet. The photo was old but protected by a vinyl cover.

"It's the only picture of Marais and me together. That was in the old days before she was famous and we both had to be so careful about everything."

They were young and smiling. Marais Grand wore a white summer dress. Her long black hair hung over her right shoulder in a single braid. Her skin looked deeply tanned, but Jo guessed it was the evening light and Marais's Ojibwe heritage. They stood in front of a white picket fence. Beyond that, a cypress tree partially blocked a dark blue ocean descending into night. They were holding hands.

"When was it taken?"

"The summer of 1970. I met her at a fund-raising rally for Angela Davis. We ran into each other at a lot of gatherings like that. I'd be there to speak, Marais to sing. The difference in us was that I believed in what I was saying."

Harris made a sound like a blast of steam from a broken pipe. He didn't bother to hide the derisive look on his face. "Cut the bullshit, Nathan. No voters here."

Jackson went on as if he hadn't noticed. "Marais, she'd sing anything people wanted to hear. Just so they'd listen and remember her. My God, she was good. And so beautiful. And so damn certain she was going to make it. I'm not sure I've ever known anybody who had a better sense of exactly what they wanted."

"That's when you were lovers?"

"The first time." Jackson took the photo back. He squinted at it as if he were trying to read the faded etching on a gravestone. "We went separate ways after that. Marais got an offer in Vegas along with Willie Raye, whom she'd hooked up with professionally. I defended the Watts Eight, and that was my ticket up." He put the photo back into his wallet.

"I didn't see her again until the Williams Commission

hearings three or four years later. She came to see me because her name was on the witness list and I was chief counsel for the commission. She was worried that if she testified it would ruin a television deal in the works for her and Arkansas Willie. She asked me to take her name off the list."

"And you did," Jo said.

He nodded, with a faint smile. "The commission was bogus anyway. Congressman James Jay Williams's version of the McCarthy hearings. Made him famous for a while. And gave me a foothold in politics. Marais and I became lovers again, briefly and very secretly. Then she told me she was pregnant. But she didn't want anything from me. She told me she was leaving for Nashville to film her television show and that she was going to marry Arkansas Willie so the baby would have a name. She asked me if I minded. What was I going to say? To marry her was out of the question. We were going in such different directions. And to make public our liaison in that way and at that time would have ruined me. I said I didn't mind. Didn't mind," he said with loathing. "It was the hardest thing I've ever done." He rolled the cigar between his fingers, studying the long ash, shaking his head faintly. "She was true to her word. She never asked me for anything. But she sent me pictures of little Shiloh once in a while. Here. This was the first. In over twenty years, it's never left my person."

He took out another photograph protected in clear vinyl. Shiloh at eighteen months in a white dress in a photographer's studio. Jo had seen one exactly like it before in the trembling hands of Vincent Benedetti. She turned it over. The words on the back were in the same handwriting as those that had appeared on the photo in Benedetti's possession.

Nathan—she barrels around like a fullback, knocking over everything. She has your nose and intelligence. My skin. My mother's eyes. Marais.

"Shortly before her murder," Jackson went on, "Marais moved to Palm Springs. She was tired of television and eager to do something different. I think she and Willie Raye were ready to call it quits. They'd played out the charade of their marriage long enough for both of them. Marais wanted to embark on a new enterprise. A recording company. She was smart. She'd investigated the angles and knew there were lots of incentives in California for minority businesses, many of them programs I'd championed. She came to see me. Told me she was prepared to do whatever was necessary to make sure she qualified. She didn't need to do anything and she knew it. She was just testing. She brought Shiloh. It was the first time I'd ever seen my daughter, ever touched her hand. You can't imagine what that felt like."

"Tell me," she said.

"It was as if from the moment Marais let me know that Shiloh was born and I couldn't share that, I'd been living with a shattered heart. But suddenly all the pieces had been brought back together. I'd have done anything Marais asked just to be able to be with Shiloh again. Then Marais was murdered."

"Why didn't you come forward about your relationship to Shiloh?"

"I was afraid. It was a very confusing time."

"And you were on a political express that might have been derailed," Jo said.

"I know it sounds callous. I had Dwight Sloane assigned to the case. Dwight and I go way back to the old days in Watts. Practically like brothers. And I pulled a lot of strings to get Booker assigned by the Bureau. Because of Benedetti's suspected ties to organized crime, they were willing to come in under the RICO statute. I had to know what was going on."

"What was going on?" She looked directly at Harris.

"A lengthy, ultimately fruitless investigation," Harris said.

"It was Benedetti," Jackson insisted. "We just couldn't prove it."

"His motive?" Jo asked.

"They'd been lovers once. He wanted to start again. She told me she'd borrowed a hefty sum from him to start Ozark Records and he'd indicated he'd be willing to accept sex in lieu of interest. She wanted it strictly business. They argued—in public, in front of witnesses—the day before she was killed. Her murder was a hit, Ms. O'Connor. And it was Benedetti who arranged it. We just weren't able to prove anything. If Benedetti's here now, it's to silence Shiloh, to keep whatever she remembers about that night from being told."

Jo said, "The men who are here with you, they were all involved in the original investigation. Why are they here now?"

"They know the case. They owe me favors, and I wanted this done quietly. As soon as the tabloids get hold of this information, every lunatic this side of the Atlantic will be here trying to spot Shiloh. We hoped to do it so that Benedetti wouldn't know either. I guess we blew that.

"If Benedetti's men are out there, your husband, the boy, the others, they're all in danger." He held out his hands, empty. "That's everything. I swear. Now you."

"I spoke with Benedetti this morning," Jo said. "He told me a story every bit as interesting as the one you've just told. Only in his version, he's Shiloh's father and you're the man who killed Marais Grand."

"What?"

Jo recapped Benedetti's version of Shiloh's origin and Marais Grand's demise. Nathan Jackson listened with his jaws working back and forth like a silent engine powered by rage.

"The lying bastard. *His* daughter?"

"His story sounds no less plausible to me than yours."

Jackson thrust the photograph of Shiloh at her. "Just look at her. She looks like me."

"Vincent Benedetti is convinced she looks like him. We believe what we want to believe."

"If Benedetti's here, Nathan, we need to talk to him," Harris said. "Maybe we'll have a better idea of what's going on out there."

"What do you mean, what's going on out there?" Jo looked from one to the other. "Don't you know?"

The two brothers exchanged a glance. Harris said, "There's a problem."

"What problem?" Jo demanded.

"I think we should go downstairs." Harris moved toward the door. "Metcalf can explain this. And Nathan, it's time we brought the sheriff in, don't you think?"

Jackson's eyes fed on the photograph of Shiloh. He looked like a man worried it would be his last meal.

Downstairs, Schanno and Metcalf were at the map. Schanno saw Nathan Jackson, but probably didn't recognize him. He looked unhappy and he looked at Jo.

"Got a problem, Jo," he said.

"So I understand."

"You told him?" Harris asked Metcalf.

"The essentials," Metcalf replied.

"Will someone please tell me?" Jo said.

Metcalf beckoned Jo to the wall map.

"The last communication we had with Dwight Sloane was yesterday. Five-oh-eight P.M. Here." He put his finger on a lake called Embarrass. "He should have checked in four hours later. He didn't. At first light this morning, I went out in a helicopter to their last known coordinates. They weren't there. I circled the area, but unfortunately with this weather, I couldn't see much."

"So the situation is, you've been out of touch with them since almost the beginning," Schanno said unhappily.

"Essentially, that's correct," Metcalf admitted. "Probably it's an equipment failure. The fact that we found no trace of them at the last coordinates indicates that they're still moving."

"But you have no idea where," Schanno said.

"No," Metcalf admitted.

Schanno rubbed his jaw and slowly shook his head. "Embarrass Lake. Not good."

"Why?" Harris asked.

"The lake's roughly circular," Schanno explained. "There are easily half a dozen trails that lead off from various points around the shoreline."

Harris said, "Then we do an aerial search along each trail until we spot them."

"In that?" Schanno indicated the weather visible through the glass doors. "You couldn't find the Eiffel Tower in that."

"Suggestions?" Harris continued, unfazed.

"We get the Tamarack Search and Rescue Team to put men on every trail," Schanno said.

"How soon?" Nathan Jackson asked.

Schanno looked at him and must have decided that whoever he was, he was in it as thick as the rest. "They could be on the ground at Embarrass Lake in a couple of hours. We should get them started right away. With this cloud cover, dark'll come early. They won't have much daylight left."

"It's better than sitting around waiting," Metcalf put in.

"Have it done." Jackson turned to Jo. "I want to talk to Benedetti."

"I can arrange that," she replied.

31

THE WATER LOOKED LIKE GRAY EARTH and the paddle in her hand felt like a spade. With every stroke, Shiloh saw herself digging her own grave.

The man in the stern of the canoe hadn't spoken except to press her for directions. She'd lied to him, tried to misdirect him to buy time. "That way," she'd pointed, leading them through a narrows between two islands. "Now that way."

His sense of direction was flawless even though the mist and the drizzle sometimes blotted out everything except the flat water fifty yards around them. "That will take us in a circle," he said quietly at her back. "Don't try that again. Which way is it?"

"There," and she'd lifted her hand grudgingly in the direction of her death.

She'd struggled with despair all her life. She knew that people envied her, looked at the trappings and thought she had it all. They were wrong. Her life was a big beautiful box with lots of ribbons and bows on the outside but completely empty within. The only love she'd ever known was from her mother and that had been wrenched from her a long time ago. Her father had given her everything she wanted except love. She'd been raised by nannies, nuns, tutors, and housekeepers. She'd never had any real friends, anyone she trusted deeply. All she'd ever had was the music.

What would be the loss? Who would even care if she never came out of the woods? She laid her paddle across the gunwales, laid her head down, and wept. The canoe didn't slow in the least.

"You disappoint me," he said. "We all die sometime. Wendell Two Knives understood that. He went as nobly as any man I've ever known. You would honor him by dying well."

"There's no honor in dying if there's no reason to die," she wept.

"Dying's never had a reason. As far as I can tell, the same is true for living."

It wasn't true about dying, she thought. Wendell had died for a reason. He'd died for her. And dying herself seemed like no way to honor him.

She whispered his name. *Wendell*. It didn't exactly fill her with courage, but it did pull her out of her self-pity.

She considered the knife in the pocket of her jeans. It wasn't much, but small as it was, she found herself wrapping her hope around it. She had the map in her vest, and a compass, and matches there, too, in a waterproof container. All she needed was a chance.

She wiped her tears and took up her paddle.

"Do you have a name?" she asked.

"Call me Charon."

"Charon? Charon. Where have I heard that name before?"

Her back was to him. She listened to his voice carefully. His words were like stones, hard in the way he said them. But not without feeling. Rather, they were like a wall behind which the feeling was hidden.

"You said Wendell died a noble death. How?"

"In the end, I cut his throat. A small, painless cut. It doesn't take much when you know what you're doing."

"Is that how you'll kill me?"

"That depends on you."

"I have money," she tried.

"I have money, too."

"Look, if you don't do this, I could make it worth your while. In other ways."

"Sex? If I wanted that from you, I'd take it."

"I don't understand this. I don't understand any of it." She hit the water with her paddle and sent a splash of silver into the gray on their left.

"'Our civilization is founded on the shambles, and every individual existence goes out in a lonely spasm of helpless agony.' William James said that. About as close to understanding any of this as I've ever come."

"I'll bet you tortured small animals when you were a child."

He was slow in responding, although the canoe slowed not at all. "I was the small animal," he said.

"I have to pee." She lifted her paddle from the water. "We need to stop."

"No stops," he said.

"If I'm going to die, I want to die with the dignity of clean underwear."

A moment later, she felt the canoe draw to the left toward a small island. As the bow touched shore, he said, "Try to run and I'll hang you by your hair from a tree limb."

She stepped out. "I'm just going over there." She pointed a dozen yards away to a gooseberry bush near a scrub pine. "For privacy."

"Right there's good enough." He nodded toward the wet ground on which she stood.

"At least turn your back."

She was thinking that when he did, she could grab the knife and use it. She was thinking she could cut his throat as he'd cut Wendell's.

"So you can hit me with a rock?"

He stared at her until she undid her jeans. She pulled them down and squatted facing him.

He stood in the canoe, tugged his zipper down, and proceeded to urinate into the lake.

Wendell had told her often that it was important to note the details around her. She saw that the man who called himself Charon was uncircumcised and she wondered if that was important.

"I'm hungry," she said when she'd finished.

"I told you you would be." He sat back down in the canoe and waited for her.

"Even the worst condemned criminal gets a last meal," she said.

He turned and drew in the yellow duckie they'd towed behind them. He lifted out his pack, opened it, and tossed her a Hershey's bar. No nuts.

"You call this a last meal?"

"I had a last meal once. Flat bread, that was all. A piece of hard flat bread and a little water in a rusty can."

She unwrapped the Hershey's bar. "How come you're not dead?"

He took a bar himself, unwrapped it, and sat back in the canoe as he ate. "They never bothered to check my pulse. Just threw me on a pile of other dead men. I let the flies lick my blood for a full day before I crawled away. Here." He tossed her a plastic bottle full of water.

She took a drink, then, as his eyes flicked down for a moment to his candy bar, she spit in the bottle. She capped it and threw it back.

"How does a man get to be like you?" she asked, her voice sizzling with her spite.

"If you believe in karma, I didn't have a choice." He drank from the bottle.

She smiled bitterly. "If I don't?"

"Then you enter the nature-nurture debate. I had a tough early life. So maybe that was it. Or maybe it was a simple genetic predisposition, because not everyone who had a tough life ends up in this line of work."

"You sound educated."

"I don't spend all my time killing people."

"How many people have you killed?"

"I'd know only if I gave that any importance. I don't. The only important one was the first."

"Your father, I suppose."

He stared at her, then a laugh, like a freed bird, escaped his lips. "Archetypal as hell, huh?" He crumpled his wrapper and put it in his pack. "Give me," he said and held out his hand for her wrapper.

"Think someone's going to find it? Think it's going to save me or threaten you? Christ, what difference does it make? You left two bodies this morning." She threw the paper on the ground.

"You never know what might make a difference. Pick it up." He spoke in that deadly, quiet way that was business and was final.

She picked up the wrapper and tossed it to him.

"Get in," he said in the same tone. "It's time to be moving."

"Charon," she said suddenly. They'd traveled for nearly an hour in a silence broken only by the splash and swirl of water as they dipped their paddles into the lake. The rain was mixing more and more with wet snowflakes that clung to her eyelashes before melting into drops that blurred her vision. "I remember. The boatman who ferried souls across the river Styx to Hades. The nuns made us study that. Charon. Funny in a grim sort of way. But that's not your real name."

He didn't reply.

"What is your real name?"

"As I understand it, an Ojibwe may have several names. The name given him by a Dreamer, the name that has come to him in his own dream, a nickname, a kinship name. Which one is real?"

"You're smart," she said, feeling the frustration and anger rise again. "And you say you don't need money. So why are you doing this?"

He spoke very carefully, as if it were important. "Your music. Why do you do that?"

Now it was her turn to refrain from answering.

"Let me suggest something to you, then. Your music is who you are. It defines you."

"You kill people to define yourself?"

"I take difficult jobs. Sometimes killing is a part of that."

"This is a job? Christ, this is just a job?"

"No. I told you. It's who I am."

"Who hired you?"

He paddled a few strokes before answering. "Do you believe in an afterlife?"

"What difference does it make?"

"Because if you do and you're right, all your questions will be answered there."

Strange, how familiar it all was. The line of hills rising west like horses lifting their heads. The island that was nothing more than a piece of bare gray rock. A hundred yards beyond that, almost hidden among ribbons of mist and rain, the place where the stream emptied into the big lake. She surprised herself by finding it so easily.

As the bow nudged the rocks along the shoreline, the stranger stepped out and drew the duckie in. When both craft had been secured, he said, "Lead the way."

She was trying to keep her mind clear, but she felt as if she were floating. Felt distanced from the feet that walked the soft bed of pine needles covering the trail. Separated from the cold that nestled under the big evergreens and gave her cheeks a vague tingling. She breathed but felt nothing enter her body.

Her thinking was thick and empty. She thought of the knife in her pocket and wondered should she try to use it. But it wasn't a real thought, a real wonder. She was heading toward something so huge and absolute it couldn't be embraced. It was as if she were already dead, had passed on in spirit, and was simply waiting for the flesh to join her.

"Up there?" she heard him ask.

They'd come to the high wall of jumbled rock that long ago had dammed the stream to create the hidden lake Wendell called Nikidin. She stared up dumbly at the rock wall, stared up out of a deep well of hopelessness.

With the toe of his boot, he tested the footing on the stones. Water seeped over everything, and the stones were covered with green slime.

"Hmm," he said. "Slippery."

32

IT WAS PAST TWO when the Lincoln Town Car pulled up in front of cabin 7 at the Quetico and parked beside Wally Schanno's cruiser. The Lincoln sat. Nothing could be seen through the charcoal-tinted windows.

"What's he waiting for?" Nathan Jackson asked.

Jo said, "If I were him, I'd feel about as comfortable with this situation as I would stepping over a rattlesnake." Jo moved toward the front door.

"Where are you going?"

"To ask him in."

"I'll go," Schanno said.

"He's not going to shoot me, Wally. Besides, he doesn't know you. I'm the one who asked him here." Before she stepped outside, she addressed Harris, who was studying the Lincoln through a lifted slat in the window blinds. "You wouldn't do anything stupid, would you?"

A bar of the gray light from outside fell across his eyes and Jo saw how tired they looked. "Ms. O'Connor, too many stupid things have been done already."

She crossed the porch and descended the steps. The air was cold and wet and her breath came out in vaporous puffs. As she approached the Lincoln, the back window slid down. Vincent Benedetti sat hunched in the seat, a small white man against the big black interior.

"What am I walking into?" he asked.

"A discussion," Jo replied. She crossed her arms and hugged herself for warmth. "One that probably should have taken place a long time ago."

Angelo Benedetti leaned into her vision. "Who's in there? Besides Jackson?"

"Do you want to talk or not?" Jo asked.

"I'll talk to him," Vincent Benedetti said.

"Pop, it could be a setup."

"Is it a setup?" The trembling little white man looked at Jo.

"No."

"Then let's go."

The driver, the big blond man Jo remembered was called Joey, got out and opened the car door for Vincent Benedetti. "I'll get the wheelchair from the trunk," he said.

Benedetti waved him off. "The braces. Give me the braces. I want to walk in on my own."

Angelo Benedetti got out on the other side. Jo saw a look pass between him and Joey over the car top. The younger Benedetti gave a shrug and a nod. From the trunk, Joey hauled out two metal crutches with arm braces. Angelo and he strapped them on the elder Benedetti and stood by patiently as he made his way toward the cabin, step by agonizing step. Pain twisted Angelo Benedetti's face as he watched his father's struggle, but he made no move to interfere. At the cabin steps, Benedetti paused, breathing heavily. He eyed the top of the steps as if he were looking at the summit of Everest, gave a grunt, heaved his right leg up, then dragged the left one after. His head disappeared in a cloud of vapor as he sucked in air and expelled it noisily. In a couple of minutes, he reached the porch, where Wally Schanno was waiting with the screen door open.

"Thanks," Benedetti managed to say.

His son was right behind him.

Schanno reached out to offer his hand, but Angelo Benedetti said quickly and sternly, "No. He'll make it."

Benedetti dragged himself across the porch, the crutches thumping one after the other on the wooden planks. Schanno opened the front door, and a moment later, Benedetti was inside.

"Here, Pop." Angelo Benedetti positioned a high-backed chair for his father, who collapsed onto the cushion, crutches splayed on either side of him as if he'd once had wings but all that remained of them were bones.

Benedetti was sweating heavily and trembling.

"Can I get you some water, Mr. Benedetti?" Jo asked.

He shook his head—a definite indication amid all the general shaking—then lifted his eyes and looked as steadily as he could at Nathan Jackson.

"You son of a bitch," he said in a hoarse whisper.

"If you were standing up," Jackson said, "I'd lay you right back down."

"This is going well," Jo said to no one in particular. She stepped between the men. "We need to cut the crap here, gentlemen. People we all care about are in trouble."

"His doing," Benedetti tried to raise his hand to point an accusing finger at Jackson, but the brace was still attached to his arm. "Get this thing off me."

Angelo unstrapped the braces and leaned them against the back of the chair. Then he stood behind his father.

"Accusations have come from both sides," Jo said.

"Where do you get off claiming Shiloh is your daughter?" Jackson leaned past Jo in Benedetti's direction.

"It's obvious," Benedetti fired back. "Just look at her. She has my eyes."

"Those are her grandmother's eyes," Jackson insisted. "And look at her skin."

"Mediterranean," Benedetti said.

"My ass. Shiloh's my daughter." Jackson thumped his chest. "Marais told me."

Benedetti smiled cruelly. "She lied. To get what she wanted from you, she told you all kinds of lies. You were easy."

"You're the liar."

Nathan Jackson started around Jo, but Angelo Benedetti moved to intercept him. As if part of a dance

choreographed in hell, Harris leaped in and warned Benedetti, "Back off."

The two men locked eyes. Their hands curled into fists.
Their bodies tensed. Schanno wedged his tall, lean, tough
frame between them. "Move back, both of you. The only
thing we're going to do here this afternoon is talk. I said move
back."

Benedetti spoke to Schanno without taking his eyes off
Harris. "Anybody comes at my father again and that sheriff's
badge you're wearing won't matter."

"Nobody wants to hurt your father," Jo said.

"Wanna bet?" Nathan Jackson gave Vincent Benedetti a
killing glare.

"Nobody's going to hurt anybody while I'm here."
Schanno used his huge hands to urge the men farther apart.

Vincent Benedetti eased himself forward on the chair,
leaned as far toward the confrontation as he could, and aimed
the venom of his words at Jackson. "Shiloh's my daughter,
you son of a bitch. I'm here to keep you from killing her the
way you killed Marais."

"I killed Marais?" The accusation seemed to hit Jackson
like a two-by-four between the eyes. "Why would I kill
Marais?"

"She put the squeeze on you one time too many. Finally
asked some favor you wouldn't grant. I'm betting she threatened to go public with the whole sordid history, so you had
her killed."

"Marais didn't have to put the squeeze on me for anything," Jackson shot back. "We loved each other."

Benedetti spat on the rug. "Politicians. Shit. You think
everybody loves you."

"You." Jackson aimed his finger at Benedetti as if he were
holding a gun. "You were the one who fought with Marais.
The night before she was killed. There were witnesses. It got
violent."

"Violent? She slapped me. She always slapped me. I irri-
tated the hell out of her because I had her number."

"You know what I think? You were trying to strong-arm

her into your bed again. When she absolutely refused, you had her killed out of some Neanderthal sense of pride."

The exchange seemed to have taken a good deal of strength from Vincent Benedetti. He sat back in the chair, trembling violently.

"You okay, Pop?" Angelo bent and touched his father's arm.

The elder Benedetti stared up at Jackson, but the fire seemed to have dwindled. "I wasn't propositioning Marais. We had a deal. I loaned her money so she could get Ozark Records off the ground. Instead of paying interest, she was supposed to let me get to know my daughter. She welched. We argued."

"You threatened her," Jackson said.

"I lost my temper. I didn't lose my mind. I didn't kill Marais."

Booker T. Harris stepped closer, but cautiously and with an eye on the younger Benedetti. "None of what you just said was in any of your official statements to the police."

Vincent Benedetti laid his head against the back of the chair. He took a deep breath. "Back then, I was doing my best to protect my daughter. I knew you cops had jack shit on me. Little Shiloh was in a bad enough way as it was. What? Was I going to add to her troubles by dragging her through the circus of paternity hearings? Besides, my wife, Theresa, threatened to leave me if I said a word about Shiloh."

Jackson paced a little, collecting himself, considering. Then he turned again on Benedetti. "Marais loved me. She told me she was afraid of you, afraid that if you ever found out how she really felt about you, you'd hurt her bad."

"She was afraid of no one. She loved no one—except herself and her daughter." Benedetti sighed, sounding tired of the whole exchange. "She used you like a carpet sweeper to clean up her messes. She told you whatever you wanted to hear."

"That's a lie."

"We're getting nowhere," Jo broke in. She turned to Nathan Jackson. "Do you really care about the woman out there?"

He looked shocked. "Of course I do."

"And you?" she said to Benedetti. "You really want her out alive?"

"I'd die for that girl," he replied.

"All right." Jo held up a finger as if asking the men to follow her in her train of thought. "Let's assume for the moment, just for the sake of getting somewhere, that neither of you was responsible for the murder of Marais Grand or for what's happening here now. The question is, if not you, then who?"

Both men appeared to be a little startled by the concept and it took a while before they stopped glaring at one another and the anger between them seemed to dissolve. Benedetti stared thoughtfully at the wooden beams above him. Nathan Jackson slid his hands into his pockets and turned toward the long windows to gaze at the gray outside. Harris put a finger to his lips and tapped lightly. Metcalf put a new log on the fire, and the bark burned quickly with a sound like someone was crumbling wrapping paper.

"It would have to be a professional in Shiloh's case," Harris finally said.

Jackson turned back to listen.

Harris went on. "The murder of Elizabeth Dobson was a clean job. Professional. Not a shred of evidence left to trace him."

"And the shrink," Vincent Benedetti said. "Whoever torched the shrink and her records knew his business."

Jackson looked from one to the other. "Same person, you think?"

"Maybe two," Angelo Benedetti offered. "Working together. Different talents, covering one another."

Harris looked toward Metcalf, who'd sat the whole time at the table that held all the electronic equipment. "Feed what we know to the computer at the L.A. field office. See what you come up with."

Metcalf moved to his laptop.

"Angelo and I will make some inquiries of our own," Benedetti said.

Jackson squared himself in front of the chair that contained Vincent Benedetti. "I've held you responsible for

Marais's murder for fifteen years. For Shiloh's sake, I'm willing to reconsider. But I'm not letting go yet."

"There's an old Sicilian saying," Benedetti replied. "'A man who drinks the wine he's made never tastes a bitter glass.' Maybe we've both been drinking our own wine too long." He leaned toward Angelo and said, "Take me out."

Angelo Benedetti gathered his father in his arms. Schanno lifted the crutches and opened the door. Jo followed them all out. Joey had the black Lincoln running, warm and waiting. He held the back door open and helped Benedetti settle his father. Then he popped the trunk for Schanno.

"I'll be at my office," Jo told Angelo Benedetti. "Or at home. Call me if you find out anything."

"I will." He looked back at the cabin. "You didn't buy that, did you?"

"All I want is to get to the truth, Mr. Benedetti. I'm trying to keep an open mind."

He looked disappointed in her. "I'll be in touch."

Schanno stood with Jo as the Lincoln pulled away. "What do you think?" he asked.

"I don't know, Wally. I get the feeling truth and lies are all jumbled up like a ball of snakes here."

"I know what you mean. Look, I've got to get back to my office, oversee the search-and-rescue. The men should be at Embarrass Lake pretty soon. What about you?"

"I'm going back to my office for a while, then out to see Sarah Two Knives. I think she should know what's going on."

"Do you know what's going on?"

Jo eyed the cabin and saw that Harris was watching through the blinds. "Does anyone?"

33

Late afternoon was on them when Louis lifted his hand and said, "She's up there."

The men feathered their paddles and stared through the mist at a ridge backed by the vague dark shape of forested hills. Cork had been in and out of the Boundary Waters his entire life. He'd never before felt menace in the land, but he felt it now as he looked at the shoreline, trying to pierce the gray veil, trying to divine what might be awaiting them when they landed.

"There's a stream," Louis said. "About a quarter of a mile back is another lake, a real small one."

Cork took out the map and studied it. "I don't see anything indicated here."

"Uncle Wendell said you'd never find Nikidin on a map. He said it was protected."

"Protected," Sloane said. "By what?"

"*Manidoonsag*," Louis replied. "Little spirits."

Cork pulled ahead. "I'll go in first. If things look okay, I'll signal you."

"I should go first," Sloane said from the canoe he shared with Arkansas Willie.

"And I'm not going to wait here." Willie Raye was firm. "Every minute is important. Now that we're this close, let's just go."

"Not until we know what we're walking into," Cork told

him. "A few hours ago, a man nearly killed us all. I don't want something like that again. All of you stay until I signal it's safe."

A lot of years as sheriff had given Cork a voice of authority that emerged now and again of its own accord. It brooked no argument.

"We'll do what the man says," Sloane told Raye. He gave Cork a thumbs-up.

No one said anything further as Cork veered away from them.

Cork had his .38 out and ready as he approached the shore. He saw the small stream Louis had spoken of, and he heard the bubble of the water as it tumbled over a scattering of smooth stones near its mouth. There was hardly any other sound. No birds. No wind. Only the susurrus of the water as the canoe glided through and the scrape of the bow against the shore. He was out of the canoe quickly, like a marine on a beachhead, and he crouched low, scanning the trees near the water. Nothing showed itself. Nothing moved. He spotted a trail that shadowed the stream and he made quickly for the cover of the brush there.

A quarter mile inland, Louis had said, was the lake where Shiloh would be. Cork moved down the trail a few yards at a time, stopping to listen, to check the deep woods around him. He came to a place at the edge of the stream where the bed of pine needles was cleared to mud. The mud was full of tracks—deer, raccoon, rabbit, squirrel—animals who'd come there to drink. There were other tracks. Ridged boot soles. Cork knelt and studied them carefully. Two distinct sets: one small enough to be a woman's; the other, larger, deeper, though not as huge as might have been made by the man who'd ambushed them that morning. The distance between strides was not great. Whoever had made them didn't seem in any great hurry. He couldn't tell if the two people had traveled that way together or if the woman had been followed.

A rush of movement to his right brought him around quickly. He had his .38 leveled belly high into the trees. He froze in that readied position, his whole body tuned to his senses, watching, listening. He saw only the deep, empty gray among the trees and heard only the ubiquitous drip of the drizzle that, having fallen silently, gathered into heavy droplets on the foliage and fell again. He caught a familiar scent, something that gave him a moment of hope. The smell of wood smoke. But he saw no fire.

The movement came again. Something big rushing left to right. Cork's finger tightened on the trigger. Then he saw the white flag of the deer's tail as it bounded away, and he nearly collapsed with relief.

He followed the trail until it broke from the trees and he confronted a high ridge. He could see that at one time the stream had worn a passage through the ridge. But that passage was blocked now by tightly packed rock fragments that formed a ragged dam nearly a hundred feet high. Water seeped among the rocks and reformed into the stream that ran to the lake. Cork found the prints again at the base of the wall. Along the top of the ridge, he saw a quivering among the last of the fall leaves. The wind was slight but evident, coming out of the west, over the wall, bringing the scent of the wood smoke from a place he couldn't see. He returned to the shore and signaled the others.

"I found tracks," he said, and pointed toward the trail. "Shiloh's, I'd bet, and someone else's."

"Uncle Wendell's?" Louis looked hopeful.

Cork said. "We'll know soon enough."

"Should we leave someone with the canoes?" Sloane asked.

"I think it's best we stay together," Cork said. "Leave the gear. Bring the weapons."

Sloane handed Stormy his handgun. "That's a nine-millimeter Glock. Think you can handle it?"

"I'll do fine," Stormy said.

Sloane lifted the rifle from his canoe.

Arkansas Willie surprised them all by reaching into his pack and pulling out a pistol of his own. "It's only a twenty-two," he said apologetically. "But I'm pretty good with it."

Cork led them to the wall.

"The lake's back there?" he asked Louis.

The boy nodded. "We have to climb. There's a trail on top of the ridge. It leads to the cabin at the other end."

"Smell," Stormy said.

"Fire." Cork looked up at the top of the ridge, anxious to check the other side.

"Think someone's cooking?" Sloane asked.

"Let's hope it's dinner and there's plenty." Cork gave him a fleeting smile.

They went slowly, one at a time, covering each other as they climbed. At the top, they found themselves looking down at a narrow lake walled by steep rock topped with aspen. The far end was hidden in mist.

"There's the trail." Louis swung his hand toward a faint parting in the brush.

Cork knelt down. "Look here."

He pointed at a place in the muddy ground where there were more boot prints. But there was something else.

"A dog?" Arkansas Willie asked.

"Wolf," Cork said.

"What do you make of that?"

"It's a good sign," Louis said firmly.

"I hope you're right, son," Raye told him. "I hope to God you're right."

They moved single file up the trail. They left the brush and entered a bared area strewn with boulders. Finally they were among the aspen atop the ridge. They'd walked into clouds, into a deep, cold mist, into the wet kiss of snowflakes on their faces. The lake below was a dark gray slit in the earth—gray from the overcast and dark from the depth of the water. The ridge on the far side was slate colored and mounted by leafless trees. The pines, just visible at the other end of the lake, seemed like another dark wall.

A wall, Cork realized, with a black snake climbing the top and crawling into the clouds.

"Smoke," he said. "Lots of it."

"Too much for a wood stove," Stormy said.

"The cabin?" Sloane asked.

"Oh, God." Arkansas Willie broke from them suddenly. He started down the slope of the trail toward the dark pines. "Shiloh!" he cried.

"Willie!" Cork called after him. "Stop!"

But he knew it was too late. Whatever it was they were moving into, they had to move quickly now.

"Stormy, stay here with Louis. Let's go, Sloane."

He broke into a run, following Raye down the ridge toward the cabin hidden in the pines. Arkansas Willie surprised him with his speed and the fluidity of his movement. The man leaped rocks like a runner over hurdles. Cork understood that if it were Annie or Jenny down there, he'd probably be running hell-bent for leather, too. As it was, he kept himself in check on the downslope. He wanted to be able to stop quickly and fire his .38 if necessary.

He glanced over his shoulder. Sloane had dropped back. That was probably best. If they were stirring up hornets, they wouldn't all get stung.

Raye disappeared among the pines. Almost immediately, Cork heard a gunshot. He reigned himself in and drew up beside the trail. Sloane reached him a moment later, puffing like a big, black steam locomotive and sweating like a racehorse.

"You . . . you . . . hear . . . that?" he stammered between breaths.

"Sounded like a small caliber," Cork said. "Maybe Will's twenty-two."

"Shooting at what?" Sloane gasped.

"I'll circle right, you go left. You okay?"

"Nothing an oxygen mask wouldn't fix. Go on," Sloane said. "I'll be fine."

Cork made first for a big rock a dozen yards distant. Then to where the ridge fell away to the lake. The ground was strewn with mossy boulders, and Cork dashed from one to another until he reached the edge of the pines. He paused and listened. A steady groaning came from somewhere ahead and to his left. He caught a flick of motion out of the corner of his eye. Sloane slipped into a kneeling position behind a big pine, leveled his rifle, and panned the woods. He glanced at Cork and shook his head. Cork signaled them forward.

They came on Arkansas Willie sprawled in the mud on the trail. His face was squeezed in pain. He held his right knee. His .22 was on the ground beside him.

"Slipped and fell," he said between clenched teeth. "Twisted my fucking knee."

"We heard a shot," Cork said.

"Gun went off when I hit the ground." Raye eased himself into a sitting position, still grasping his knee.

Sloane asked, "Can you walk?"

"Christ, I'll crawl if I have to. Just get me to her."

"What's up?" Stormy and Louis approached on the trail behind them.

"I told you to wait," Cork snapped.

"We only heard one shot," Stormy replied. "Didn't figure that was enough to kill you all."

"We might as well stay together now," Sloane said. "We're sure not going to surprise anybody, and we can cover one another."

"What about him?" Cork nodded impatiently at Raye.

"Here." Sloane handed Cork his rifle. "Come on, Willie. Lean on me."

Sloane helped Raye to his feet and let the man slip an arm around his big shoulders.

"Thanks," Raye said.

"No problem, man."

"What's ahead of us, Louis?" Cork asked.

"A stream. The cabin's just on the other side."

Cork made sure there was a round chambered in the rifle, then he said, "Let's see what there is to see."

The stream lay only a few dozen yards ahead. Cork paused when he reached the bank. The others moved up around him and stood silently.

On the other side, the remains of the cabin stood smoldering in the drizzle. A charred, ragged suggestion of walls enclosed a jumble of collapsed roof beams black as old chicken bones. A big potbellied stove stood in a heap of ash near the center, its stovepipe jutting up into nothing. Flames had bared the lower branches of the pines nearest the cabin and sooted the bark of the trunks, but the thick, wet air had saved the trees from fully catching fire.

"My God," Raye whispered. "Shiloh."

They found no sign of the woman. Sloane moved carefully among the ash and char, sifting and poking with a long stick. Much of the area still glowed with embers, and licks of flame danced up here and there. Sloane stayed clear of the hot spots. He came out shaking his head.

"Nothing here."

"What do you mean?" Arkansas Willie sat on a stump that had a webbing of ax bites across the top where wood had been split for kindling. He was obviously in pain far greater than any caused by his wrenched knee.

"He means," Cork said quietly, "there's no indication that Shiloh was in the cabin when it burned."

"Bones don't burn so well, and teeth not at all," Sloane said. "And there's a smell to burned flesh that's unmistakable. What I'm trying to tell you, Willie, is that there's still a lot of reason to hope."

"Why did they burn the cabin?" Louis asked.

Cork shrugged. "I don't know. Maybe they were trying to cover up something."

"Or destroy something," Sloane suggested.

"Or drive Shiloh out," Arkansas Willie said miserably.

"What do we do now?" Stormy asked.

Cork looked up at the sky. Dark wasn't far away. The temperature was dropping and what came out of the clouds now was mostly white. "Let's get back to the canoes and set up camp before dark comes, try to figure what our next move should be."

"Shouldn't we look around?" Raye said. "Maybe she ran into the hills. Maybe she's hiding somewhere."

"The woods are big, Willie. And it'll be dark soon. We're hungry and tired. It's best to regroup and see what we can figure. Can you walk?"

Louis had found a long birch pole and offered it as a walking stick. Raye stood up, leaned on the stick, and took a few tentative steps.

"It'll be slow, but I can make it." His voice and long hounddog face were full of despair.

The clouds were charcoal and the darkness among the pines had turned deep black by the time they reached the place where they'd beached the canoes. As they came out of the trees, Cork stopped abruptly.

"One of the canoes is gone."

Once again, his .38 was in his hand, and he crouched to scan the trees along the shoreline.

"Stay here." He motioned the others back.

He crept to the two canoes still drawn up on the shore.

"Goddamn it," he said.

"What's wrong?" Sloane called to him.

He turned back to them grimly. "Someone's put an ax through the hulls."

34

Jo HAD MEANT TO GO straight to her office after she'd left Benedetti and Harris. Instead, she found herself heading to St. Agnes. She wasn't sure if praying was what a strong lawyer would do at that juncture, but it felt right for her. More and more in the last year, she'd found herself seeking answers in a way that law books could never address. The church was empty and was dimly illuminated from the light above the altar.

As she prayed, she heard the soft creak of the front doors. She glanced back and saw that Angelo Benedetti had entered. He crossed himself and stood in the dark at the back of the church, waiting respectfully. She finished her prayers.

"I didn't mean to disturb you," he said when she approached.

"What is it?"

The quiet of the church seemed to touch something in Benedetti. His eyes moved over the soft curves of the pews, lingered on the stained-glass windows, drifted through the dark along the outer aisles. He reminded Jo of a boy at First Communion. In a muted voice, he said, "My mother used to take me to church with her every day. St. Lucia. She'd light candles for all the dead relatives back in Italy. There were a lot of them, believe me. I'd curl up on a pew, go to sleep. I remember how safe that felt. The church big and quiet. My mother murmuring her prayers. The candles like tongues of angels

203

speaking back to her. I still go whenever everything seems all jumbled up. I'd guess things seem pretty jumbled to you right now."

"Is there something I can do for you, Mr. Benedetti?"

He wore an expensive waxed canvas slicker that was wet from the drizzle outside the church. The slicker crinkled when he moved.

"I just wanted to make sure you weren't fooled by Jackson. He's slick as raw oysters."

"And that's why you followed me?" She didn't bother to hide her irritation.

"Mostly I wanted to tell you that I've seen his brother before. Booker T. Harris. Just after Shiloh's mother was killed."

The quiet in the church changed. The peace in it felt crushed by something ominous. Jo sat down in the last pew and Benedetti joined her.

"Go on," she said.

"The papers were going crazy. Dredging up all the stuff about the old days when my father and Marais Grand had been a hot item. There was a lot of speculation flying around about their starting up their affair again and about Marais Grand's death having something to do with a love thing gone wrong. It was hard on my mother. She spent a lot of time at St. Lucia. She was so upset she couldn't even drive, so I'd take her. I was sixteen then. I didn't have the same patience I'd had when I was little. Usually I'd drop her off and go get a burger or something, come back in an hour or so. Generally she was still inside lighting candles, praying. I'd have to tell her it was time to go.

"One day I come back, step inside, and there she is at the candles, but she's not alone. A man's with her. A black man. And they're whispering hot and heavy. I think something must be wrong, so I go to help her. She yells at me. There in church. Tells me to get the hell out. So I do. I'm waiting outside for her, wondering what can be going on. A few minutes later, the guy comes out and I get a good look at him. It was that Booker T. Harris. I'd swear to it on my mother's grave. A little later, my mother comes out. Usually church soothes her, but she's shaking like she just had a visit from the Devil himself. She's real quiet. Doesn't say a thing the whole way home."

Jo waited, but Benedetti seemed to have finished. "What do you think it means?" she finally asked.

"I don't know. I'm just trying to tell you these men have been harassing my family for years. Now I realize it extended even to violating the sanctity of the church. Maybe I'm just saying that being a lawyer, you may be disposed toward believing them because of who they are. Me, I wouldn't trust any of them any farther than I could throw this church."

Jo stood up as if to leave. Benedetti did the same.

"I'm interested. In your line of work, just how do you know who to trust?" she asked.

"My line of work?" He laughed and it sounded loud in the empty church. "I'm just a businessman, Ms. O'Connor. I manage my father's casino."

"You didn't answer my question."

"About trust, you mean? All right, I'll tell you who I trust. Family."

"Family," Jo considered. "And this is all family business because, of course, Shiloh is family."

"My father believes she is." Benedetti looked down at the dark water spots on the carpet where rain had dripped from his slicker. "He loves her like a daughter, whatever."

"He's had a strange way of showing it all these years."

"Love isn't always about hugs and kisses. Sometimes it's about doing what's best for the person you love. I guess Pop always figured her life was complicated enough without his throwing her another curveball. You should see his office. Plastered with pictures of Shiloh. Plays her music all the time. He's been to every concert she ever gave."

"Does that bother you?"

"I beg your pardon?"

Jo shook out her umbrella in preparation for heading outside. "You're familiar with the story of the prodigal son? I'm just wondering. The good son who did all his father asked of him, how do you think he felt when he saw the love that was lavished on the other?"

Benedetti shook his head in a disappointed way. "This isn't about me."

"Why should I believe anything you tell me? I mean, if, as you say, family is all that can be trusted."

"Whether you believe me or not doesn't matter," he said. "What matters is that you don't buy that slop Harris and Jackson are trying to sell you."

"But disbelieving them is part of the package you're trying to sell. Do you see my dilemma?"

Angelo Benedetti regarded her for a moment, and something like regret seemed to enter his face. He shrugged. "Believe what you want to believe. Your funeral." He walked away from her. When he opened the front door, a shaft of gray light entered the church, but it didn't make things any brighter.

She spent a few minutes at the office clearing her schedule. She called Rose, let her know she'd be late for dinner. Finally, as dark settled over Aurora, she climbed into her Toyota and headed toward the Iron Lake Reservation. She had to tell Sarah Two Knives that the men who'd forced her husband and her son into the Boundary Waters had lost contact with them and had no idea where they were.

Heavy white flakes began to plaster themselves against the windshield. In her headlights, the wet snow mixed with the drizzle like moths among a swarm of gnats.

On the outskirts of Allouette, she pulled up and stopped at the turn-in to the trailer home of Wendell Two Knives. The trailer and the outbuildings were almost lost in the dark and the precipitation. But beyond the buildings, visible through the boughs of the cedars near the lake, was a flickering light.

Jo left the car at the side of the road and stole into Wendell's yard. She crept between the dark, empty trailer and the big shed where Wendell kept his truck and the materials he used to make his canoes. She passed a small garden full of bared cornstalks and emptied pumpkin vines. A light wind came off the lake and moved through the branches of the cedars, coming toward her with a long sigh. Another sound came with the wind, a sound that to Jo seemed like crying.

She hid herself behind one of the trees and peered cautiously through the thick branches. The light, she realized, was a fire. And the crying was a song. Henry Meloux sat on a stump near the deep vast black that was Iron Lake and sang in the language of The People. As she watched, he lifted his hand and sprinkled something into the wind. He stopped suddenly and listened intently, then he looked directly at the place where she stood concealed. She stepped from cover.

Meloux grinned. "Jo O'Connor." He didn't seem surprised in the least, but Jo had never known the old *midewiwin* to be surprised by anything.

"*Anin,* Henry," she said, offering him the traditional Anishinaabe greeting.

"*Anin,*" he replied. He beckoned her forward and indicated a big chunk of saw-cut birch as a seat.

Jo liked Henry Meloux immensely. The old man seemed to favor her with the same affection. It probably had something to do with the fact that Meloux credited her with saving his life the year before. She'd been lucky with a rifle and had prevented a murderous man in a jeep from running Meloux down. But she also suspected that anyone who approached him in true need would have felt embraced by his affection. Jo's own feeling about Meloux was deeply embedded in respect. The old *midewiwin* understood a kind of law Jo appreciated more and more all the time, a law for which nothing was written and no courts existed.

Meloux wore an old plaid mackinaw that, in the firelight, glistened with rain. On his head was settled a red billed cap with CHIPPEWA GRAND CASINO printed across the crown. Water dripped from the bill. His breath, when he spoke, fogged the air. Jo looked at his hands, dark old hands where the veins ran like rivers, and she saw that he held a pouch.

"What are you up to, Henry?"

"Fishing," the old man told her. "Among the spirits." He lifted a bit of cedar bark and added it to the fire. "I have been asking the *manidoog* of the woods to bring my old friend Wendell Two Knives back safely to his home. And I have been asking that the other men come home safely, too."

"Henry, do you know what's going on out there?"

The wind rose suddenly. The fire stirred and grew brighter. The cedar bark flamed up in a small explosion of embers that, lifted on the wind, scurried into the night like fireflies.

"It's an old battle," Meloux said. "If I were a younger man . . . " But he let it drop.

"You know about Cork and the others?"

Meloux nodded.

"Do you know where they're going?"

"No." He reached out as if touching the air. "I only know everything is connected, like the threads on a spider web. And time is like the wind. The wind blows, the web moves, but the connections do not break. Only, now I feel something tearing through, something big. Threads are breaking. I don't know why."

Jo leaned toward the fire and spread her cold hands to its heat. "I don't know what's going on, Henry. It's like I'm downwind of the Devil. I can sense something awful out there, but I can't tell what it is or what it wants. I don't know how to fight against something I don't understand."

"We do what we can." Meloux spoke quietly, but without defeat. "I burn sage and cedar. I offer tobacco. You? You have become a hunter. Maybe a warrior, too?"

"Maybe."

"I know you as a warrior, Jo O'Connor. I owe you my life."

"I was lucky, Henry."

"I do not believe that." Meloux took a bit of sage and cedar bark and put it in Jo's hand. His fingers were thin and hard, the skin rough, the nails yellow. "In your own way, burn cedar and sage. And remember, the thing about a devil is that Grandmother Earth will refuse to hide it. It will be revealed. Be ready."

"I'll do my best, Henry." She stood up to leave. "You're a long way from home. Can I give you a lift?"

The old *midewiwin* smiled. "You already have. As for getting home, when I am ready, that I can do on my own."

She headed back toward Aurora. Until she knew more, what good would speaking with Sarah Two Knives do except add to the woman's burden of worry? There was nothing anyone could do that night anyway. Best let those who could sleep in peace.

She pulled into the garage of the house on Gooseberry Lane. When she opened the back door and stepped into the kitchen, the smell of fried chicken rolled over her like the scent of heaven. Rose stood at the sink with Stevie, doing dishes.

"Mommy!"

Stevie threw his dish towel down and jumped off the chair that had given him enough height to reach the counter. He ran to Jo and gave her a big hug. It was the best thing that had happened to her all day.

"We saved you some dinner," he told her.

"In the oven," Rose said, using the hem of her apron to wipe suds from her hands. "Hungry?"

"I wasn't until I smelled the chicken. Now I'm starved."

Jo took a hot pad from a hook near the stove and pulled the plate from the oven. A chicken breast with a light golden breading, baked potato, fresh green beans, and yellow squash. She put her nose into the steam that rose from the plate and breathed in the wonderful aroma of Rose's cooking. Stevie gave her flatware and a napkin and she sat down at the kitchen table.

"Where are the girls?" she asked.

"Annie's at church," Stevie answered. He knelt on a chair at the end of the table, set his chin on his folded hands, and his dark eyes followed her every move. They were Cork's eyes. The deep, watchful eyes of the Anishinaabe.

"She's helping mark things for the bazaar next Saturday," Rose explained. She put butter and salt and pepper on the table for Jo, then took up Stevie's dish towel and set about drying the remaining dishes.

"And Jenny's at Sean's," Stevie finished, eager to share what he knew.

"Sean's folks invited her to dinner. They're studying afterward," Rose added.

Stevie picked up the salt shaker and tapped a little onto the table. He tried to get the shaker to stand at an angle on a few grains, something he'd seen his father do. The shaker fell over.

"Will you play Legos with me tonight?" he asked.

"I'm sure your mother is very tired—" Rose began.

But Jo reached across the table, angled the shaker successfully on a pinch of grains, and said, "Of course I'll play. Let me eat first and change my clothes, okay? Why don't you go gather all your Legos and decide what we'll build."

Stevie disappeared. Rose poured a cup of coffee and sat at the table with her sister.

"Delicious," Jo said with her mouth full.

"Thanks." A small, satisfied smile appeared on Rose's plain, wide face. "I remember Mom used to come home from the base hospital and I'd have dinner ready. We'd sit down, and you'd always have something interesting or funny to tell her. You know, a place to start the conversation. I used to love that time, all of us at the table together."

"Mom would start her drinking then," Jo reminded her.

"Not always."

"Too often."

"She was alone. Taking care of us alone."

"We did the caretaking, Rose."

Rose stared at her. At first the look held hurt and mild anger, but that passed quickly.

"You're too hard," she said.

"I just try to be realistic."

Rose stood up and looked down at her. "Maybe you should try being forgiving instead." She took her coffee and headed back to the sink to finish the dishes.

The food in Jo's mouth seemed tasteless all of a sudden. "I'm sorry, Rose. I'm just worried."

Rose came back and sat beside her. "What is it?"

"They've lost contact with Cork and the others."

"How?"

"Equipment failure, they say."

"But you don't believe them."

"Oh, Rose, I don't know what to believe. Or who."

Rose put her plump, wonderful arms around Jo, who could smell the lilac powder her sister always used after her afternoon bath.

"What does your instinct tell you?" Rose asked.

"Never trust a man. Period."

They both managed to laugh. Jo briefly related the events of the day, the Benedettis, what Schanno had discovered, the confrontation at the Quetico.

"Somebody must be lying."

"But who?" Jo asked.

"Do you think Cork and the others are in real danger?"

"My instincts say yes. But I don't know how to help them." Jo pushed her plate away, put her arms on the table, and laid her head down. "God, Rose, I feel so tired, so confused, so fucking responsible. For everything."

"First-child syndrome. And Catholic to boot." Rose stroked Jo's hair gently. "When I said you should be forgiving, I meant you should try it on yourself as well. Look, you've always been the smartest woman I know. You'll figure something out."

Jo hugged her sister tightly and for a long time. "You're the best, you know."

"I know." Rose finally pulled away. "I'll finish the dishes. I think you've got a construction job waiting for you in the living room."

Jo spent the evening building a Lego castle with Stevie. She put him to bed at eight and read to him from *The Indian in the Cupboard.* Annie came home at nine, Jenny on the stroke of ten. Jo was at the kitchen table drinking herbal tea. When Jenny breezed through the door, her face was bright as a harvest moon.

"How did the studying go?"

"Oh, fine."

Jenny smiled from a distant place. She went to the refrigerator, pulled out a carton of milk, and poured herself half a glass. She took a couple of cookies from the cookie jar and leaned back against the counter.

"Mom, how old were you when you got married?"

"A lot older than you."

"How did Dad propose?"

"Badly." Jo sipped her tea and smiled as she remembered. "He took me out on a cruise on Lake Michigan. I'm sure it cost him half a week's pay. He'd never been on a boat like that before. The lake was a little rough. He got seasick. He proposed to me and threw up."

"No."

"Oh, yes."

"Did you accept? I mean, right then and there?"

"Uh-huh. He looked so pathetic, I couldn't say no."

Annie stepped into the kitchen from the other room. The concern in her voice stopped the conversation dead. "Mom, there's someone outside again, watching. In the shadow of the lilac hedge."

"Turn out the light," Jo said.

Annie hit the switch. Jo went to the kitchen window and peered out. She saw the figure, black against the shadowed hedge, motionless, nearly lost in the night.

"What is it?" Rose asked. She came into the kitchen knotting the tie around her robe. "Why's everybody standing in the dark?"

"Call the sheriff's office, Rose," Jo said. "Get someone over here right now."

Rose didn't pause to ask why. She went straight to the wall phone.

In less than five minutes, a sheriff's department cruiser

rolled up the street and stopped near the lilac hedge. Two deputies with flashlights converged on the figure, which had not moved. Jo couldn't see a face, but whoever the lurker was, he didn't resist. The deputies brought him between them toward the kitchen.

"Your Peeping Tom," Deputy Marsha Dross said, presenting the offender at the back door.

"Sean?" Jenny peered around her mother.

"Hi, Jen."

"What were you doing out there?"

"Nothing. Just—you know—looking at your house."

"Why?"

"Sean, were you out there last night?" Jo asked.

He was dressed in a black leather jacket, black pants, black boots. Long and lanky, dripping wet, and chagrined.

"It's all right, Sean. I'd just like to know."

"Yes," he said. He looked at Jenny to gauge the degree of his transgression. "I just didn't want to go."

"Parting is such sweet sorrow," Annie said dramatically from somewhere in the kitchen.

"Thanks, Marsha," Jo said.

"No problem. 'Night."

"I'm sorry, Mrs. O'Connor," Sean said.

"Good night, Sean. Go home."

From the kitchen window, Jenny watched him walk away. She turned back. "Kind of embarrassing for him."

"It could have been worse." Jo smiled. "He could have thrown up."

In her nightgown, she switched off the bedroom light and stood at the window. The rain had turned completely to snow. By morning, everything would be covered in flawless white. All the faults of the earth would be invisible, as if forgiven.

Forgive yourself, Rose had advised. Jo wished it were that easy. But when the wounds you'd inflicted went so deep, was there anything that could heal them? When your own soul felt so broken, could anything make it whole? She closed her eyes and said a prayer again for those out that night in the wilderness. Then she crawled under the covers. It was a large bed, and she'd taken a long time to become accustomed to lying in it by herself. Usually, she was fine sleeping alone. But sometimes, especially on nights like this when she lay a long time staring at the ceiling, the bed still felt far too big for her and too empty.

35

THEY'D PITCHED THEIR TENTS along the shore and eaten in a quiet that was the result of fatigue and a general hopelessness. Now they sat at the fire while the snow began to turn the ground around them white. Willie Raye, who was particularly subdued, had also developed stomach cramps and diarrhea. He confessed that he'd drunk lake water. Cork informed him that he'd probably ingested a parasite, *Giardia,* sometimes present in the urine of beavers. It caused just such symptoms in humans. Although Cork assured him that however uncomfortable it might be it wasn't deadly, Raye seemed less and less convinced each time he hobbled into the bushes.

Cork stirred the fire idly with a basswood stick. "We have plenty of food," he said. "And there are enough old logging roads that we shouldn't have any trouble finding one and walking out."

"Without Shiloh?" Louis asked.

The men looked at one another.

"I'm not sure there's anything more we can do, Louis. Whoever it is, they've made sure we couldn't follow them." With the glowing end of the basswood, Cork gestured toward the canoes.

Sloane sat hunched toward the fire looking tired and perplexed. "I don't get it. Why'd they do the canoes but leave us our gear? That seems pretty frigging polite."

"In a hurry," Stormy speculated. "Slow 'em up too much to do anything more than slam an ax through the hulls."

"How much more time would it take to grab our gear and throw it all in the canoe?" Sloane pointed out.

Arkansas Willie Raye, who looked like death, said quietly, "They did what they came for. They grabbed my girl. Now all they want to do is get away."

Cork wished there were some shred of hope he could offer, but it finally looked like they'd hit a dead end as far as hope was concerned. They'd been too late. In a wilderness the size of the Boundary Waters, the body of a woman could easily be hidden so that it was never found.

Stormy finally stood up. "I'm going to get some more firewood. Give me a hand, Louis?"

With an electric lantern lighting their way, father and son headed down the shoreline toward a stand of mixed hardwoods a short distance away. Cork watched them go and felt the hollow place in his own spirit as he thought about how much he missed his son, Stevie. He wondered what was happening that night in the house on Gooseberry Lane. He envisioned the living room lit with the warm glow of lamps, the smell of Rose's cooking suffusing every breath, Stevie sprawled on the rug with his trucks or Legos. The girls would be studying, probably. Annie anyway. Jenny—who knew? She was changing so fast he always felt like he was seeing her from a distance as she left him behind. And Jo? She would have everything under control. She always did. It was always hard when he realized how well they managed without him.

Cork swung his attention to Sloane, who sat staring into the fire, his hands tightly clasped. Cork imagined what must be going through his head. He'd lost an agent in his charge, maybe a friend. They hadn't saved the woman they'd come for. Cork figured Sloane was probably going over it all, revisiting his mistakes, every bad decision, and feeling responsible and regretful. Cork understood. He'd been that route himself, and not that long ago.

"Look!"

Louis came back into the firelight with his father. Between them they held something big and flat and yellow.

"What is it?" Sloane asked.

"Lay it out," Cork told them.

He stepped to the other side of the fire where Stormy and Louis set the thing on the ground, took the electric lamp, and studied their find carefully.

"It's an inflatable kayak," he said. "And check this out." He stuck his index finger into a couple of slits that ran for several inches along one side. "Clean cuts. Probably with a knife. Where'd you find this?"

"Stuffed in some bushes in the trees," Louis said. "Hidden, kind of."

"It's a one-man kayak," Cork said.

"A one-man kayak." Sloane's eyes narrowed as he thought. "And one set of prints besides Shiloh's. Maybe we're down to dealing with one guy out here."

"Everything points that way," Cork agreed.

"What do you think? Somehow," Sloane went on, speculating, "he locates Shiloh, so he doesn't need Louis anymore. He radios the dude who attacked us this morning and tells him to make sure we don't interfere."

"Then what about that?" Stormy pointed to the kayak that had been rendered useless by a knife blade. "Why would he do that, then steal one of our canoes?"

"Maybe he didn't do it," Cork said.

Sloane looked at Cork, and life leaped into his eyes. "Shiloh."

"You lost me," Arkansas Willie said.

"It's like this, Willie," Cork explained. "As far as we can tell, there's only one man after Shiloh now. Suppose Shiloh was able to get away from him. She puts a couple of slits in the kayak to make sure he can't follow her. Strands him here."

"How does she take off?" Sloane considered.

Cork looked to Louis. "Did she have a canoe of her own?"

"Uncle Wendell said she did. I never saw it."

"There you go." Cork was walking back and forth in the firelight now, envisioning it all. "Whoever this guy is, he burns the cabin. Who knows why? Spite. Evidence. Anyway, he knows he's stranded. Then we come along. He hides until we're on the ridge, then puts an ax through the hulls of those two canoes so we can't follow him, and he takes off in the other."

Sloane rubbed his hands together in excitement, but he said cautiously, "It's an awful lot of speculation."

"Seems to me we've got two choices," Cork said. "We can give up and say we're beaten. Or we can decide we've still got a fighting chance at finding Shiloh."

"I'm all for giving it a go," Sloane told him, "but I've gotta point out to you that that guy's done a good job of punching holes in any rescue effort we might want to mount." He jerked his head toward the damaged canoes.

"Yeah." Cork hit his palm with his fist. "Damn. If I'd just brought some duct tape along, I'll bet I could patch those holes."

"Maybe Louis could help," Stormy offered.

The men turned their attention to the boy. He seemed small, and when he looked down, his face was shadowy in the firelight, uncertain.

Stormy knelt and spoke to his son, although his dark eyes never moved to the boy's face. He seemed to be speaking to the fire. "Louis, I never much believed in the things your Uncle Wendell taught you. I thought being a Shinnob was mostly a hard thing and the best way to handle it was to ignore it as much as possible. Well, I was wrong. What you know, what Uncle Wendell taught you, can help Shiloh. What do you say?"

The boy spoke quietly. "I don't know if it will work."

"If what will work?" Arkansas Willie asked.

Stormy said, "My uncle builds canoes. Birch-bark canoes."

"Ours aren't birch bark," Sloane pointed out.

"Maybe they could be patched as if they were. What do you think, Louis?"

From far behind them came the howling of a wolf. They all turned toward the inland dark. The howl came again, from somewhere high along the ridge they could not see, a cry that seemed to be seeking an answer.

Louis turned back to the men. "I'll try," he said.

The ground was fully white by the time they drew the canoes up to the fire and Louis sat down to work. Following the boy's instructions, Cork and Sloane had cut several strips of bark from a number of birch trees in the stand of mixed hardwoods. The canoes were tipped with the hulls to the fire. Louis spread one of the strips across the first of the damaged hulls. The ax blade had been swung twice, making an X near the bow. Louis trimmed the strip with a knife so that it covered the entire area with a couple inches to spare. He'd told them he needed an awl. Uncle Wendell, he said, used a *migos*, an awl made of deer bone. Cork offered his Case knife, which had a reamer/awl among its many blades. Louis also said he'd need something like thread to sew the birch-bark patch to the hull. Cork never entered the Boundary Waters without a small tackle box and collapsible rod. He dug the small tackle box from his pack and offered Louis nine-pound-test fishing line.

Louis tried to punch the awl through the Kevlar without success. The rend in the hull had weakened the integrity of the material and the whole area simply gave as he pushed. He looked up at the men, wounded with defeat.

Arkansas Willie sat down heavily. "Guess that about corks it."

Stormy reached toward his son. "Give me the knife, Louis." He took the knife and nudged the tip of the awl into the coals at the fire's edge. He put on a glove. After a minute, he pulled the awl from the coals, pressed the red-hot tip gently to the canoe, and melted a deep indentation near the rend.

"Hold this against the inside," he said and gave his son a flat chunk of wood. Sloane and Cork held the canoe on its side while Louis braced the wood chunk against the Kevlar hull. Stormy gave the awl a whack and punched a clean hole right through the melted indentation. In this way, within half an hour, Stormy and Louis had the damaged area outlined. Cork straightened a fishhook and tied on the fishing line. Stormy pressed the patch to the hull and held it in place. Louis worked from inside the canoe and Raye from the outside, pushing the straightened hook and line through the holes and the bark.

After they'd secured the patch in this fashion, Louis took hold of the cooking pot he'd placed earlier on the fire. The pot contained pieces of pitch-covered spruce bark he and his father had gathered while Cork and Sloane were cutting the birch-bark strips. Louis had made a sack from the mesh inner pocketing of Cork's down vest, filled the sack with the pieces of spruce bark, and sunk the whole thing in water to boil. The pitch lifted from the spruce bark, filtered through the mesh sack, and rose to the surface of the boiling water where Louis carefully skimmed it off with a spoon. He placed it in another, smaller pot, which he put on the fire as well. While that mixture boiled, he ground some charcoal powder from partly burned cedar chips and added that to the liquid pitch. The powder, he said, would help the resin mixture to firm up after it had been applied.

He told his father he needed a *cijokiwsagaagun*, a small spatula for spreading the resin mixture over the seams of the birch bark to seal it. Stormy split a birch branch and whittled a small, flat blade. Louis took the liquid resin mixture and, using Stormy's makeshift spatula, carefully applied it to the edges and awl holes of the birch bark to seal the patch.

When they were done with the first canoe, they all stood back and studied it in the firelight. Willie Raye's long face seemed to have grown longer with weariness. "Do you really think it'll work?" he asked.

"I think it's got a hell of a chance," Cork replied. "Birch bark is watertight. And Kevlar is basically a resin derivative, so Louis's pitch blend has a reasonable chance of making a good bond. And if it doesn't, what have we lost but a little sleep?"

"And we'd have lost that anyway," Sloane added.

Stormy put his hand on his son's shoulder. "Louis, you've done a good job."

The boy smiled at his father's praise, and he looked down, embarrassed by the attention of the other men.

"How about some coffee before we start the next one?" Sloane suggested.

He made the brew and they all took some, including Louis, and they sat around the fire. Cork was tired to the bone and could see it in the faces of the others as well. They'd had a long, hard paddle. Two men had met brutal deaths. And it had come down to this: The life of the woman they'd come for might well depend on a couple of thin strips of birch bark. But Cork felt a quiet pride at that moment, in the company of these men and the boy. For despite the terrible odds against them, they had not backed down.

"If you're right, Cork," Sloane said, finally breaking the good quiet that had come with the coffee, "and Shiloh got free, where would she go from here?"

With his index finger, Cork snagged a bit of ash that was floating on the surface of his coffee. "I've been thinking about that. Louis could probably back me up, but I'd guess if she knows anything at all, she's headed for the Deertail River. It would begin to complete the circle back to the place we put into Boundary Waters yesterday. The river heads southeast, ultimately to Lake Superior."

"Wouldn't she have passed us on our way here?" Willie Raye asked. "I mean, wouldn't we have seen her?"

Cork shook his head. "In this weather, with all these islands, we could miss the *Queen Mary* going by."

"So," Sloane went on, "she makes this river, the Deertail, then she's home free?"

Cork swung his gaze to Louis.

"Animkiikaa," Louis murmured.

"I don't know what you said," Sloane told the boy, "but it don't sound good."

"It means 'thunder,'" Louis said.

"On a white man's map, you'll see it called Hell's Playground," Cork said.

Arkansas Willie asked, "What is it?"

"As bad a stretch of rapids as you'll find anywhere in the Boundary Waters," Cork replied. "Class four. Deafening when you're near it."

"Wouldn't she know about Hell's Playground?" Sloane asked.

"If she's got a map," Cork said. "And if she knows how to read it."

Willie Raye rubbed his hand across his mouth in a nervous way. "If she doesn't know and she gets herself into them . . . " He couldn't finish his question.

Sloane set his cup down. "Maybe we'd better get started on the other canoe."

They all moved toward the work, all except Arkansas Willie Raye, who doubled over suddenly and hobbled desperately toward the trees.

36

SHILOH KEPT THE FIRE SMALL. A compromise between fighting the cold and risking that the stranger, should he find a way to follow her, might see the blaze. She hauled the canoe well away from the shore of the island and covered it with evergreen boughs. She built the fire in the lee of the canoe and bent close to warm herself.

She had no food. Everything she had, she'd brought in her pockets. Matches, knife, map. But she didn't care that she couldn't eat. She was alive. God almighty, she was alive.

She'd climbed the slippery rock wall ahead of the man who called himself Charon, hoping he'd fall. He didn't. He was agile as a mountain goat, even with the heavy pack on his back, and he was never farther from her than arm's reach. She made it to the top first, a few seconds ahead of him. He mounted the wall and stood poised there, the floor of the forest below him on one side, the long narrow lake Wendell called Nikidin on the other. She turned to face him. And what she saw behind him made her eyes go huge.

He glanced at her face, saw the surprise there, and spun around to confront—

A gray wolf.

The animal was tensed as if to leap at him, focused on the stranger with a fierce intensity in its yellow eyes, its teeth bared. A threatening growl rumbled in its throat.

Charon went for his gun. As his hand disappeared into his vest, Shiloh lunged at him, pushed into him with all her strength. She would love to have shoved him so that he fell to the forest floor, but her vantage point gave her only the option of the lake. As he plunged into the water a dozen feet below, Shiloh turned and fled up the trail along the ridge.

The trail led eventually to the cabin, but she didn't stay with the trail. After fifty yards, well out of sight of the place where the stranger splashed, struggling to climb from the lake, she hid herself. Her gut said to put distance between them, but she'd lived with fear long enough now not to be shoved around by it foolishly. She pressed herself flat on the wet ground behind a low growth of blackberry vines. Two feet to her right, the ground ended in a twenty-foot drop to the lake. She knew it wasn't a likely spot for hiding—open and with no escape. In her mind, however, she saw him running past her, bolting toward the thicker woods atop the ridge where the cover was better.

In the still, wet air, sounds carried easily. She heard him grunting as he heaved himself from the water up the rock wall. Heard him swear softly. Heard the squish of his wet leather boots and the swish of his wet jeans as he bounded up the trail toward her.

She stopped breathing and squeezed shut her eyes, as if plunging herself into a dark silent place might blind him to her. She held her breath until she began to feel dizzy and to hear only the sound of her own blood throbbing in her ears.

Then she exploded. Sucked in air like a big machine sputtering to life. And when she could hear again, she heard the sound of the man who called himself Charon running far up the trail near the top of the ridge.

She should wait, she knew. Give him time to move farther on. To be lost for good among the trees above her. But the panic she'd kept at bay finally was on her. She sprang up and leaped the blackberry vines and ran as fast as she could for the rock wall that dammed the stream. She slipped twice scrambling down but felt no alarm at the near plunges. What did she have to lose? She reached the bottom and didn't look back as she raced for the cover of the woods. When she reached the big lake, she shoved her canoe into the water and paused only long enough to pull the knife from her pocket, whip out the blade, cut free the yellow duckie, and put two long slashes in its side. She hopped into the stern of her canoe, grabbed the paddle, and dug hard at the water.

She imagined him on the shore, aiming his gun. She felt the place between her shoulder blades where the bullet would rip through. But she didn't risk a glance back until she was more than two hundred yards out. Then all she saw was the empty shoreline, the flat yellow at the water's edge where the deflated kayak floated like a pat of melted butter, and, among the pines where the stream ran, a gray shape that moved low to the ground and vanished the moment her eyes found it.

She'd paddled ceaselessly, with a strength that came from a place inside her she'd never known existed. Two hours, three, she didn't know. Somewhere along the way, the rain turned completely to snow and the gray light to a deep charcoal that was early night. She bumped into an island and realized she could go no further. With what suddenly seemed the last of her strength, she dragged the canoe from the water. With her knife, she cut evergreen boughs and hid the craft. The rain had wetted everything, but she found a fallen birch, broke off some branches, stripped the wet outer bark, and shaved some dry kindling.

She was beyond tired. She entered a place where her thoughts and actions seemed to bubble up of their own accord from some well of primordial knowledge. She realized she was humming to herself and thought probably her music had always come from the same kind of place. The best of it anyway.

Feeding the flames sparingly, keeping the fire small, she thought about the stranger, the man who called himself Charon. Why had he come for her? What purpose would her dying serve? Who wanted her dead? And what did it have to do with the work she'd hidden at the cabin? Whoever was behind it, they'd learned about the work from the letters she'd written poor Libbie. What was it she'd put in those letters that would drive someone to murder? Was it the past? She'd been so vague in what she told Libbie about the secrets of her therapy, both with Dr. Sutpen and on her own in the deep woods. The future? She'd been more explicit about that, full of an excitement she could barely contain. No drugs, no running from the past, no longer being nothing but a piece of dandelion fluff borne on the strongest wind. She was going to shape her future, change her life. Oh, she had such visions. And The People—Wendell's people, her people now—would be a part of everything.

But there could be no future until she freed herself completely from the menace she'd only just escaped, the man called Charon. It was as if the Dark Angel had stepped from her dreaming and had become flesh and blood. Well, if this was the Dark Angel, if this was the horror of the past rising, then she would be ready. This time she would fight back.

She realized she was beginning to nod, the exhaustion finally overtaking her. But there was one chore left before she slept.

She unfolded the blade of her knife. Grasping a handful of her long black hair, she severed it near her scalp. She took another handful and cut. Again and again and again. The knife moving over her whole head. Long swathes of her beautiful hair lying about her as if she were in the midst of slaughter. Hacking away. Cutting shorter and shorter. Until she could grasp her hair no more. Until there was so little left, no one could.

37

Jo was startled awake by the ringing of the phone in her bedroom.

"Jo. Wally Schanno."

"Yes." She rose up in bed, struggling to shake off her sleep. "What is it, Wally?"

"I'm sorry to bother you so early."

She glanced at the clock on the nightstand: five-thirty A.M. "That's all right."

"They found a body. One of the search parties did. Last night. Out in the Boundary Waters. A helicopter's airlifting it to the morgue at the community hospital right now."

"Have they identified it?"

"No. Only a brief description."

It was like seeing the flash from a muzzle and waiting for the bullet to strike.

"Go on."

She heard him take a deep breath. "Male. Caucasian. Red-brown hair. Brown eyes. Medium height and build. Age probably mid- to late forties. It's vague, Jo."

"No, it isn't, Wally." The bullet had struck. Dead center in her heart.

"You don't have to come down. I—just thought—"

"I'll be right there."

Her blood was racing when she hung up. Her breath

227

came rapidly and with effort. Her throat was taut and dry. *Dear God, let it be someone else.*

The hall light went on. Rose stood in the doorway.

"I heard the phone ring," she said.

"They found someone. In the Boundary Waters. A body."

"Oh, dear." Rose put her arms around herself as if she were suddenly cold. "Do they know who?"

"No."

"Do they—?" It sounded as if Rose's throat had gone tight, too, and she'd choked a moment on the words. "Do they know how?"

"I don't know. They're bringing the body in by helicopter." Jo was up and looking for clothes, anything. "I'm going down to the hospital. I need to be there when it comes in." She pulled on jeans, thick socks, a sweater, no bra. She stopped dead and looked at Rose. "The description fits Cork."

"Oh, my God, Jo."

"That doesn't mean it's him."

"No," Rose agreed.

Jo lurched toward the closet, grabbed a pair of boots. She sat on the floor and jammed them on. The laces wouldn't cooperate. "Fuck."

"Jo, it'll be okay." Rose knelt beside her and took her in her arms.

Jo buried her head in her sister's chenille robe. "Oh, Rose. I think of all the things I never said, the good things. And I want to take back all the hurt."

"I know. I know."

Jo gathered herself, wiped her eyes. "Not a word to the kids."

"Of course."

She pushed herself up. "When I know something, I'll call."

"All right."

Jo was out the door, down the stairs. She pulled her coat from the closet and headed through the dark kitchen to the back door. As she opened it, she felt Rose come up quickly to her side and put a hand on her shoulder.

"I'll be praying."

Jo closed her eyes a moment. "Me, too."

A light snow had fallen in the night, covering Aurora in a thin layer of white. Like the sheet over a corpse, Jo thought as she drove to the Aurora Community Hospital. Morning was crawling up the eastern horizon. The snow clouds had moved on. The sky was a pale blue-white, the color of deep, hard ice on a lake.

Because the hospital served a large, rural area, a heliport had been constructed on the eastern side of the building. In summer, especially, the heliport got a great deal of use—accidents with axes or chainsaws, drownings, cardiac arrests in city men who eagerly shed their suit-and-tie identities and, envisioning themselves as latter-day voyagers, embarked on canoe expeditions far more demanding than their flabby, cholesterol-ridden bodies could endure.

Wally Schanno was in the parking lot near the heliport, hunched up in his leather sheriff's jacket, hands sunk deep in the pockets. Booker T. Harris and Nathan Jackson were there as well, sitting in a blue Lumina, engine running to keep them warm. Schanno walked over to Jo's Toyota when she parked it.

"I'm real sorry about this," he told her as she got out. "I probably should have waited until I knew something for sure."

"I'm glad you didn't," she said.

She scanned the sky. Lots of stars were still visible, particularly in the north, the direction from which the helicopter would come.

Schanno looked at his watch. "ETA about ten minutes."

"How'd they find the body?"

"One of the search parties set up camp at nightfall at a landing on the north side of Embarrass Lake. Guy gets up in the middle of the night to relieve himself and stumbles over a pile of rocks. He pulls off a few and sees that there's a newly dug hole underneath. Digs down a little and finds the body."

Dear God, Jo found herself praying, *please don't let it be Cork.*

"You okay?" Schanno asked.

"No."

"Yeah." He nodded sympathetically.

"Wally—" She wanted to know, but couldn't bring herself to ask.

As if he'd read her mind, he said, "It wasn't an accident, Jo." He studied the sky with undue interest and the muscles at the back of his long jaw twitched. "An ax blow. To the neck."

"Jesus," she said. "Oh, Jesus."

Lights around the heliport came on. The double doors of the hospital opened and two orderlies in parkas appeared, pushing a gurney. They moved into the glare of the lights, men Jo didn't know, looking tired, as if they'd been on duty all night. There was no doctor with them. What the helicopter was bringing was far beyond healing.

"Here it comes." Schanno motioned toward the north.

Jo heard it, too. Then she saw it, coming in low over the trees, its lights tracking across the sky like shooting stars. Harris and Jackson got out of their car and waited. Harris cast a glance in Jo's direction. The helicopter came down in a swirl of blowing snow. Jo could see the body bag on a sled secured to one of the runners. A couple of men jumped from the helicopter. They wore jackets that had TAMARACK SEARCH AND RESCUE printed across the back.

"Wait here," Wally Schanno said.

Jo nodded, barely able to breathe and unable to talk at all. Schanno went to the helicopter, joined by Harris and Jackson along the way. They gathered around the sled. Jo saw them zip open the body bag and confer. Schanno turned, remained hunched under the blades of the chopper that hadn't stopped spinning, and started back toward Jo. She turned away. She didn't want to try to read his face.

Schanno put his hand lightly on her shoulder. "It's not Cork."

Jo almost collapsed. Tears of relief blinded her momentarily. She put her hands over her eyes a minute, then she faced the sheriff. "Who is it?"

"The man named Grimes."

The orderlies wheeled the gurney with the body of Grimes across the parking lot and into the hospital. Harris and Jackson approached Jo and Schanno.

"I want a meeting with Benedetti," Harris said. "And I want it now."

"You don't think Vincent Benedetti is responsible for this?" Jo asked.

"What I think is that there are six more people out there and I'm scrambling for answers before any of them show up dead. Get Benedetti. We'll be at the Quetico."

38

THE WORLD FELT NEW TO CORK. Like Easter morning. Like hope had been born again.

The sun was up, bright as a vision of God. The lake was blue as heaven. Snow lay thick on the evergreens and made them white as angels' wings.

The patches on the canoes were holding.

Cork and the others had hit the lake at first light—Raye in the bow of Cork's canoe, Sloane, Stormy, and Louis in the other. They spoke little, putting all their effort into their strokes, into making distance. They'd set Louis, whose eyes were young and hawk sharp, to the duty of watching for any sign of Shiloh or the man who pursued her. The morning was so clear that had it not been for all the islands that obscured the horizon, Louis could have seen for miles.

The contrast struck Cork powerfully. In the midst of a beauty so pervasive and dramatic it made his soul quiver, they were racing against a faceless, depthless evil. If Shiloh's life hadn't been the stake, he would have allowed himself to exalt in the thrill of the chase. It was a day for doing battle, and he couldn't help but feel that God and Kitchimanidoo, the Great Spirit, were on the lake with them. When he heard the blaring of a line of Canada geese coming over the treetops, it was as if Gabriel had sounded his horn. He believed—believed absolutely and for no other reason than the day was glorious and their luck was holding—that they were meant to beat the evil. It could easily have been a false euphoria, he admitted to himself, born of exhaustion and the strain of the last two days. But it felt like a gift, a sign, a revelation, and he bent his will to what seemed a greater will that guided them.

He knew the feeling was not just with him. The others were on fire, too. Their faces may have been hollow, sunken with fatigue, but in their eyes burned a light as illuminating as that morning sun. They'd reached deep inside themselves, deep into a place where warriors reached for extraordinary courage. Cork was glad—immensely proud—to be in the company of such men. In a grim way, he was pleased for Louis. The boy had seen terrible things, it was true. But he'd also been given a chance to experience this rare companionship, to feel this rare emotion that lifted them all up and carried them forward together.

They moved swiftly through the morning hours. The lake remained calm and the canoes flew across the water like swallows through air. He'd worried about Arkansas Willie at first, but the illness of the previous night seemed to have passed and Willie made no complaint.

Midmorning, as they approached the Deertail River, Louis cried out, "Over there!"

He pointed toward a jut of land ahead of them and a little to the north dominated by a tall lightning-scarred pine tree. Cork ceased paddling, shielded his eyes against the glare, and squinted where Louis had indicated.

"What is it?" he asked, for he saw nothing.

"A camp," Louis said. "A tent and a canoe."

Once Louis had defined the images, Cork could see them, too. The tent was covered with snow and blended almost invisibly into the snow-covered evergreens behind it. The canoe was a long white finger pointing out from the whitened shore.

"Do you see anybody?" Cork asked.

Louis shook his head. "Looks deserted."

"Let's check it out," Sloane said.

"Why don't Willie and I go first. That way you can cover us with the rifle."

Sloane chambered a round. "You're covered."

They moved in cautiously. As the bow nudged shore, Raye and Cork stepped out. Everything was lightly layered with snow, and the snow was crisscrossed with animal tracks, mostly those of birds and rabbits. Cork went to the tent and pulled back the flap. Two sleeping bags were laid out inside, both empty. He headed to the lightning-struck pine and studied the tracks around the shredded remains of a pack.

"Food," he said over his shoulder to Raye. "Looks like bears got to it."

But bear tracks were not the only tracks he saw there. He examined the rope that had at one time held the pack suspended from a high branch of the pine. The end had been cleanly cut with a knife.

"Was this bears, too?" Arkansas Willie asked behind him. He was staring down at a lump of snow sparkling at his feet.

Cork stepped up next to Raye, knelt, and brushed the snow away, revealing eyes as lifeless as agates. He carefully cleared the snow from the rest of the body. Over the dead man's heart, his blue flannel shirt was hard and black with frozen blood.

"Not a bear," Cork said grimly. "Unless someone taught it how to fire a gun."

He moved to a second lumping of snow next to the circle of stones that formed a fire ring. The snowfall hadn't covered the body entirely, and one arm lay exposed like a severed limb on a white sheet.

"Another one," he said, wiping the snow from a face dull and white as lard.

"How long have they been dead?" Arkansas Willie asked.

"Hard to tell. A while."

Cork waved the others to shore.

"Louis, you stay in the canoe," he called.

Sloane entered the camp and stood beside Cork.

"Two bodies," Cork told him. "Caucasian males. Multiple gunshot wounds to the chest on both. Dead . . . a while."

"Today, you think?"

Cork shook his head. "Snow's completely covered them. Maybe yesterday."

"Think they have anything to do with Shiloh?"

"All the death we've seen up here has to do with Shiloh. Let me show you something else." He led Sloane to the shredded pack. "She's been here. Look, same small boot tracks as at the cabin."

The tracks led from the shore to the pack, where they were mixed with the tracks of the bear. Boot tracks also led back to the shore, in the same unerring line that had been followed in.

"Food," Cork said. "She was after food. Cut down the pack from the tree and either took what she wanted and left the rest or she was surprised by the bear and had to leave it."

Sloane looked at the evidence. He slung the rifle over his shoulder, knelt, and picked up some snow. The warmth of his light brown palm turned the snow quickly to water that trickled through his fingers.

"How long ago?" he asked.

"The sun's had time to melt the edges of the prints, so I'd say a few hours."

"Shit!" Arkansas Willie doubled over a moment. "Good Lord, here it comes again." He hurried to the canoe, grabbed his pack, and raced to the cover of the trees.

After Willie had gone, Stormy called quietly, "Cork." He stood near the shoreline, beckoning.

When Cork reached him, he saw what Stormy saw. At the edge of the water, near Shiloh's tracks, were the tracks of the other.

"He's been here, too," Cork said.

"Prints are clear," Stormy pointed out. "Edges clean. The sun hasn't had time to melt them. He was here after her. And not that long ago."

Sloane said, "We should move out quickly."

"What about taking their canoe?" Louis suggested.

Cork stepped to the dead men's canoe. "Good idea, Louis, but we can forget it. He took care of this one, too."

Arkansas Willie emerged from the woods looking ashamed. "Sorry."

"Not your fault," Cork assured him. "Up here, it happens. But if you can, hang on a bit. I think we're almost there." He nodded toward the Deertail, a wide drift of silver in the morning sunlight that led into the pines a hundred yards down the shoreline. "He thinks he took care of us. He thinks he's home free. But we're about to nail that son of a bitch, Willie. We're about to nail him good."

39

SHE ATE THE DEAD MEN'S FOOD.

Long before she reached the place where she knew the bodies lay, she'd begun to think about the bag that hung from the tree branch. She'd never been so hungry. Her stomach curled in on itself as if desperately searching the emptiness there. She felt weak as well. The hunger she could live with, but the weakness scared her. It would slow her down, and she had to keep moving. She didn't know how he'd do it, but she knew the man who called himself Charon would find a way to follow her.

So she steeled herself. And when the jut of land with its lightning-struck pine—just a stone's throw from the Deertail River—came into view, she made for it with all the strength she could muster.

The sun hadn't yet risen above the trees and the camp lay in the cold blue shadow of the forest. Fate had been kind, in a way. The snowfall had covered the bodies. Almost. She tried not to look where the dead men lay, graveless, sheeted in a cloth the sun would soon strip away, but her guilt betrayed her. She stopped in horror when she saw that some quirk of nature had kept one man's outstretched arm bare. It was almost as if he were reaching out to her from a place that should have been hers. She fought back tears, fought back the weakness of her legs, and forced herself toward the pine with its long lightning scar and its hanging bag. She cut the rope wrapped around the tree trunk and the bag dropped heavily. She was on it like the creature she was, a starved animal. She found plastic bags containing freeze-dried stew, powdered eggs, jerky, pancake mix, and dried fruit. Her mouth watered so fast her jaws ached. She nearly screamed with delight when she pulled out a plastic jar of peanut butter and a big Baggie full of white bread.

She had the peanut butter and the bread in her hand when the black bear entered the camp. The wet snuffle as the animal investigated the tent made her turn suddenly and startle the bear. The animal rose up on its hind legs, let out a menacing *woof* that shook the silence of the camp, and clawed the air in her direction. She clutched the bread and the peanut butter as she backed away. The bear dropped to all fours, shuffled to the bag, and began to rummage. Shiloh bolted for her canoe and hit it on the run. The little craft shot into the lake. She nearly tipped it, but she never let go of the food. She scrambled to the stern, dropped the food into the hull, grabbed the paddle, and dug at the water hard, not daring to look back until she was fifty yards from shore. When she did look back, she saw the bear seated on its haunches, breakfasting noisily on the rest of the dead men's food.

The bread and peanut butter seemed like a feast. She was sure she'd never tasted anything so good. Afterward, as the current of the Deertail swept her away from the big lake, she sat back a while and let the river carry her. The sun was high now, and warm, and she felt as if she'd come out of a long, dark tunnel into the light. She finally let herself consider her dream the night before. Stiff, hugging herself for warmth, drifting in and out of sleep, she'd been visited again by the Dark Angel.

This time she'd been in a shower, a small stall full of steam with hot water flowing over her, cleansing her. She felt safe. She'd let her fear wash away, let herself relax. Then, turning, she'd seen the Dark Angel, its faceless form coming at her through the steam. She pressed herself back against the wet tiles; in the small stall, there was nowhere to escape.

She awakened with a scream trying to tear itself from her throat.

The Dark Angel had been a part of her dreaming all her life. Dr. Sutpen—Patricia—had been very interested in this faceless figure of terror. In the course of the therapy, she'd finally guided Shiloh back to the night when the Dark Angel first entered her life. That had been the night Marais Grand was murdered.

Shiloh had been awakened from her sleep. Her room was in the center of night, a place of dim shapes and deep shadow. The night-light in the hallway misted the door and the carpet with a dull yellow luminescence that sifted toward her bed like the creep of a moonlit fog. She rubbed the sleep from her eyes, enough to see that the man crouched by her doorway was really only the rocking chair. She lay back down, let her eyelids start to close. Then she heard it again, the sound that had awakened her. An angry voice somewhere downstairs. It frightened her. It was not her mother's voice. It was no voice she knew. Her mother's voice was there, low and crooning, the way she sounded when Shiloh was scared and her mother held her and whispered everything was all right. But the angry voice didn't sound all right.

She slid from the covers. The tile of the floor was cool beneath her feet and made her think of Hershey's bars, cold and hard from the refrigerator. In the hallway her shadow, cast by the night-light, crept beside her along the wall. At the top of the stairs, she stopped and listened. Below, the great living room spread out so large she couldn't see the walls. The floor was red tile covered with a thick, ruby Oriental rug. The room looked empty. But the angry voice was there, just out of sight. Her mother had stopped crooning now. The voice Shiloh didn't recognize suddenly vaulted into a shriek. Her mother gave a little cry: "No!" She stumbled into view and fell near the bottom of the stairs. She didn't look up, but Shiloh could see her face, could see the red on her skin that was like the tile on the floor. And then the Dark Angel appeared. Dressed all in black, the figure carried a golden sword streaked with red. The Dark Angel swooped toward

Shiloh's mother, who raised a feeble arm. The golden sword descended. Again and again it struck, until Shiloh's mother no longer tried to fend off the blows, until the red tile glistened with a deeper, wetter red.

The house seemed filled with the sound of heavy breathing. Whether it was her or the Dark Angel, Shiloh couldn't tell. The Dark Angel slowly turned and raised its head. There was no face, only a blackness where the face should have been. Shiloh shrank back. She could hear the Dark Angel ascending. She turned and ran to her room, ran to her closet, wedged herself into the farthest corner amid her stuffed animals and her shoes. She knew when the dim glow from the night-light blacked out a moment that the Dark Angel had entered her room. Pee soaked her pajamas and spread out on the floor beneath her. She could hear the Dark Angel breathing just outside the closet doorway. She closed her eyes.

She felt the touch of a hand on her cheek, but she dared not look.

"We're angels, you and I," the voice said. "Little innocents."

Shiloh drew back from the touch. Her eyes were still shut as tightly as she could force them.

"I won't hurt you, child."

Slowly, Shiloh opened her eyes and looked where the pool of blackness lay instead of a face. The Dark Angel lifted a finger toward that blackness, a bar across the place where lips should have been. A sign for silence. Then the Dark Angel vanished.

The memory of the Dark Angel had vanished, as well. Except in Shiloh's dreams. Then Patricia had guided her back.

"A dark stocking," Patricia suggested when they spoke about the blackness where there should have been a face. "Or maybe a veil. And the golden sword? The brass poker from the fireplace that was used to kill your mother."

It was odd. The Dark Angel was her mother's killer, but her mother was only memory, and who killed her wasn't as important to Shiloh as discovering that the Dark Angel was, in fact, human.

They'd spoken of other things, of Shiloh's loneliness, her feelings of abandonment, of her disconnectedness.

"Why *Shiloh?*" Patricia had asked. "When you chose your professional name, why only that one name?"

Shiloh hadn't replied.

"Think about it. No last name. No connection. No family. No history. Just Shiloh."

Wendell Two Knives had said much the same thing in his letters to her. She began receiving them after the tabloids had made big splashy headlines about her arrest and conviction and sentencing for substance abuse.

He was, he reminded her in the first letter, the husband of her grandmother's sister. He'd guided her mother and her into the Boundary Waters once long ago. Shiloh had remembered him and the trip into the Boundary Waters the summer before her mother died. She remembered the canoe. Birch bark. And the quiet of the forest. And all the things Wendell Two Knives had known and shared with them. She remembered how peaceful her mother had seemed, a rare thing. It was a good memory. One of the last.

Wendell invited her to come again. He knew of her problems. The woods, he'd written, had healed her people for generations. *Her people*. Was he accepting her as Indian even though she'd lived her whole life in the white man's world?

It was weeks before she wrote back, well into her therapy with Patricia and ultimately at Patricia's urging. Wendell replied. They spoke on the phone. His voice was kind, slow, soothing. He told her stories of her mother and her grandmother. Wonderful stories that filled her with longing. He invited her again, told her he knew of a place she could be alone for as long as she wanted, alone to remember who she was. Had she ever been alone? he asked.

"I've always been alone," she heard herself confiding. "And afraid."

"I can help you not be afraid," he promised.

He'd kept his promises, every one. The cabin had been

wonderful. The woods had been healing. In her aloneness, after a time, she heard her own voice speaking to her truly.

She asked Wendell for a tape recorder. And she let the voice speak. The truth of her life that she'd turned away from through drugs and sex and a hundred forms of forgetfulness. It all poured out of her. And then her plans began to form. Such wonderful plans for the future that included, now, The People. Her people.

As the current of the Deertail carried her away from the hidden cabin and back to the world, she was excited by the thought of returning. She felt strong in her resolve to carry out the plans she'd created, had dictated carefully onto the tapes, had written to Libbie about. For the first time in her life, she felt truly herself and in control of her destiny.

There was only one thing that kept the moment from being perfect. She looked back, knowing the man called Charon was somewhere behind her.

She pulled out the map. The arrows followed the Deertail River for quite a way. She was headed toward something called the Deertail Flowage, where she would portage briefly to a round patch of blue called Embarrass Lake. She hoped she would know what the flowage was when she got there.

She put the map away and let the current carry her. Occasionally she paddled, but the river seemed to know its way and to welcome her as a companion. The sun was warm. She was tired, drowsy, and she closed her eyes. Until she heard the roar, she didn't even realize she'd fallen asleep.

She woke with a start. The canoe was moving fast. Less than twenty yards ahead, in an angry crashing of white water, the river funneled into a long corridor of dark rock. She tried to back paddle, but it was useless. The river dragged her in.

The canoe leaped from under her, then tipped hard to the right. She threw herself in the opposite direction and dug at the water with her paddle. The bow glanced off the sharp edge of a rock half submerged and surrounded by roiling white. She was launched toward a place where the river climbed high and furious as if desperate itself to escape the corridor, and even above the din of the crashing water she heard a scraping that made her certain the canoe was being ripped apart. The world tilted. The bow lifted as if the craft were raising its head in the throes of a noble death. Water poured in at the stern, and she thought for sure she would swamp. Weighted now, the canoe spun sideways and slammed broadside into a huge rock that split the river. She grabbed the gunwales as the canoe began to tip. Then suddenly, miraculously, she swung out, canoe and all, bow downriver, and she was free of the corridor.

She was not out of danger. Great chunks of fractured rock littered the water before her, and around them the river foamed like a rabid dog. She grasped her paddle with both hands and drove the canoe to the right of a long, ragged spine of rock. She hit a whirlpool, fought to stay on the outer edge, and rode the spin for a dozen feet before she broke away. For another thirty yards, the water grumbled under the keel, but its real fury was past.

The river opened up again in a smooth, broad flow. Overhead, a brown hawk rode the thermals along the canyon walls, easy as a dream against the sapphire blue sky. In the bottom of the canoe, water sloshed gently over her boots.

Once again, she'd beaten a thing that thought it had her. She lifted her paddle above her head and let out a warrior's yell. The echoes of it came back to her from the canyon walls like the voices of her ancestors crying her on.

40

ANGELO BENEDETTI CARRIED HIS FATHER into cabin 7 at the Quetico. When the trembling, white-haired man had been ensconced in a leather easy chair, Booker T. Harris stepped toward him. Harris's hands were clasped behind his back as if they'd been cuffed, and his face glistened with the sweat of a worried man.

"One of my men is dead out there. I want to know why."

Nathan Jackson, who'd stood at the long glass windows that overlooked the lake, fuming silently, threw his hands up in exasperation. "For God sake, Booker, you know why. The son of a bitch is afraid Shiloh's going to help nail his fucking ass for Marais's murder."

"Are we back to that?" Benedetti said. "I thought we were done with it."

Jackson started across the room. "I'm not done until I've put you in the gas chamber."

"Back off, Nathan."

Harris reached out to grasp his brother's shoulder, but Jackson pulled loose.

"The hell I'm going to back off."

Benedetti furiously motioned to his son. "Get me out of here, Angelo. This place stinks of bullshit."

"You're going nowhere." Jackson lurched toward the quivering man in the leather chair, but Angelo Benedetti thrust himself between them, chest to chest with Jackson. Harris grabbed his brother and yanked him back.

"Nathan, for Christ's sake, use your head. Let me handle this."

Jackson wrestled free and glared at Harris. "Oh, yeah. No problem, brother. Go right ahead. Handle it like you've handled everything else here. Got one man killed already and God only knows what's happened to the others out there. Doing a stellar job, Booker. Downtown Saturday night."

A small earthquake seemed to pass through Booker Harris, and whatever had held him in check collapsed.

"Fine," he hollered. "Fine. You want to kill the man, you go right ahead. You've been throwing other people's asses in jail for years—time maybe you had a visit there yourself. For thirty years, you've been dead set on undoing the good things I've done for you. So go ahead, throw it all away. And while you're at it, you can double-kiss my ass, little brother."

"Fuck you," Jackson said.

"Yeah, and fuck you right back." Harris slammed his hand down on the coffee table. The coffee cups jumped like startled little men. "I told you to stay away. God damn it, I told you I'd handle this. I'm going to let you in on something, Mr. Next Governor of the Golden State. I don't know what all this is about out here, but I sure as hell know it ain't got nuthin' to do with Marais Grand."

Nathan Jackson froze. He looked hard at his brother's face until Harris guiltily turned away. "How do you know that, Booker?"

Jo, who'd stood back silently taking in all the sound and the fury, said quietly, "Because he's always known who killed her."

The men in the room—Schanno, the Benedettis, Jackson, Metcalf, and finally Harris—turned their full and amazed attention to Jo. She was a little amazed herself. But suddenly, it had all made sense.

Vincent Benedetti grabbed his son's sleeve. "What am I missing here? Angelo, do you know what's going on?"

"Hang on a second, Pop. I think we're about to find out. Go on, Ms. O'Connor."

"You all thought this was about men, about the two of you. But it was really about women, wasn't it, Agent Harris?"

"What are you talking about?" Benedetti complained. "Speak plain."

"Pop, will you just give her a chance?"

Jo moved closer to the leather chair from which Benedetti eyed her irritably. "You said your affair with Marais Grand began shortly after she came to perform at your casino. Is that right?"

"Yes."

"And your wife threatened to leave you when she found out?"

"That's right."

"In fact, you said she threatened to kill you if you ever cheated on her with Marais Grand again."

Benedetti shrugged. "She had a temper."

"You ended that affair. But you had another fling with Marais Grand, shortly before she left for Nashville, and Marais claimed that Shiloh was the result."

"So?"

"Did your wife know about the second affair?"

"Hell, Theresa knew about everything. I don't know how. It was lucky for everybody Marais went to Nashville."

Jo went on, "When Marais came back with little Shiloh and the tabloids were stirring up rumors of the old flame's being rekindled, how did your wife react?"

Benedetti said, as if it were only natural, "She went berserk. I told her it was all lies."

"But she didn't believe you."

"Who could blame her?"

"The night Marais Grand was killed, you were in Los Angeles. There were witnesses." Jo looked up at the younger Benedetti. "What about you? Where were you that night?"

"Me? On a houseboat on Lake Mead with Joey and his folks. He'd just graduated from high school."

"What about your mother?"

He thought a moment. "She stayed home, I guess. She was pretty upset back in those days. Didn't go much of anywhere except to St. Lucia to light candles and pray."

"Then she was alone?"

"I guess."

"What are you getting at?" Vincent Benedetti sounded as if his patience was nearly exhausted.

"Angelo told me yesterday about a meeting between your wife and Agent Harris that took place in St. Lucia shortly after Marais Grand was killed."

"In St. Lucia?" He glared at Harris. "She never told me."

"There was a reason for that," Jo said. "And there was a reason Agent Harris never looked officially in her direction during the homicide investigation. Think about it a moment. Wouldn't an irate wife be a reasonable suspect in the killing of a woman reputed to be her husband's lover?"

Everyone looked at Harris. He faced them like a man before a firing squad.

Jo said to him, "You must have had something pretty solid on her before you met her that day."

"I don't know what you're talking about."

"Do you deny you spoke with Theresa Benedetti in the church?"

"I was involved in a homicide investigation."

"In a church?" Nathan Jackson cried. "Bullshit, Booker. Look at me. I said look at me, God damn it." He studied his brother's face, then his own face opened up in horror. "My God. Oh, my God. It's true." He looked as if he were going to fall over. "Why, Booker?"

"Why? Because you're my brother. Because I've spent my whole life covering your ass, Nathan. It just came naturally." He turned away from Jackson and bent to a table where the coffee server and cups had been set out. He poured coffee, took a sip, and seemed disappointed. "Cold," he said. He put the cup down and looked at Jo. "We grew up in Watts, Ms. O'Connor. A lot of people never make it out of Watts, and a lot of those who do never look back. We were lucky, Nathan and me. We had a mother—she was a seventh-grade history teacher—who believed fiercely in ideals and in us. Dwight, he was lucky, too. When his own mother abandoned him, we took him in. Mom raised him like her own." Harris glanced at his brother. "Christ, she believed in you, Nathan. Believed you were destined for greatness. Believed you could do something for black people. Dwight and me, we grew up covering your thoughtless antics. Covering you for her sake. Feels like we've been fighting a rear-guard action all our lives. You surely do know how to talk the talk. And you even do a damn good job of making it look like you walk the walk. But I know you, brother. And I know you got all the substance of a soap bubble. You want to know why we did it? I'll tell you. Family, that's why. In the end, that's all that matters. Not ideas—they change. Not justice—hell, I don't even know what that is. Family, Nathan. In the end, family's all that abides."

"What did you have on Theresa Benedetti?" Jo asked.

Harris took a deep breath and plunged in. "MURs for starters. Phone records. A call had been placed to Marais Grand from the Benedetti residence a few hours before she was killed. I knew Benedetti was in L.A. at the time. A little investigation made it clear that Mrs. Benedetti had been home alone that night. It didn't take a genius to put two and two together."

"Why did you approach her in church?" Jo asked.

"I wanted the meeting in private and in a place where the truth might matter to her."

"I don't like the way this is going," Vincent Benedetti said.

Jo ignored him. "What did you say to her?"

"I told her about the phone call. I told her it seemed an odd thing that Marais Grand had been killed but the little girl, who was a potential witness, hadn't been harmed. I told her I thought it was touching, something a mother might have done. I told her I wouldn't blame a woman for trying to keep her family together, whatever it took. I also told her we had a bloody fingerprint pulled from the girl's closet door."

"Did she confess to killing Marais Grand?"

"She claimed it was in self-defense. I told myself that, in a way, it probably was. She also revealed to me that her husband had fathered Shiloh."

"Did that surprise you?"

"Yes. I knew Nathan believed Shiloh was *his* daughter."

"You struck a deal with Theresa Benedetti, didn't you? Silence for silence."

He nodded. "If she guaranteed that her husband would never say a word about the child, never lay a claim to Shiloh, I'd make sure the investigation didn't touch her. She was safe."

"Jesus fucking Christ," Nathan Jackson whispered.

"I did it to save your political ass, Nathan. I was sure if you knew that Benedetti believed the child was his, if he made any claim to her, you'd spill everything. Son of a bitch, you were on your way. You had it all ahead of you. You had looks, brains, a golden tongue, and more luck than any man had a right to. But I knew you, and I knew you'd throw it all away to lay your own claim to that child." He gave his brother a cold look. "So yeah, I crossed the line. Kept everything clean, kept your name from ever coming up. Like I'd done a hundred times before. And I'd have done it again, here. All you had to do was stay away and let me handle this."

"What about the other men involved in the investigation?" Jo went on. "Dwight Sloane, Grimes, Mr. Metcalf over there? They would have known, wouldn't they?"

Harris nodded. "They knew."

"I understand Dwight Sloane." Jo looked toward Metcalf. "What did it take for you?"

Metcalf offered her only an enigmatic smile.

"The promise of a better salary than they'd ever have as cops," Harris answered for him. "As consultants, the business that comes their way from the state and the feds has been more than generous. Dwight and I have seen to that."

"I didn't know," Nathan Jackson said, as if pleading his case to Jo.

Harris shook his head angrily. "No, you only chose not to see."

Vincent Benedetti wore a strange expression, somewhere

249

between confusion and amusement. "Let me get this straight. You're saying my wife, my Theresa, killed Marais?" The idea seemed to take hold and not displease him especially. "She had the guts for it, God rest her soul."

Nathan Jackson sat down. "All these years," he said, but he didn't go on.

The fire in the room crackled and no one spoke. Hard silence, Jo had observed, often followed hard truths.

Harris walked to the window and stared out at the lake, an icy blue in the sunlight. "It's beautiful out there," he finally said. "God's country. How does the saying go? Where God builds a church, the Devil builds a chapel."

The telephone rang. Metcalf answered it. "Sheriff Schanno, it's for you."

Wally Schanno took the phone and said, "Yeah?" He listened a moment, said, "I'll be there," and hung up.

"What is it?" Jo asked when she saw the dark countenance of his face.

Schanno said, "They've found another body."

A big man, the word finally came. Caucasian. Thirty to thirty-five years of age. Shaved head. Dressed in camouflage military fatigues. Three gunshot wounds in the upper torso.

It wasn't Cork or Louis or Stormy. Not any of the men who'd gone into the Boundary Waters together to look for Shiloh.

Harris accompanied a sheriff's deputy in the helicopter. Two hours later, they were back, the body delivered to the morgue at Aurora Community Hospital, where it kept company with the corpse of Virgil Grimes. Harris had a full set of fingerprints that Metcalf relayed via the computer to the Los Angeles field office. In the meantime, Wally Schanno had ordered the search-and-rescue teams to head to Wilderness Lake with all due speed. He requested the U.S. Forest Service have their De Havilland Beaver begin flying over the lake where it would be joined soon by the helicopter.

It was early afternoon. Jo knew there was nothing more

she could do at that point. She told Schanno she was heading to the Iron Lake Reservation to talk to Sarah Two Knives.

First, she stopped by the house on Gooseberry Lane. She'd called Rose early that morning when she knew the first body wasn't Cork. Now the children were all at school. The house smelled of baking bread. So normal. But at the moment, nothing felt normal to Jo. Dead men were being hauled out of the Boundary Waters like cut wood. Cork and Louis and Stormy were still unaccounted for.

"My God," Rose gasped when Jo told her the situation. "No wonder you look like hell. Does Sarah know?"

"I'm on my way there now."

"She may already have heard something," Rose said cautiously. "Word's leaked out about the man they found this morning. People have been calling all day to see if I know something."

"I hope nobody's said anything to the kids. Listen, Rose, if they ask, just let them know their dad's all right."

"Is he?" Rose asked.

"It's what they should hear right now," Jo said. She sat down in a kitchen chair, feeling quite weak.

"Have you eaten?"

"Not a bite all day."

"Let me put something together. A sandwich, at least." Rose pulled out bread, roast beef, tomatoes, lettuce, cheese, and mayonnaise and went to work. "It's a good sign in a way, isn't it?"

"What?" Jo asked.

"That the man they just found isn't one of . . . the good guys."

"I honestly don't know what it means, Rose." She laid her head in her hands. "I never thought I'd be happy to see a dead man, but twice now I've been almost ecstatic when they brought out the bodies and neither of them was Cork. I suppose that's wrong."

"That's just human. Let it go. Here." She handed Jo the sandwich in a Baggie. "I don't suppose we should plan on you for dinner."

"No." She stood up and gave her sister a hug. Rose smelled of the baking bread, and Jo wished she could take that smell with her wherever she went. "Thanks for covering here on the home front."

Rose smiled sympathetically. "I've got it easy. You have to tell Sarah Two Knives that it looks like her son and husband have stumbled into hell."

41

AFTER THEY HIT THE DEERTAIL, they made a plan and then they talked no more. The sky stayed nearly cloudless. Although the air was crisp, by early afternoon the sun began to melt the snow, and all along the riverbank, trees dripped glittering pearls.

The wind blew directly upriver. Although normally that would have made the journey more difficult, in a way it was good. If they were lucky and the man they were after was careless, the wind might bring to them his sound. Cork found himself listening so intently that the sudden cry and flap of an osprey in an overhanging spruce made him jerk hard and he nearly dropped his paddle.

His jacket hung heavily to the right from the weight of the .38 in the pocket. Willie Raye had his .22 stuffed in his belt. Sloane, in the bow of the canoe with Stormy and Louis, kept the rifle propped against the gunwale. Stormy had the nine-millimeter Glock in his down vest. They'd agreed that as soon as they spotted the man, they would drop Louis on the riverbank and pick up the pursuit.

By the time Cork heard the dull distant roar he knew to be Hell's Playground, he was concerned. He'd believed they would overtake the man before the rapids. If the footprints in the snow had been a true indication, he hadn't been that far ahead. They'd paddled hard but hadn't been given even a glimpse of their quarry.

Hell's Playground was clear from a distance. It lay in the middle of a long, narrow valley—almost a canyon—where the water was deep. An old lava flow that had at one time blocked the river formed two tall palisades of dark rock on either bank. Beneath the cool October sun, they looked like the black wings of a fallen angel. The closer the canoes came, the louder was the sound of the water crashing through. Cork hadn't been on the Deertail in years, but the portage around Hell's Playground was a thing you didn't forget. He spotted the landing, ahead fifty yards on the right. As he turned to signal the second canoe, he saw Sloane pitch back and left as if he'd been hit by a bus. The canoe flipped, plunging Sloane, Stormy, and Louis into the river. For a moment, it made no sense to Cork; then the sound of the shot reached him. In the next instant, Willie Raye seemed to mirror Sloane. He flew back as if kicked, and as he toppled into the river, he tipped the canoe, taking Cork along with him into the swift, cold current of the Deertail.

Cork surfaced, spitting water. Over the sound of thrashing men, he heard the report of more shots. He didn't wait to see where they were hitting. He dove. In the sunlight, the river water was clear and golden. He tried to move to help Willie Raye, but his clothes soaked up the river and he felt heavy and awkward in the current. Raye was swept out of his reach. Again he rose, broke the surface like a leaping trout. In the glimpse he got of the river around him, he didn't see the others, and he realized he was being drawn inexorably toward the rapids.

He swam hard for the nearest riverbank. Grasping the gnarled white root of a birch at the river's edge, he pulled himself out and rolled immediately to the cover of the trees. He felt for his .38. The gun was still in his coat pocket. He drew it out and peered around a tree trunk. Shielding his eyes with his hand, he looked southwest, directly into the glare of the sun. As he watched, the canoes swept between the palisades and vanished in the white water there. He didn't see Stormy or Louis or Sloane or Raye.

In his mind, he tried to fix where the sound of the shots had come from. He remembered both Sloane and Raye had pitched back and left, which meant the shots had come from ahead and to the right, somewhere on the opposite side of the river from where he now crouched. The bank looked peaceful, unbroken forest all the way to Hell's Playground. He eyed the wall of rock through which the river had carved its course. The flat top on the far side would have been an ideal location from which to fire. Good field of vision, and hidden in the glare with the sun behind it.

Cork kept to the woods along the eastern bank and worked his way downriver. He'd covered thirty yards when he heard Stormy call softly, "Cork."

Stormy was hunched behind the cover of a loose curl of big moss-covered boulders next to the river. Louis was with him. Sloane lay on the ground between them, the thin blanket of snow beneath him staining a deep crimson. As Cork knelt, Sloane looked at him.

"In the rocks," he said quietly. "Other side."

"That's what I figure, too," Cork said.

"Lost the rifle."

"I've got my thirty-eight." Cork held it where Sloane could see. To Stormy, he said, "Did you see Arkansas Willie?"

"No."

"You still have your Glock?"

"Here." Stormy pulled it from his vest.

"The shooter's on the other side. If he's coming for us, he'll have to cross. Probably downriver from Hell's Playground. I'm going to do my best to discourage him. I think you should stay here, cover Louis, and . . ." He glanced down at Sloane who'd closed his eyes. "Do whatever you can."

Louis was on both knees beside the wounded man. He took Sloane's hand. "He's real cold." Louis looked grim and a lot older than a boy his age ought to have looked.

"I know," Stormy said. "We'll build a fire as soon as we can."

"I'll be back," Cork promised, and turned downriver.

255

He shivered from the wet and the cold, but there was a fire in him that licked up from his gut and burned all the way to his brain. Whoever the son of a bitch across the river was, Cork wanted him dead.

Sam Winter Moon, who'd been like a father after Cork's own father died, had taught him that anger was no companion on a hunt. Cork didn't care. He'd had enough of being a day late and a dollar shy with this guy. He wanted to see him plainly, wanted to see him in a gun sight so bad it fried his thinking. He dashed through the woods, ignoring the slap and claw of low-hanging birch branches, keeping his eye on the dark rock walls rising like a fortress in front of him. He broke from the trees at a dead run and hit a bare stretch in advance of the palisades where broken rock had tumbled from the canyon side. Big stone slabs lay shattered in jagged pieces with snow cradled in the shadowed crevices. Cork had maybe twenty yards of reckless dancing before he reached good cover. He didn't make it.

The bullet caught the ragged crown of a boulder as he passed. Rock shards bit through the air around him and stung his jaw and neck. He stumbled, falling headlong onto unforgiving stone. But his .38 was grafted to his hand and he wormed behind the squat protection of the nearest rock. His tiny sanctuary provided barely enough cover that became less as the bullets picked away at the edges. Cork figured it was a game with the man. Left side, right side, then left again, each round within a few inches of the round before it. The son of a bitch was showing off, letting Cork know he'd be nailed the minute he abandoned his cover.

Shit. Sam Winter Moon had been dead on. As usual.

But Sam had offered Cork another piece of wisdom. Never hunt alone.

He recognized the bark of the nine-millimeter coming from the trees behind him. Squinched low, he half turned and made out Stormy kneeling behind the root end of a wind-felled beech, taking careful aim at a target high across the river. Stormy squeezed off another round.

When a fist-sized chunk of tree three inches left of

Stormy's head disappeared, Cork took the opportunity to bolt. He ran a desperate zigzag, hunched like a troll, toward the shadow of the eastern palisade. The hotshot on the far side of the river had enough time for only one pull, and that round split rock a foot behind Cork.

Breathing hard, Cork began to climb. The rock had endured centuries of freeze and thaw, but it was not unscathed. The back side of the palisade was cracked and wrinkled, and Cork had no trouble finding handholds and footholds as he scaled the wall. Near the top, a thirty-foot climb, he held up. Stormy had fired a few more rounds, but his shots hadn't been returned. Cork swung his gun arm over the lip and swept the far flat-topped palisade. The sun was no longer in his eyes; he could see everything in sharp detail. Except for a few tenacious tufts of weed, the rock was bare. He saw several golden glints near the upriver edge. Spent shell casings.

The shooter had vanished.

Cork heaved himself over the top. Along the edge that plunged to the river, he began a brash lope. The old lava flow was a hundred feet wide and Cork reached the down-river end in a few seconds. From that vantage, he could see the whole river all the way to a blind bend a couple of hundred yards south. Below him the Deertail churned over the last of Hell's Playground, a wide, angry stretch of white water strewn with huge rocks. Beyond that, the river became peaceful again, as if it had instantly changed personalities. In the trees along the bank there, Cork caught a glimpse of movement. Someone running. He raised his .38 and sighted. It was a long shot but within range. Still, he held off firing. What if it wasn't the shooter? What if he dropped someone innocently caught in all this hell? He lowered his gun.

He recrossed the top of the palisade, feeling tired, feeling old and worn as that ancient lava flow, feeling utterly defeated. It was beginning to be a familiar sensation. Somehow the son of a bitch was ahead of him again in his thinking. Cork realized the shooter had probably never intended to cross the river and come for them. He'd accomplished what he wanted—held Cork and the others up, separated them from their canoes and their supplies, and now he was back on the track of Shiloh without anyone on his own back. Christ, who was this guy?

Majimanidoo. That's what Henry Meloux had said about him. A devil. Cork was beginning to believe it was true.

Stormy still hunkered behind the fallen beech. He kept his Glock trained on the far side of the river as Cork made his way over the open stretch where earlier he'd been pinned down.

"I didn't hear any more shots," Stormy said. "I guess you didn't get him."

Cork shook his head. "I think I saw him hightailing it downriver."

"Think he'll keep going?"

"He's after Shiloh, not us. Yeah, I think he'll keep going."

"Maybe we held him enough for her to make it out okay."

"Maybe," Cork said.

"You're bleeding."

"Chunk of rock. At least it wasn't a bullet. Christ, I'm freezing." He hadn't noticed during all the excitement, but now the wet clothes and the brisk air made him shiver. His hands were purple from the cold. "We need a fire going. Fast."

They began back through the trees along the river. They hadn't gone far when they moved into the smell of wood smoke. Ahead, they saw a gray billowing, and a minute later they found Louis feeding dead wood onto a roaring blaze he'd built against the curl of rocks. Cork saw that the boy had constructed a council fire, the sticks of wood in a cross-hatched square so the fire would burn big and hot and fast. The heat had already melted the snow several feet from the flames. Louis had somehow managed to move Sloane as near to the fire as he safely could.

Sloane's eyes flickered open when Cork and Stormy arrived. He managed a weak smile. "You got some boy there, Two Knives."

"I know."

"You get him?" Sloane asked Cork.

"No," Cork answered.

He heard the awful quiver in Sloane's voice, saw how his body shook. The fire wasn't doing a lot of good yet. Cork threw off his wet jacket and pulled off his wool sweater. He handed it to Louis. "Hold this near the fire and get it warm." He took off his pants and socks and pulled his wet wool hat from the pocket of his coat. "Can you handle these, too, Louis? Stormy, help me get Sloane out of those wet clothes."

Sloane made no protest as they undressed him. Cork was sure the man was going into shock. But one problem at a time. When they had Sloane's clothes off, Cork quickly checked the wound. Entry was a penny-size hole through the bottom of the rib cage, right side. The exit wound was a huge explosion of flesh out of the lower back, full of jagged bone fragment.

"In my left coat pocket, Stormy, there's a red bandanna."

Stormy got it. Cork folded the bandanna into a compress and put it over the exit wound. It wasn't going to be enough, he knew, but there wasn't much else he could do.

"How're those clothes, Louis?"

"Warm."

"Let's have them."

The wool was steaming when Louis handed the clothing over. Cork and Stormy pulled the things onto Sloane's cold body. Hat, sweater, pants, socks. Finally they put him against the rocks that were beginning to feed back the heat of the fire.

Cork stripped off his thermals and stood stark naked so close to the flames that he smelled the hair on his legs singeing. He turned himself frequently, letting the heat hit his whole body. Stormy and Louis did the same. Cork shook his head. Men reduced to one of the most basic and primitive of relationships. Cold naked flesh and fire.

Their clothes hung on sticks thrust into the ground and leaned toward the flames. Their boots ringed the fire. They sat against the heated rocks with Sloane lying between them. For a long time, they hadn't spoken. Cork was tired beyond words. Even so, he found himself thinking, remembering.

He was remembering the day Marais Grand had left Aurora, the day she'd started the long train of events that would ultimately bring him and the others to this juncture.

They'd gathered at Pflugelmann's Rexall Drugs where the Greyhound bus stopped on its way to and from Duluth. Ellie Grand was there, and Marais, and Cork's mother, and Cork. Marais had a backpack, a guitar case, and a one-way ticket to L.A. Ellie Grand was sure her daughter would be back within a few weeks. Marais was just as positive she was leaving for good. She looked down Oak Street, the main street of town, and predicted, "Someday they're going to put up a sign that says 'Hometown of Marais Grand.' People are going to come just because I used to live here. They'll point to this spot and say, 'That's the last place she stood before she left for good.'" She smiled at Cork. "And they'll beat down your door, Nishiime, just because you knew me."

She kissed him when the bus came. Her eyes were bright with expectation. Her mother's eyes, Cork recalled, were green pools with streams spilling from them. They all stood waving in the cloud of stinking diesel as the bus pulled away. Except on the screen of his television, he never saw her again.

He wondered now if anyone could have foreseen that her life would end as suddenly as a stone dropped in water, or that the rings of tragedy that swept outward from that death would overtake so many lives fifteen years later.

"Thirsty," Sloane said.

Cork danced across the cold ground to the river and tried unsuccessfully to bring back water in his cupped hands.

"Wait a minute," Louis said. He disappeared into the trees and came back a few minutes later with a strip of birch bark roughly folded into a vessel. He dipped it in the river and brought it back full. He knelt down.

Sloane grinned slightly and said, "Is this water okay? Don't want to get sick."

Cork laughed quietly. "It's fine. Drink all you want."

Sloane sipped a little, looking Cork over with his droopy

eyes. "Used to make fun of the idea of men dancing naked in the woods. Where's your drum?"

"Don't talk," Cork advised.

Sloane said, "Won't make any difference. We both know it." He closed his eyes a moment. "Can you do something about these clothes? They're itchy and they smell."

"Are you warm?" Cork asked.

"I'm done on this side. You can turn me over." Sloane rolled his eyes toward Louis. "Sorry about all this, son. Tough trip for you."

Louis said, "It's okay."

Sloane closed his eyes and was quiet again.

Cork felt his thermals. They were almost dry.

"I'm going to get dressed and go downriver. See if I can find any sign of Arkansas Willie and take a look for the canoes and our gear. You okay staying with him?" He nodded toward Sloane.

"Yes," Stormy said.

The sun was level with the treetops by the time Cork left the fire. Another couple of hours before hard dark, he figured. With the sky so clear, the temperature would probably drop fast.

He scaled the palisade, crossed the top, and worked his way off the downriver side. He followed the river to the bend, then another quarter mile until he spotted the canoes. They'd hung up among the branches of a pine that had fallen, half blocking the river. They were overturned, nudged against one another and bobbing in the current like mating beasts. Cork shinnied out along the trunk of the pine tree. He saw that the hulls had been smashed, the bows shattered beyond anything the river or pine branches could have done.

Majimanidoo, he thought darkly.

Because the hulls were upturned, he couldn't tell if the packs were still secured to the thwarts. He knew he'd have to get wet again. The prospect was disheartening. He eased himself into the icy flow of the Deertail and went under. Threading his way through the branches that had snagged the canoes, he felt under the stern thwart of the canoe he and Raye had paddled. The pack was there. He surfaced, took a deep breath, and went back under. Wetted, the knots of the cord that held the pack were impossible to untie. Once again, he surfaced for air. This time when he went under, he undid the pocket of the Duluth pack and pulled out the old Case knife he kept there. He unfolded the blade, sliced through the cord, and hauled the pack out. After he'd wrestled it to solid ground, he returned to the canoe and cut the cord holding the supply pack that had been secured under the bow thwart.

That was enough. The cold had cramped his hands. He dragged himself onto the riverbank, knowing he had to get back to the fire quickly. He shouldered both packs, awkwardly. Waterlogged, the load seemed twice as heavy as it would have dry. Cork stumbled to the palisade, but once there, knew he couldn't drag both packs over. He abandoned his own and started up with the supplies.

By the time he reached the fire, his hands felt rigid as a couple of frozen pork chops. Stormy quickly helped him strip off his wet clothes. Cork had to hold himself back from walking right into the flames.

"The canoes?" Stormy asked.

"No good. Smashed. *He* did it. Packs are there." Cork spoke in a quivering staccato, his voice on the edge of breaking. "Tried to bring mine up. More wool clothes for us. Left it on the other side of Hell's Playground."

"How about Arkansas Willie?"

Cork gave his head a dismal shake.

"It'll be dark soon," Stormy said. "I'll get your pack. Louis, put something hot together for this man."

After Stormy left, Louis pulled a pot from the wet supply pack and some dehydrated vegetable soup tightly sealed in a plastic bag. In a few minutes, he had a pot of soup on the coals at the fire's edge and the smell was like heaven to Cork.

"How has he been?" Cork whispered to Louis, and nodded at Sloane.

Louis shook his head. "Quiet." He stirred the soup. "Do you think he'll be okay?"

He's got a hole in him a rat could crawl through, Cork thought. *And we're in the middle of a wilderness. And it's going to be cold night soon. No, Louis, there's no way in hell our friend is going to be all right.*

But he said, "That's in the hands of Kitchimanidoo."

42

THE RANGER WASN'T IN THE DRIVE at the home of Sarah Two
Knives, nor did Sarah answer Jo's knock at her door. Jo headed back into Allouette to LeDuc's, the small grocery store that
also sold bait and tackle and fishing licenses and served as the
reservation post office. At the counter where the cash register
sat, George LeDuc paused in his restocking of a candy bar
shelf and greeted Jo with a smile.

"Hey, counselor."

George LeDuc was not only an elder but also a member
of the tribal executive council, and Jo knew him well. He
was nearing seventy, had thick white hair, white teeth, a
broad face, and a strong, broad build. He'd outlived two
wives already and was on his third. He wore a gray sweatshirt that had printed across the front KEEP YOUR LAWS OFF MY
BODY.

Francine, George's wife, a woman in her midthirties and
seven months pregnant, stepped in from the back room. "Hi,
Jo."

"Francine, you look wonderful."

"That's what George says, too." She laughed, and covered
her mouth.

"Like a garden getting close to harvest." George put his
arm around her and smiled.

"I'm looking for Sarah Two Knives," Jo said.

"I figured," George replied. "We heard there's bad shit

going down in the Boundary Waters. *Majimanidoo,* the old ones are saying."

"You're one of the old ones," Francine said.

"Young enough still." George patted her swollen belly.

"It's not good," Jo said.

"Federal agents is what we heard." George looked as if he'd taken a drink of vinegar. "That's never a good sign."

"Do you know where I can find Sarah?"

"At the community center," Francine said. "She and Lydia are working on the Iron Lake Initiative."

"Migwech," Jo said. *Thanks.*

The community center was a new brick building constructed with profits from the Chippewa Grand Casino. It housed the reservation administration offices, a clinic, a gym, and a day-care. Jo found Sarah Two Knives and her mother, Lydia Champoux, in a conference room set up with computer equipment. Sarah was at the computer. Lydia was scanning a sheet coming off the printer. The Iron Lake Initiative, a program to which many men and women on the reservation gave time, was an effort to consolidate reservation land. Like many reservations in Minnesota, Iron Lake was a patchwork of holdings—tribal trust land, land allotted to tribal members, land that had been sold or leased to non-Indians, and land belonging to the county, state, or federal forest service. The purpose of the initiative was to buy back land wherever possible in the hope that ultimately the reservation would exist again in the configuration spelled out in the original treaty of 1854. Jo had supplied legal counsel when the initiative was first being established, but since then, the Iron Lake Anishinaabe had carried on the work entirely on their own.

Men, Jo had noted long before, tended to smoke or drink or pace when they were worried, feeding their bodies to the anxiety. Women were more likely to find something to occupy themselves. It didn't surprise her that Sarah and Lydia were working on the initiative.

"Anin, Lydia. *Anin,* Sarah," Jo said in greeting.

"Anin, Jo."

Lydia Champoux taught Native American studies at Aurora Community College, and her courses were among the most popular of the college's offerings. She was a small woman with braided silver hair and light brown eyes. She was dressed in jeans and a denim shirt. Tiny blue ceramic feathers dangled from her ears. Normally, Lydia—a woman of refreshing intelligence and wit—would have smiled, but Sarah had no doubt informed her of the situation, and Lydia, like Sarah, appeared braced for the worst.

"It's bad, isn't it," Sarah said. She swiveled in her chair and the bearings squealed.

"I wish it were better," Jo admitted. She sat near Sarah and explained the situation.

"So they've found no sign of Louis and Stormy," Lydia summed up darkly.

"Not exactly. They found trail signs left where the first dead man was discovered. Sheriff Schanno believes they're the kind Boy Scouts use."

"Wendell's doing," Lydia speculated. "He was always teaching Louis the old ways. The Boy Scouts learned everything from Indians."

Jo said, "The search plane and helicopter are concentrating on Wilderness Lake now. Sheriff Schanno's pretty sure that's a good bet."

"Wilderness is a very big lake," Lydia observed. "Although they are big in our hearts, as far as that country is concerned, Louis and Stormy and Cork are quite small." She took an unhappy look at the sky outside the conference room window. "And there isn't a lot of daylight left."

"I'm sorry to have to bring you such bad news," Jo said.

"Thank you," Sarah Two Knives told her. "It's more than those *majimanidoog* would offer us."

"Have you seen any sign of Wendell?" Jo asked.

Lydia shook her head. "I watch the stovepipe on his trailer home. When there's smoke, I visit. There's been no smoke for a long time. Let's hope he's burning a fire somewhere else."

"I'm going back to Aurora, back to the men who're responsible for all this. Would you like to come?"

"What for?" Sarah said. "It won't change what's happening out there. Will you let me know when you get any news?"

"Absolutely."

"Jo." Lydia reached out and laid a hand on Jo's arm, an unusual thing for an Anishinaabe. "I've seen alcohol and despair cause men to kill one another senselessly. That's a sad, sad thing. But this is different. This feels like a battle."

"I think probably it is."

"Then we should pray for our men to be strong and cunning and ruthless in destroying whatever evil is out there against them."

Jo nodded and said, "Amen."

The sun, as it set, struck fire to the trees along the shoreline of Iron Lake. High above the water, a flight of Canada geese, late in migrating, pointed themselves south in a long dark finger, and fled the North Woods. The lake surface was still and empty. Across it lay the reflection of the low sun, like a long fiery crack, as if the placid surface were only a thin shell over a molten sea beginning to break through. As she passed the trailer of Wendell Two Knives, Jo checked the stovepipe. No smoke.

Driving back to Aurora, she considered the situation as it stood. Fifteen years earlier, Marais Grand had been murdered. Now people associated with her daughter had died—two in California and at least one in the Boundary Waters, the man named Grimes. Benedetti and Jackson and Harris had all thought the recent deaths were tied to the old murder, the result of someone trying to cover tracks. But the death of Marais Grand had been explored and explained, so what was the motive for these other killings?

Cork had once told her that in his opinion most murders occurred for one of three reasons—fear, anger, or greed. She wasn't entirely certain she agreed with him, but for the sake of argument, she decided to start there.

If fear was the motive, what was there about Shiloh that would generate enough fear in someone to drive them to murder, not once but several times? Benedetti and Jackson had believed it was a fear of the memories Shiloh's therapist had dredged up. That would have explained everything nicely, including the death of the therapist. The only problem was that they all now knew the truth of the murder of Marais Grand. With Theresa Benedetti dead, there seemed nothing significant left to fear about that incident.

So maybe fear wasn't the motive. What about anger, then?

She dismissed it almost immediately. Anger was an emotion of the moment, a flare of destructive passion. Everything about the current situation felt too well planned, too carefully executed. For the time being at least, she would put aside the consideration of anger.

Which left Jo, as she entered Aurora, wondering about greed.

She made a stop at her office. Fran had left a stack of phone messages and notes on her desk, most dealing with rescheduled appointments. Jo glanced over them but couldn't make herself concentrate. She called the sheriff's office. Deputy Marsha Dross answered and told her Schanno wanted her to call the cabin at the Quetico. She gave Jo the number. Metcalf answered when Jo called. She asked to speak with Schanno.

"I think you should come over. Now. Interesting news," Schanno said.

They were all at the Quetico. Harris, Jackson, Metcalf, Schanno, and the two Benedettis. The place smelled of fried food. On the table sat a nearly empty tub of broasted chicken from the Pinewood Broiler and a greasy sack of fries.

Harris wiped his mouth with a napkin when Jo walked in. "Ms. O'Connor, we have some information." He sounded more cautious than Wally Schanno had on the phone.

"Here." Angelo Benedetti stepped forward to help her with her coat.

"What have I been missing?"

"An information exchange," Jackson said. He held a bottle of Leinenkugel beer in his hand. "We've come a distance."

"What kind of information?"

"The name of the man we found in the Boundary Waters, for starters," Harris replied. "Have a seat." He waved his hand toward an empty wing chair near the fire. When Jo was seated, he went on. "The prints match those of a man known as Papa Bear. Real name's Albert Lowell Bearman. He's a former marine, saw action in Grenada and the Gulf War. Since then, he's gone into business for himself. Soldier of fortune kind of thing. As nearly as we can tell, he's been involved in insurrections in Africa and South America. Now he's plying his skills domestically."

"I made some calls as soon as we knew his name," Angelo Benedetti explained. "This guy's not our kind. He's got no loyalty except to himself. No family ethic, no accountability. He's more the kind the government would use." He gave a cordial nod to Harris, who paid him no heed. "Still, people I know know about him. He usually works alone, but the word is he's out on a big contract and he's teamed with a guy nobody knows from nobody except he calls himself Milwaukee."

"We checked out this Milwaukee," Harris broke in. "Nothing on the NCIC computer about a man with that name or using that alias. In any event, it appears that somebody has put a contract out on Shiloh. The question is why."

"I've been thinking about that," Harris said. "I think we've been wearing blinders that have kept us looking too much at the past. Maybe this has nothing to do with the past and everything to do with the future."

Jackson looked at his brother, confused. "I don't understand."

"Oh, but I do," Jo said. She eyed Harris. "Because I've been thinking along those lines myself. I think it would be very interesting to know who would benefit financially from Shiloh's death."

Harris cocked a finger at her and fired off an imaginary round. "Bull's-eye."

Jackson squinted a moment, rolling things around in his head. Then the light came on in the attic. "Oh."

"Family usually benefits, don't they?" Vincent Benedetti

said. "She doesn't have any family she knows about except Arkansas Willie Raye."

Jo tapped her fingernail on the arm of her chair as she considered this information. "Raye owns Ozark Records, is that correct?"

"No," Benedetti replied. "Shiloh owns the company. He just runs it. When I loaned Marais the money to start Ozark, I insisted that Shiloh be the sole beneficiary should Marais die. I wanted my daughter well taken care of. It turned out Marais was way ahead of me on that. But when Marais died, Raye did become executor of the estate and took charge of running Ozark Records. He's done a good job, I gotta give him that. Built the best label in the industry, they tell me. But Shiloh owns it all."

"If Arkansas Willie Raye is Shiloh's beneficiary, I'd say you have a pretty good motive. But how would Raye contact a man like Papa Bear?"

"I can answer that," Metcalf said, "if you'll step over here a minute, Ms. O'Connor."

Jo walked to the table and looked over Metcalf's shoulder as his fingers flew across the keys of his laptop. He accessed the Internet and went to a bookmark called Papa Bear's Lair. A moment later, a home page appeared complete with a cozy photo of Papa Bear himself—a huge man with a shaved head, dressed in military fatigues, holding an assault rifle in his hands, and sporting a wicked combat knife hung from his belt. The header on the text read DISCREET ENFORCEMENT. I'M SO DAMN GOOD IT'S SCARY. His résumé read like a ticket through hell, with time spent in Nicaragua, El Salvador, Angola, and Bosnia. Foreign and domestic service, the text indicated. Every reasonable offer considered. The final page of the web site was an e-mail form readers could use to communicate with Papa Bear.

"Hired over the 'net?" Jo said.

"Or at least this was where contact was probably initially made."

"It's legal?" She looked at Jackson.

"Not much governance over what's on the Internet," Jackson said.

"Arkansas Willie Raye." All the muscles on Vincent Benedetti's body seemed to ripple—whether from anger or disease was hard to tell. "I'll tear his heart out."

"You don't know for certain that he's responsible," Jo warned. "It's only speculation at this point."

"Fucking good speculation." Benedetti narrowed his eyes on her. "I hate lawyers. But you, I like."

Harris said, "I'll get someone working on a check of Raye. It seems as reasonable a lead as any."

"What good does it do us?" Jo asked. "We still don't know what's going on out there. Has there been any more word?"

"It's dark now," Schanno said. "The search plane's landed, but the helicopter's still in the air, looking for campfires, anything. Mostly we wait now until morning. The good thing is this: If the information from Benedetti's contacts is accurate, we have only Raye and one other man to worry about out there. The odds are getting better."

"We don't have a lot of time," Harris said. He held up a rolled copy of a tabloid, chewed and ragged as an old bone. "Tomorrow this piece of shit that calls itself a newspaper hits the stands with a front-page story about Shiloh. Every asshole who's got nothing better to do will be up here making this a hell of a lot harder than it already is."

"There are going to be reporters. What are you going to tell them?" Vincent Benedetti asked Nathan Jackson.

Jackson lifted a poker and rearranged the burning logs in the fireplace. He worked carefully, positioning the logs so that hot flames rose up, climbing into the chimney. "If Shiloh is my daughter," he asked Benedetti, "would you still care?"

"I suppose I've cared too long to stop now."

"Me, too." Jackson put down the poker. "I'll tell the reporters the truth and see what happens."

Schanno leaned to Jo. "You look tired. Why don't you go on home. I'll keep you posted if we get any news."

Angelo Benedetti helped her on with her coat. "It's dark out," he said. "I'll walk you to your car."

Schanno started to say something, but before he could get a word out, Jo said, "All right."

Outside, night was bringing a deep chill to the air. Jo pulled her coat tightly around her. Benedetti's shoulder brushed her own. He smelled of a good limy cologne.

"Mind if I ask a question?"

"Go ahead," Jo said.

"Who are you most worried about out there?"

"What kind of question is that?"

"I've heard things about your husband. If your concern is for him, I'm thinking you must be quite a forgiving woman."

"You've been listening to gossip."

"People love to talk about other people. Hard to stop them. And you can learn a lot that way."

"Do they gossip in Las Vegas?"

"Does a flush beat a straight?"

"And do they always get it right?"

"Ah, more to things than meets the eye?"

"Always."

"You know, I thought people here would be different."

Jo reached out to open the door, but something rich and warm in Benedetti's voice held her back.

"I came here expecting . . . I don't know . . . "

"American Gothic in flannel?" she said.

"Something like that. I don't get out of Vegas much, so for me if it doesn't glitter, it's not exciting, you know."

"Mr. Benedetti, the only things that glitter here are the stars. And frankly, I like it that way." She looked down at the keys in her hand. "But for the record, you're not exactly what I would have expected of a—"

"Gangster?" He laughed softly. "You know, I've seen the law played a lot of ways. So much depends on the side of the table where you happen to be standing. For the record, you look good on your side of the table. Good night, Ms. O'Connor."

He headed back toward the cabin. For a moment, she stood alone under the stars and let herself enjoy the ghost of the compliment Angelo Benedetti had left behind.

43

DARKNESS SPILLED ACROSS THE SKY above the Deertail, bringing cold that threatened a bitter night. As the fire dried and warmed their clothing, Cork and Stormy slid pants and shirts under Sloane, coats and sweaters over him. They kept the flames leaping high, with a huge bed of coals beneath giving out heat. Sloane's wounds bled and soaked the dried clothing; there was nothing any of them could do. They tried their best to make him comfortable. He ate a little soup Cork spooned through his lips. But Cork knew they were losing him. And when Sloane's brown eyes held on Cork's face, the look in them said he knew it, too. They didn't talk about the other man who was lost to them and probably dead. Except Louis, who said, "I hope Arkansas Willie is okay."

"We all hope so," Stormy said.

"He liked my stories." Louis added a handful of sticks to the fire. "Maybe we'll find him waiting downstream."

Stormy glanced at Cork. "Maybe we will," he said quietly.

"Are you warm enough?" Cork asked Sloane.

"Enough," Sloane murmured.

Louis brought over a fire-dried wool sweater and laid it on Sloane. "Is that good?" he asked.

Somehow Sloane managed a smile for the boy. "Fine, Louis. It's fine."

Stormy had a pot of coffee on the fire's edge. Cork poured a cup and sat down beside Sloane.

Although Sloane's face glistened, a chill passed through him that made his body shake so violently he couldn't speak. When the tremor passed, he breathed a sigh and closed his eyes. "I like your stories, too, Louis. How 'bout one now?"

"About what?"

"Anything," Stormy told him.

Louis looked into the dark where the Deertail ran. He said, "How about the story of the river?"

His father nodded and Louis told this story.

Small Bear was a proud man. More than proud. He was vain. He was generally known to be the most handsome man in the land of the Anishinaabe. His hair was long and black, his eyes red-brown like cedar bark, his face more pleasant to look on than a summer lake. Village maidens dreamed of becoming his wife. All except one. Her name was Morning Sun. She was a young woman who loved the beauty of the forests more than the face of any man. Her lack of interest stung Small Bear's pride—and intrigued him. He sought Morning Sun whenever she went for solitude into the forest, but she always hid from him. Desperate to possess the maiden who shunned him, Small Bear appealed to Nanabozho. Nanabozho understood Small Bear's passion, but he was also fond of Morning Sun, whose love of the forest and respect for the *manidoog*—the spirits—were well known to him. Nanabozho decreed that Small Bear and Morning Sun should race. If Small Bear won, Morning Sun would be his wife. If Morning Sun were the victor, Small Bear could never again speak to her.

Small Bear was afraid, for Morning Sun was reputed to be as fleet of foot as he was handsome. He sought the help of a magician, who gave him a deerskin pouch containing three leaves. Eat the leaves just before the race begins, the magician instructed him.

The day of the race, moments before they began to run, Small Bear ate the leaves. Immediately he changed into a river. He began to flow swiftly, leaving far behind him Morning Sun, who had to leap fallen trees and avoid raspberry thickets and climb high hills. The sound of the water bubbling smoothly along was the laughter of Small Bear in his delight, for soon Morning Sun would be his wife.

Morning Sun cried out, appealing to Nanabozho that Small Bear had cheated. Nanabozho agreed. He caused the spirits of the valley to throw down a wall of rock to block Small Bear's way. Small Bear hit the wall with a sound like thunder. Angrily, he threw himself against the rocks again and again, slowly breaking through. But not soon enough. Morning Sun ran past him and finished the race long before Small Bear. To this day, the sound of Small Bear's anger can be heard in the thunder of the rapids.

Sloane opened his eyes when the story was finished. "Thank you, Louis. Small Bear was an asshole. Glad Morning Sun won." He looked at Cork. "A runner. Like you, Cork. A marathoner, right?"

"I've run one."

"Always told myself I'd do a marathon someday. Never got around to it. Lot of things like that. Too much left undone."

"Don't talk," Cork said.

"Think it'll make a difference?" Sloane made a sound that might have started off as a laugh but came out as a faint coughing. When he spoke again, it was only the ghost of a voice drifting from his lips. "Truth is, I won't be leaving much behind. Divorced ten years. Daughter doesn't speak to me anymore. Got a grandson I've never even seen. Funny . . ." But he didn't finish. "O'Connor, do me a favor."

"What is it?"

"Make sure my daughter knows I love her. Will you do that?"

"I'll do it."

Sloane shifted his gaze to Stormy and Louis. "Sorry I got you into this."

"Forget it," Stormy said.

"Bet this trip was easier when it was just you and your uncle, Louis."

"Yeah," Louis replied. He tried to smile. "Me and Uncle Wendell and the letter."

275

"Letter?" Sloane's face folded into creases of concentration.

"We always brought out a letter to mail for Shiloh."

"The letters she sent to Elizabeth Dobson in California," Cork reminded Sloane. "And to her father in Tennessee."

"No," Louis said.

Cork threw a quick, troubled look at Louis.

"Not to Tennessee," the boy clarified. "Only to California. To Los Angeles. To a woman named Libbie."

"Are you sure?" Cork asked. "Wendell went into the Boundary Waters without you sometimes. Could he have brought out letters on those trips that he mailed to Willie Raye in Tennessee?"

Louis shook his head. "He waited for me. We always walked together to LeDuc's to mail the letters. They all went to California."

Cork stared into the fire a while, but he wasn't seeing the flames. "Raye told me he'd received letters from Shiloh. That's how he knew she was up here."

"How could he?" Stormy asked.

"I don't know. Unless . . ."

"Unless what?" Louis asked.

Sloane looked at Cork and the same thought seemed to pass between them.

"Unless Raye was responsible for the letters' being stolen from Libbie Dobson in the first place," Cork replied.

"That—what did you call it, Louis? *Majimanidoo?*—of yours. Maybe he's got a name now." Sloane breathed shallow and fast. "Arkansas Willie Raye."

Stormy took a stick and began to stir up the coals so that flames broke out at the edge of the fire where he sat. He tapped at them, making more and more flickers of fire, like Mickey Mouse's ever dividing brooms of *The Sorcerer's Apprentice.* He said, "If that's true, then it probably means he's been working with the men who've been out here after us."

"Bet he's been in communication with them the whole time," Sloane said in a venomous whisper.

"It would explain a lot," Cork said. "I've been wondering how they tracked us so well."

"That's how they knew Grimes was waiting and where," Stormy said.

"Sorry I ever blamed you," Sloane told him.

"Forget it."

"Of course," Cork said suddenly.

"What?" Sloane asked.

"Remember when we were ambushed and I wondered why that guy didn't just kill us? We were carrying the canoes on our shoulders. Our faces were hidden, so he couldn't tell which of us was Raye. He didn't know who not to shoot."

"The shooter on the rocks today," Stormy put in. "That explains Raye's diarrhea. Every time he disappeared into the bushes, he was probably on a radio to the son of a bitch."

"But Arkansas Willie was shot, too," Louis said

Cork shook his head. "I'm pretty sure not, Louis. He went into the water as if he'd been shot. That added to the general confusion and gave him a chance to slip away from us."

"He's alive," Sloane said, and even in his weakened state, his anger came through strong.

"Not only alive," Cork added, "but joined up, I'd bet, with the guy who's after Shiloh. Shit."

Cork picked up a stick and threw it down hard among the coals of the fire. Blazing embers leaped away like little demons afraid of his anger.

"Maybe we held them up enough here so that Shiloh can get away from them." In the firelight, Louis's young face seemed bright with hope.

"I wish that were true and the end of it, Louis," Cork said. "But those men have gone to a lot of trouble to try to kill her. I don't think they'll stop at the edge of the Boundary Waters. And if Raye is smart, he knows where she'll go once she's out."

"Where?" Stormy asked.

"Wendell's trailer. I'd bet on it. Her car's there. And she probably believes it's safe."

Sloane's hand slipped from under the clothing that covered him and he grasped Cork's arm. "We've got to do something."

"Yeah," Stormy agreed. "But what?"

They sat silently for a long time, thinking, sat as people had for thousands of years, around a fire that lit a very small place in a very great dark.

"Maybe there is a way," Cork finally said. "Maybe I can make it to Shiloh before they do."

"How?" Louis asked.

"First thing in the morning, I run my second marathon."

"You don't exactly have a clear course here," Stormy pointed out.

"Let's take a look at the map."

From the pocket of his pack, which was still wet, he pulled the map of the Boundary Waters. The map was wet, too, and he opened it carefully to avoid tearing the paper. He spread it on the ground near the fire, and he and Stormy hunched over it.

"The Noodamigwe Trail is east of here." Cork put his finger on a black dotted line. "Looks to be about four miles."

"Closer to five," Stormy said.

"If I can connect with it, I'll follow it until I catch the old Sawtooth logging road here. What is that? Ten miles? Then another eight or so to County Road C. If I can catch a ride there, I could be at Wendell's by noon."

"Lot of ifs," Stormy said.

"I'm open to other suggestions."

Stormy sat back and offered nothing. Louis was looking at Sloane, whose eyes danced with firelight. Sloane saw him watching. He smiled, real and true.

"Don't worry about me, Louis. No way I'm going to miss the end of this. How 'bout a little more of that soup?"

44

SHILOH BUILT A SMALL FIRE on the southern shore of a boot-shaped lake the map called Desperation. On the map, she was only two inches from the place where she would leave the Boundary Waters, and only another four inches from the X that marked Wendell's place. She could have calculated it in miles, but inches were far more comforting.

The peanut butter and bread she'd taken from the dead men's pack had provided what felt like a sumptuous feast. Funny, she thought, how little it took to be happy when there was little choice. She knew she was still learning the lessons of the wilderness. To breathe, to eat, to sleep, and to do so fearlessly—how much more did anyone need to be happy? Wealth, Wendell had impressed on her, was not a value the Anishinaabe held. Sharing was the way of The People.

When, in the little cabin, she'd discovered how happy she could be with almost nothing, she'd made a profound decision. She intended to divest herself of the holdings that had given her wealth but never a moment of happiness. The decision filled her with more joy than she ever thought possible. Over the course of several weeks, she solidified a plan. She would begin by establishing a foundation for the preservation of Indian culture. Not just the culture of the Anishinaabe, but all Native American people. She would call it Miziweyaa, which Wendell had told her meant all of a thing—whole—for that was how she felt. After that, she would reorganize Ozark Records, make it a venue for Native American music. The voice of The People would be heard at last. And not just music, but the words of storytellers as well. She'd learned so much from Wendell's stories. But why stop there? Why not include the music and stories of indigenous peoples everywhere? Despite all the noise technology could manufacture and send to the farthest reaches of the earth, Shiloh believed there had been a great silence in the world for too long.

Her last decision was to change her will. She intended to leave everything, whatever still existed of her wealth when she took to the Path of Souls, to the Iron Lake Anishinaabe.

She'd journaled extensively, talked the whole thing out on tape, and finally, unable to contain her zeal, had written to Libbie Dobson, pouring forth the whole plan.

To possess nothing but the full abundance of her heart, even now the very idea brought her to tears. Real tears of happiness.

She wiped her eyes and saw among the trees, glowing with the reflection of her fire, the eyes of a gray wolf. They'd frightened her the first time they'd appeared in this way, but she felt differently now. She'd faced her death and her fear of it and had come to the other side of an understanding. All things were connected. Trees, water, air, earth, gray wolf, Shiloh. Life and death. Happiness and sorrow. All elements of the Great Spirit, Kitchimanidoo. If the man called Charon found her and if he killed her, she would still be a part of a great whole. As was Wendell. As was her mother.

All her life she'd felt utterly alone. But she would never feel that way again.

She began to sing softly, "The water is wide, I cannot cross o'er . . ."

The wolf drew itself back into the night and was gone.

"Is that you, Jo?" Rose paused in the dark doorway of the kitchen, a ghost in her white chenille robe.

"Yes. Don't turn on the light."

"Can't sleep?"

"No," Jo answered. "My brain's working overtime."

"Worried about Cork?"

"About all of them."

"How about some tea? Herbal."

"Thanks."

Jo stood at the kitchen window that overlooked the driveway and the lilac hedge beyond. The moon had risen, what little there was of it, only a scrap of light amid all the debris of heaven.

"It's cold out there tonight," she said.

"There are lots of good people looking for them." Rose filled the teakettle with tap water and set it over a flame on a burner of the stove.

The Burnetts' dog, a big German shepherd called Bogart, began to bark two houses down. The sound was dim through the glass of the closed window. It was often the only sound at night, a dull constant yapping that caused the neighbors to complain but made the Burnetts, an elderly couple, feel protected.

Whatever it takes, Jo thought.

She crossed her arms and leaned against the kitchen counter. "I've been thinking about Dad."

"What about him?"

"Trying to remember things."

"Like what?"

"I remember he was always up early. I'd wake sometimes. The house would be dark except for the bathroom. He'd be in there shaving, humming to himself, tapping his razor against the sink. I'd fall back asleep. When I woke later and went into the bathroom after he was gone, I'd still smell the Old Spice aftershave he put on. I've always loved that smell."

"You never told me before." Rose stood next to Jo so their arms touched. "Cork uses Old Spice."

"I know," Jo said.

The teakettle began to whistle. Jo took it from the stove

and poured steaming water in the cups Rose had set out. From the cinnamon smell that drifted up on the vapors, Jo could tell Rose had chosen Good Earth.

"I don't remember him much," Rose said. "Every once in a while, I dream about a man. He doesn't look like the pictures of Dad, so maybe it's not him. But he makes me feel safe." Rose stirred her tea. The spoon rang against the side of the cup. "The men I remember are mostly shadowy guys in the middle of the night. You know, you'd hear their voices, maybe see a big dark figure pass by your door, and they'd be gone in the morning."

"They were spooky," Jo said.

Rose lifted the tea bag out and took a sip from her cup. "For Mom, they passed as companionship, I guess. But I think she never loved another man."

"Rose."

"Yes?"

"I'm glad I'm not alone in this. Thanks."

"That's what family is for."

Dwight Douglas Sloane died quietly in the night. The last thing he said was, "Across the river," spoken to no one.

Cork was feeding birch limbs to the fire. Stormy and Louis sat together against the tall rocks warmed by the flames. Louis slept, his head laid against his father's arm.

Sloane gave a small groan and spoke his final piece. His chest rose high in one last struggle for breath, then fell and rose no more. His eyes were half open. The reflection of the fire danced in them and made them seem alive. But Cork knew, and so did Stormy.

"What did he mean?" Stormy asked.

Before Cork could answer, from the far side of the Deertail came the mournful howling of wolves. The crying woke Louis. He straightened up and looked at Sloane.

"He's dead, isn't he?"

"Yes, Louis," Stormy said.

The boy listened to the wolves, their sound like a sad song in the dark beyond the river. "He was wrong."

"What do you mean?" Stormy asked.

"Remember, he said the wolves weren't his brothers. But listen to them. Uncle Wendell told me that the wolves only cry for their own."

"*Ma'iingan,*" Stormy said. "I'd be proud to call him my brother."

45

WHEN THE GHOST OF SUNRISE first began to haunt the sky, Cork ate a light meal. He and Stormy talked quietly at the fire while Louis slept. Stormy agreed it would be best to stay where they were until Cork sent someone back for them. If no one came by the following morning, Stormy and Louis would walk out, following the same route Cork proposed to take along the Noodamigwe Trail to the old logging road. Cork left Stormy both weapons.

"I don't need extra weight on this run," he said. "I don't think you and Louis will need all that firepower either. Raye probably doesn't suspect that we're on to him. I'll bet he has a story already concocted about being washed downriver and getting lost in the woods. But I'd feel better if you kept the guns."

Cork stretched his muscles in preparation for the run. He discarded his jacket, so that he was dressed in a thermal top, sweater, jeans, socks, and his boots. "I know you'll keep him safe," he said, looking down at Louis as the boy slept.

"Cork, I've been hard in my thinking about you for a long time. It was easier for me to blame you, you know. I'm sorry."

"Forget it."

"Get to the woman before that *majimanidoo* does."

"I'm on it."

"When you get to Wendell's, if you need a firearm, he

keeps a rifle in the tall cabinet in his shed. And you'll find cartridges in a Quaker Oat container on the shelf."

"Quaker?"

"My uncle's sense of humor. Good luck." He offered his hand.

Cork took the strong hand. "To you, too." He turned away and began to run.

The morning air was crisp, and Cork, as he breathed, left a trail of vapor that vanished within moments of his passing. The light was still gray, but the sky was a clean blue, and within an hour, the tips of the tallest pines burned like candles set to fire by the light of the rising sun. Cork followed the Deertail south to its junction with Raspberry Creek, and there he turned east. The creek ran between low, rugged hills covered with jack pines. The bed was nearly dry, but, here and there, Cork splashed through small pockets of water trapped behind a fallen log or rock dam. He ran through ragged patches of sunlight clean of bugs in the autumn cold, and he startled big ravens that flew up in a drumming of wings, cawing their complaints as he passed under them. He ran more slowly than he wanted, but the creek bed was an obstacle course littered with rocks and limbs and sudden mud that threatened to snap an ankle if he placed a foot unmindfully. Normally when he ran, his thoughts moved in a different world. Now he kept his concentration riveted to the dozen feet of ground directly in front of him.

He almost missed the Noodamigwe Trail. He broke into a sudden wide bar of sunlight, and by the time he looked up, he was already beyond the four-foot swath of cleared forest. He backtracked and picked up the Noodamigwe heading south.

The Noodamigwe Trail was one of the oldest through the Boundary Waters. Voyagers loaded with beaver and mink pelts had traveled the route two hundred years before, and the Anishinaabe long before that. The trail was little used anymore—most visitors to the Boundary Waters came by canoe—and was covered with porcupine grass. Where the edges of the trail touched the forest, clusters of yellow buttercups and bluebells grew. The grass was wet with melted frost and glistened ahead of Cork like a carpet covered with jewels.

He was sweating heavily, and he shed his sweater as he ran, tying it around his waist by the arms. His legs were fatiguing already, the result of too little sleep, the extra weight of his boots, and clothing ill-suited to a run. He couldn't think about the fatigue or he would begin to feed himself to it. So he thought instead about Arkansas Willie Raye.

The man had fooled him, but not without Cork's complicity. Raye had woven truth and lie into an appearance that was seamless. Not a particularly difficult trick. Even the worst people weren't pure evil. They were selfish, greedy, thoughtless, prejudiced, afraid. But these weren't traits of the Devil, only human weaknesses, and most often Cork had found them paired with some balancing virtue.

So Arkansas Willie had fooled him. But Cork had been ripe for fooling. Raye had played a worried father, concerned that he'd let his child down. And that was Cork all over, bound up in a confusing guilt about his own children. He knew Aurora saw him as a philanderer, a man who'd abandoned his duty and his family. Although the truth was far different, far more complex than anyone would guess, he still felt vulnerable. Being seen unfairly as having abandoned the ones he loved, he was more than willing to believe that no father would. Willie Raye had played to that vulnerability, enlisting Cork in his quest to locate Shiloh, using Cork as a perfect dupe. Cork didn't know why, what Arkansas Willie had to gain, but it was obvious the man's purpose all along had been murder.

I should have seen, he thought, castigating himself silently as he ran. The theft of the letters at Grandview had been a fraud, a setup. And that same night, he'd given Raye Stormy's name, all the son of a bitch needed to plant money at Wendell's cabin that would incriminate both Stormy and Wendell. And Raye, running down the hill toward the burning cabin where Shiloh had stayed, firing his pistol, warning the man he'd hired to kill her. *Christ, how could I be so blind?*

He paused where the trail crossed a running brook, cupped his hands, drank, and did a quick calculation. Five miles to the old logging road, another ten to County Road C. Less than halfway home. He checked his watch. Reaching Wendell's before noon had been a ridiculously optimistic appraisal of the task ahead of him.

But there was nothing to be done except suck it up and keep going.

A mile short of the Sawtooth logging road, the Noodamigwe crested a hill and dropped at a steep angle through a stand of quaking aspen. The trail was a river of leaves a foot deep, wetted from the melted snow, slick as ice. As he started downhill, Cork braced himself against the pull of gravity that tried to accelerate his descent. His left foot, as he planted it, slid from under him and the world did a sickening flip. His view was a blur of flying leaves, bone white tree trunks, and chill blue sky webbed with the bare branches of the aspen. He tumbled uncontrolled, then stopped abruptly when his left shoulder rammed a stump solid as petrified wood.

He lay on the ground, wet leaves stuck to his face like leeches, a dull fire burning in his left shoulder. When he tried to sit up, the fire blazed, burned white hot all over, and he cried out. After another minute, he did a slow roll to his right and worked his way to his knees. Gently, he felt his left shoulder at the socket and touched a place that was like punching an elevator button to the top floor of the Agony Building.

Dislocated, he figured. Shit. It had happened to him once before during a high school football game. He was out for the season.

He spent the next minute reviewing his options. There were only two. He could quit. Or he could do his best to move beyond the pain and finish what he'd set out to do. No choice at all.

He stood up carefully and, just as carefully, slid his left hand into the front of his jeans and pulled his belt tight to hold it there. He knew of no sure way to keep his arm from moving, but he had to try to immobilize it as best he could. The belt would have to do. He completed his descent of the hill at a cautious walk, an excruciating preview of what was ahead.

46

SHILOH LEFT THE CANOE drawn up on the shore and walked along a path into tall marsh grass. She crossed wood planking laid over muck. A couple of minutes later, she stepped into a large square of gravel and yellow dirt where several empty vehicles sat parked. The sight of windshields and tires and the familiar glint of sunlight off chrome moved her to tears. Her body, whose strength had not failed her in all the long journey, suddenly felt weak and she sat down, weeping with relief.

She was out.

Redwing blackbirds flitted among the cattails near the parking area. Small white clouds, delicate as angels' breath, drifted across a pale blue sky. Two days before, she'd been certain she was a dead woman. Now, like Lazarus, she was alive again. From somewhere down the road came the drone of a chainsaw. Shiloh stood up and began walking toward the sound.

After a quarter mile, she came to an old yellow pickup, leprous with rust, that had been parked to the side of the road. From the pines beyond came the song of the chainsaw, the sound rising and falling as the teeth bit through timber. Forty yards into the trees, Shiloh found a short man with a thick gray beard, dressed in biballs and a red flannel shirt, his hands covered with brown leather gloves. He was cutting a small, felled pine into sections. He concentrated on his labor and didn't see her at first. When he did, he eyed her a while before killing the engine.

"Yah?"

"Could you help me?" she asked.

"Well, young lady, dat all depends. What ya need?" The saw hung heavy in his right hand, and the muscle of his forearm humped along the bone solid as a small rock ridge.

"You see," she said, "I've been lost a while. I need a ride."

He didn't answer.

"I can pay," she offered.

"Pay? If ya got money, then I'm Jiminy Cricket." He shook his head and ragged teeth smiled through his beard. "Ya look like somethin' a bear sharpened his claws on. Pay, ya say? I'll take ya, but I won't take none of your money. Where 'bouts is it you're goin'?"

She told him.

He lifted a metal thermos and started toward the road. "You Indian?"

"Part Anishinaabe," she replied. "The best part."

"Me, I'm Swedish and Finn. Da worst of 'em both, my wife says. Nils Larson." He shoved the thermos under his arm, pulled off his glove, and offered his hand.

"How do you do, Nils."

"Didn't catch your name dere."

"Just call me grateful," she said.

Nils Larson dropped her off at the trailer of Wendell Two Knives. True to his word, he refused to consider payment. She'd told him nothing of her ordeal. She was safe now. Soon enough, she would have to deal with Wendell's murder and the murder of Libbie Dobson, offer the police the information the man called Charon had given her, provide a description, do all she could to see that the murderer was caught. But for now, for just a little while, she wanted to think of nothing.

In Shiloh's heart, Wendell's place was heaven's doorstep. She walked down the dirt drive. The birches along the way had been thick with summer green when she'd last seen them, and the air had smelled of honeysuckle. Now, all the limbs were bare and what Shiloh breathed was the smell of wet earth and decaying leaves. But everything was heaven to her still. She went to the shed and tried the door. It opened easily. Wendell had told her he didn't believe in locks. On the rez, nobody did. The red Mercedes was there, fine dust powdered evenly over the finish. Around it hung the tools of Wendell's craft—handsaws, planes, mallets, wood chisels, and buckets—all of it steeped in the scent of evergreen pitch. She crossed to a shelf along the wall, reached into a tin can spattered with dried paint, and pulled out the keys to the car.

She crossed the yard. The grass was still a deep green. Down a gentle slope on her left, cornflower blue behind a line of cedars, lay another lake, the one called Iron. She mounted the two steps to the door of the white trailer home. Out of habit born of a lifetime of cultural hammering, she knocked politely. Did she expect Wendell to answer? Something in her resisted still the idea he was gone forever, and she waited, as if a few breaths of time would make a difference. But nothing would, not for Wendell, not ever. Finally, she stepped in.

The trailer had a large main room separated from the kitchen by a counter. A bathroom and bedroom were down a short hallway. The place was clean, well kept, the furniture simple. A soft brown sofa, a green easy chair, a television, a table with a couple of chairs where Wendell ate. White curtains, glowing with sunshine, hung in the windows. A compact metal fireplace with a glass door stood in one corner. It was what Wendell used for heat when his propane burner was on the blink. Next to it sat a wood rack that held a few logs and kindling.

She hadn't grieved for Wendell. There'd been no time. At the moment, she didn't feel sadness. In fact, what suffused all her being was a profound sense of relief and a deep gratitude at still being alive. In this place that reflected Wendell's spirit so evidently—right down to the birch-bark lampshade and the smell of sawed wood that had come to be like perfume to her—she still felt wonderfully safe. Grieving would come, she knew, in its own time. Right now, she was too damn tired.

The trailer was chilly, holding in the cold of the last few

days. Wendell, even when it was warm, laid a fire in the fireplace most evenings. He'd told her that he'd spent so much time around a campfire, the smell of wood smoke was almost as essential to him as the air itself. Shiloh put kindling and wood in the fireplace and lit a fire. Now the place seemed well and truly full of Wendell.

She checked the refrigerator, took out bologna and bread, and wolfed a dry sandwich washed down with a Coke. She caught sight of herself in a small mirror that hung on the wall and she nearly leaped back in horror. Her hair jutted out in short, ragged splashes. Her face was smeared with mud and charcoal. She looked down at her hands. Grime had worked under the fingernails, giving her five black crescent moons on each hand. A grout of dirt filled the creases at her knuckles. The lines of her palms were black as poisoned veins.

She went to the bathroom, the first indoor plumbing she'd seen in weeks. She ran water in the sink until it was hot, then took the soap from the small green dish and began to scrub. The hot water felt wonderful. It ran down her cheeks, long hot fingers stroking her neck. She glanced at the tub only a few feet away. A hot shower called to her like a lover. She hesitated. Ten minutes, she thought, no more. What difference could this small indulgence make? She quickly stripped off her clothes and dropped them where she stood. Reaching into the glass shower stall, she turned the water on and adjusted the knobs until hot vapors filled the air. The water startled her when she stepped in, the heat nearly unbearable. But she quickly settled into the liquid luxury she'd forgone so long, let the water run hot over every part of her, lifted her breasts to the stream, opened her mouth and took it in, joyously filling her senses.

So enraptured was she that there was no way she could have heard the front door opening.

47

THE MORNING BEGAN with a beautiful sunrise and went sour from there.

Jo had been drinking coffee in the kitchen waiting for toast to pop up when the phone rang.

"Jo. Wally Schanno."

His voice was beveled with caution, and Jo felt sick to her stomach. "What is it?"

"We—uh—we just got word from the search plane." He held up a moment, as if he'd come to a big jump he wasn't sure he could make. "They've spotted two bodies."

"Two bodies." Jo repeated the words, although she'd heard them well enough. Her mind was trying not to see the image the words conjured. "Do they . . . know who?"

"Not yet."

Her throat had closed. She could barely swallow, and when she spoke again, it was in a hoarse whisper. "Are you at the department?"

"Yes."

"I'll be right down."

She hung up and slowly turned. Jenny stood near the refrigerator, her eyes afraid. "Two bodies? Mom, what's going on?"

"Nothing," Jo answered automatically. "It's nothing."

"Bullshit."

Rose was in the doorway, listening, too. Jo glanced at her,

trying to decide if between them they could dull the cruel, sharp edges of the truth. Rose shook her head.

"Would you get Annie?" Jo asked her sister. "Let Stevie sleep."

Rose came back with Annie. Annie had a hairbrush in her hand, half her red Irish tangle brushed smooth. She glanced at Jenny and, as if it were contagious, Jenny's worry appeared on Annie's face. "What's going on?"

"Sit down," Jo said. "Both of you."

She related the salient events of the past few days, and when she was finished, the girls sat motionless and silent.

"Isn't there anything someone can do?" Annie finally blurted.

"They're doing all they can right now," Jo said.

"Those two bodies?" Jenny asked.

"They don't know yet. I'm going down to the sheriff's office now."

"What can we do?" Annie asked.

"I'm not sure there's anything we can do."

"We can pray," Rose suggested.

Jenny stared at the tabletop. "I'm not going to school."

"All right," Jo said.

"Mom?"

"What is it, Annie?"

"Does Dad know there are, like, these other bad guys out there?"

"I don't know what he knows. But I'll tell you this: If I were Shiloh, I'd want someone exactly like your dad out there trying to help."

"I know he's going to be okay," Annie said.

"How do you know?" Jenny shot back.

"I just know."

"Oh, I suppose God talked to you."

"Shut up."

"Girls," Jo said. She took them both in her arms, felt their fear as she held them, and knew it was her fear, as well. "I wish I could say everything's going to be fine, but nobody knows. Rose is right. Praying is good. Holding on to each other helps, too. We're a family. We all need to be together in this, okay? We need to be there for one another." She kissed the tops of their heads. "I have to go to the sheriff's office. Don't worry about school today. I'll let you know as soon as I know something."

Wally Schanno hadn't received any additional word when Jo reached his office. The bodies had been spotted on a point of land on a southeast arm of Wilderness Lake. The search plane was going to attempt a landing and investigate. The helicopter, which had one of Schanno's deputies on board, was proceeding there as well.

"Have you told Agent Harris or Nathan Jackson?" Jo asked.

Schanno said he had.

"I'll phone the Benedettis."

Angelo Benedetti took the call. "Where are you?" he asked after she'd explained the situation.

She told him.

His end of the line was quiet. She wasn't sure if he was waiting for her to say something more. Then he surprised her by asking sincerely, "Are you okay?"

"I'll be better when I know what's happened up there."

"Sure."

She heard him turn from the phone and speak briefly in response to a voice in the background.

"I'm coming down there," he said to her.

He showed up fifteen minutes later, was buzzed through the security door, and was escorted to Schanno's office. Just as Benedetti entered, Deputy Cy Borkmann rushed in behind him. "S-and-R on the air, Sheriff."

Schanno hurried to the dispatch desk where Borkmann had been monitoring the frequency used by Search and Rescue. Jo and Benedetti were right behind him. The airwaves crackled with static. Borkmann said, "They're standing by."

Schanno took the mike. "This is Sheriff Schanno. Do you read me? Over."

"Loud and clear, Sheriff. This is Dwayne."

"What's the situation up there?"

"We've ID'd the bodies from their driver's licenses. Roy Alvin Evans and Sander Carlton Sebring. According to their licenses, they're residents of Milaca. From the looks of their gear, I'd say they came to fish."

"How'd they die?"

"Gunshot wounds to the chest on both of 'em. The cold makes it hard to tell, but I'd say they've been dead a while. Looks like they got snowed on after they died, and the snow's pretty well melted off 'em now."

"Any sign of Cork and the others?"

"Negative. But someone's made sure the canoe these guys came in wasn't going to take them or anybody else out of here. Big hole's been punched through the hull from the inside. What do you want us to do, Sheriff?"

"Stand by," Schanno said into the mike.

He stepped to the wall where a map of Wilderness Lake and the surrounding section of the Boundary Waters had been posted. He ran his finger over the map and tapped the place where the bodies had been discovered. His finger moved slowly southeast, following a blue line that indicated a river. He nodded to himself and lifted the mike back to his mouth.

"Schanno coming back at you, Dwayne. Do you read me? Over."

"Still loud and clear, Sheriff."

"This is what I want you to do. You stay with the bodies and keep the scene as undisturbed as you can. Get the plane back in the air and have it head down the Deertail River. That's the start of the circle route out if any of these people are coming out where they put in. Once the plane hits the Deertail Flowage, have it head west to do another flyover of Embarrass Lake. You copy all that?"

"Ten-four, Sheriff. Over and out."

Schanno's gray eyes offered Jo a look of relief. "Not Cork or the others."

Jo sat down and let out a deep breath. "I want to say thank God, but those two men may have families, too."

Benedetti asked Schanno, "Do you think it had anything to do with Shiloh?"

Schanno let out a short, bitter laugh. "Since that woman went out there, people have been doing nothing but dying. Yeah, I'm sure it has everything to do with Shiloh. I just don't know what." He turned to Borkmann. "Give Hans Friedlander a call. See if he'd be willing, at county expense, to fly his float plane out to Wilderness Lake with a couple of deputies aboard. If he agrees, you and Dross take the evidence kits and get out there to give Dwayne a hand with the crime scene. And tell Les to give Gus and Jake a call to come in. I'm running out of officers." Schanno rubbed his temples. "I'd better give Harris the word."

Jo used the phone at the dispatcher's desk to call home. "Rose? It wasn't Cork." There was a slight catch in her throat, and she saw Benedetti smile sympathetically. "Tell the girls, all right?" She listened and replied, "Two fishermen, it looks like. Sheriff Schanno doesn't know how it's related." She shook her head. "No, no word about the others yet. I'll keep you posted, okay?" She hung up, stepped out of the dispatch area, and started slowly for Schanno's office. "You look tired," she said to Angelo Benedetti, who walked at her side.

"I didn't sleep much last night. Too worried. That's a new one for me. I didn't eat any breakfast either. The truth is I'm starved and tired and I'd kill for a cup of good coffee." As soon as the words were out, he grimaced. "I'm sorry. I didn't mean—"

"That's all right," Jo said.

In the doorway of Schanno's office Benedetti stopped. "Have you eaten?" he asked her.

"No."

"Would it be inappropriate, Ms. O'Connor, to offer to buy you . . ." He checked his watch. "Brunch?"

"I appreciate the thought, really, but I'd rather not leave."

"Sure, I understand." He glanced around the department. "Maybe there's a vending machine where I could get us a couple of Twinkies and the battery acid that passes for coffee?"

Jo smiled. "There's a good coffee place two blocks down.

The Moose Juice. Cappuccino, latte, whatever you'd like. And delicious bakery goods."

"Great. Can I get you something?"

"Latte, made with skim. And a scone. Thanks."

"A scone? It's yours, whatever it is. Sheriff?"

Schanno looked up from a map on his desk. He reached down and lifted into view a big metal thermos. "Got everything I need right here, thanks."

"All right, then. I'll be back."

Schanno's eyes trailed Benedetti out of the department. When he looked back at Jo, she asked, "You don't like him?"

"I don't trust him."

"Nor do I. But that's not what I asked."

Schanno thought it over. "He stands by his old man. He doesn't back down easy. If he were Lutheran, I guess he'd be just fine."

Deputy Borkmann stuck his head in the door. "Sheriff? Sorry to interrupt, but there's a reporter for the *Duluth Register-Guard* on the phone. Says he's got word that the country singer Shiloh's lost up here and we got us a manhunt mounted to find her. He wants to talk to you."

Schanno took a deep breath. "Patch it through." He looked at Jo like a man about to eat raw squid. "It's starting."

Fifteen minutes later, as Schanno appeared to be winding up his conversation with the Duluth reporter, Borkmann thrust himself into the doorway, looking excited. Schanno said, "That's all I've got to say at the moment," and hung up quickly. "What's up?"

"Search plane's spotted smoke from a campfire on the Deertail just above Hell's Playground. Guess the trees made it hard to see but it looked like several people. On the second pass, a man and a boy come out waving their arms. Appeared to be Stormy and Louis."

"Any sign of Cork?" Jo asked.

"Like I said, search plane reported several people at the campfire in the trees. No reason for all of them to signal the plane. I'd say we found 'em." He offered a reassuring smile.

"Get on the radio to Dwayne. Have the helicopter pick them up."

"I already did."

"Wally, may I use your phone?" She felt like Christmas had come two months early.

"Be my guest," Schanno beamed.

Rose wept at the other end of the line when Jo gave her the news. Jo hung up and said to Schanno, "Now Sarah Two Knives."

When Sarah didn't answer her phone, Jo grabbed her coat. "I'm going out to the rez. Sarah needs to know. I'll be back in an hour."

"They'll practically be home by then," Schanno said. Relief filled every hollow of his long, gaunt face.

Angelo Benedetti pulled into the parking lot just as Jo stepped from the building. He got out carrying two lidded hot cups and a white bakery bag.

"Where are you going?" he asked.

"They've found the men. I'm on my way to tell Sarah Two Knives."

"Mind if I come along?" Benedetti gave a nod to the items in his hands. "I've got breakfast."

"Be my guest," Jo offered with a broad smile and a sweep of her hand, hallmarks of that brief moment when all seemed well.

48

How long he'd been running, Cork couldn't say. An hour? Three? He felt as if he'd been tortured for a century. Each stride was like drawing a rusty saw blade across his shoulder. He moved no faster than a rapid walk. The old road hadn't been used for logging in years and was overgrown with rye grass and wild oats and timothy. Two swathes of crushed stalks straddled the center as if two huge snakes had passed there, side by side, an indication that a vehicle had traveled that way recently. Forest service, Cork guessed, or maybe mushroomers. He tried to keep to one of the swathes. Whenever he strayed, his feet tangled in the tall grass and threatened to trip him. Another fall would put an end to what little resolve he had left.

Under a blue-white sky and a brilliant autumn sun, the North Woods had warmed again. Cork was soaked with sweat. He knew if he kept on this way he'd dangerously dehydrate. It was rapidly becoming a question of which of the hellhounds that pursued him would bring him down first.

He had to think about something besides the pain, something to drive him on. He pulled up the image of Grimes fallen among the dripping raspberry vines. Next, he conjured the giant with the shaved head and saw him again, laid out under a gray sky, leaking dark red blood onto wet rock. Dwight

Sloane materialized—a good man—with a hole blown clear through his body and the knowledge of his own death rising up into his brown eyes like water in a spring. Cork imagined Elizabeth Dobson, dying alone, afraid. He saw these things clearly, the tragic images falling over his eyes, blinding him to the trail in front of him, curtaining him from the beauty of the woods around him. He was deep in death, slogging through a quagmire of blood. It was like one of those awful nightmares when he tried to run but his feet would not move. And ahead of him, beyond the reach of his hand or voice, he could see Shiloh. She stood in an empty room, in the silence that was the music of death. He saw her turn toward an opening door where light burst through like the flash of fire from the muzzle of a gun. A shadow darkened her face. He heard her screaming.

And the screaming broke through his vision. He was seeing the trail again, and the blue sky and the evergreens. The screaming became a horn honking at his back. He stumbled to a halt and turned around.

A black pickup nearly half a century old rolled slowly to a stop and a head crowned by a wild rag of white hair poked out the driver's window.

"Hell's bells, if it ain't Corcoran O'Connor."

Cork recognized Althea Bolls, a widow who'd lived alone in a cabin in the Superior National Forest since the pickup she drove was new. He hobbled to her truck.

"Lord, boy, I've seen roadkill looked better'n you."

"I need to get to Allouette." His throat was parched, and the words came out thin and brittle as autumn leaves.

Althea patted the good arm he rested against her door. "Sure, I'll take you. You just get yourself in this truck before you fall right over."

Cork got in the passenger side. On the seat next to Althea were a pair of Leitz binoculars, a copy of Palmer's *Handbook of North American Birds,* and a notebook. Althea was head of the local chapter of the Audubon Society and often made excursions into the deep woods to chronicle the birds. She shoved the truck into gear and lurched forward.

"There's coffee in that thermos there on the floor," she said. "Help yourself. Sorry I didn't bring anything stronger. Looks like you could use a snort. What happened to you anyway?"

"Long story," Cork said, and, for everyone's sake, left it at that.

49

SHILOH INDULGED HERSELF. She let the hot water from the shower run over her until her skin felt parboiled and her palms and fingers began to wrinkle. She sucked into her lungs the luscious air, hot and moist, as if she were in a steam bath in a Beverly Hills spa. At last she soaped and rinsed, and when she stepped from the shower, she felt clean and new.

She pulled a folded green towel from a shelf above the toilet and began to dry herself.

That's when she heard the creak of the floor in the living room and she stopped dead still. She listened intently. She'd relaxed, closed the door to caution, and now she felt trapped again and afraid. She draped the towel around her, tucked in the corner to hold it in place. Quietly, she dug into the pocket of her jeans on the floor and pulled out the knife Wendell had given her. She opened the blade. Warily, she peered around the threshold of the bathroom. What greeted her made her step back in surprise.

A woman—slender, blond hair, ice-blue eyes—stood caught in midstep less than a yard down the hallway.

"Who are you?" Shiloh demanded.

The woman stared at her, astounded, as if she were looking at an elephant who'd managed to squeeze into the trailer. "My name's Jo O'Connor. And unless I'm crazy, you're Shiloh."

"What're you doing here?"

"I saw smoke from the stovepipe." Jo O'Connor motioned vaguely toward the roof. "I thought it might be Wendell."

Shiloh leaned back against the door, weak with relief, heavy with regret. "It won't ever be Wendell."

"Did I hear the name Shiloh?"

Behind Jo O'Connor, a man appeared. He looked at Shiloh with deep interest.

"So you're the spark that started the fire," he said.

"Who are you?" Shiloh asked.

He smiled. "Some people think I'm your brother."

Shiloh folded the knife blade and retucked the end of the towel. "That doesn't make any sense."

"Just give us a few minutes to explain things," Jo said. "Did you know you've got a whole county looking for you?"

"Yeah? Well, they missed me." She gave the man a closer look. "What did you mean you might be my brother? I don't have any of that kind of family."

The man scratched his head and seemed almost ready to laugh. "You have a lot more than you imagine."

"You've been in terrible danger," Jo said. "Were you aware of that?"

"Oh, yeah. That was made very clear to me. How did you know?"

Jo said, "Tell you what. Get some clothes on. I'll make some coffee. And we'll talk."

In the tiny kitchen, Jo found a coffeemaker.

"She looks different," Benedetti said.

"Her hair's been butchered." Jo found filters in the cupboard. In the refrigerator was a bag of beans. Kona Blend. On the counter was a small Braun electric grinder. She hadn't realized Wendell was such a coffee connoisseur. But it seemed that nowadays everyone was.

"She looks pretty good otherwise," Benedetti noted with an interest that sounded not at all like brotherly love.

"She's your sister," Jo reminded him.

"Allegedly."

Jo ground the beans, put the coffee together, and was just

finishing as Shiloh came into the small living room. She wore clean clothes—a large work shirt and overalls rolled up at the cuffs—that Jo suspected belonged to Wendell.

"Sit down, Ms. . . ." Jo hesitated, uncertain how to address a stranger with but one name. "Sit down, Shiloh. We'll explain some things. It's a little complicated. First, I'd like to call the sheriff's office and let them know we've found you."

"Fine." Shiloh shrugged. "Whatever."

Jo lifted the receiver from the phone hanging on the kitchen wall. "That's odd. No dial tone."

Behind her, the door to the trailer home opened, and she heard Shiloh exclaim, "Willie."

Jo turned quickly. In the doorway, with the sun at his back, stood a man in dirty jeans, a torn flannel shirt, and a green down vest. He took them all in carefully.

Shiloh stood up. "What are you doing here?"

A smile suddenly graced the face of Arkansas Willie Raye, and he replied, "Why, I was worried sick about you, darlin'. Lots of folks was." He stepped in and closed the door.

"That's what these people have been saying." Shiloh swung a hand back to indicate Jo and Angelo Benedetti.

"How do?" Raye said.

Benedetti took a step forward and the look on his face was hard as brass knuckles. Jo jumped in quickly. "Mr. Raye, Jo O'Connor. Cork's wife. I thought you were with him in the Boundary Waters."

Arkansas Willie scratched at the silver grizzle on his jaw. "Got separated looking for my girl, here. I came on back. I suppose Cork and the others'll be along shortly. Christ almighty, it's good to see you, Shiloh. Have you let anyone know you're here and safe?"

"Of course we have," Jo said. "In fact I just finished speaking with the sheriff's office." Jo waved at the wall phone.

Willie Raye gave that a thoughtful nod, then said, "That woulda been kinda hard, seein' as how I cut the line a bit ago." He reached behind him, lifted his vest, and pulled a pistol from his belt. "Why don't y'all just get together with Shiloh over there and rub shoulders."

"Willie?" Shiloh frowned at the gun, then looked at Raye with puzzlement.

"When were you goin' to tell me, girl? After you took my child and butchered it?"

"Tell you what? What child? What are you talking about, Willie?"

"I created Ozark. Ozark is mine, not yours. You can't just take it and destroy it."

"I own Ozark. Mother left it to me."

Raye began to pace, but he kept his eyes on the others. He passed through a bar of dusty sunlight and his shadow leaped toward them.

"She left you a debt and a dream," he cried. "I paid the debt. I made the dream come true. It was my sweat, my worry, my lost sleep that made it happen. Ozark is my baby. You think I'd just stand by and let you inflict on it whatever misery happens to creep into your head?" He turned and paced the other direction. The hand that held the pistol was beginning to become more animated, the barrel slicing the air like a conductor's baton.

"Shiloh's your child, too," Jo tried gently.

"Like hell. She was never my child, only my responsibility." His eyes snapped toward Shiloh like whips. "Gettin' close to you, girl, was like tryin' to hug a bunch of nettles. You never let me love you."

"You never gave me anything to love," she shot back. "When I needed comfort in the night it came from nannies and nuns."

"I tried."

"No, you didn't. You didn't have to. I wasn't yours. And nobody had to tell me that. Whenever you touched me, your hands were hard. Whenever you spoke, your words were slippery. You were one big lie, Willie, and you can't hide a lie from a child. I always knew."

"I took care of you." He emphasized his point by thrusting the barrel of the handgun at her. "I made sure there was a roof over your head. A damn good roof. Several of them. And I did that by building Ozark Records into something I was proud of."

"And something you'd kill for. It was you." Shiloh's voice carried the wonderment of a revelation, but her face carried all the lines of pain. "Libbie, Wendell. That was your doing."

"Libbie Dobson?" He laughed scornfully. "Now there was a true friend. She agreed to send me copies of all your letters. We had us an understanding. A debut CD all her own. She was easy. Cheap."

"You killed her."

"Had her killed. Had to. She knew where you were, knew your intentions. And she was goin' to sell that information, make it all public. Death of Ozark right there."

"And Shiloh's therapist, Patricia Sutpen. That was you?" Jo asked.

"Patricia?" Shiloh looked like the wind had been knocked out of her.

"I figured it would focus attention on the past, which I had nothing to do with."

Raye's boots thudded heavily as he paced and the whole trailer shook under him. "And that Wendell, hell, that son of a bitch trusted me until we were 'bout halfway out there, then somethin' happened. Somehow he knew and refused to take me any farther. So he's dead."

"No, he's alive, Willie," Shiloh said, and she took a fast, angry step nearer. "He's alive in everything he passed on to others."

"Shut up and get back."

Shiloh took another step. "He'll be alive a long time after you're gone. He was more a father to me—to a lot of people—than you could ever have been. His concern was never about what I could do for him. That's what a father should be all about, Willie."

The gun was trued on her heart. But Willie Raye didn't fire.

Jo asked, trying to keep her voice quiet with reason, "What do you expect to accomplish here?"

"What do I expect?" The question seemed to stump him. He searched the beige carpet where he'd tracked bits of dried mud. Finally he replied, "What I set out to do in the first place—and then some, looks like."

The coffeemaker grumbled suddenly and Raye swung his gun that way. When he realized what it was, he smiled and the moment seemed to give him some relief. "When they find your bodies, I'll be back out in the Boundary Waters, hopelessly lost. Your husband will attest to that, Ms. O'Connor."

Angelo Benedetti stood up. "The first thing my father ever taught me about gambling was never draw to an inside straight. You're missing an important card in the middle of the hand you're holding, Willie."

"Who the hell are you?"

"Angelo Benedetti. Vincent's kid."

"So what am I missing, Vincent's kid?"

"They know about you. My father, the FBI, the sheriff here. They put it all together. You've lost the pot, friend." Benedetti gave his shoulders a shrug as if it were the end of a game they'd all been playing strictly for the fun of it.

"I'm not your friend, you sow-littered wop."

Raye fired. Angelo Benedetti stumbled back from the impact and toppled over the chair in which he'd been sitting. At the same moment, the door to the trailer flew open. Cork rushed in and threw a blow with his good right arm. He caught Arkansas Willie Raye hard on the side of the head before the man could turn. Raye went down. Jo stomped on Arkansas Willie's hand, then pried the pistol loose from his fingers. She stood up, breathing hard.

"Oh God, Cork. I've never been happier to see anyone in my life."

"You okay?"

"Yes."

Cork touched his shoulder gently. Knocking Willie Raye down had hurt. "I could hear him ranting from halfway across the yard. Sorry I didn't get here sooner."

Shiloh had moved quickly to Benedetti's side. "Somebody get a doctor here."

"I don't think so."

Shiloh looked up. A figure had stepped into the doorway, dark against the brilliant sun outside, the face lost in deep shadow. Even so, Shiloh knew who it was—or at least what he called himself.

Charon.

50

"Put the gun back on the floor." The man called Charon motioned with the big automatic he held in his hand. "Do it slowly."

Jo did as she was instructed. "Who are you?"

He ignored her question and looked down at Arkansas Willie Raye who was gathering himself in an effort to stand. Raye touched his head where Cork's blow had connected, and he grimaced. "I thought you were going to cover me from the outside." He eased himself up.

"You're covered."

Raye took his pistol from the floor and scowled. He appeared about to speak, but instead, he lashed out and struck Cork on the side of the head with the gun barrel.

The blow turned Cork, wrenched his shoulder, and he cried out. His ear rang afterward, and his jaw felt like Arkansas Willie had hammered a nail through the bone.

"Now you got a mornin'-after headache, too, you son of a bitch. What the hell're you doin' here anyway?"

Talking wasn't easy, but he replied through gritted teeth, "We figured you out, Willie."

"You're the one I had pinned down back there at Hell's Playground." The man called Charon looked Cork over intently. His eyes were hard brown. There was something old about them, though not particularly wise. "How did you get here?"

"Ran mostly," Cork replied.

"When you came down the road out there, I saw you holding yourself like you were hurt."

"Dislocated shoulder."

The man's interest deepened and his face seemed to shift as if the very structure beneath had altered. "You ran out of those woods with a dislocated shoulder?"

"It was dislocated for only half the way."

Raye butted in. "Let's get on with what we came here for and get out."

"Angelo Benedetti told you the truth," Jo said. Cork was amazed how calm she sounded. "Killing us does no good now. Everyone's looking in your direction, Willie. And those men in the Boundary Waters know about you. You have no alibi."

"Shut up." Raye jabbed the gun at her.

"Is that true?" The man called Charon focused on Jo so intensely she felt as if her thoughts were being pierced.

"You must be Milwaukee," she said.

"Son of a gun." Milwaukee looked at Arkansas Willie wistfully. "I do believe they're on to you."

"No evidence," Raye said hastily. "This gun is untraceable. I go back into the woods, who's to say I wasn't lost out there the whole time?"

"Don't do this, Willie," Shiloh said. "Good people are going to suffer."

Milwaukee looked at her and it appeared as if a smile almost touched his lips. "I thought going out there would be a picnic. I was wrong about you. And I'm not often wrong."

With his pistol, Raye frantically motioned toward Shiloh, who still knelt beside the fallen Angelo Benedetti. "Everyone over there."

No one moved.

"Do it," Milwaukee said. There was death in his voice, deep and empty as a waiting grave. "This man's paid for the game. We play the cards however he deals them." He leveled his automatic at Jo's heart.

Cork stepped next to Jo and stood with his shoulder pressed against hers. He tried to think what he could say that would alter the trajectory of that moment. But his mouth was dry and his voice was caught somewhere between his intention and his tongue, and all he could do was stand there as the barrel moved toward him like a compass needle that had found north and the man called Charon and Milwaukee poised himself on the edge of an act that would send them all plummeting into unknowable dark.

"Shoot him," Raye shrieked.

Milwaukee hesitated.

"I said shoot him, you chickenshit bastard. Or I will."

Raye swung his own gun toward Cork.

Milwaukee lashed out faster than Cork had ever seen a man move. He grabbed Arkansas Willie's arm and twisted it at an unnatural angle so that the gun dropped from his hand. Then he delivered a sharp, precise kick to the side of Raye's right knee and the bone or cartilage gave an audible pop. Raye crumpled to the floor. Milwaukee did all this without the barrel of the automatic he held veering in the slightest degree from its dead-on aim at Cork's heart.

Arkansas Willie clutched his knee and stared up at Charon/Milwaukee with pain and anger and disbelief. "Are you fucking crazy?"

"I won't take disrespect from any man."

"It's broken," Raye whined.

"Consider yourself lucky."

"I paid you."

"Tell you what," he said. "When I see you in hell, we'll talk about a refund."

In no more time than it took to strike a match, everything had changed. Cork looked at the hard brown eyes and wondered what it was that made the man kill or decide not to. It didn't matter. If Cork had to live forever not knowing why, he could do that.

"You think you're out of this?" Raye screamed. "You think you can just walk away? They know who you are."

"No, they only know a name. I have lots of those."

Milwaukee bent and picked up the pistol Raye had let fall to the floor. As he straightened, he noted the consternation in the eyes of Cork and the others. "I prefer to let you live," he said simply. He backed toward the door and stepped outside into the sunlight. He looked up, squinting, then into the dark of the trailer. "'Long is the way and hard, that out of hell leads up to light.'" He turned and, as if he'd walked through a doorway into another dimension, vanished.

"What was that all about?" Jo asked.

"Milton. *Paradise Lost*." With Shiloh's help, Angelo Benedetti had eased into a sitting position, his back against the trailer wall. Seeing Jo's surprise, he managed a faint smile. "Minor in English lit at UNLV."

Cork went to Benedetti and checked the wound. It was high on the right shoulder, clean entry and exit. "Small caliber, and the angle was just right. Seems to have missed almost everything, including bone. You're pretty lucky."

Benedetti laid his head back. Even with his California tan, his face looked pale. Shiloh held his hand. "I never had a little sister to protect before," he told her. "All things considered, it pretty much sucks."

Shiloh kissed the top of his head. "Thanks."

"Get some towels to press against those wounds, Jo," Cork said. He went to check on Raye.

Arkansas Willie tried to stand as Cork approached, but he cried out and flopped back to the floor. His face contorted and he howled, "Christ, the son of a bitch shattered everything."

"Best thing you could do for yourself now, Willie, is stay there and stay quiet. Shiloh, think you can make sure he does that?"

"My pleasure." She took the knife she'd dropped into the pocket of Wendell's jeans, opened the blade, and stood over Arkansas Willie Raye. "I have a whole lifetime of reasons, Willie. All I need is one more," she threatened.

Cork moved to the doorway of the trailer home just as Jo returned with the towels. "Where are you going, Cork?" She knelt and opened Benedetti's shirt and pressed a towel to his wound.

"Wendell keeps a rifle in the shed."

"You're not going after that man, are you? You don't have to do that. Cork, you're not the sheriff anymore." She seemed torn between tending Benedetti and rising to hold back Cork.

Cork stared in the direction Charon/Milwaukee had disappeared. There was only the empty drive leading through the bared birches toward the main road.

"He killed Wendell and he killed Dwight Sloane," Cork said to her over his shoulder.

"And he killed Libbie and two men who were only trying to help me," Shiloh added. She looked at Cork as if she understood him perfectly.

"You all stay here and lock the door after me," he told them. "The sheriff's people should be on their way. Althea Bolls went into Allouette to phone them."

"Cork—"

He heard her call to him, but it was too late. He was out the door and moving swiftly toward the shed.

He found the tall cabinet and inside the rifle—a Remington 700 ADL bolt action. As Stormy had said, the cartridges were in an old Quaker Oat container: 30-06, 180-grain bronze point, enough power to bring down a small bear. Cork pulled out half a dozen and fed them into the magazine, worked the bolt—not an easy thing with his injured shoulder—and chambered a round. Then he headed outside, where he stood a moment in the sunlight, considering.

The man had disappeared down the drive toward the road. That made sense. To have reached the trailer as quickly as they had, he and Arkansas Willie must have driven a vehicle of some kind, probably one Charon/Milwaukee had left somewhere they could easily reach when they came out of the Boundary Waters. And now it would be parked somewhere hidden from the road but accessible. Not toward Allouette. Too great a chance of being seen. More likely the other direction, somewhere south along the shore of Iron Lake.

Cork recalled that a quarter mile south of Wendell's trailer was an old boat launch. It was seldom used anymore because proceeds from the casino had allowed the Iron Lake Anishinaabe to develop a fine park just north of Allouette that included new launch facilities. The old boat launch still showed on maps, but hardly anyone ever used it. It would be a good place to stash a vehicle.

Cork circled Wendell's shed, moved past the empty canoe racks, and headed quickly into the cool shadow of the trees that bordered Wendell's yard, thinking, *He'll be watching the road. He'll be looking for me to come from the road. But I'll take him from the cover of the trees.*

He carried the rifle with his right hand only. Although he attempted to keep his left side as immobile as possible, every step was like twisting a knife in his shoulder. He tried to formulate a plan as he went, keeping his mind on his calculation rather than his pain. All he could come up with, however, was to reach the launch before the man drove away. In the back of his mind, he knew that even if he missed Charon/Milwaukee, the man would have a hard time making a clean getaway in Tamarack County. The main roads were few, and as soon as Schanno got word, he'd lock those roads up tight using his own men and the state highway patrol.

That brought Cork to a sudden stop.

Charon/Milwaukee had been ahead of him in his thinking all along. Some of that was Arkansas Willie's doing, but more, it was because the man anticipated well. He knew his adversaries and knew how they thought. He'd know the roads would be watched closely and that his description would be out over every police radio in northern Minnesota. He wouldn't risk the roads.

Then a detail flashed into Cork's thinking. As he'd moved past the canoe racks at Wendell's shed, he'd noted, without really thinking about it, that the rack was empty. When he'd been there two days ago with Arkansas Willie, there'd been one canoe left.

For a man like Charon/Milwaukee, a man who knew how to survive in the wild, heading into the protection of the great North Woods was a perfect choice. Within a few days, he could be across the border into Canada. Or ease his way west or south until he was beyond whatever net the law had thrown across the roadways to snag him.

Cork turned toward the wide, sparkling blue of Iron Lake.

The shoreline near Wendell's place was a ragged edging of small, rocky inlets dotted with pines. Stepping quietly, his rifle readied, Cork made his way to the water. He paused a moment, listening. The lake was calm, lapping very gently at the rocks. Just north of where he stood, in the direction of Wendell's trailer, rose a big slab of gray rock about the size of a pickup truck. From the other side came the almost imperceptible bass note of a canoe hull tapped lightly with a paddle. Cork eased to the rock, and around it, until he saw Charon/Milwaukee leaning over the canoe. The man stood bent, caught in a netting of shadow cast over him by the branches of a big red pine. He appeared to be securing a pack under the stern thwart. Cork stepped up behind the trunk of the red pine and leaned himself against it to help his left arm support the weight of the rifle as he brought it to bear. A fire raged in his shoulder. He prayed he wouldn't have to hold the rifle that way for long.

"Put your hands on your head and don't turn around."

The man paused. "O'Connor," he said, as if Cork were not unexpected at all.

"Hands on your head. Now."

Charon/Milwaukee complied, pressing his palms to the back of his head.

"Turn around slowly."

As the man came around, Cork could see he wore an affable grin. "I guess I should have killed you."

"With your left hand, using only your thumb and index finger, take your weapon from its holster and drop it on the ground."

When the handgun lay flopped on a bed of pine needles, Cork asked, "That's Willie's twenty-two. Where's your weapon? The automatic. What was it? A Sig Sauer?"

"In the pack." He gestured with a jerk of his head toward the canoe behind him.

"Sure it is."

"Care to frisk me?" Charon/Milwaukee gave a very small,

very real laugh. "A little tough holding that rifle. And with a bum shoulder."

"We're going back to the trailer."

"You'll be dead before we get there."

A slight wind made the water roll and the bow of the canoe went up and down like a little head nodding in agreement.

"You make the tiniest move and I'll shoot you," Cork warned.

"How quickly can you swing that rifle and aim with a dislocated shoulder?" Charon/Milwaukee asked. "That's a bolt action. You'll be lucky if you even get one good shot, because I'll be moving. I can imagine the pain you're in, O'Connor. The pain's already eaten into your normal ability to aim, to react. It would be the same for any man." He lifted his hands from his head, only a few inches, a gesture of reasonability. "Look, you've fought a better battle than anyone I've faced in a very long time. Let's call it a truce, you and me. Go back to your wife. I'll fade away into the darkness I came from. We'll never see one another again." Something sharp and pointed entered his words as he finished, "I've given you your life once already."

"Let's go," Cork ordered.

Charon/Milwaukee didn't move. His face lost any trace of reasonableness. He narrowed his gaze and a deep line appeared between his eyes like a sudden streak of war paint. "If you don't back down now, this is what will happen. I'll kill you, and after I kill you, I'll return to that trailer and kill everyone in it. Is it worth that risk to you?"

Cork was silent.

"I thought not." Charon/Milwaukee smiled, but almost sadly, as if the victory had been a cheap one. "Then it's good-bye, O'Connor."

He took a step backward, still smiling. He turned toward the canoe. As he pivoted, he made his move quickly, diving left, rolling on the soft pine needles that covered the ground along the shoreline, reaching for the automatic stuffed in his belt under his vest. Cork didn't fire until the moment the man called Milwaukee and Charon came up to one knee and braced to shoot.

The bullet from Wendell's rifle blew off most of Charon/Milwaukee's left hand. It plowed a wide, messy path through his chest and exited his back along with large splinters of his shoulder blade. The force knocked him backward. He lay on the ground, his arms spread wide, his face turned toward the sky. The automatic had fallen near his feet, unfired. With difficulty, Cork worked another round into the chamber of Wendell's rifle. Carefully, he approached the downed man.

Charon/Milwaukee's eyes were open. The hard brown, Cork saw, was flecked with gold. He was still breathing, small gasps that sounded like hiccups. Cork bent to him and said, "I've hunted all my life. One good shot is all you ever get."

Charon/Milwaukee tried to speak, but he seemed to be addressing someone behind Cork, above him. Cork almost turned to see who it might be. Then the hiccuping stopped, and the brown eyes became sightless as a couple of marbles.

Cork's legs gave out and he sat down hard. His shoulder hurt like a son of a bitch. Whatever it was that had sustained him was gone. His ability to focus, to think at all, had fled. If the dead man had risen up like Lazarus from his pine-needle bed, Cork wouldn't have been able to lift a finger to defend himself. He was empty.

He barely turned when he heard the crackle of twigs breaking underfoot. He saw George LeDuc come from the trees cradling a rifle. George knelt beside him. When he spoke, his breath smelled of spearmint gum. It was like the scent of an angel.

"You okay?"

Cork nodded.

"That him?" George pointed the rifle muzzle at the body.

A thought crept out of the haze in Cork's mind, a clear wonderment. "What are you doing here, George?"

"Woman came into the store, used the phone to call the sheriff. Seemed like somebody should get here quicker'n they could."

Cork looked at him dully. "The others?"

"They're fine. Up at Wendell's trailer. Jo wanted to come, but I put my foot down. Wasn't sure what I'd find out here. Come on. Can you walk?" He offered his hand.

As they approached the trailer, the whine of sirens rose from the distance. The trailer door opened and Jo rushed into the sunlight.

"He's okay," George called out to her as she came.

"Thank God." She put her arms around Cork.

"Gently," he cautioned, although her arms felt good.

In a moment, two cars from the Tamarack County Sheriff's Department skidded onto Wendell's drive and kicked up dirt and gravel as they sped toward the trailer. Behind them came the blue Lumina and the Lincoln Town Car.

Wally Schanno bounded out. "You okay?"

"Alive anyway." Cork gestured toward the trailer. "Some folks in there need help. Get an ambulance."

Schanno hollered instructions to a deputy in the other car. He took inventory of Cork. "You look like you could use some medical help, too."

"At this point, Wally, I'm just happy to be alive. There's a body down at the lake. George can show you where. Not one of the good guys."

The big man Joey approached them, carrying Vincent Benedetti in his arms. "My son?" Benedetti asked.

"Inside," Cork said. "He'll be fine."

"And Shiloh?" Nathan Jackson came up beside Joey, Harris right behind him.

"She's in there, too. Unharmed."

Cork and Jo followed them inside. Schanno went to check on Arkansas Willie, who sat hunkered in a corner, holding his knee and looking like a trapped varmint. The others went directly to where Shiloh sat on the floor next to Angelo Benedetti.

"Shiloh," Angelo said, gesturing toward the man in Joey's arms, "meet your father." She looked up, confused. Then Benedetti waved toward Nathan Jackson. "And . . . meet your father."

Nearly a dozen bodies were packed into the small living room of the trailer home. Cork backed out, and Jo with him. "Let them sort it out," he said.

Schanno accompanied them. "We're going to need a full statement, Cork."

"First we're getting him to a doctor," Jo said. "He may have a broken collarbone."

"Want to wait for the ambulance?"

She shook her head emphatically. "I'll take him."

They walked away from the trailer. Across Iron Lake, through the cedars near the shore, over grass still greening under the October light, came a breeze that smelled of the North Woods. Of evergreen and deep, clean lakes. Of sun-warmed earth. Of desiccated autumn leaves. Of the cycle of dust to dust. Of things seen and half seen, things unseen but sensed. Fragrances that had gifted Cork all his life, that had become as common to him as the scent of his own body. Pay attention to what blows across the water, Henry Meloux had advised Cork early on. In his wisdom, the old man had offered more than just a warning about the coming of the *maji-manidoo,* and Cork found himself taking in the air with a renewed sense of wonder.

"You're grinning like this was Christmas morning," Jo said.

"Am I?"

"I'd have thought you'd be in a lot of pain."

"You hurt long enough, you almost forget it's there."

"I know." She stopped walking.

"What is it?" he asked.

"I was just thinking. You'll need some tending while that shoulder heals. Why don't you come and stay with us."

The smile on her lips seemed as delicate as a snowflake and as easily melted.

"You mean . . . at the house?"

"Yes." The breeze pushed a wisp of yellow hair onto her forehead. She swept it back with her small hand. "You can stay in the guest room to begin with. We could see how things go while you heal. While we all heal."

It was a day of miracles. Of two suns. One crowning a cloudless sky and the other rising new in Cork's heart.

"Hey, Cork!" Schanno called to him. "If I want to reach you, where will you be?"

For a moment, Cork was lost in the blue of Jo's eyes. Then he answered, "Home, Wally. I'll be home."

EPILOGUE

IN HIS FORECAST based on the coats of muskrats, Charlie Aalto had been correct. Two days before Halloween, a heavy snow fell over the North Woods. The weather came gently, moving in just before nightfall, and hour after hour, snow drifted silently down until it covered the ground deep as a man's calf.

The weather did not deter the Anishinaabe. Quiet as the snowfall, they filed past the white trailer home, past the harvested garden, through the line of cedars, and gathered around a fire on the shore of Iron Lake to honor Wendell Two Knives.

The *midewiwin* Henry Meloux beat the *mitigwakik*, the Mide drum, and spoke to the spirit of Wendell Two Knives, guiding him on the Path of Souls, cautioning him against the dangers and distractions on his way west to the Land of Souls. Wendell Two Knives was guardian of tradition, respectful of the old ways. Tradition dictated that a man be buried with the implements that had defined his life. There was no burial for Wendell Two Knives; his body was never found. Instead, Meloux placed on the fire a strip of birch bark, Wendell's deer-bone awl, a wooden bowl of pitch, and a *cijokiwsagaagun*, the small spatula Wendell had used to seal the seams of his canoes.

"Our brother, you leave us," Meloux said in the language of the Anishinaabeg. "Our brother, to the Land of Souls you are bound."

George LeDuc stepped forward. He was not ashamed to let his emotion show in tears.

"I knew Wendell Two Knives all my life. As boys, we wrestled. Wendell was stronger and smarter and usually beat me. I was a better shot. When we hunted, Wendell was never envious and was always glad for me when I brought home the deer. He was a good man who never turned away when someone needed his help. All of us on the rez, we're better people because of him. I will miss my friend."

Others spoke, each in their turn honoring Wendell Two Knives. Then Henry Meloux said, "Our brother was *aadizookewinini,* a storyteller. In our stories do we remember who we are. In our stories do we tell our children's grandchildren about the ways of our people. Wendell Two Knives gave the gift of his stories to the Anishinaabeg. He gave his stories as a trust to his nephew's son, Louis. The snow has fallen. It is winter. The time for telling stories."

For one so young to be asked was an honor. Louis came fully into the firelight, a small boy with a great heart. The snow had whitened his hair, making him seem an old man already. Cork, who was watching, knew there was indeed something wise in the boy, far beyond his years.

Louis told this story.

"There was a man who knew Noopiming—Up North in the Woods, the Boundary Waters—better than any other man. He knew not only the lakes and rivers, but also the rocks and trees and animals. He loved all life there, held sacred the belief in the *manidoog,* the spirits who dwelled in that place. And he was blessed in return with a skill in building canoes that glided across water smoothly and swiftly as birds in air. The man was called Ma'iingan, for he was brother to the wolf.

"A woman came and asked Ma'iingan for help. She asked for a place to hide in Noopiming, for she was being pursued by a terrible *majimanidoo.* The good man Ma'iingan led her to a special place and hid her there. He brought her food and he kept her safe.

"One day the *majimanidoo,* in the shape of the woman's father, appeared before Ma'iingan and begged to be taken to her, claiming he was worried and wanted to see with his own eyes that she was well. At first, because his heart was so good that he did not recognize evil in another, Ma'iingan was fooled. But the true spirit of the *majimanidoo* could not be hidden for long, and before they reached the woman's hiding place, Ma'iingan saw the *majimanidoo* for the evil it was. He refused to go any farther. Using all his terrible magic, the *majimanidoo* tried to force Ma'iingan to tell him where the hiding place was, but to no avail. In anger, he killed good Ma'iingan.

"The spirit of Ma'iingan stood on the Path of Souls but did not want to make the journey yet. He cried out to Kitchimanidoo, imploring the Great Spirit to let him stay a little longer in Noopiming, to keep safe the young woman, to fulfill his promise to her. Kitchimanidoo heard the good man's plea. The spirit of Ma'iingan was given the shape of a gray wolf, for that was his totem, and allowed to return.

"In the meantime, brave hunters from several tribes had joined to track the *majimanidoo*. The evil spirit was powerful and many hunters lost their lives. And all the while, the *majimanidoo* drew closer and closer to the young woman. But Ma'iingan, in the form of the wolf, prowled the woods, guarding and guiding the woman, keeping her just out of reach of the evil that tracked her. Not until the hunters finally killed the *majimanidoo* and the woman was safe did the noble spirit of Ma'iingan begin the journey to the Land of Souls.

"But the wisdom of Kitchimanidoo grants the return of Ma'iingan in the shape of his brother the wolf whenever there is someone in Noopiming in need of help. And you can still hear the voice of Ma'iingan raised with his brothers, singing in the wilderness, in the land he loved so well."

Louis stepped back, and his father laid a hand proudly on the boy's shoulder.

"What a good man leaves behind him is forever," Henry Meloux said. "Until the trees no longer touch the sky, Grandmother Earth and her children will hold with respect the memory of Wendell Two Knives."

The snow fell softly on Meloux and melted. Drops gathered along the deep lines of his skin and reflected the firelight in a way that made the old *midewiwin*'s whole face seem aflame as he spoke in the language of The People:

> *K'neekaunissinaun, ani-maudjauh.*
> *K'neekaunissinaun, cheeby-meekunnaung.*
> *K'neekaunissinaun, kego binuh-kummeekaen.*
> *K'neekaunissinaun, k'gah odaessiniko.*

> Our brother, he is leaving.
> Our brother, on the Path of Souls.
> Our brother, do not stumble.
> Our brother, you will be welcome.